Eleanor & Grey

BRITTAINY CHERRY

Published: Brittainy C. Cherry 2019
brittainycherry@gmail.com

Editing by C. Marie, Ellie at Love N Books, Jenny Sims at Editing for Indies, LBEdits
Cover Design by Hang Le
Paperback Formatting by Elaine York, Allusion Graphics, LLC

Eleanor & Grey

To Mama.

Thank you for believing.

Part One

"When I was a boy and I would see scary things in the news,
my mother would say to me, 'Look for the helpers.
You will always find people who are helping.'"

-Fred Rogers

Prologue

Eleanor

April 8, 2003

Everything my mother knew about life she learned from Mister Rogers.

She called him the greatest teacher of life lessons, and she swore up and down that he'd saved her life countless times. Whenever she was upset, she worked through her problems using her words. Whenever she was happy, she embraced it fully. Whenever she was hurt, she studied what led to her aching.

I'd never met a woman so in control of her own energy. Her awareness of self was something to be applauded. She never raised her voice, and she had the calmest demeanor of anyone in the whole world. You couldn't be around my mother and be angry. I truly thought it was impossible.

It was because of her that we had Tuesdays with Rogers.

Only on Tuesday nights would we eat away from the dining room table, and pull out the TV trays. There was never a Tuesday that passed where she, my father, and I weren't watching an episode of *Mister Rogers' Neighborhood*. It was an odd tradition, yet it was something Mom had been doing since she was a kid. She'd watch the show every week with Grandma, and when she met Dad, she made him promise he'd keep the tradition going if they ever had kids.

I loved it, too. There probably weren't many sixteen-year-old kids who knew, let alone loved, Mr. Rogers, but honestly, they were missing out. Even though it was an older show, its life lessons were still pretty relevant.

That Tuesday afternoon was no different to me. We ate meatloaf and mashed potatoes, we talked about music, we laughed at Dad's bad jokes, and we chatted about Mr. Rogers's cardigan collection that looked very similar to mine, seeing how Mom made me a new one every year for my birthday.

Everything was fine and dandy until three words rocked everything sideways.

"I have cancer."

My body reacted in a way I didn't know was possible. I slumped back against the couch cushion as if someone had slammed a fist straight into my gut, forcing all air to evaporate from my body.

I turned to my mother, confused, stunned, aching. My palms grew clammy, my stomach knotted up, and I felt like I was going to vomit.

"What?" I whispered, the word hardly falling from my lips.

Three words.

It was just three words. Three words that changed my mood. Three words that cracked my heart. Three words that I never wanted to hear.

I have cancer.

My eyes fell to Mom's lips as she spoke to me. At least I thought she spoke to me. Did she say anything at all? Did I make it up? Was I hearing things? Were the echoes of my past haunting me?

Grandpa had cancer.

He struggled with cancer.

He died from cancer.

There was nothing good that came from that word.

I shook my head back and forth, confusion swirling as tears began to slowly fall down Mom's cheeks. I looked to Dad to see him on the verge of crying, too.

"No."

That's all I could say.

That's all that came to mind.

I shook my head. "No. No, that's not true."

Dad pinched the bridge of his nose. "It's true."

2

"No," I repeated. "It's not."

There was no way Mom had cancer.

People like her didn't get cancer. She was the healthiest woman in the world. I mean, heck, her idea of a crazy snack was juicing carrots, apples, and a cucumber. If you cut her, she'd probably bleed out broccoli. Healthy people like Mom didn't get sick. They only got healthier. There was no way...

Oh, no...

Now Dad was crying, too.

Dad didn't cry. I could count on one hand how many times I'd ever seen him shed a tear.

"Eleanor..." He called me Eleanor when things were serious, and my father was hardly ever a serious man. He sniffled and shut his eyes. "This is hard for us all. We wanted to tell you when we found out, but we didn't know how. Plus, there were more tests to do and—"

"How bad?" I asked.

They both answered with silence.

That couldn't have been good.

My heart felt as if it was being ripped piece by piece from my chest.

Mom's hand flew over her mouth as the tears kept falling.

Dad spoke again. Saying my full name—*again*. "Eleanor...please understand. We'll have to all stand together to get through this."

"We're going to fight it," Mom promised, her voice shaky and scared and unsure and fragmented. "We're going to fight this, Ellie, I swear. You, your father, and me. We're going to fight back."

I couldn't breathe. I wanted to run. I wanted to stand up and dash out of the room, out of the house, out of that reality. But, the way Mom's eyes stared into mine. The way I could see how she was hurting. The way every inch of her body shook from fear and pain.

I couldn't leave her.

Not like that.

I leaned toward her on the couch and wrapped her with my arms. I burrowed myself into her, placing my head against her chest, hearing her heart beat wildly. "I'm sorry," I whispered as tears burst from my eyes and sadness overtook me. I didn't know what more I could do, so I just held her tighter and kept repeating the words. "I'm sorry. I'm sorry. I'm sorry."

She pulled me tighter, and held on as if she wouldn't ever let go. Then, Dad's arms wrapped around the two of us, and we all held on for dear life.

Our tears fell in sync, and we stayed locked together as one unit.

As the hurt kept hurting, Mom placed her lips against my forehead and softly spoke words that made me cry even harder. "I'm so sorry, Ellie."

But everything would be okay, because we were going to fight it.

We were going to fight it together.

And we were going to win.

1

Eleanor

June 21, 2003

Everything I knew about life, I learned from Harry Potter. I called him the greatest teacher of life lessons, and I swore up and down that he'd saved my life countless times. When I was upset, I wrote spells to turn people into rats, slugs, or toads.

Needless to say, my people skills were lacking, which was fine, because I was really great at avoiding humans—well, at least until I was forced to interact with them.

"You're grounded from your room," Mom stated as she stood in my bedroom doorway rubbing her palms against her face. Her brown hair was tossed up in a messy bun, and her painting apron was tied around her waist, hiding her Pink Floyd T-shirt. Her neon-green Chucks were covered in paint, and her pink thick-framed glasses sat on top of her head as she gave me the brightest smile.

She'd been painting all day in the garage, because the weekends were when she could let loose and dive into her love for art. During the week, she was just your everyday friendly nanny, saving kids from lives of dullness. On the weekends, though? She let her hair down.

It had been two months since her cancer diagnosis, and I loved whenever she was painting. As long as she was painting, I felt like things were okay. As long as she was still herself, every day was easier.

And for the most part, she was herself. Sometimes she was tired, but still, she was Mom. She just took a few more naps than normal.

I narrowed my eyes, looking up from my novel. "You can't ground people from their bedroom."

"Yes, you actually can. Your father and I talked it over, and we are grounding you from these four walls. It's summer vacation! You need to hang out with your friends."

My eyes darted from her to the book then back to her. "What exactly do you think I'm doing?" I loved my mother to death. Out of all mothers, she was top of the line, but that afternoon she was being completely inconsiderate. It wasn't just any summer day, after all. It was June 21, 2003, the day I'd been counting down to for the past three years.

Three. Long. Painful. Years.

She was truly acting as if she didn't recall that *Harry Potter and the Order of the Phoenix* had released that day. The fact that she even had the nerve to speak about anything other than Harry, Ron, and Hermione was mind-blowing.

"Eleanor, it's your summer vacation and you haven't even left your bedroom yet."

"That's because I had to reread the first four *Harry Potter* books in order to prepare for this one." Truly, she should've understood. It was like back in her day if a new Black Sabbath album came out and, instead of letting her listen to it, Grandma told her to go pick up milk from the corner store.

Totally uncool.

Black Sabbath > milk.

Harry Potter > social life.

"Shay said there's a party happening tonight," Mom commented, plopping down on my bed. "There will probably be pot and alcohol," she joked, nudging my arm.

"Oh, joy," I mocked. "How could I pass up such a grand time?"

"Okay, I know you're not the party animal yours truly was as a teenager, but I feel like every sixteen-year-old should go to an unsupervised party at least once in their life."

"Why would I want to do that? Why would *you* want me to do that?"

"We haven't had sex since summer break began," Dad said matter-of-factly, joining the conversation.

"*Daddd*," I groaned, covering my ears. "Come on!"

He walked into the room, sat down on the bed behind Mom, and wrapped his arms around her. "Ah, come on, Ellie. We all know sexual intercourse is a beautiful, natural act, one we should all celebrate when it is had in a consensual, respectable fashion."

"Oh, my gosh, please stop talking. Seriously. Stop." I tightened my grip on my ears, and they laughed.

"He's just teasing you, but we *were* hoping to have a horror movie marathon, and I know how you hate horror movies," Mom said, and I was actually thankful for the heads-up.

One time when I was a kid, I'd walked in on them watching *Chucky*, and for weeks I was convinced my dolls were out to get me. I got rid of every stuffed animal I owned. You never really notice how creepy Cabbage Patch Kids are until you envision them with butcher knives in their hands.

Don't even get me started on the time Dad thought I was old enough to watch *The Shining*.

Spoiler alert: I wasn't.

Ever since then, when they had a horror movie night, I made sure to go to Shay's house. I would've been fine with it, too, if it hadn't been that night of all nights.

"Can't you guys just wait a few days?" I asked.

"We would, but seeing how it's our anniversary..." Mom's words trailed off, obviously thinking that would be enough to convince me.

Spoiler alert: it wasn't.

"Oh, man, that's today?" I asked. "Didn't that just happen last year?"

Dad smirked. "It's insane—you can remember book release dates, but not your own parents' anniversary."

"You would understand if you ever read these books, Dad."

"It's on my to-do list," he joked. He'd been saying that since the first *Harry Potter* book had come out. I wasn't holding my breath.

"I'm just saying, Ellie, it would be great for your father and me to have the house to ourselves tonight. Plus, you know how hard it is for us to find alone time to...well, you know," Mom commented.

"Have sex," Dad said, making it clear as day. "Honestly, you're welcome to stay here, but you do know how thin these walls are. So, if you want to go from hearing horror movie characters' scream to hearing your mother's screams, by all means, stay."

"For the love of... I just wish you'd stop talking now."

My parents' favorite pastime was making me as uncomfortable as possible. They were ridiculously good at it, too. They always got such   pleasure from my pain.

Dad couldn't stop himself from teasing me more. "If you want, you can just get earplugs while we are—"

I leaped up from my bed and shouted. "Okay! Okay! You win. I'm going to the party with Shay."

They smiled, pleased.

"Though I do think it's rude that you use sex talk to make me uncomfortable enough to get your way."

"Oh honey." Mom smiled and rested her head on Dad's shoulder as he tightened his arms around her. They were so grossly in love. "The best part of parenthood is making your teenager uncomfortable. Remember that."

"I'll keep it in my back pocket. I'll be back by ten, so wrap it up by then."

"Okay, but make your curfew midnight for tonight! You're young! Now go, be free! Be wild!" Dad shouted. "And keep an eye on Shay, will you?"

"Will do."

"Oh, and do you want some condoms?" Mom asked, making me cringe. She loved every second of it.

"No, Mother Dearest. I'm good."

———

"Are you good?" Shay asked, looking into her handheld mirror and applying another pound of lip gloss as we stood on the front porch of some random kid's house. My cousin Shay was beautiful. She was the kind of beautiful that didn't seem fair for a high schooler, and she'd been that way her whole life. My aunt Camila was a gorgeous Hispanic woman, and Shay took after her more than she did my uncle Kurt, which was a blessing, since Kurt was an asshole. The less connection Shay had with her father, the better, really.

But man, had she gotten her mother's looks. I was sure the day Shay had been born, she'd rolled out on a red carpet with paparazzi asking her what she was wearing, and I could just see her replying, "Onesie by JC Penney."

Her hair was Snow White–black, and her eyes were deep chocolate with lashes every girl dreamed of. She had curves in places where I had flat tires, but the best thing about Shay was that she didn't rely on her beauty. She was one of the most down-to-earth and funniest people you'd ever meet. Plus, she was all about girl power thanks to her piece-of-crap father.

We didn't really talk about Kurt a lot since Shay's parents had gone their separate ways, and I thought it was best that way. Whenever Shay used to mention her father, she'd just call him the shitty shithead who shit on her and her mother's lives.

Dad still called Kurt his brother, though he wasn't proud to do it. It was just like how Mufasa still claimed Scar, even though Mufasa knew his brother was an evil prick.

Though, maybe things would've been different if Mufasa had blacklisted Scar.

Hakuna matata, I suppose.

Shay didn't call herself a man-hater, but she did tag herself as a woman-lover.

I liked that about her, because way too many girls our age despised one another in order to get guys to like them. What a waste of energy. It truly felt as if high school had made them completely forget all of their Spice Girls training from elementary school.

Shay stood tall in her high heels, and boy, could she wear high heels.

My calves hurt at the thought of even trying them on.

"Yeah, I'm fine," I replied, looking down at my yellow cardigan with dragonflies Mom made me. Beneath it was an old-school Metallica T-shirt that I stole from my dad because it hadn't fit over his gut since 1988. My favorite ripped blue jeans and yellow Chucks completed the outfit.

My cocoa-colored hair was brushed back in a ponytail, and the closest thing to makeup on my face were lingering microscopic remnants of the bar soap I'd used to wash it that morning. At least my braces were nice and shiny.

I should've worn a push-up bra. Not that it would've helped any. Push-up bras only really worked if there was something to actually push up.

My handwoven crossbody bag—also made by my mom—was tossed over my shoulder, and I was already counting down the hours until the party would be over.

"It's pretty much just guys from the basketball team and their friends," Shay commented, as if that would make a difference in my mind about the party I was about to hate.

"That's fine."

"There's some nice people, though," she said. "They aren't all assholes."

"That sounds promising."

"Okay, let's rock this," Shay said, opening the front door and walking into a house filled with people I wished I didn't have to see. Seeing my fellow classmates outside of school felt like a cruel form of punishment. I'd seen them enough during the school year, and the last thing I wanted was to be packed in like sardines with them.

My idea of a party was more like watching reruns of *Whose Line is it Anyway* in pajamas with my parents while eating a stupid amount of popcorn and greasy cheeseburgers. Mom would have a vegan burger, obviously. She'd watched a documentary on the treatment of animals years back and it had changed her for life.

Dad had watched it too, but he still ate his steak medium-rare.

"I'll find you a Coke," Shay said.

"Are you drinking?"

She shook her head. "Not since what happened with Landon. I'd rather be sober than drunkenly make out with him again."

"That's really smart, but if you did end up drunk, I'd make sure you didn't kiss the jerk."

"That's why you're my favorite cousin."

"I'm your *only* cousin. See if you can find some ice for the Coke, will you? I'll be in—"

"A corner." She smirked. "I bet you five bucks I'll find you in a corner with a book in your hands."

"It's like you've known me my whole life or something."

She laughed and hurried away, though, not with ease. Every time Shay walked into a room, everyone clamored for her attention—and she was nice enough to give it to all of them.

I would've just kept walking.

It would be a while before I got my drink, but I was lucky enough to score myself a nice nook right under the staircase—a very Harry Potter-ish spot to read.

I tossed on my headphones, not because I was listening to anything, but because people tended to leave you alone if you had headphones on. It was a great introvert hack: look busy to avoid human interaction. Doubling up on two activities was even better.

A book alone isn't always enough to get people to ignore you, but a book *and* headphones? Well, you might as well be a ghost.

It was so hard being an introvert in an extrovert world, one where the social norms involved house parties, school clubs, spirit week, and getting together with people didn't care to see just to say you were "living life to the fullest."

Society was the worst for introverts, but I was sure a changing of the tides was on the way. I couldn't wait until the day the media pushed the idea that staying home was the new cool thing to do and socializing with people you hated was a thing of the past. All of us introverts would rejoice!

Quietly...alone...with a good cup of coffee, a solid read, and our faithful cats.

I made myself comfortable on the floor with my legs crossed like a pretzel and rested my back against the wall. The more tucked away I was in my tight corner, the less people would notice me. *Carry on, muggles. I'm not even here. I am just a part of the wall.*

Reaching into my bag, I pulled out my novel and fell back into the world of magic. It took me a few minutes to tune out the noise surrounding me, but J.K. Rowling made it easy for me to become fully invested in every single word she wrote.

Surprisingly, the party wasn't that wild. Some people were drinking, but more seemed to be into the music choices and poor dancing.

Two people a few feet away from me talked about basketball stats and workouts.

I thought more people would be tongue-locked. Though, I guess I'd gotten most of my preconceptions of school parties from television shows and over-the-top rom-coms.

It actually didn't seem so out of the ordinary for a girl to be reading. Oddly enough, I kind of fit in.

It wasn't until I heard two guys trying to whisper as they talked about Shay that I looked up from my book. Because they weren't just talking about Shay—they were talking about me, too.

Me.

That wasn't the norm. All throughout my years in school, I had been able to keep my head down and be left alone for the most part. I was almost certain no one even knew who I was, other than me being the random, oddly dressed girl Shay ate lunch with every day.

"Dude, Brace Face is here," one of the voices whisper-shouted over the bad music.

"You don't gotta call her that," the other groaned.

"Uh, have you seen her mouth? I think we do. She's Shay's cousin, right?"

"Yeah, that's her. Eleanor," the other replied.

Hmm...

He'd used my actual name. Most people called me Brace Face or Shay's cousin.

Weird.

"Go butter her up and get on her good side. Then Shay will see that I get along with her family. It will make her and me a sure thing again."

I glanced over at the two guys, trying to act nonchalant, before looking back to my book.

Of course it was Landon Harrison trying to find his way into my cousin's heart—or more accurately, her pants.

The two had been the leads in the school play the previous year. They'd hooked up during tech week while Shay was a bit intoxicated. After that, she'd made the most cliché mistake as an actress—she'd fallen in love with the fictional character the actor was portraying. Rookie mistake.

Landon was definitely no Mr. Darcy.

They'd dated for a week before he'd cheated on her on opening night of the show. Once she'd broken things off with him, he'd made it his mission to get her back, presumably mainly because he struggled with the idea of a girl not wanting him and his cheating ways.

Too bad Shay was too strong of a woman to put up with his crap. She hardly even looked his way, except when vodka was involved.

"Shouldn't you be talking to her to make a connection?" the other guy asked.

I discreetly glanced up at him. Greyson East was one of the top-tier students in our class. He, like Shay, was loved by all.

Greyson was annoyingly handsome, well dressed, and, the star basketball player who could have any girl in the world. When I thought of high school popularity, Greyson was the one who always came to mind. I mean, it was his face on the homepage of the school's website, after all. He was a big deal at our high school.

"Dude, I can't talk to that thing. She creeps me out. All she ever does is read and wear those weird sweaters."

I would've been offended by him calling me a thing, but I simply didn't care. It was just a muggle being a muggle. They didn't know any better. Sometimes they acted out in idiotic ways.

"What a waste of life," Grey mocked his friend, sounding bored.

I almost smiled at the level of sass in his voice, but my hatred pushed away my grin.

"Just do me a solid," Landon requested.

"I'm not doing that," Greyson argued. "Just leave her alone."

"Come on," Landon persisted. "You owe me for Stacey White."

Greyson sighed. He sighed again. Then one more long, dragged-out exhalation. "Fine."

Oh, no.

No, no, no, no...

I tried to absorb the words of my book, but my peripheral vision stared at his shoes as he approached. Of course, he was wearing Nike shoes, because everything about Greyson was a cliché. He might as well have been modeling them for an ad. When those crisp, not-even-creased-yet shoes paused in front of me, I reluctantly looked up.

Now his eyes were staring at me.

Those gray eyes...

They were the kind of gray you thought only existed in over-wrought romance novels where the hero looked a little too perfect. No one truly had gray eyes. I'd been alive for sixteen years and I had never come across a boy with a gray stare other than Greyson. Light blue? Sure. Green? Yeah, sometimes, but Greyson's eyes were so far from anything else I'd ever seen. I understood the appeal.

On the receiving end of his gray stare and *that* smile, I understood why most girls melted into a puddle of helplessness around him.

Oh, God, make it stop.

He gave me a slight wave when we made eye contact, along with a tiny crooked smirk, and it annoyed me. Those smirks might've worked on the Stacey Whites of the world, but they didn't work on me. I looked down at my book, trying to ignore him.

But those shoes stayed in place. Then, out of the corner of my eye, I saw him lowering, and lowering, and lowering his body before he was kneeling right in front of me. He waved again, with the same forced smile.

"Hey, Eleanor, what's up?" he said, almost as if we'd always talk-ed and he was just checking in to catch up.

I muttered under my breath.

He arched an eyebrow. "Did you say something?"

For the love of all things right in the world, did he not see my headphones and my book? Did he not know it was June 21, 2003? Why did no one seem to understand the importance of binge-reading a novel the second it hit your fingertips?

I hated this world sometimes.

"I said don't." I took off my headphones. "Just don't do this."

"Do what?"

"*This.*" I gestured between us. "I know Landon told you to come talk to me to get to Shay, but it's a lost cause. I'm not interested, and neither is Shay."

"How did you hear what we were saying with headphones on?"

"Easy—I wasn't playing anything."

"Then why wear the headphones?"

OHMYGOSHCANYOUJUSTGOAWAY?

There was nothing worse than when an extrovert tried to understand the deep corners of an introvert's mind.

I released a heavy sigh. "Look, I get it—you're trying to be a good friend and all, but I'm honestly just trying to read my book in peace and be left alone."

Greyson ran his hands through his hair like a freaking shampoo model. I swore he did it in slow motion as the nonexistent wind blew through it. "Okay, but can I, like, just hang here next to you for a few minutes? Just so Landon thinks I'm doing him a favor?"

"I don't care what you do. Just do it quietly."

He smiled and *holy crap*, it was an easy smile to like.

I went back to reading my book as Greyson sat beside me. Every now and then, he'd say, "Just talking your way so Landon thinks we're buddies."

I'd respond with, "Just replying so you don't look as ridiculous as you're actually being right now."

He'd smile again, I'd notice that smile, and I'd go back to my book.

Finally, Shay walked up with my Coke and held out a plastic cup with a frozen Popsicle in it. "I couldn't find ice, but I figured a Popsicle could keep your drink cold for a bit. Plus it's a cherry Popsicle so, voila! It's a cherry Coke." She shifted her stare to Greyson and raised an eyebrow. "Oh, Grey...hey, what's up?"

"Oh, nothing. Just getting to know Eleanor." He did that grin thing and Shay totally fell for it like a freaking gazelle in a lion's den.

"Oh, how neat! She's my favorite person in the whole wide world, so you're in for a treat. I'll let you guys keep chatting." Shay waved to me as if she didn't see the panic in my eyes that pleaded "Abort, abort! Save me." She wandered off to be the social butterfly she was, and I was left stuck in my cocoon with Greyson.

"How long does this have to go on?" I asked him.

He shrugged. "I don't know. As long as it takes for Landon to stop throwing the Stacey White situation in my face."

"What did you do to Stacey White?"

He narrowed his eyes and cocked a brow. "What do you mean, what did I do to her?"

"It just sounds like something happened."

He shifted around in his seat and broke eye contact. "It's actually the opposite. Nothing happened, though, it's not really anyone's business."

"It kind of feels like my business since it's making you stare at me."

"Yeah, I get that." He went quiet for a moment then parted his lips. "Why doesn't Shay give Landon another shot?"

"He cheated on her. After a week."

"Yeah, I know, but—"

I shut my book. It was clear I wasn't going to be getting much more reading done any time soon. "There are no buts. It just blows my mind that you guys think you can get a shot with anyone and everyone because of how you look. Shay isn't an idiot, though. She knows what she deserves."

Greyson pushed his tongue into his cheek. "Did you just kind of call me handsome in a roundabout way?"

"Don't let it go to your head."

"Trust me, it already did." He started drumming his fingers against his legs. "So, what's your deal?"

"I thought we were only pretend talking."

"Yeah, but I got bored with that. So, you're into...reading?" He nodded toward the book.

"Great observation, Captain Obvious," I remarked.

He laughed. "You're sassy."

"I get that from my mother."

"I like it."

My face heated up, and I hated that it happened. My body was reacting to his annoyingly cute-without-even-trying personality, even though my mind had been taught to dislike him. I'd spent the past year observing guys like Greyson and the way girls melted in their hands without any thought process involved.

My brain never wanted me to be that girl, but clearly my heart didn't care what the mind wanted.

I looked away, because my heart raced when we locked eyes.

"I've never read *Harry Potter*," he said, and for the first time in my life, I felt bad for Greyson East. What a sad, sad life he lived.

"That's probably a good thing," I told him. "Because if you did read it, I would probably have to form a stupid unrealistic crush on you that goes against everything I stand for."

"You're sassy *and* straightforward."

"The straightforwardness comes from my father."

He smiled.

I liked it.

Whatever.

"So, books and dragonflies?" he asked me.

I cocked an eyebrow. "How did you know about the dragonflies?"

"Well, your sweater has dragonflies on it, and your hairclips are dragonflies, too."

Oh, right. I'd have bet good money I was the only girl at the party who had dragonfly clips in her hair.

"It's kind of mine and my mom's thing."

"Dragonflies?"

"Yes."

"That's a weird thing."

"I'm a weird girl."

He narrowed his eyes as if he was studying me, trying to scan my DNA with his eyes.

"What is it?" I asked as my stomach flipped.

"It's nothing. I just...I swear I know you from somewhere."

"Well, we do go to school together," I commented sarcastically.

"No, yeah, I know that, but you just..." His words trailed off and he shook his head. "I don't know. You probably weren't at Claire Wade's party, huh?"

"That's a big no."

"Kent Fed's?"

Blank stare from me.

"Right. It's just weird, because I swear—" Before he could finish his sentence, he was cut off as Landon came rushing over.

"Mission aborted, dude. Shay's just a bitch," he said with a grumpy frown. It was clear my cousin had bruised his ego.

"Call my cousin a bitch one more time, and I'll show you a real bitch," I barked.

17

Landon glanced at me and rolled his eyes. "Yeah whatever, weirdo."

"You don't have to be an ass, Landon," Greyson said, standing up for me. "And she's right—Shay didn't do anything to you. You're the one who cheated on her. It doesn't make her a bitch because she doesn't want you back."

Wait, what?

Did Greyson East just stand up for me and Shay?

Well, okay then.

I guess I'll be having his kids someday.

Those stupid butterflies in my stomach wouldn't leave, so you can imagine my relief when Greyson stood up to go. My skin was pretty pale and when I blushed, it was obvious. I turned into the ripest tomato known to mankind. I didn't need him to witness that.

"Whatever, man. Let's go," Landon said, looking past me like I didn't even exist. That was fine, though. I looked at him the exact same way.

"I'll talk to you later, Eleanor." Greyson waved goodbye as he walked away. "Enjoy the book."

Under my breath, I said bye before going back to my novel. Every now and then, though, Greyson would float around in my head along with Ron Weasley.

Not much later, Shay reappeared, and we started our walk home. "So, it seemed you and Greyson were having a good conversation," she remarked.

I shrugged. "It was fine."

"He's a really nice guy, Ellie. Nothing like Landon. Greyson is genuine."

She said it as if she was trying to talk me into allowing the butterflies in my gut to remain, while I was trying to somehow rip off their wings.

I shrugged once. "He's fine."

"Just fine?" she mocked, nudging my arm, probably seeing my reddened cheeks.

"Yup."

Just fine.

Shay was crashing in my room that night, and when we walked into the house, the living room television was glowing bright. Some horror movie was playing so I hurried over and grabbed the remote, quickly shutting it off. There they were, passed out on the couch. Dad was lying out flat and Mom was wrapped in his arms.

"Should we wake them?" Shay asked.

I grabbed a blanket and covered them up. "Nah. They always end up in bed by the morning."

This was a normal sight with my parents—Mom wrapped in Dad's arms after they'd fallen asleep watching television. Whenever she would shift around on the couch, Dad would smile, readjust his arms around her, and get comfortable again. I'd never seen two people who'd merged so completely as one. If it hadn't been for my parents, I'd have thought soul mates were a lie.

2
Greyson

"I'm just saying, I don't get it. I'm real good-looking, she's real good-looking! I just don't get why she wouldn't want to be with me," Landon said, tossing his hands around like a madman as we walked home from the party. "I mean, we're pretty much the Nick Lachey and Jessica Simpson of Raine, Illinois. We're meant to be together!"

He said it so passionately, I could hardly tell if he was kidding or not.

Honestly, he would've done a lot better dating Shay if he'd been this obsessed with her while they were dating. He pretty much shot himself in the ass by acting like one.

"I think you should let the idea of you and Shay go, man. I don't think she's interested."

"She just doesn't know she's interested yet. You'll see. You'll all see!"

I rolled my eyes, but let him keep talking. There was no point in trying to reason with someone as wasted as he was right now.

"Anyway, sorry I made you talk to her weird cousin," he said, running his hand through his hair.

"She's not that weird."

"Cardigans every day. Head always in a book. Weird."

"Just because someone is different doesn't make them weird," I said, getting a bit defensive about Eleanor. Sure, she had her quirks, but so did Landon. He bit down on forks and pulled them out of his mouth, making an unbearable sound. He couldn't watch a movie without going "Wait, rewind that, I missed something." He couldn't get the hell over his infatuation with Shay because she bruised his massive ego.

Sure, maybe Eleanor wore a lot of cardigans, but at least she wasn't a jerk.

"Alright, alright. I see you made a new friend today," he said, tossing his hands up. "I still think she's a weird loner, but whatever."

I guess in a way Eleanor was a loner. She was a professional at keeping to herself, outside of Shay.

Sometimes I wished I could be more like that.

It seemed less complicated.

Landon lived on the same block as me, and when we walked up to my house, his over-the-top chatty persona faded as he took in the howling that was coming from my house.

Mom and Dad were home.

That was always a treat to partake in.

Landon stuffed his hands in his pockets and he gave me a pathetic smile. "You wanna crash at my place tonight?"

I shook my head. "Nah, it's fine. I'll just hurry to my room. I'm sure my dad will find a reason to storm off soon enough."

"Are you sure?"

"Yeah. Night."

He scratched the back of his neck, hesitant about my choice, but he started walking away. "All right, night, Greyson." He paused, then turned back to me. "I'll leave the window to the first floor guest room open tonight if you need it, okay?"

Even though he was sometimes a crappy human, he was a damn good best friend.

"Thanks, Landon."

"Yup. Night."

Once I reached my front porch, I hadn't gone inside. I knew nothing good would come from walking into that place.

My parents were in yet another screaming match.

That was nothing new. Whenever they were both home, fighting was what they did best. Mom was probably wine-drunk, cussing out Dad, and Dad was probably whiskey-drunk, telling her to shut her piehole.

Though, I was pretty sure whatever was going on was Dad's fault. He was pretty good at screwing up and making it look like Mom made the mess. I'd never met a person who was so damn good at gaslighting another person. Mr. Handers taught us that word last year in English class—*gaslighting*—and the moment I heard it, I knew it was my father to the T.

He was a professional manipulator. Both at work, and at home. He was so good at making my mother think she was completely mad. If she smelled perfume on his clothes, he'd say it was hers. If she found lipstick on his shirts, he'd convince her that she placed it there. If he told her the sky was green, she'd doubt her own eyesight.

He once forced her into the hospital to test her psyche.

The tests showcased that she was sane. She'd married an asshole.

Dad stayed eerily calm during Mom's meltdowns, too. Which was another mind game of his—making her seem as if she was crazed, even though he was the one driving her to the looney bin. Sometimes I thought he left other women's numbers in places just so she'd find them. I wouldn't put it past him.

When I was younger, he'd try to get me to side with him—to use me to throw Mom under the bus. But I never did. I'd always known that the only thing Mom had done wrong was fall in love with a monster.

My father was a liar, a cheater, and a messed-up man.

Actually, there was one other thing Mom had done wrong. She stayed.

I never understood that.

I didn't know if it was because she loved him, or loved the comfortable life he created for us. Either way, it wasn't healthy. I guess that's why she was hardly ever home. Maybe she got comfort from seeing the world on Dad's dime. Maybe spending his money made her feel as if she was somehow winning.

"I know you're messing around with her, Greg!" Mom hollered as I sat on the top step of the porch. I rolled my hands over my ears, and tried my best to drown out the sounds.

I wished Grandpa was still around. For the most part I tried my best not to think about him being gone, because it really messed with my head, but some nights I just wished I could sneak off to his house and watch old kung fu movies with him and eat insane amounts of popcorn.

The best thing about my grandfather was the fact that he was nothing like my father.

He was a good man through and through, and the world sucked that much more now that he was gone.

It had been a few weeks since I'd lost him, and honestly, I still didn't know how to stop missing him.

The guidance counselor at school told me that over time it would get easier dealing with loss, but I didn't find that true. It didn't get easier; it just got lonelier.

I glanced back and looked through the window. Something shattered in the living room. Mom had thrown a wine bottle at Dad's head, but she'd missed—she always missed.

Housekeeping was going to have the time of their lives getting that red wine out of the carpet again.

"Just leave, Greg! Go!" she hollered at him. "Go be with that whore!"

Like always, Dad stormed out of the house.

I think it worked best for him when she told him to leave. Then he was free to go to whoever he was sleeping with behind Mom's back.

He paused when he saw me sitting on the front porch. "Greyson. What are you doing out here?" He pulled out a cigarette and lit it.

Avoiding you.

"Just got home from hanging with Landon."

"Your mom's acting like a nutjob again. I'm wondering if she's been taking her pills."

I didn't comment, because any time he called her crazy, I wanted to punch him square in the face.

Dad narrowed his eyes and nodded my way. "I heard Landon started an internship at his father's law firm."

"Yeah." I knew where this conversation was headed.

"When are you going to come down to EastHouse and learn something, huh? I can't run that place forever, and it's about time you figured out the basics. The sooner you learn, the sooner you'll be ready to take over one day."

Here we go again.

My father was determined to have me work at EastHouse Whiskey headquarters, because he was certain I'd be taking over the company one day. My grandfather had started EastHouse, and he'd run it with all his heart and soul for years until his retirement. My father had followed in his footsteps.

It was a family business, and I intended to take over someday to honor Grandpa.

I just didn't want to do it any time soon.

"Are you deaf, boy? Am I not speaking English?" he hollered.

I stood up and stuffed my hands into my pockets. "I just don't think I'm ready for that yet."

"Not ready? You're sixteen years old, and you don't have any time to waste. If you think this basketball thing is going be your one-way ticket out, you're fooling yourself. You don't have what it takes to make it on basketball alone."

There were three things to note about his comment:

1. I was seventeen, not sixteen.
2. I didn't want to be a basketball star.
3. Piss off, Dad.

I pinched the bridge of my nose and walked past him and straight into the house. He hollered that we weren't done talking about the internship, and we'd pick it up at a different time, but I wasn't too worried about it. He never stayed home long enough to really hammer into me.

As I walked inside, I saw Mom picking up the shattered pieces of glass from the bottle.

"Mom, here, let me get that before you cut yourself," I said, watching her sway drunkenly back and forth.

"Back off," she said, pushing my arm away. She looked up at me, with mascara cruising down her cheeks, and frowned. She placed her wine-soaked hand against my cheek and parted her lips to speak. "You look just like your father. You know how angry that makes me? It makes me hate you almost as much as I hate him."

"You're drunk," I told her. She was the kind of drunk where she didn't even look like herself. She looked wild in the eyes, and her hair was tangled. "Let's get you to bed."

"*No!*" She pulled her hand back and slapped me across the face, muttering, "Fuck you, Greg."

My eyes shut as my cheeks stung. Her eyes watered and she placed both of her hands over her mouth. "Oh, my gosh. I'm so sorry, Greyson. I'm so sorry." She began to sob into her hands, shaking. "I can't do this anymore. I just can't do this."

I wrapped an arm around her, and squeezed lightly, because I was pretty sure if I didn't hug her, she wasn't getting any hugs at all. "Yeah, it's fine, Mom. You're just tired. Just go to bed. Alright? Everything's okay."

I gathered the large pieces of glass and tossed them into the trash can as she wandered off to bed. She'd probably be gone before I woke the next morning, off to catch a flight to her next adventure. But we'd cross paths again when she needed her monthly fight with Dad, and a bottle of wine to toss.

I headed to the bathroom to wash the wine from my hands and face, and when I glanced in the mirror, I hated what I saw.

Because I did look like my father, and I kind of hated myself for it, too.

When I went to bed, I tried to shake my parents from my mind, but when I did shake them, Grandpa entered my head, and that just made me sadder.

So I thought about Eleanor Gable.

The girl who read books at parties, and really liked dragonflies.

Those thoughts weren't as heavy as all my others.

So, I let them stay.

3
Eleanor

It had been two days since the party, and I hadn't even finished reading *Harry Potter and the Order of the Phoenix*. My focus was shot, and I couldn't shake Greyson from my mind.

It wasn't even the way he looked or the things he said. It was just small things about him.

I didn't talk to a lot of people, but I noticed them well enough.

I noticed the way he became uncomfortable with certain things, the way he'd tap his fingers against his legs and never stood still.

I noticed the way he kind of smelled like red licorice.

Thinking about him was like a bad daydream I couldn't wake up from. A part of me wondered if he thought about me, too.

This was a whole new concept for me.

I didn't do crushes, unless we were talking about fictional characters. I always found guys my age to be idiotic and shallow. Everything about high school was the worst kind of cliché.

To me, everything seemed so contrived and fake. It was all based on superficial things like looks, popularity, and how much money your parents made. I just didn't want any part of it.

Until Greyson and that stupid grin showed up. Now I was one of those girls, wondering about him when I shouldn't have been, and reading one too many articles about having a crush.

"Hey, Snickers," Dad said, popping into my room while twirling a pencil between his fingers.

"What?! Nothing. Stop. Huh?" I huffed quickly, hurrying to close the internet browser on the desktop computer. My breaths went in and out as I tried to cover up my nerves. "Hi, Dad," I said on an exhale, giving him a wide, toothy grin.

He cocked an eyebrow. "What are you hiding?"

"Nothing. What do you need? What's up?"

He rubbed his hand against his stomach and narrowed his stare. My father had a nice gut on him, and he called it Doritos, after the cause of the creation of said gut. Mom was a vegan and she always tried to get him to go down that line with her, but he was completely against giving up bacon—which I understood.

For the most part, Mom was good at keeping Dad's diet in check. He'd been pre-diabetic before she'd gotten him to somewhat follow her eating plan. She'd tell him it would make her happy if he had a salad with dinner, so he'd have the salad, because making her happy was his favorite activity.

I always giggled a bit when he'd rub Doritos as he tried to figure something out, as if his belly was a magic lamp with all the answers.

"I just wanted to let you know it's just you and me for dinner tonight. Your mom's not feeling great."

My gut tightened as worry took over. "Oh? Is she okay?"

"Just a little tired." He smiled. "She's all right, Ellie. I promise."

He called me Ellie and not Eleanor, so I believed him.

He scratched his chin. "So, dinner?"

"I can't tonight. I'm babysitting Molly." I'd been babysitting Molly Lane twice a week, Mondays and Fridays, for the past few months after school. She was a spunky five-year-old girl who lived a few blocks away, and she kept me on my toes. "I should actually head over there soon."

"Oh, it is Monday, isn't it?" He wiggled his nose. "Well, I guess it's just me, *Frasier*, and Mickey D's for dinner tonight."

"Does Mom know about the McDonalds?" I asked, knowing about Dad's latest diet plan.

He pulled out his wallet and held up twenty bucks. "Does she have to know about it?"

"Are you bribing me?"

"I don't know—is it working?"

I walked over and took the money from his grip. "Yup, it sure is."

He wrapped his hands around my head and kissed my forehead. "I always knew you were my favorite daughter."

"I'm your only daughter."

"That we know of. There were a lot of rock concerts in the early eighties."

I rolled my eyes, a small chuckle coming from my lips. "You know Mom will smell the French fries on you. She always does."

"Some things are worth the risk." He kissed my forehead one last time. "I'll see you later. Tell Molly and her parents I said hi!"

"Will do."

"Love you, Snickers." He'd nicknamed me after his favorite candy, a term of endearment.

"Love you, too, Dad."

After he left, I began getting ready to head over to Molly's. I always took some of the old chapter books I'd loved as a kid to read to her before she went to bed. Molly loved books almost as much as I did, and I secretly felt a bit of jealousy that one day she'd get to read the *Harry Potter* series for the first time ever.

What I wouldn't have given to once again experience the feeling of reading those books for the very first time.

———

Raine, Illinois was split into two parts, divided by a bridge—the east side and the west side. I lived on the west side, but Molly was on the east, off Brent Street. Even though I lived only a few blocks away, once you crossed over the small bridge, you could tell the difference in income level. My family was well-off, but we weren't as well-off as those east of the bridge.

All the houses on Molly's block were worth insane amounts of money. They were mansions—really big mansions. Raine was a pretty middle-class town, except for when you walked the east side. It was where all the wealthy people who worked in Chicago, but wanted a semi-suburban lifestyle lived. Mom nannied for families on that side of the bridge, and she made a pretty great income. I swore even the air smelled like hundred-dollar bills. If it hadn't been for Molly, there would have been no reason I'd ever be caught on that side of town.

"You're Molly Lane's babysitter!" a voice shouted as my sneaker landed on the first step of Molly's porch. I quickly turned to see where it was coming from. Across the street, three houses to the left, stood a boy with a stupid great smile. Greyson waved.

I glanced over my shoulder to make sure he was waving at me, and for goodness' sake, he was.

I brushed my hand across the back of my neck and said, "Oh, yeah."

Those were the only words I could think to say. When he started down his porch toward me, my heart started doing cartwheels in my chest, and it beat faster and faster the closer he got.

He did that slow-motion hand-through-his-hair move again, and my heart somehow both stopped and sped up at the same time.

"You've been watching her for a while?" he asked.

"Yeah, a few months." My hands were clammy. *Why are my hands clammy? Can he see the guilt all over me? Can he tell that I've been thinking about him? Does he smell my fear?! Oh, gosh, are my elbows sweating?* I hadn't even known elbows could sweat!

"I used to go to church with her when she was younger. She was the best part because everything was so structured, and when it was quiet, she'd just scream, 'A clue, a clue!', quoting *Blue's Clues*, then she'd run to the front of the church and just dance."

I snickered. Sounded like the Molly I knew and loved.

He stuffed his hands into the pockets of his sweatpants, and rocked back and forth in his Nikes. "But that's not where I know you from. I figured it out the other day."

"Oh? And where's that?"

"The Sherman Cancer Clinic." His smile kind of evaporated while my heart kind of cried. "I've seen you there a few times, coming and going."

Oh.

Well, that was awkward.

I went to the Sherman Cancer Clinic with my parents whenever Mom was having chemotherapy appointments. For the longest Mom didn't want me to go, because she thought it would upset me, but honestly, I felt more upset not being there.

I didn't say a word.

"Are you sick?" he asked.

"No. I'm not."

He crinkled his nose. "Is someone you know sick?"

"Um, my mom. She has breast cancer," I breathed out, and the moment the word *cancer* left my lips, I tried to suck it back in. Every time I said it, my eyes had a way of watering over.

"I'm so sorry, Eleanor," he said, and I could tell he meant it because his eyes were so sincere.

"Thanks." He kept staring at me as my stomach flipped over and over again. "Is someone you know sick?"

This time he grew uncomfortable.

"He was. My grandpa. He passed away a few weeks ago." His eyes did something I didn't know Greyson East's eyes could do: they grew sad.

"I'm so sorry, Greyson," I said, and I hoped he could tell I meant it by looking at how sincere my eyes were.

"Yeah, thanks. Everyone keeps saying he's not in pain anymore, but I don't know. I just feel like he left some pain behind for me to take on." He brushed his thumb against the base of his jaw, and I was stunned.

Greyson was sad.

Really sad. That was shocking to me because I never noticed his sadness when I looked at him before. To me, he just always seemed like the free-spirited popular kid that everyone loved.

Turned out popular kids could be sad, too.

Greyson shook off the grimaced look and smiled. "So, I've been thinking...we should hang out."

He said it so casually, as if the idea of us hanging out wasn't insanely absurd.

I laughed sarcastically to cover up my nerves. "Yeah, okay, Greyson."

"No, I mean it. We should hang out."

I glanced up and down the block, just to make sure he was speaking to me. "You don't want to hang out with me."

"Yes, I do."

I tugged on the bottom of my purple cardigan. "No, you don't."

"I do," he pressed.

"To get to Shay?"

He cocked an eyebrow and stepped closer to me. "Not everything is about your cousin. Some things are about you."

"I mean, it just doesn't make sense. Why would you want to hang out with me?"

"Why wouldn't I? You were interesting at the party, and I'd like to get to know you more."

"I was reading a book and wearing headphones at a high school party. That's not interesting. That's weird."

"I like weird."

I laughed. "No, you don't. You like *not* weird."

"How do you know what I like?"

I glanced around and shrugged. "I'm just assuming."

"Well, you shouldn't. If you want, you can hang out with me and really get to know me," he offered.

"We don't really come from the same kind of world, Greyson. You're you, and I'm me. I mean, look at the size of your house, and your popularity, and—"

"Listen, if you don't want to hang out, just say so. No need for excuses," he cut in, making me stand up straighter.

"No, that's not it. I'm just saying...we don't have much in common, I don't think."

"Well, we can find out, and go from there."

I narrowed my eyes. "Okay, well, once you discover something we have in common, I'll hang out with you."

He narrowed his eyes, almost as if he didn't believe me. "Pinky promise?" he asked, holding out his pinky finger.

"Are you kidding?"

"No. I mean it. I need your word. If I find something we have in common, you'll hang out with me. Pinky promise."

"*Fineee*," I groaned as I wrapped my pinky with his. I tried to ignore the feeling his touch brought me. "I promise. I gotta get to Molly now."

He smiled, pleased. "Okay, I'll talk to you later." I smiled back before I could stop myself and he noticed it. "More of that, Eleanor."

"Whatever. Bye, Greyson." I turned away from him, and I felt my cheeks heating up as I hurried up the steps, still smiling from ear to ear. As I reached the porch, I paused and I turned back toward him. "People call me Ellie. You can, too, if you want."

"Okay, Ellie." The way the name fell from his lips made me blush even more. "And you can call me Grey."

"Just Grey?"

"Yeah, just Grey." He turned away and tossed a hand up in the air. "Bye, Ellie."

The corners of my mouth turned up as I watched him walk away and I softly spoke to myself, unsure what exactly was happening in my life lately. "Bye, Grey."

"Is that your boyfriend?" a small voice asked.

I looked up to see a sassy Molly standing in her doorway with her hands on her hips. Her curly red hair hung to her shoulders, and she was tapping her foot repeatedly.

"What? No. He's not my boyfriend."

"Then why did your face turn red?"

"My face isn't red."

"Uh-huh. You look like an apple."

"Some apples are green," I argued, walking over to her.

"But you're the red apple, because of your *boyfriend*," she mocked. Suddenly she started dancing around on the front porch and singing loudly. "Ellie has a boyfriend! Ellie has a boyfriend!"

"Molly, knock it off!" I whisper-shouted, looking over my shoulder and seeing Greyson staring at us. My God, I was horrified.

"Why don't you go kiss him? Go kiss your boyfriend!" She kept pushing the boyfriend agenda, making me groan as I rubbed my hands against my face.

"He's not my boyfriend!" I argued once more.

"If he's not your boyfriend, who is he?" she asked, her hands still on her hips in that sassy pose.

"He's Grey." I sighed, tossing my hands up before walking over to her and lifting her nosey self into my arms. "He's just Grey."

"He doesn't look gray," Molly remarked. "He looks tan."

I chuckled. "No, he's not gray, but he's Grey. Like...his name is Grey."

"People's names can be colors?"

"Well, yeah, I guess."

"Can I be pink?"

I shrugged my shoulders. "Okay, Pink."

"And you're Red! Like your face right now."

Well, that felt fitting.

4

Eleanor

Y ou know those first few minutes after finishing an amazing book?

Those moments when you aren't quite sure what to do with yourself?

You simply sit there, staring at the last words, unsure how to move on with your life.

How can it be over?

How can those characters just fade to black?

For you, the characters are still imprinted on your soul. Their actions, their dialogue still alive and strong in your mind. Your tears haven't even dried, and you crave another fix.

I loved that feeling—the bittersweet love story between a person and a novel coming to an end.

That's what happened to me after I finished *Harry Potter*.

I didn't really know what to do with myself. Mom was still recovering from her cold and Dad was off watching TV, so I did the only thing that felt natural: I thought about Greyson.

I was officially a teenage cliché.

Every time I headed over to watch Molly, I grew more and more nervous about the idea that Greyson could've been sitting on the porch across the street, three houses down. I knew it was stupid, but on those days, I might've started combing my hair a little more, and I might've asked Shay for makeup tips.

I might've overplucked my eyebrows, too.

Each time Greyson wasn't there, I let out a sigh of relief, but then I felt a little sad.

When Friday came three weeks after our first interaction at Molly's, my heart raced as he came jogging across the street toward me.

"I'm a Gryffindor," he declared, waving the book he had gripped in his hand.

I cocked an eyebrow and tugged on the bottom of my cardigan. "What?"

"I said I'm a Gryffindor. I'm pretty sure, at least. It was a tossup between that and Ravenclaw, but then I read some articles online and I'm pretty sure I'm Gryffindor."

"You read *Harry Potter*?"

He nodded. "Yup. Sorry it took me so long to get back to you, but these are long."

"You..." My heart pounded against my rib cage. "You read *all* of the books?"

"All five, and now I'm counting down the days until the next one releases."

Same, Grey, same.

"Why did you read them all?"

"So we'd have something in common. Plus, I wanted you to form a stupid, unrealistic crush on me that goes against everything you stand for." He began flipping through the book, pointing out a few of his favorite quotes, which he'd highlighted. He talked quickly, going over his likes and dislikes for each of the books. He told me his favorite characters, he told me his pet peeves, and he spoke as if he truly understood what he was talking about.

I was still stuck on the fact that he'd read all five of the books simply so we would have something in common.

If he were a book character, he'd be the hero.

After he showed me his last highlighted quote, he closed the book and gave me a slight shrug. "So, what are you?"

"Hmm?"

"What's your Hogwarts House?"

"Oh." I traced the sidewalk with the toe of my shoe. "I'm a Hufflepuff."

"That's what I thought."

"Yeah, most people think it's the worst house."

"Hufflepuffs seemed silently strong, and loyal. There's nothing wrong with loyal and patient people. I think there should be more of that."

I smiled.

He smiled back and said, "More of that, Ellie." He tapped his fingers against the spine of his novel. "So, now that we have something in common, does that mean we can hang out?"

"Well, I did make that promise, and as a Hufflepuff, I have to keep my word."

"All right. So, what are you doing next Tuesday?"

"Um, nothing?"

"Okay, awesome. You want to meet me at my place? I'll plan something for us to do."

I shrugged, trying to play it cool. "All right." *Note to self: knees can sweat, too.* "Well, I have to get to Molly."

"All right. I'll see you Tuesday!"

He headed off, and for a few seconds, I wondered if I was stuck in a dream. I was too afraid to pinch myself, though, because I worried I'd wake up. If this were a dream, I wanted to live in it a little bit longer.

———

"I like a boy," I blurted out Sunday afternoon as Mom and I sat in our hidden location at Laurie Lake. We'd been going there as long as I could remember, even sometimes all bundled up in our winter gear to be near the water. If there was one thing Mom loved, it was the water. She said it was because the water healed her. Her dream was to someday place her feet in the ocean and stand with her arms wide open, but since we were in Illinois and there was no ocean to be found nearby, that dream had to wait a little bit longer.

For the time being, small lakes and ponds worked fine for us. We always made it our mission to go sit by our hidden pond and watch the dragonflies pass around us. Laurie Lake was normally packed with people during the summer, but, one day during our exploring, she and I found a smaller body of water hidden between the trees, and we'd always go there to sit and chat.

After feeling a bit off, she was finally feeling well enough to get out of the house, and I was happy to get back to our regular scheduled mama-daughter dates. She still looked tired, but not sick-tired. It seemed like the kind of tired people got when they overslept.

Still, in the back of my mind, I worried. Couldn't help it. That worry would probably always linger.

Mom tilted her head toward me, and her blue eyes lit up with joy at my words. There were two things we never really talked about with each other: sports and boys. I'd never had any interest in either one, but that afternoon, I knew I had to tell her, because she was my person. I told my mother everything. We were a regular Lorelai and Rory Gilmore.

"Oh, my gosh, who? How? From where?!"

"His name is Greyson East. We talked at the party you and Dad forced me to go to a few weeks ago."

She tossed her hands in the air with excitement. "I knew I was being a good parent forcing you to go to a party with drugs and alcohol!"

I snickered. "Something like that."

"So, tell me everything. What is he into? What does he look like? If he were to be an animal, which animal would he be?" She placed her chin in her hands and stared at me with eyes wide and filled with wonder.

So, I told her everything—everything I knew, at least.

She raised an eyebrow. "Is that why you've been wearing my makeup lately?"

"You noticed?"

"Honey, I'm sick, not dead. Plus, we really need to have a makeup lesson because the way you curled your eyelashes was a bit wild."

I laughed. "I just wanted to, I don't know, girly-up a little."

"Wearing makeup doesn't make you a girl. Were you wearing makeup when you first met him?"

"No..."

"Then there's no need to wear it now, unless you want to. Do things for you, Ellie, never for others. He obviously liked you just the way you were."

My stomach flipped as I fiddled with my thumbs. "He's the complete opposite of what I thought my first crush would be like."

"How so?"

"I don't know. I thought I'd go for a nerdy type guy, or like, an artist, or a musician. Greyson is popular."

"You say it like he has an STD," Mom joked. "People like him—so what? That's not a bad thing."

"Yeah, but it's not just people, it's *everyone*. He could have any girl he wanted, so it's hard to think he'd want—"

"No." Mom placed her hand on my knee. "We don't do that. We don't put ourselves down." She combed my hair behind my ear and placed her hands on my cheeks. "Not only are you beautiful on the outside, Eleanor Rose, you are stunning on the inside. You are creative. You have the best laugh I've ever heard. You are kind, giving, and brave. Don't ever think you aren't good enough based on what the magazines define as beauty. You. Are. Beautiful."

Mom always did this whenever I slipped into my random teenage doubts.

It was easy for me to not feel beautiful in a world of prom queens, yet my mother was always reminding me of how worthy I was.

I was a lucky daughter.

"Plus, it sounds like you caught his attention with your looks *and* your mind," she commented. "That's the most important part."

"Can we just not tell Dad? He's a bit dramatic about things like this."

"Your father has never shot a gun in his life, but I feel like you having your first crush would be enough to push him over the edge, so I'll keep it between you and me."

"Thanks."

She started to reply but broke out into a coughing fit instead. She couldn't catch her breath for a while and my gut filled with worry. When she stopped, she shook her head. "I'm fine, Ellie."

I heard her words, but sometimes I felt like they were lies just to keep me from hurting. I had a feeling moms would do anything to keep their children from feeling any form of pain.

I rested my head on her shoulder as we stared out at the water and three dragonflies flew by. "He read *Harry Potter*, all five books, because I told him we had nothing in common, and he wanted to make sure we did."

Mom's eyes widened, and her mouth dropped open. "He read your favorite series?"

"Yup."

"Eleanor?"

"Yes?"

"Marry this boy."

5

Eleanor

I wore my dragonfly cardigan when I headed over to Greyson's on Tuesday. It was what I'd been wearing the first time we talked, and I figured maybe it was a good luck charm. I went with no makeup, because that didn't matter, and also I was tired of poking myself in the eye with the mascara wand.

As I walked down Weston Street, I tried my best to tame my nerves. It was just us hanging out, anyway, not a wedding.

There was no need for me to be overthinking things.

I walked up Greyson's front porch and rang his doorbell.

Fiddling with my fingers and tapping my shoes, I waited a few seconds for him to come to the door. It was the longest time it had ever taken for anyone to answer the door, but then again, with the size of Greyson's house, it made sense.

When he opened it, he was holding a big, fluffy black cat in his arms.

My eyes widened with excitement. "Oh, my gosh, who is this?"

"This is Meow, my best friend," Greyson explained, allowing me to pet him. "He's an old fart, but he's the coolest dude out there."

I smiled at the feline. "Hey there, Meow. I'm Ellie."

Meow meowed before leaping out of Greyson's arms and walking back into the house, completely uninterested in me. I couldn't help but laugh.

"He's sweet," I said.

"Yeah, he is. So, are you ready to go?" Greyson asked, grabbing a hoodie from his foyer.

"I am, but where exactly are we going?"

"I figured I learned about something you like by reading those books, so I wanted to show you something I like. We're going to the movies."

"Oh? Which one?" I asked as we walked down the porch steps.

"Well, on Tuesdays they play old kung fu movies at Cameron Theater. This week they're playing *King Boxer*."

"You go watch old kung fu movies?"

"Yeah. I used to watch them with my grandpa before he passed away. Then, I just kept going." He shifted around in his shoes and did his *I'm uncomfortable so I'm fiddling with my fingers* thing. "If you hate the idea of going to the movie, we can do something else, like go get ice cream or something. I just thought…"

My heart…

I smiled and gently shook my head, rubbing my left hand up and down my right arm. "I think this is perfect."

He smiled back.

"More of that, Grey," I said with a grin as I used his words.

We walked to the theater, and he ordered popcorn and candy. I couldn't really eat any of that due to my braces, but it was fine. I had enough butterflies in my stomach to keep me full.

His favorite candy was red licorice, and he said he'd learned to love it from his grandpa.

The butterflies in my stomach didn't fade as we sat in the theater. If anything, they just grew in size. I swore his arm moved closer to mine, and mine inched closer to his throughout the movie. My heart stopped beating completely as his pinky brushed against mine.

When the nerves became too much, I placed my hands in my lap and tried my best not to overthink the small touch. I kicked myself for moving my hand, though, because what if I had left it? Would he have linked our pinkies together? Would we have held hands? Would he have felt my pulse racing throughout my body?

Every time Greyson laughed at the movie, I laughed, too, because he had the kind of laugh that made you think you'd just met the happiest person alive. The movie was great, but the best part was watching how much Greyson enjoyed it. His eyes stayed wide on the screen, and he'd toss his head back at the parts that tickled him while stuffing handfuls of popcorn into his mouth.

It was wild to me that I had thought I knew who the popular boy in the hallways was whenever we saw each other at school, but clearly I was wrong. There was more to Greyson than his basketball skills, and his Nike shoes, and his good looks.

He had a personality that wasn't seen at school, from his love of his cat to his love of kung fu movies, from the way he missed his grandpa to the way his eyes sometimes looked so lonely.

I felt silly for having judged him before really knowing anything about him.

Everything I learned was making my crush grow more and more. Greyson had so many layers to him, and each time he revealed one, I felt like I was being let in on a big secret.

"Did you like it?" he asked me, sounding uncertain.

"It was amazing! I've never seen a kung fu movie before."

He sighed, relieved as he rested a hand on his chest. "Good. I was really worried. Most girls think it's weird that I watch them, but I love it."

"I love that you love it."

"So, now what? Do you want to go get some food or something?"

"I could always eat," I agreed.

We headed to an ice cream parlor, where I found something else we both had in common: vanilla ice cream with chocolate fudge. We weren't shy about stuffing our faces, either. As we ate, I couldn't help but wonder about something, though.

"What made you want to hang out with me?" I blurted out, feeling my face heat up a bit after the words left my lips.

He held his spoon filled with ice cream midair and cocked an eyebrow at me. "What do you mean?"

"It just seemed a little random, that's all."

"Oh." He ate the bite he'd scooped up and then spoke with his mouth full. "You didn't seem impressed with me at the party."

"And that made you want to hang out with me?"

"Yup."

"But why?"

"Because most girls act like everything I do and say is magic when really I say a lot of stupid things. I would say a good ninety percent of what I say is just bullshit."

"I'd round it up to a hundred," I joked.

He snickered. "See? Things like that. Other girls would never say that. It's like they like this guy they made up in their head, and they have no clue who I actually am. You didn't care about me at all."

"You want to hang out with me because I don't care about you?"

"Yeah, exactly."

I chuckled. "That seems messed up."

"Maybe, but it's true. Plus...with your mom being sick..." His words trailed off and I felt a strange tug in my gut.

"I don't want you to hang out with me because you feel bad for me," I told him. I didn't need his pity.

"No, it's not that. I mean, I do feel bad, but I don't know how to explain it." He raked his fingers over his forehead. "I guess, I just mean, when my grandpa was sick, it was all I could think about, and I remember wishing I had someone to take my mind off of him being sick for just a little while. I wanted to do that for you. I wanted to give you something else to think about, and I didn't want you to feel alone."

I wasn't certain that this boy was real.

Even in my novels the heroes weren't that sweet.

I bit my bottom lip as I ate my ice cream. "Oh."

That was all I could say, because my emotions were choking me.

"Which brings me to our next topic." He linked his fingers together and stretched out his arms before placing them on the table. "I have a proposition for you."

"Oh? What is it?"

"We have to keep seeing one another, at least once a week to keep you from going insane."

"What do you mean?"

"You're going to drive yourself crazy worrying about your mom seven days a week. Trust me, I know. I have lived that life."

"I'm fine," I argued.

He cocked an eyebrow. "How often do you do internet searches on cancer?"

Hmm...

One, two, skip a few...

"Only a couple of times," I lied.

He smiled. "Every day, huh? I bet it leaves you feeling worse, too. Therefore, once a week, you have to take your mind off cancer. That's why my grandpa had me go with him to the movies on Tuesdays—to clear my head. It helped a lot."

"You want me to go to the movies every Tuesday with you?"

"Nah, we'll do different things. The main point is to get you to stop overthinking sad things at least for a few hours. After that you can return to your sad internet searches," he semi-joked.

I narrowed my eyes. "Only once a week?"

"Yup, I just need three or four hours of your time. It's a win-win deal for both of us."

"How is it a win-win deal for you? I mean, I get why it is for me, I get a break from reality, but you don't really get anything from it."

"I get to hang out with you, which means I don't have to be so lonely."

I laughed. "You're always surrounded by people. I doubt you even know what loneliness feels like."

His brows lowered and he brushed his thumb against his nose. His stare moved to his almost empty bowl of ice cream. "You ever stand in a crowded space and feel like no one knows a single thing about you?" he asked. "Everyone talks about you in a way that feels so phony. Everything they know about you is random lies they made up in their own heads, but they don't really *know* you. They just know the fictional character they created. That's what loneliness is—living in world where no one really sees you."

Wow.

He just described my entire high school experience.

"Well, maybe you do know what it feels like," I said.

"So, what do you say? Are you in?" he asked, clasping his hands together.

"Yes," I quickly replied, and I didn't care how fast the word flew out of my mouth, didn't care how eager I sounded. "Yeah, I'm in."

He smiled.

I liked it.

Whatever.

"All right. I'll come up with a list of things we can do! I think it will be a lot of fun." He truly appeared excited, which made me excited, too.

We finished our ice cream, and then he walked me home. I was glad Greyson had a chatty personality, because there were so many times I ran out of things to say. He was great at keeping the conversation going strong.

"Thanks for coming today, Ellie. I had a really great time," he told me, shifting around in his Nikes.

"Yeah, I did, too."

"How about we meet up next Wednesday?"

"It's a date," I said, then I felt my cheeks heat up. "I mean, not like a date-date, but like, you know...just two people hanging out...I didn't mean like—"

"It's a date." Greyson smirked, smooth as ever. "I'll talk to you later. Also stay off the internet, will you?"

He turned to walk away, but I called after him.

"Yeah?" he questioned.

"I just wanted you to know I see you, you know, the you that the rest of the world doesn't see."

He scrunched up his nose and rubbed the back of his neck. "Good, because I see you, too."

I'd spent so much time hiding in the shadows. I'd avoided people, because it felt safe being invisible. If I was invisible, people couldn't judge me. If I was invisible, people couldn't laugh in my face. I always thought that was the right choice—to stay hidden.

That afternoon my thoughts slowly shifted in a new direction, because Greyson took the time to look my way.

Who knew being seen could feel so good?

6
Greyson

Mom and Dad were fighting again. It was late into the night and I had nowhere to escape to, so I locked myself in my bedroom and put my headphones on, turning up my music real high. It was almost impossible to drown them out, but I tried my best to do it.

As I sat in my bed, staring at my ceiling, I thought about ideas of things Eleanor and I could do when we hung out again. I thought about places she might like to see, and things she might like to do.

I tried to figure out foods she could eat with braces, so she wouldn't be annoyed when I devoured pizza. I thought about if maybe I should bring her flowers to make her day a little better, but then I thought maybe she didn't like flowers. Not all girls liked flowers, though a majority of them did.

Then I thought about her smile.

She always had a tight grin, and she hardly showed her teeth. Maybe because she had braces and she was insecure. But she had nothing to be insecure about. When Eleanor smiled a real smile, it was the prettiest thing I'd ever seen.

Mom called Dad an asshole, and I heard something shatter.

I turned up my music, and focused my thoughts more.

Skating.

I wondered if Eleanor liked roller skating.

I'd really love to take her skating.

Even though I'd probably fall on my butt.

That night I just kept thinking about Eleanor. Lately thoughts about her seemed to be the only thing that kept my mind from spiraling. I knew I told her that I wanted to be her friend to keep her from being lonely, but maybe I needed a friend just as much as she did.

Maybe I needed her even more than she needed me.

"Okay, pick out as many books as you want, then we'll head off to part two of today's adventure," I told Eleanor as we walked down the fantasy aisle of a used bookstore. It had only been a week since the last time I saw her, but I swore it felt a lot longer.

"Oh, Grey, you should never say those words to a bookworm. We'll need a U-Haul to carry the books out of here," she semi-joked.

"All right, then let's just stick to two for now and then we'll move on to the next stop. There's no rush, though. Take your time."

She headed off to find her two books while I tried my best to narrow it down to five.

I went with a fantasy and a horror, and she chose a historical and a comedy.

I was definitely going to borrow her novels from her once she finished reading.

"Okay, where to next?" she asked, holding her books to her chest.

"We're gonna go to a coffee shop and read our books. I figured that's what people do—drink coffee and read."

She blushed but she tried to keep me from noticing her reddening cheeks. She turned away from me a bit, and it was fucking adorable.

"Oh, cool," she said. "I've never really had coffee, though."

"What?! And you call yourself a bookworm?" I laughed. "I haven't really drank coffee either, but we can learn what our favorites are."

She smiled, and that was fucking adorable, too.

I loved it when she smiled, and I meant *really* smiled, showing me all of her braces. Her real smiles meant she wasn't sad for a moment, and that was good. It was so important in life to have a few moments when you weren't really sad.

We headed to the coffee shop a few blocks away. After we walked in, we tried almost all of their specialty drinks.

I wondered if Eleanor noticed my eye twitching from the caffeine high I was experiencing.

Though, she probably missed it, because she was busy being really talkative. Maybe that was what happened to her when she had caffeine—she became less shy.

I learned that I liked mochas. Eleanor was more specific about her likes, though: two sugars, one pump of vanilla, extra cream.

After we found our beverages of choice, we stopped talking so much because we were both too busy drinking coffee and reading books. Every now and then, though, she'd glance my way and smile, making me smile back.

Her smile was really growing on me. I could get used to seeing it once a week.

After a few hours, we made the walk back to her place. I loved how she hugged the books against her chest as if she was cradling babies.

"You know what I didn't think about over the past few hours?" she asked as we reached her front porch.

"What's that?"

"Cancer."

I grinned.

Good.

———

We started seeing each other more and more, and if we weren't seeing each other, we were talking on AOL Messenger. I'd tell her my favorite kung fu films, and she'd toss me her favorite novels. Then, we'd do the homework of watching the films or reading the books and we'd report back to each other with our thoughts.

When she'd babysit Molly, she'd first walk to my house, where I'd be sitting on my front porch, waiting for her arrival. Then I'd escort her three houses down, cross the street with her, and walk her to Molly's. Then, as I walked back to my place, I'd think about her smile.

I'd think about her laugh, and her favorite cardigans, and how she'd light up when she talked about a good book. I'd think about how her smile looked more like a frown whenever I asked for an update on her mom. I'd think about the things that made her happiest. I'd think about the things that made her sad.

Everything.

I'd think about it all.

I kept making lists of different things we could do together. Different ways to keep her mind busy. Different ways to have her around me.

Eleanor was beginning to be my first thought in the morning, and the last thought before my head hit the pillow at night.

I didn't know it was possible...

I didn't know how quickly your heart could begin beating for someone who had been nothing but a stranger a few weeks before.

7

Eleanor

Finally I decided to show Greyson the dragonflies. We met in the parking lot of Laurie Lake, and when he arrived, I swore he was more handsome than ever before. He was just wearing a white T-shirt and dark jeans, but to me, he looked amazing.

"Hey." I smiled.

"Hey," he replied, and then he hugged me.

He walked straight up to me, wrapped his arms around me, and hugged me.

Yup.

He hugged me.

Our first hug.

He did it so effortlessly, too, as if hugging was our normal way of greeting. I hugged him back, and probably held on for longer than I should have, but I didn't care. It seemed like he didn't care either, because he held me tight until I let him go.

When I pulled back, I cleared my throat and wouldn't even look at him because I was so nervous. What did the hug mean? Did the seconds we'd held on mean more than a normal friendship hug? Did he get nervous, too? Was I overthinking every single second of every single day since Greyson East had put himself into my life?

"So, where are the dragonflies?" he asked, breaking me away from my dramatic thoughts.

I cleared my throat and rubbed my left hand up and down my right arm. "Oh, this way. Come on."

We walked through the more popular park areas where people were having cookouts and playing volleyball. The lake was always packed during the summer days. Raine didn't get many warm days, and we made it our mission to soak up the sun as much as possible.

When Greyson and I reached the hiking trail, he was determined to pet every dog that crossed our path. Each time he discovered a new pup, his eyes would light up as if it were the only dog on the whole planet, and he'd turn to me and say, "Look at his nose, Ellie! Oh my God! He's smiling." It was as if he'd just discovered his new best friend—until the next one came along.

The way he loved animals made it even harder for me to control my ever-growing feelings for the guy.

Can you just not be so perfect, Greyson? That would be great, thanks.

When we were about halfway down the trail, I nodded to my left. "Okay, now we have to cross through the trees."

He cocked an eyebrow. "You're not trying to take me out into the woods to, like, kill me, right?"

I laughed. "Don't be silly, Grey. If I wanted to kill you, I would've done it ages ago."

"Well, that's comforting."

We went through the trees, and the branches hit us repeatedly. It took about three minutes of getting scraped up from rough foliage before we approached the clearing, and when we did, Greyson smiled ear to ear.

"Wow," he said, staring out at the body of water. Compared to the actual lake, it was tiny, but seeing it isolated made it look massive, especially when there were only two people around it. There were some large logs, which was where Mom and I always sat and talked. Wildflowers were fully in bloom, and the grass was the greenest it would be all year.

"I know, right?"

I led him over to a log, and we sat down beside each other.

For a while, we were just quiet, looking at the natural beauty that surrounded us. Greyson didn't say much, but his grin spoke loud enough for me to know he didn't hate it.

Then, a dragonfly flew right past us.

"I see why you love it here. It's peaceful," Greyson said.

"Yeah, plus being near water helps my mom with inspiration for her artwork."

He raised an eyebrow, intrigued. "Your mom's an artist?"

"Yeah. She's been doing it all her life for fun. She's amazing."

"And that's like, her job?"

"Well, she's a nanny by day, artist by night. She could do it full-time if she wanted to, but she's really in love with being a nanny."

"That's pretty neat."

I frowned. "Yeah, I guess."

"What is it?"

"It's just that she recently stopped nannying for her last family. And she hasn't been painting as much as normal," I told him, shifting around on my seat. "I think she's getting too drained from chemo-therapy to do it."

Greyson's smile slowly faded. "I'm sorry, Ellie."

"Yeah, me too." The less she painted, the more her illness became real in my mind. But, I tried my best to shake off those thoughts. If I slipped down that rabbit hole of sadness, I wouldn't come back from it. "What about your parents? What do they do?" I asked, changing the subject.

He shrugged. "My dad's the CEO of a whiskey company, and my mom's always traveling for fun. They aren't around a lot. I haven't seen my mom in a few weeks, and Dad just comes home sometimes and sleeps. Most of the time he stays at the apartment he has in Chi-cago, though, instead of driving home."

"So, you're just alone most of the time?"

"Yup. I mean, before I had Grandpa, but since he passed away... it's just me."

"Do you miss them?" I asked. "Do you miss your parents being around?"

"Doesn't matter. Missing them isn't going to make them stay. I just always promise myself I'll be different, you know? I want to be different when I have kids someday. I would never abandon them. I'm supposed to take over the whiskey company when I'm older, but I'd do it different than Dad. I'd make time for my family. I'd show up. My grandpa was able to do both, be a parent and run a business. He showed up all the time."

"I think people underestimate how important just showing up is."

"It's everything," he agreed.

"So, you're taking over your dad's company?"

"Yeah. My grandpa started it. It's a family tradition, I guess."

"Is that what you want to do? What do you want to be when you grow up?" I asked Greyson.

He effortlessly replied, "Happy."

"Happy?"

"Yeah. That's all. It's what my grandpa always told me. He'd say, 'Greyson, listen close. You can be anything in the world, and it would be good enough. Job title doesn't matter as long as you have food on your table, and heat on your stove. What matters the most is being happy. So, when you do grow up, make sure you're happy. Everything else will fall into place.' So, yeah, I just want to be happy. I don't care what I'm doing as long as I'm happy while I'm doing it."

I liked his answer more than I could say.

"What about you, Ellie? What do you want to be?"

"Happy," I said, stealing his answer. "I think I just want to be happy, too."

He smiled at me and gently nudged my shoulder with his. Then his head tilted up and he looked at the sky. "I like this place a lot."

"Yeah. It's a good escape from the muggle world," I commented.

He smirked. "You're really into this *Harry Potter* stuff, huh?"

"It's only the air I breathe," I said matter-of-factly.

I couldn't really imagine what would've happened to me if I hadn't had *Harry Potter* to get me through the past years. If I hadn't, I might've believed the lies people told about me.

I would've thought I wasn't magical, and that would've been a shame.

It was sad that so many people went through life without knowing they were filled with magic.

"I think it's cool that you're so into it," he said. "And I really am excited for the next one to come out."

"Me too," I agreed. "I can't wait."

We sat there watching the dragonflies buzz around, and I took a deep breath and then exhaled slowly. "Can I ask you a question? You don't have to answer if you don't want to."

"Anything."

"What's the story about Stacey White? Again, you don't have to answer, but I feel like since she was the one who kind of brought us together..."

He brushed his finger against his nose. "It's embarrassing."

"You don't have to say, really. I'm just curious."

He clasped his fingers together, rolled his shoulders back, and cracked his neck. "Well, yeah, I'd be curious, too, I guess. It's really embarrassing, though."

"I wear crocheted cardigans with dragonflies on them, Greyson. Embarrassing is my middle name."

He sighed and nodded, turning to face me. He clapped his hands once. "All right. So, Stacey and I were dating for a short period, not long, and I wasn't even sure if she was someone I should've dated, because, well, she's not really my type. She's a bit self-absorbed, but, whatever. Everything was going good with her, until she was ready to, well, you know..." His cheeks reddened, and for the first time ever, I witnessed Grey get flustered.

Finally, we were on an even playing field.

"Yeah, I know." I nodded, trying my best to ease his nerves.

"When I told her I'd never done it, she laughed, thinking I was joking, so I laughed too, trying to play it off. But then when we went to do the act, I couldn't..." He dropped his stare. "Well, I mean, my nerves...I couldn't get it...up." The last words were whispered, and I swore I'd never liked him more.

"I was just nervous, and overthinking, and I know it's embarrassing that I'm seventeen and I haven't—"

"I haven't either," I cut in.

He looked up to me, shocked, which was shocking to me. The *Harry Potter*-loving, cardigan-wearer was a virgin?

No way!

"Really?" he asked, clearly feeling hopeful that he wasn't the only one of us left on the planet.

"Really, really. It's not shocking. I've never even been kissed."

"You're wrong," he disagreed. "That *is* shocking."

I shrugged. "I think people our age make it out to be a bigger deal than it is."

"Which is exactly what Stacey did. She laughed in my face, and mocked me, saying that the most popular guy in school couldn't even get her off. So, I broke up with her. She didn't take that too well and threatened to tell everyone about my, um...performance issues. I told Landon, and he handled it. He had some dirt on Stacey that she didn't want to get out, so she shut up about it, which led to me owing Landon."

"I see."

"Yeah. He's a dick, but he's my best friend, so at least he's a loyal dick."

"Wow. That's actually really nice of him...you know, until he forced you to talk to a weird girl at a party by blackmailing you."

"I don't regret that," he said matter-of-factly.

Sigh. "Me either."

"I owe you thanks, Ellie."

"For what?"

He cleared his throat and scratched the back of his neck. "The past few weeks since my grandpa passed away, I've been really lonely and sad, even when I'm around other people at parties and stuff, it's been hard. But, when I'm with you, I'm not lonely anymore. When I'm with you, I feel like I belong. So, I owe you for that. I almost forgot what it felt like."

"You almost forgot what what felt like?"

He shrugged a shoulder. "Being happy."

8

Eleanor

"What's our grand adventure today?" I asked Greyson as he walked up to my house one Saturday afternoon. I really needed the break from reality, because Mom had a rough night. She was currently resting while Dad looked after her.

I asked if she wanted me to stay home, but she told me to go off with Greyson and have fun. She'd rather me be having a good time instead of worrying too much.

Greyson smiled as he stuffed his hands into the pockets of his jeans. "I was thinking I'd win you a stuffed animal down at the county fair."

Sounded good enough to me.

There were so many things I loved about being around Greyson. I loved how when he talked about things, he expressed himself with massive hand gestures. I loved how he hummed tunes whenever he was happy. Sometimes we'd just be walking down the street, and he'd start tapping his foot as he hummed some random song.

I loved how when he looked at me, he really stared my way, as if I were the only girl he would ever look at again. I loved how when I spoke, he listened and responded with questions to deepen the conversation. I loved how he had a small dimple in his left cheek that showed whenever he smiled.

I loved how his hand accidentally slid across mine as we held the bar on the Tilt-A-Whirl ride at the fair. I loved how he could eat three corn dogs and then crave cotton candy. I loved his laugh.

Gosh, I loved his laugh.

I also loved his determination to win me a freaking stuffed animal.

"It's really okay, Grey." I laughed as we stood in front of a carnival booth where he'd been trying his hardest to hit a bullseye with a baseball in order to win me a stuffed animal.

"No! I can do this." He huffed, seemingly more resolute than ever, even though he'd already missed the target fourteen times. He picked up the baseball, took a step backward, rounded up his arm, and threw it with all his might.

He missed by a few inches.

"Dammit," he muttered.

"Five more bucks for five more balls," the booth guy mentioned.

"It's not worth it," I said, lightly touching Greyson's arm. "These things are made to lose."

Greyson narrowed his eyes and reached into his wallet, pulling out five more dollars. With the way things were going, the poor guy was going to have to tap into his college fund in order to win me that stuffed panda bear.

He started tossing the balls once more, and, of course, he kept missing. At one point the booth guy even frowned at Greyson's attempts.

"This is the one," Greyson said as he held the twentieth ball in his grip. "This is the one that's going to be different than all the ones before," he promised.

In a way, he was right.

He pulled his arm back and swung it forward, and in a freak accident, the baseball hit the corner of the bullseye and bounced off of it, flinging the ball directly back at him, hitting him square in the face.

"Oh my gosh!" I screeched as Greying went flying backward and crashing to the ground. I hurried to his side and bent down. "Grey, are you okay?"

"Did I win?" he asked with his left eye closed tight. The redness from the impact of the ball was already in place as I helped him to his feet.

"No, not at all."

"Damn, I thought I had it that time."

"Here, man. Just take the panda," the carnie said as he held the stuffed animal toward us. "Anyone who tries that hard to impress a girl deserves to give her a stuffed animal."

Greyson smirked with his quickly bruising eye. He took the panda bear and handed it to me. "See? I knew that time was lucky!" he exclaimed.

I laughed. "Yeah, well, let's just go find a place to sit so I can find ice for your eye."

He held the stuffed animal to me, and I took it and hugged it tight. *Thanks, Grey.*

I led him to a bench and forced him to sit down while I wandered off to find ice for his eye. When I came back, the guy was sitting there with a black and blue eye and a stick of cotton candy, smiling like a fool.

I liked him so much in that moment—so, so much.

He kept funneling cotton candy into his mouth as I sat down beside him.

"Hold still," I ordered as I placed the cloth filled with ice against his eye. He cringed a bit as it touched his skin. "Sorry," I said, pulling the cloth away from him. My fingers gently touched the swollen area of his eye. "I just want to get some ice on it before it gets worse." I put the ice back against the skin, and he smiled.

"I like that," he told me.

"The ice on your face?"

"No. I like it whenever you touch me."

My heart stopped beating, I stopped breathing, and Greyson kept smiling.

I didn't respond, because I had completely forgotten how to form words, but I was certain my reddened face told him exactly how his words had made me feel.

"So, I know today has been eventful, but if you're up for it, I got one of my grandpa's favorite kung fu movies on DVD. I figured maybe we could watch it at my place," Greyson offered.

"Sure, that sounds fun."

We headed back to his house, and even though I kept looking toward Greyson's bruising eye, he seemed unfazed by it all. He simply began humming a tune, so I began humming along with him.

We hummed the whole trip back, right until we walked up to Greyson's house and his smile faded away.

There was shouting coming from inside the house, and I could see his parents hollering at one another through the front windows.

Greyson's whole demeanor shifted as embarrassment took over. He turned to me and rubbed the back of his neck. "Uh, maybe we should hang out another time."

"Yeah, it's fine, not a big deal."

"I'll talk to you later?"

"Yeah, of course."

I turned to walk away, but then glanced over my shoulder to see him staring at his house with such a look of defeat. It was clear he didn't want to go into the house with the screaming.

"Hey, I'm still not ready to go home," I said. "Do you want to maybe go to Laurie Lake to just hang out for a little bit longer?" He needed the break. He needed something to shut his mind off of his own sadness.

Maybe he needed me just as much as I needed him in order to not be so broken.

He looked up at me and I saw a flash of relief wash over his face. "Yeah, okay. Let's go."

"Are your parents always like that?" I asked as we sat on our log at Laurie Lake.

"Even more so lately. I just don't get it. If they hate each other that much, then why even bother being together? I can't even think back to a time when they actually liked one another."

"I'm so sorry, Grey. That has to be hard for you."

"It's easier when they aren't home, and luckily they are hardly ever home. Besides, next year I'll be off to college and it won't matter much at all."

"Still, I'm sorry."

I couldn't imagine living in a home without a strong type of love. My parents swam in each other's love as if their hearts were oceans. They held one another up whenever times were hard. Their kind of love made the world a better place to be in. I couldn't imagine them ever not being completely head over heels with one another.

They were the greatest love story I'd ever witnessed, and it was so hard to even imagine the two of them being apart. I swore their hearts beat together as one.

If there was one thing that I knew for sure, it was the fact that there was no Kevin without a Paige.

"I just never want to be like that," he confessed. "When I fall in love, it's going to be real. It's not going to be a love for convenience, it's going to be a forever kind of love. Otherwise, what's the point?"

"I agree."

"But I do have to thank my parents. If anything, they taught me what love isn't, therefore I'll know what it is when it comes."

He kept doing his nervous fiddling thing with his hands, and I swore my heartbeats were directed straight to him.

"Sorry. We can talk about something else," he offered. "Maybe we can talk about us."

Heart skips and heart flips.

"Yeah? What about us?"

"I've been thinking about it a lot lately, you know." Greyson's head tilted toward me, and we locked eyes. "About what it would be like to kiss you."

I swore he controlled my heartbeats with those words. We hadn't really talked much about things like that, about us and if there were any feelings involved other than friendship. The most we'd ever done was hug, for goodness' sake, and a hug from him was enough to set my world on fire.

For a while, I'd thought my crush on Greyson was a one-sided thing, so to hear those words come out of his mouth somewhat felt like a dream.

"Do you ever think about that, Ellie?" he asked.

I inhaled slowly. "Only always."

He inched a little closer to me, and I let it happen. He tucked my hair behind my ears, and I let it happen. His smile melted every part of me, and I let it happen.

"I think about it a lot. After we hang out sometimes, I beat myself up for not just doing it. I overthink it. Like, it should've happened when we got ice cream, or when you first brought me here. Or on Molly's steps." He scrunched his face. "Probably not on Molly's steps, but still, I think about it."

"Me too. All the time." I paused. "Well, not all the time, but yeah... all the time."

He placed his hand in mine and gave it a slight squeeze.

"I just want it to be perfect, you know? Especially now that I know it's your first kiss. That's important. In the novels you've had me read, it always happens naturally," he said softly. "I take notes when I'm reading on how the hero does it, on where it happens, on how comfortable or uncomfortable both the characters seem."

I felt his hands trembling slightly—or was it my hands that were shaky? It was becoming hard to tell what were his feelings and what were mine.

That was okay, though.

I liked the confusion.

"I know," I agreed. "There's always a moment..."

"When the timing is just—"

"Right." I finished his sentence, knowing his thoughts the same way he knew mine.

"Ellie?"

"Yes, Grey?"

"Would it be cliché of me to ask if I can kiss you?"

"Yes." I scooted closer, so close that his lips were millimeters from mine, so close that his exhales became my inhales, so close that my mind had already decided it was going to be the best first kiss of my life. "But do it anyway."

And then he did.

9

Eleanor

"He's so goofy!" I exclaimed as Mom and I went grocery shopping. I wandered in front of her as she pushed the cart. "He kept trying to win me the stuffed animal, and ended up with a black eye. Even with the black eye, he seemed proud, though."

"That's so sweet, honey."

"It was sweet, in a really dorky way." I walked toward the fresh fruit, moving on my tiptoes as I thought about Greyson. Every now and then I'd start humming. "We're supposed to go out for Mexican food next week, and I'm really excited about it." My hands moved across the oranges.

Did Greyson like oranges?

I'd have to ask him. I wanted to know everything about Greyson East. The good, the bad, and his opinions on fruit.

"Oh, and I forgot to tell you—"

Crash.

I whipped around quickly at the loud sound which snapped me from my current dreamy state.

"Mom!" I hollered, rushing over to her side. She was lying on the floor, and her eyes were crossing before they shut. I shook her body, but she wasn't responding. "Mom, mom! Someone help!" I shouted.

She completely blacked out, and my heart shattered into a million pieces.

An ambulance was called to the scene, and I cried harder than I'd ever cried as I sat beside her and tried to wake her up.

When she came to, she was dazed and confused. She tried to speak, but she was too shaky. I just stared at her, wide-eyed and terrified. I watched as my tears splashed her cheekbones so prominent under her thin skin. I couldn't stop. I couldn't stop sobbing. I couldn't stop shaking. I couldn't let go of the hopelessness I felt.

We were rushed to the hospital, and Dad met us there.

He forced me to sit in the waiting room as he searched for answers.

I sat, I waited, and I cried.

I sat, I waited, and I cried some more.

Mom was released a few hours later and the whole ride home was completely still.

That was the day when it became real for me. That was the first time since finding out about her cancer that I was really afraid. For a while, I was naïve enough to think that she was getting better than worse, then a wake-up call hit me in the fresh produce aisle.

———

The next morning, Mom walked into my room and gave me a small grin. She wore a Janet Jackson T-shirt with overalls, and her hair was wrapped in a bandana. For the most part, she looked like her regular self. You could hardly tell anything was wrong just by looking at her. From the looks of it, she didn't seem like a woman who had just blacked out the day before. I thought that was the hardest part to wrap my mind around: how could she look okay but not be?

"Hey, beautiful," she said.

"Hey, Mom."

"So...yesterday was tough."

"You should be in bed," I told her. "You need rest."

I sat up a bit. "Sorry about that. I—"

She shook her head. "It's fine, really. I just want to make sure you're okay. I'm sorry if I scared you."

"You shouldn't be worried about me."

"I'm a mother, sweetheart. Worrying about my child is all I ever do."

I lowered my head. "I'm scared, Mom."

"I know." She moved into the room and sat on the edge of the bed beside me. She wrapped an arm around me and I rested my head against her shoulder.

"I just need you to be okay, alright? Can you do that?"

She combed her fingers through my hair but didn't reply.

Mom was never one to make promises she couldn't keep.

"Your dad went out to clear his head and will probably be out for a while. You want to drive over to Laurie Lake?"

"Are you okay enough to travel?" I asked warily.

"I promise, Ellie. I'm okay."

"Okay."

We headed to the lake and walked out to our secluded area. It was hot that late morning. The high was supposed to be around ninety-five degrees, but it already felt like it was triple digits.

We sat under the sun, melting and drinking from the water bottles we'd brought. It was quiet for a while. I wondered if we were quiet because we didn't have anything to say or because we didn't know how to say it.

Mom tilted her head up to the sky with her eyes closed and felt the sun beating against her skin. "I was thirty-three the first time I found out I had cancer. You were two years old."

I turned to face her, stunned. "You've had cancer before?"

"Yes. You were so young, and I remember crying with you in my arms, because the idea of leaving this world was too hard to face. You were so new to me, and your father and I had fought so hard to have you in our lives. You were just becoming your own person. I was watching you grow into this beautiful little girl with her own personality. I thought about all the things I'd miss, all the firsts you hadn't even discovered. Your first day at school, your first dance...your first boyfriend, your first kiss. Your first heartbreak. I remember getting so mad at the world, at my own body for bringing you to me only to take me away. It felt unfair. I felt as if I'd betrayed myself. One day when my worries were so loud and my heart was breaking, do you know what your father said to me?"

"What?"

"'You're still here, Paige. You're still here.' That changed everything for me. I just need you to know that, too, okay?" She took my hand into hers and patted it gently. "I'm still here, Ellie."

"I can't stop thinking about if you weren't, though. I thought yesterday was..." I shut my eyes and inhaled hard. "I thought you were gone..."

"I know, but even if a day comes when you can't physically see me, I'm still here. Always."

I took a breath.

That was a difficult concept.

"I'm really scared, Mom," I confessed.

"Fear's okay, as long as you don't let it drown you." She looked down at her hands. "Do you know the story behind the dragonflies?" she asked. "Do you know what they stand for?"

"No. You've never told me."

"In almost all parts of the world, the dragonfly stands for change and transformation. They live most of their life as a nymph. Do you know what that means?"

"Like a fairy?"

She smiled. "Well, that's one of the meanings, but in this case it means an insect with incomplete metamorphosis. It's the stage before it gets its wings. Dragonflies only actually fly for a small fraction of their lives."

"I didn't know that."

"Crazy, right? When you see dragonflies, you would believe they fly all their lives, but you don't take into account the number of flightless days that came before. The dragonfly never gets down on itself for not having wings, though. It never overthinks when they will come. It just lives fully in the moment. That's what they mean to me: living in the moment. They live each day moment by moment, not overthinking the future."

I knew what she was getting at. "I'm not a dragonfly, Mom. I can't help but overthink everything."

"I know. I've been overthinking things, too, but I also want to find the good moments. I don't want the next however-many days to be filled with sad times, Ellie. I want to know the good things. I like to think you can find a reason to smile every single day if you look hard enough. So, can you do that for me? For us? Can you find a reason every single day to smile?"

"Yes," I promised, even though I didn't know if it were true. For her, I'd try. I fiddled with my fingers as dragonflies buzzed around in the distance. "You didn't miss one of the firsts," I told her. "Greyson kissed me two nights ago."

Mom's eyes lit up, and for the first time in the past twenty-four hours, she smiled, a real smile filled with happiness. "Oh, my gosh." She placed her hands on top of mine. "Tell me everything."

As I told her, she kept smiling ear to ear, and I realized I was smiling too, not because Greyson had kissed me, but because she was it for me that day. Seeing her glow felt so amazing. Seeing her not crying was what made my lips curve upward.

She was my reason to smile.

10
Eleanor

After Mom blacked out, things became harder. She made me stop going to chemotherapy treatments with her, even though I fought her tooth and nail about it.

At first, we were all doing okay. We found our daily reasons to smile.

Then, things progressed.

She stopped painting in the garage.

Her hair thinned.

Her movements were becoming slower.

One night after Mom's chemo, she became extremely sick. It woke me up in the middle of the night, and there was no way I was going back to sleep. While Dad helped her in the bathroom downstairs, I sat at the top of the staircase, listening. She was crying, telling him she was tired.

I didn't know if she meant physically or mentally.

Maybe a little bit of both.

I hugged the railing as Dad helped walk Mom back to their bedroom. Afterward, he came back into the space and stood still in the middle of living room. He stared forward, looking at the blank television screen, and then he covered his mouth and began to sob uncontrollably. He muffled his tears with his hands, trying his best to keep his hurting contained in order to not worry Mom or me.

My father was the master of putting on a brave face. He'd always take care of Mom and then check in on me to make sure I was okay. Yet, if I asked how he was, he'd always reply, "Great," even though I knew that was a lie. My father was heartbroken. He refused to admit it to anyone, but I could see it even before he'd begun to cry.

The next day, we could hardly find a reason to smile. Then the following one, it became even harder. Our reasons for joy were decreasing day in and day out. We all knew it, but we tried to hide from each other the fact that we were all cracking more each day. Our reasons for smiling were so very few, yet we were all too tired and too stubborn to admit it.

———

"Hi, Ellie," Greyson said while standing on my porch one Saturday afternoon. He was holding some canvas in his hands and smiling brightly. I was confused about why he was there. Truth was, ever since everything with Mom worsened, I'd been a bit antisocial. I didn't have a clue why he'd still want to be my friend, or whatever it was that we were. We hadn't even had a chance to really talk about anything between us after our first kiss.

He never brought it up, and neither did I.

If we were hanging out together, I was quiet on the outside while my insides screamed.

He hadn't signed up for a sad friend, but still, he kept showing up.

Something should be said about the people who show up for the depressed souls. They never receive enough credit for being brave enough to stay.

"Hey. What are you doing here?" I asked him.

"I just thought I could stop by to officially meet your mom. I wanted to see if she'd like to teach me some of her art skills."

"That's really nice, but she's not feeling too great today."

"Oh. Well, maybe..."

"I'm feeling good enough for that," Mom interrupted.

I turned around to see her standing in the foyer, looking skinnier than I liked.

"Are you sure?" I asked. She had bags under her eyes, her hair was wrapped up in a bandana, and she looked nothing like herself.

"Of course. Come on in, Greyson."

He walked past me and followed Mom into the living room. He set his materials on the table, and then sat beside Mom on the couch. "I'm sorry we haven't officially met yet, Mrs. Gable, but I'm Greyson. I just wanted to stop by and see if you could give me some art tips. I'm not an artist at all, but Ellie has told me you're the best artist in the world, and I'd love to pick your brain about techniques and stuff."

Then, for the first time in days, Mom smiled.

More of that.

For a moment in time, Greyson took her mind off of her illness and accompanied her back into the world she loved more than anything. She spoke about curves and lines, pastels and chalks, paper drawings versus canvas.

She had him paint and then she critiqued his work, but with a gentleness Mom always maintained. She didn't give critiques without offering solutions. Her eyes lit up when she talked about art.

After a while, they headed to Mom's studio in the garage, and they stayed there for hours. I didn't join them, because everything they were talking about pretty much just went over my head.

Mom needed it—she needed to feel inspired.

When they finished, they both came back into the house covered in paint. Mom was wearing an apron, and a paintbrush was balanced behind her ear. She looked a little like herself.

"Thank you, Grey," I told him as he was getting ready to leave.

"For what?"

"Being you."

I didn't know why he'd come into my life all those weeks before. I didn't know why he chose to stay. I didn't deserve a friend like him. Honestly, I wasn't sure anyone deserved Greyson East in their life, but I was so thankful he was in mine.

Mom walked up to me after Greyson left and wrapped her arm around my shoulder. "You know what I like about that boy?" she asked.

"What's that?"

"Everything."

11

Eleanor

By the time Mom's sixth chemotherapy appointment came around, school was back in session. I'd never thought I'd say it, but being back at school was the kind of normal activity I needed in my life. It distracted me from worrying, and I needed a break from worry.

Shay and Greyson made sure to keep my mind busy, too. They'd come over to my house and read books with me, and they'd sit with me during lunch. They'd talk about anything and everything to keep me laughing. Turned out Greyson was the master of telling really bad jokes that didn't make sense but, somehow, were still funny.

Even on the days when I wasn't feeling happy, I'd give them a small chuckle.

If Shay wasn't checking in on me, Greyson was looking for an update.

I needed that. I needed their check-ins to remind me that I wasn't alone.

One Saturday afternoon, I sat at my computer researching cancer. My parents told me not to search anything on the internet anymore, but I couldn't help it. It was like an odd addiction that I couldn't break. Even though it made me sadder, I kept hitting enter on the search engine.

When the doorbell rang, I sat up a bit as Mom called my name. I hurried into the living room, and I stepped back a bit when I saw Greyson standing there in a suit and tie with a corsage in his hands.

"Hey, Ellie," he said with that Greyson smirk of his.

I raised an eyebrow. "Hi...?" I lowered an eyebrow. "What are you doing?"

"Oh, I was just in the neighborhood and wanted to see if you wanted to be my date to homecoming."

"Uh, homecoming is tonight," I told him, confused.

"Yeah. I bought the tickets a few weeks ago, but didn't want to tell you, because I was pretty sure you'd find a way to talk yourself out of it. So, now it's too late to say no, and seeing how I'm already in a suit, you have to come."

Mom snickered a little while I shifted around on the carpeted floor. "I can't go to homecoming with you."

"Why not?"

"I don't know, I just can't. I'm actually busy doing some research."

"On what?" Mom asked with an arched eyebrow.

"Nothing," I sharply responded, knowing she would've killed me if she found out. "Plus, I don't even have a dress."

"You can borrow one of mine," Mom said, giving me a smile. "I'll even help you get ready."

"But what if you need something? What if you and Dad need my help?" That was my biggest fear: something going wrong while I wasn't around.

"I'm fine, Ellie. Still here," she said as she walked over to me. "Now, I think you have to give this nice boy an answer. Are you going to homecoming with him?"

I bit my bottom lip as my stomach twisted up with butterflies and worry all at once. I glanced over to Mom and then over to Greyson. Then back to Mom. "Are you sure you're okay?"

"One hundred percent."

"And if you need anything you'll call?"

"One hundred percent."

I sighed and let the worry kind of slide away as more butterflies came in. I turned to Greyson and smiled. "I need a few minutes to get ready."

"Take your time." He walked over to the couch and took a seat. "I'll wait."

Mom took me to her bedroom, and she started rummaging through her closet for opportunities for me to wear.

I'd never been to a dance.

I didn't even know if I knew how to dance, honestly.

If I knew anything about myself, it was the fact that I wasn't the best at social gatherings. Ask me to read a chapter out loud in class, and I'd nail that. Ask me to go be social, and I'd melt into a puddle of anxiety.

But it was with Greyson.

How could I say no to those eyes and that smile?

"How about this one?" Mom asked, holding out a black dress with a low drop back. "You can even wear your Chucks with it, because you're you, and that's awesome."

"It's beautiful," I told her. "I think it's perfect."

"Good. Now, go change. There's a really sweet boy waiting out there for you."

I hurried out to my room and changed into the dress. It fit me pretty okay, but Mom was a safety pin queen and made it tighter where it needed to be tight, and she hemmed up the bottom so I wouldn't trip over the dress all night long. Then, she helped me with my hair, and gave me a touch of makeup. She even sprayed me with her favorite perfume.

"You look like a goddess," Mom said, tearing up. "You look like a beautiful goddess, Ellie."

"Thanks, Mom."

She hugged me tightly, and then walked me out to the living room, where Dad and Greyson were sitting and waiting. They both stood up instantly when we walked out and both of their jaws dropped.

"Wow," they said in unison.

"Ellie, you look—" Dad started.

"Beautiful," Greyson finished.

I felt my cheeks heat up as I looked away, feeling bashful. Then Greyson walked over to me with the corsage and asked for my wrist.

"Wait! Pause! I need to get the camera!" Mom shouted, waving her hands. It was fun watching how excited she was getting about it all. Lately every time she smiled, it felt a bit like a blessing.

She hurried back, holding a camera, and she started snapping photographs of Greyson and me.

"Watch that hand placement, Greyson," Dad warned.

"Yes, sir," Greyson replied, moving his hands a bit higher, hardly touching my back. I think Dad kind of made him nervous, which was funny, seeing how Dad was nothing but a big teddy bear.

"If you want we can drive you two to the school dance and then pick you up later on," Dad offered, and we took him up on it.

As we drove, Mom kept glancing back and smiling at the both of us. "You two look adorable," she kept repeating, shaking her head in awe. "Just adorable."

"Thanks, Mrs. Gable," Greyson said, and I swore his face was even a little red from embarrassment. At least I wasn't alone.

We pulled up to the school, and they dropped us off. "All right, you two, have so much fun!" Mom exclaimed.

"But not too much fun," Dad added, pointing at Greyson.

Greyson swallowed hard and hopped out of the car.

As I got out and started walking away, Mom called after me, rolling down her window. "And Ellie?"

"Yeah?"

She held her hands out toward me and I walked over to her, taking them into mine. I leaned in and she squeezed my hands lightly. "Live in this moment, my dragonfly. Live fully in this moment."

"I love you, Mom."

She pulled me closer and kissed my cheek. "I love you, too. Now go. Have the time of your life."

I walked over to Greyson, who looked so handsome in his suit. There were a ton of people standing around the entrance of the school, dressed up and laughing.

"Nervous?" he asked me.

"Terrified," I replied.

This was kind of our first outing in public. Our reveal, of some sorts. Sure, we ate together at lunch, but Shay was always there. We never looked like we were a thing, but walking into that building together would definitely make it seem that way.

I didn't even really know what we were, but I didn't see a need to find out, either.

It was pretty simple, actually.

He was him, I was me, and we were us. This was our story.

"Don't worry, Ellie. I got you. And also—" he took my hand into his, linking us together as one— "you look beautiful tonight."

Chills.

Chills all across my body.

"Ready?" he asked.

"Ready," I replied.

When we entered the gymnasium, a few people whispered about the two of us being together, but Greyson didn't seem to pay much mind to it. I didn't either, because if he didn't mind, it didn't matter.

He looked at me every now and then like I was the only girl in the room, and that meant everything to me. In a room filled with Stacey Whites, his eyes were on Eleanor Gable.

"Do you want to dance?" he asked as an upbeat song began.

My heart started pounding against my rib cage. I shifted my feet. "Oh, no. I don't know how to dance."

"You don't have to know how to dance in order to dance." He stood in front of me and started kicking his arms and legs around like a wild man. "You just do it."

I laughed. "You look crazy!"

"So?" he said, still kicking, still jumping. Then he held his hand out toward me. "Look crazy with me?" he asked with the silliest smirk ever and I swear, I just thought about kissing him in that very moment.

I took his hand in mine and stood up.

Okay, Greyson.

Let's go crazy.

———

The night was perfect in every way, shape, and form. When it came time for the last slow dance, we walked to the dance floor and Greyson placed his hands on my lower back. We swayed back and forth just like every other couple around us, not really doing anything, but feeling like we were doing everything.

"Why did you want me to come to the dance with you?" I asked him.

"Because there's no one else I'd want to go with. Plus, well, I kind of got the idea from your mom."

"My mom?"

He nodded. "When we were painting, I asked her what she was looking forward to with you. You know, like your wedding someday, or your college graduation, or things like that. And she mentioned school dances. So, I wanted her to have that experience."

My eyes filled up with tears as I stopped swaying. "You did this for my mom?"

"Yeah, I mean, it seemed really important to her." He paused and cringed a little. "But I mean, just to be clear I did it for me, too. I really wanted to dance with you, Ellie."

My mouth parted and my sigh fell between my lips as I went back to swaying with him. I rested my head on his shoulder and breathed him in. "Grey?"

"Yes?"

"Would it be all right if I kept you forever?"

When my parents picked us up, we dropped Greyson off first, and when he was out of the car, Mom turned around and gave me the biggest grin. "So, how was it?" she asked.

I sighed, and I was certain she could see the stars in my eyes and the cheese in my smile.

Her grin widened as if that moment was the happiest moment she'd ever lived. "Yeah?" she asked.

I sighed, smiling with the kind of delirium that could only be described as happiness.

Yeah.

12
Eleanor

One day during the first week of November, I walked home from school, and when I headed inside, I was surprised to see Mom and Dad sitting in the kitchen. "Hey, I thought you had a doctor's appointment,"

Mom rubbed her tired eyes. "We decided to miss it."

"Miss it? You can't just miss treatment like that, can you?"

Dad frowned. "We actually came to the decision to stop treatment, Eleanor. After getting some results back, we realized this was the best choice."

"Well, what do we try now? What do we do?"

"Honey, I'm tired," Mom confessed. "I'm so tired, and nothing we're trying is working. I'm only getting worse, and I don't want to spend these days feeling like this. I just want to be with you and your father."

"You're giving up?"

"No. I'm giving in. We've exhausted all of our options."

I went quiet. I didn't know what they wanted me to say. I didn't know what to even think.

Dad rolled his shoulders back and cleared his throat. "I asked Paige what she wanted, and she said the water. We found a nice place on the beach down in Florida. It's beautiful, Ellie."

"You want us to go to Florida? For how long?" I asked.

Mom smiled. "For however long we're able to be down there. I know that changes things for you. You'd have to switch schools during your senior year, and things with Greyson—"

"Whatever you want," I blurted out. Mom had worry in her eyes about hurting me, and I couldn't let that be her fear. My biggest concern was her. "Whatever you want, Mom."

Wherever she wanted to be, I wanted to be there, too.

———

"A cancer vacation?" Greyson asked as we sat on the top step of his porch.

"Yeah, that's what my dad called it. It would be a family trip to Florida for a few months because Mom's treatment is over."

His eyes widened with hope. "Because it worked?"

I frowned.

He lowered his head. "I'm sorry, Ellie."

"Yeah, me too. Her dream has always been to take a trip to the ocean, and well, it looks like now is the only time that will be possible."

He was quiet for a while.

Then he said, "That's good for her. She deserves that."

"Yeah."

I was quiet next.

"I'll probably have to finish senior year down there."

"Oh. Yeah." He grimaced and rubbed his hands against his legs. "Is it selfish of me to ask about us?"

No, it wasn't. I'd been wondering the same thing. Truth was, after everything with Mom, Greyson had been the next thing to cross my mind.

"We've never really talked about us since my mom got sick."

"Yeah, but it just kind of felt like we were...I don't know, just us, you know?"

I knew exactly what he meant. It was as if we didn't need labels to describe whatever it was we had between the two of us.

We just were.

It was that simple.

"I've been thinking about asking you to be my girlfriend, you know," he told me. "And I mean, just because you live in Florida for a while doesn't mean you can't still be that until you get back home."

I wanted to be selfish about it. I wanted to ask him to wait for me, wanted to do the long-distance thing for a while, but I also knew that was wrong. Greyson had just begun his senior year. He was going to play his last high school basketball season. He was going to want to go to school dances and participate in different activities and go to his last ever prom, and I couldn't be a part of any of that with him.

I didn't want to get in the of any of it. I didn't want to stop him from living his final year of high school to the fullest because he felt he couldn't because of me.

"I really like you, Grey."

He kept his head down. "But?"

"I..." I swallowed hard, somewhat shocked that I was actually going to say the words I'd been dreading so much. "I just don't think it's smart to try to be in a relationship right now. You have such a great year coming up, and I don't want to stop you from living it to the fullest. You deserve to be happy."

"You make me happy."

I wanted to cry.

I wanted to crawl into his arms and just cry.

I wanted to be childish about it. I wanted to stay in Illinois with him so we could be us, whatever it was that we were. I wanted ridiculous laughter and kung fu movies and *Harry Potter* references and Greyson.

I wanted Greyson so bad.

But sometimes a kid is forced to grow up faster than they like.

"I'm not going to be okay, Greyson. The next few months of my life are going to suck, and I'm going to cry, and I'm not going to be the weird girl who reads books at parties. I'm just going to be sad."

"You shouldn't have to be sad alone."

I wished he weren't a good guy. It seemed much harder to walk away from a good guy.

"You deserve more than this," I said.

"So, you're breaking up with me before you even give us a chance," he whispered, his voice tight. "Just say it and get it over with."

I stared at him. His hands were clenched tightly together and he tapped his foot repeatedly on the step. The more I waited, the worse it was going to be for the both of us, so, I parted my lips and spoke so softly, hoping he actually heard me. "I can't be your girlfriend, Grey."

He stood up quickly and nodded. "Okay."

"Greyson." I leaped to my feet, feeling my heart pounding against my chest. "Wait—"

"No, it's fine. Really, Ellie. It was stupid for me to think anything other than this. I hope the move goes okay." And with that, he went into his house.

No real goodbyes.

No true closure.

Just a slamming door.

I wanted to die.

The whole walk home, I moved with regret, but I knew it had been the right choice to make. If it had been the wrong one, it wouldn't have hurt so much.

I walked into the house, and Mom was lying on the couch. She sat up a little, and I hated how long it took her to get comfortable. I didn't want her to get up because of me but she always got up.

"Hey, Ellie. How did the talk with Greyson go?"

I smiled. It was forced and fake, and she knew it. "It was fine. I'm just going to lie down for a bit."

She narrowed her eyes and looked concerned, but I turned on my heels and darted to my bedroom. I shut my door behind me and collapsed onto my bed. My arms wrapped around my pillow, and I buried my face into it. I silenced my cries, because I didn't want my parents to feel bad. They were already going through enough; the last thing they needed was to feel like I was broken because we were moving.

I was, though.

As I cried, a hand touched my shoulder. I looked to my right and saw Mom standing there. She was skinny, fatigued, and sick, but she was still there.

She's still here.

She wiped my tears with one finger and sighed. "Oh, baby..."

"I'm sorry, Mom. I'm okay." I tried to promise her that I was fine, wiping my eyes. "You go rest."

She didn't listen, though. She climbed into bed with me and wrapped her arms around me. That made me cry even more because she was in pain and hurting yet still wanted to comfort me. It blew my mind how a mother could be the strongest person in a room, even at her weakest.

———

We moved the third week of November, after my parents figured out all the details for me transferring to a new school. Dad booked first-class tickets to Florida, even though Mom said it wasn't worth it. It was as if Dad felt helpless so he was doing anything he could to try to make Mom a little more comfortable.

I was able to sit next to her on the flight, and the whole time I held her hand. She fell asleep pretty easily, and I was happy about that. Every time she'd awaken, she looked for my hand, and it was still in hers.

"Still here, Mom," I'd whisper as she went back to sleep.

I'm still here.

13

Greyson

FROM: GreyHoops87@aol.com
TO: EGHogwarts@aol.com
DATE: November 23, 4:54 PM
SUBJECT: Timing

Ellie,

You've been gone for a week, and it feels so weird without you here.

I'm a jerk, and I handled things really badly. I'm sorry. In my head, I just thought we could at least try to make it work. I haven't felt like this about anyone before, and I just hate that you're gone. I didn't know caring about someone could happen so fast, and I'm just not sure I know how to shut off the caring. My life has been lonely for a while now. I thought lonely was the default option, though being lonely was normal. Even though I've always been surrounded by people, it's as if no one really knew me. And then came you.

I didn't mean to storm off and slam my door like that. Sometimes my head just gets so clouded I'm not sure

81

how to handle my own thoughts.

I'm really going to miss you, and I'm not used to feeling this way.

I know that's selfish, and I know you're going through so much worse, and I know it's stupid for me to even be this sad about it when your life just flipped upside down, but it hurts.

Hopefully you can forgive me and we can be friends.

-Grey

———

FROM: EGHogwarts@aol.com
TO: GreyHoops87@aol.com
DATE: November 24, 8:00 AM
SUBJECT: Re: Timing

Grey,

You'd have to be crazy to think I wouldn't still want to be your friend.

-Ellie

———

FROM: GreyHoops87@aol.com
TO: EGHogwarts@aol.com
DATE: December 2, 8:54 PM
SUBJECT: Father figures

My father's such a freaking tool.

He's hammering down on me to start interning at his company, but I just want to finish my senior year without that extra stress.

He called me a pussy for not having any drive.

I never want to be like him. I never want to be that cold.

I hate him...at least that's what I tell myself, because that makes it easier. Truth is, I kind of still want his approval. It doesn't make sense, right? He's never around, and when he is he's an asshole. He hardly knows me, and what he does know he doesn't approve of. Still, I have this deeply rooted need to make him proud.

Being human is weird.

I'd much rather be an alien.

How are things in Florida?

-Grey

———

FROM: EGHogwarts@aol.com
TO: GreyHoops87@aol.com
DATE: December 2, 9:30PM
SUBJECT: Re: Father figures

I'm sorry about your dad, that's tough, but you gotta do whatever makes you happy in this moment—that's what your grandpa would've said, right?

Things down here are fine. It's been quiet, but it still feels loud. Mom is doing okay, but Dad is struggling. It's like he's screaming in silence, and his echoes are bouncing off the walls. I hate it. I can only take so much, which led to my next life choice: I'm going to pick up some new hobbies, just to keep me out of the house.

I hate being home now, which is weird because it used to be my favorite place in the world. It's just too sad.

I'm thinking of taking a crocheting class downtown with Mom, if she's feeling strong enough to do it. I figured it might be nice to do something she's into.

Did you know she learned to make cardigans from my grandma? That's where all of my cardigans came from. The dragonfly was the last one she gave me. It's my favorite one.

I'm also thinking of taking karate, because I just watched *Enter the Dragon*, and now I'm pretty sure I have to learn how to break a piece of wood with my foot.

Do you think alien teenagers get annoyed with their alien moms and dads?

I really want to imagine angst-filled adolescent aliens rolling their one eye at their overprotective parents.

Can you imagine the fights?

"Clean your room. Brush your hair. Stop taking the spaceship out at night to party on Mars."

Anyway. Watch *Enter the Dragon*. You won't be sorry.

-Ellie

———

FROM: GreyHoops87@aol.com
TO: EGHogwarts@aol.com
DATE: December 3, 7:13 AM
SUBJECT: Enter the Dragonflies

Ellie,

I'm kind of hurt that you'd think I haven't seen *Enter the Dragon*.

Me! Of all people! Ellie, I've seen that movie about fifty times, and I never get sick of it. It's a classic. If you're into that watch *The 36ᵗʰ Chamber of Shaolin* next. It's *so* good!

Also, I'm happy you're picking up hobbies. I'm going to feel really lost when the basketball season is over.

What will I do with all the free time? Maybe I'll pick up a hobby, too. Or hell, maybe I'll just take the internship. Who knows?

Also, the idea of you kicking ass while knitting sweaters is pretty badass.
My kind of woman.
-Grey

P.S. Saw a dragonfly last night. Reminded me of you.

14

Eleanor

I wished I could say things magically turned around once we got Mom near the water, but it wasn't true. Her health only declined more each day. For months, it felt like an uphill battle we were losing over and over. After a while, we had to push her around in a wheelchair. Some days, she couldn't even get out of bed, and others we had to rush her to the hospital because she couldn't breathe.

After her last trip to the ER in late April, we all knew time was running out. We never talked about it, though, because talking made it more real than any of us were ready for it to be.

Ding ding.

I finally signed online late one evening in April. I'd been avoiding doing it for a while, because whenever I signed on, Greyson was there waiting for updates, and I hated that lately the updates were getting sadder and sadder.

That night, I needed him. I just needed to talk to him, and like the loyal boy he always was, when I signed on at ten at night, he was there.

GreyHoops87: Hey, Ellie! Just checking in on you. You haven't been online a lot, so just a heads-up, you're going to have a whole inbox's worth of emails filled with my mindless random thoughts.

EGHogwarts: Hey, sorry. Things have been a bit crazy.

GreyHoops87: It's okay. I get it. Any update?

EGHogwarts: Just sad ones.

GreyHoops87: I'll listen to the sad ones, too.

I sighed, running my hand over my face.

EGHogwarts: I'm going to put on a five-minute timer, and that's all the time we're putting toward the sad stuff, okay? Otherwise, I'll drown in it. So, I'm going to word-vomit and get it all out all at once. You don't even have to reply. I just…if I say the stuff to you, I'll feel like it's not just waiting to explode inside of me.

GreyHoops87: Five minutes on the clock. Annnd go!

EGHogwarts: I think today's the first day I realized my mom is actually dying. Before there was an unrealistic belief that she was going to get better, a belief that there would be a day she didn't need the wheelchair anymore, or that she'd stand up and be able to dance again, or paint. But today we sat by the water, and I felt it. I felt the ending closing in. I felt that our goodbyes are a lot closer than our good mornings. I've never been so scared in all my life, and I have these terrible thoughts that make me feel like the worst daughter ever. If she were gone, she wouldn't have to struggle anymore. If she died, she'd be free of the pain. What kind of monster does that make me? How can those thoughts even cross my mind? Anyway, I guess that's where I am right now, and I completely understand if that makes you want to pull back a little from talking to me. Because right now this is me: I'm sad. I'm hurting. I'm so sad that sometimes I just want to stay in bed. I'm so sad that sometimes I have dark, dark thoughts and I don't really know how to control them, and that can be a lot. I can be a lot. My sadness is a lot right now, and I don't even know how to handle it, so I don't expect you to know, either.

I hit send and waited for a reply. And waited. And waited.

GreyHoops87: What else?

EGHogwarts: What do you mean what else?

GreyHoops87: That was only two minutes of our five. You have three more minutes to spill out your heart on this open canvas. I'm not going anywhere, Ellie. I'm here.

Tears rolled down my cheeks, and I took a deep breath. I had been given permission to express myself wholeheartedly. What a freeing thing that was to have.

EGHogwarts: I think that's it. That's everything I'm feeling.

GreyHoops87: Do you want my reply?

EGHogwarts: No, not now. Not yet. I just needed to get it all out, I think. So, if we could do anything but talk about sad stuff, that would make me feel better.

GreyHoops87: Okay.

GreyHoops87: So, what did the fish say when he swam into a wall?

EGHogwarts: What?

GreyHoops87: Dam.

I smiled.

Thank you, Grey.

———

FROM: GreyHoops87@aol.com
TO: EGHogwarts@aol.com
DATE: April 29, 10:54 PM
SUBJECT: I know you said

Ellie,

I know you said you didn't need my reply, but being the stubborn guy that I am, I wanted to email you after our talk tonight. I just wanted you to know that you're not too sad for me. If anything, you are the perfect amount of sad, because you are going through a really shitty thing. Honestly, I would feel a bit scared if you were happy.

Be sad.

Happy can come later.

And you don't have to push me away. You aren't too much for me. I want to be there for you, and I'm not going to stop just because you tell me to. This is what being my friend means. It means me being too much sometimes, me checking in on you and wanting to know about the bad days. It means when you're drowning, I drown, too.

It's okay for you to lean on me, even if I'm a thousand miles away.

Also, and I cannot make this clear enough: you not wanting your mom to suffer doesn't mean you are evil in any way, shape, or form.

If anything, it makes you a good person because you don't want your loved one to hurt anymore.

That's not a monster—it's a saint.

Don't let those thoughts eat you up at night.

You're a good person, Eleanor Gable.

And if you ever forget, just check for my emails.

I'll be there to remind you.

-Grey

15

Eleanor

On a quiet afternoon after I returned home from school, Mom and Dad were sitting outside near the ocean, looking out at the waves crashing against the shore.

I walked toward them and smiled. Dad looked at me, his eyes dripping with tears, and my smile quickly disappeared. "What is it?" I asked.

Dad couldn't even speak.

He just shook his head and covered his mouth with his hand.

"Mom?" I moved over to her. She was resting her head against the back of the wheelchair, and her eyes were closed. I took her hand into mine. "Mom."

She ever-so-lightly squeezed my hand.

"Still here, Eleanor Rose," she said.

I exhaled in relief. "I was nervous."

"It's okay." She slowly opened her eyes and raised a hand to my cheek. "Can I have a minute alone with Ellie, Kevin?"

He cleared his throat and sniffled. "Yeah, of course."

Dad walked away, and I sat down next to Mom's wheelchair. The light breeze brushed against our skin. She was so tiny, nothing but skin and bones. Sometimes I worried if I touched her even softly, she'd just shatter into a million pieces.

"Do you need another blanket?" I asked.

"I'm good."

"Maybe you're thirsty? I can get water."

"I'm good."

"Or maybe—"

"Ellie, it's okay. I'm okay."

But you're not.

We sat there, staring out at the afternoon sky in complete silence. Hours passed, and the sun began to set. The sky was painted with vibrant colors, and it was beautiful watching how they blended into the ocean.

"Your father's going to need you," she said. "More than he knows, he's going to need your light, Ellie."

"I'll be there for him."

"I know you will." She inhaled deep and exhaled slowly. "I once read a tale about dragonflies, life, and death. Can I share it with you?"

"Yes."

She closed her eyes, and I watched each breath she took. "It spoke about how the dragonfly is born a larva, but when it's ready, it sheds its casing and becomes the beauty we see flying around us. In many stories, this is seen as the process of both life and death. The dragonfly emerging from its casing is just like when the soul leaves the body. There are two stages to the dragonfly. The first stage is when it is an insect that lives underwater. This is their life on earth. The next is when they emerge and find their flight. They become airborne and find a new freedom. That's when their soul is freed from the restraints of their body. Isn't that beautiful, Ellie? Isn't that an amazing thought? That even after death our spirits live on?"

Tears were rolling down my cheeks, but I was quiet.

I couldn't reply.

It hurt too much.

"I won't be in pain," she promised. "It won't hurt anymore. I will be freer than ever before, and you know what? I will still be here. Whenever you see a dragonfly, I need you to know it's me."

"Mom..." I kept holding her hand, and the tears kept flowing. "It's too soon."

"It's always too soon, baby, but I just want you to know..." She tilted her head in my direction and opened her eyes. "You are my heartbeats. You are my masterpiece. In a way, I feel as if I cheated death, because I get to live on within you, in your smile, in your laugh, in your heart. I'm there for it all, Eleanor. I'm eternal because of you. So please, do all the things. Take risks. Find adventures. Keep living for me and know that it has been the greatest honor being your mother. I am so lucky to have loved you."

"I love you, Mom. More than words, I love you."

"I love you, baby girl. Now, can you do me a favor?"

"Anything."

"Can you walk me to the water?" I hesitated for a minute, and looked back toward the house where Dad had headed. I was positive she wasn't strong enough to make it to the shore on her own. She'd been so weak lately, yet she placed a hand on my forearm. "It's okay. I know you got me."

So, I bent down and took off her slippers and socks, and then I removed my shoes and socks, too. I took her hands in mine and, slowly but surely, walked her to the edge of the water. It was freezing that afternoon. The water was chilled beyond words, and we both squeaked as it touched our toes and rose to our ankles.

We laughed, too.

I'd never forget that, hearing Mom's laughter.

At one point, she asked me to let her go, and she stood where her feet met the ocean. Her eyes shut, and she held her hands up in the air, her arms forming a V, and tears rolled down her cheeks as the setting sun kissed her face. "Yes, yes, yes," she cried, feeling every part of the world around her, seeming to feel more alive than she had in quite some time. Then she reached out to me, and I took her hand in mine. She leaned on me, and I was strong enough to hold her up on my own. We stared out into the night, finding a new kind of comfort.

She was okay in that moment.

She was happy.

And I swore, for a short period of time, the water healed her soul.

Two days later, Mom took her last breath.

Dad held her right hand, and I held her left.

The clock in the bedroom ticked, but time stood still.

I thought there would be some kind of comfort that came from knowing she was no longer in pain. I thought since we had seen it coming, it wouldn't hurt as much. I thought I would be somewhat okay.

But I wasn't.

Every single part of me ached.

Nothing can prepare a person for death.

You can't speed past the hurt to reach the closure.

You are simply overtaken by sorrow. Grief shows its face and it unforgivingly drowns you, and for a while, you wonder if staying under the water would be better than ever breathing again.

When my mother took her last breath, I wanted to take my last one right there beside her, but I knew that wasn't what she had wanted. She wanted me to emerge from the darkness, to swim again.

And I would.

Just not that night.

That night, heartbreak won the battle as I steadily fell apart.

16
Greyson

FROM: GreyHoops87@aol.com
TO: EGHogwarts@aol.com
DATE: May 1, 4:33 PM
SUBJECT: Sorry

I ran into Shay at school today, and she told me about your mom. She said she and her mom were heading down to Florida to help your dad and you out. I'm sorry, Ellie. I'm so damn sorry and I know that doesn't do anything or change anything, but I just wanted you to know. There's not a day that passes that I don't think about you guys, about you. I just wish there were something more I could do.

I remember when my grandpa died, I just sat around, uncertain of what to do. I'd never lost anyone before, and it fucked me up for a good minute. People told me to pull myself together and man up about it. "Death happens, kid. Better get used to it," my uncle Tommy said. "Real men don't cry," my dad echoed.

I think that's bullshit, though.

Be fucked up for a good minute.

Don't pressure yourself to feel better until you're ready.

I just wanted you to know I'm sorry.

She was what every kid dreamed of having as a parent.

I know I did a million times over.

I'm just really fucking sorry.

-Grey

—

FROM: EGHogwarts@aol.com
TO: GreyHoops87@aol.com
DATE: May 2, 2:02 AM
SUBJECT: Re: Sorry

Grey,

It's two in the morning and everything hurts. By everything, I mean every single thing.

My legs ache. My back is sore. My throat is dry. My eyes burn.

I can't breathe.

Every time I think about it, I fall apart, and I can't stop thinking about it. It's just a nonstop cycle of falling apart over and over again.

I just want her back.

I'm going to be fucked up for a good minute...maybe even for quite a few.

-Ellie

17
Eleanor

"Hello?" My voice cracked as I said the words. It was three in the morning as I answered my cell phone, and after a day of crying, my vocal cords were exhausted.

"Hi, Ellie." Greyson's voice was low and tired. For a minute, I thought I was dreaming. "Were you sleeping?"

"No." I sat up a bit in bed. "I can't."

"Yeah. That makes sense."

"What are you doing up so late?"

"I couldn't sleep. So, I checked my email and figured I'd call. I just wanted to make sure you were breathing."

Tears began rolling down my face as I clenched the phone to my ear. "I can't talk, Grey. It hurts too much to talk."

"That's fine. We don't have to talk. We can just keep our phones pressed to our ears. Okay?"

I nodded as if he could see me. "Okay."

I lay back down and kept the cell phone glued to my ear. His breaths were light through the receiver, but I was thankful for them. At some point, I fell asleep, and when I woke up again, his snores were still coming through the speaker.

It was quiet, and he was snoring, and tears were falling down my cheeks as I listened.

That was the very minute I knew I loved him—when I was broken-hearted at four in the morning and he still showed up for me.

Even though he hadn't said it, I was certain he loved me, too. People didn't have to talk about love to know it existed. Love wasn't only real because someone said it out loud. No, love just kind of sat there quietly, in the shadows of the night, healing the cracks that lived in our hearts.

18
Eleanor

Dad hadn't left his room in days.

I'd lost track of how many times I'd checked on him just to make sure he was remembering to breathe. Camila and Shay came down to help with the funeral service, and I was thankful for that. Without my aunt, nothing would've gotten done.

Shay stayed by my side day and night. She made sure I was eating, even though I didn't want to, and she'd check on Dad for me when it was too hard for me to see him like that.

There was a bottle of whiskey that sat on his nightstand, and each time I looked in, more of it was gone. He was self-destructing, and I didn't know how to help bring him back to life.

Truth was, the only person able to keep my father grounded was now gone.

The love of his life had left his side, and he didn't have a clue how to live in a world where she no longer resided.

There was no Kevin without a Paige.

There was an eerie quietness that filled our house, an uneasy feeling over everything. So, at night, I'd go stand by the water and listen to the waves crash against the shore.

That was where I felt her most—near the water. It was as if somehow she'd cheated death and landed within the waves.

On the day of the funeral, I walked by to see Camila forcing Dad out of bed. "There's going to be a lot of days when you are down, Kevin," she assured him, "but not today. Today you have to get up."

Somehow, she convinced him to get out of the bed and to get dressed. I was thankful for that.

It wasn't a big funeral, just the four of us. The service took place right there on the beach near the water.

It was what Mom had wanted, a celebration near the waves.

As I stood in the sand, my chest tightened when I saw a certain boy walking my way. The closer Greyson grew, the more confused I felt.

"Hi, Ellie," he said with the saddest eyes ever.

"What are you..." I glanced over my shoulder toward Shay and she gave me a smile that was meant to reassure. I looked back to Greyson. "What are you doing here?"

He gave me that small smile I'd missed so much and shrugged a shoulder. "You would be shocked by how easy it is to book a plane ticket with your parents' credit card. Sorry I'm late. My taxi driver got lost."

I leaped into his arms without any thought. Without hesitation. Without words.

Luckily, he didn't need words. He wrapped me in his arms and held me tight.

"I'm so sorry," he whispered. "She was the best."

Yes, she was.

We walked over to the shore right as the ceremony was about to begin. In my left hand was Shay's hand, and in my right, Greyson's. Every time my body began to shake, they kept me steady. My stare stayed on Dad the whole time, but he didn't look at me. He hadn't looked at me in days. I tried not to think too much about it.

I knew he was hurting, and I knew I had Mom's eyes. I could hardly look at myself in a mirror without tearing up.

Afterward, we were given Mom's ashes, and we took the urn inside and set it on top of the mantel. That was where it'd stay until we figured out where to spread the ashes.

I snuck off to my bedroom to get a breath of air, and it didn't take long for Greyson to find me.

"Are you okay?" he asked, standing in the doorway.

"No, not really."

"Do you want to be alone?"

"No...not really."

He walked over and sat on the edge of the bed with his hands gripping the side of the mattress. "I'm sorry," he said. "I know I keep saying it, and I know it doesn't do anything at all, but I am. I'm so sorry, Ellie."

He placed his hand on top of mine, and so many feelings raced through me. I knew in my heart he'd always be one of the most important people in the world to me.

"Thanks, Grey. That means a lot."

"I just wish I could do more."

If only he knew how much just being there meant. That was enough.

We lay down in bed facing each other and didn't really say much, because there wasn't much that needed to be said. He was there, I was there, and we were us.

"He doesn't plan to go back," I whispered, my head resting on the pillow.

"What?"

"My father. I heard him talking to Camila. He's thinking about selling our house back home."

"But I thought...I thought you guys would come back. I thought you'd be coming home."

"Yeah...I thought that, too."

The fairy tale part of me had thought I'd go back to Illinois, had thought Greyson and I could fall back together. I figured I'd be going to college up there, and even if we hadn't gone to the same university, we'd be close enough to at least be with each other.

But, fairy tales aren't real, and the reality of it was that I couldn't leave my father, not when he was as broken as he was. If he was staying in Florida, I was going to stay right there with him. I'd made a promise to my mother, and I had no plans of breaking it.

"I just thought we'd have the summer, at least," he said softly as he placed his hand on top of mine. "But it looks like we only have now."

"I'm sorry," I whispered.

"Don't be. Now is enough."

"You go home tomorrow?" I asked after Greyson yawned, which made me yawn, too.

"Yeah. Pretty early. Camila said she'll take me to the airport," he told me.

"Grey?"

"Yes, Ellie?"

"How long will I be sad?"

He shrugged his shoulders before he combed my hair behind my ears. "For as long as it takes. There's no rush to be happy, that will come when it's ready." I yawned again, and he smiled. "Get some sleep, Ellie."

"You'll stay with me?" I asked.

He moved in closer and wrapped his arms around me. "I'm not going anywhere."

I slept awful that night. My sleep had been bad since Mom passed away. I'd randomly wake up from panics, in sweats, after twisting and turning nonstop.

When I awakened, Greyson was there to soothe me. He held me tight as I cried against his T-shirt. He told me it was fine to break, because he was there to pick up every broken piece of me.

"Still here, Ellie," he whispered as my head lay against his chest.

He was still there.

———

When morning came and it was time for our goodbyes, I wasn't ready for him to go. Truth was, I'd never be ready to say goodbye to him.

He held me in his arms, and I held him back. "Thank you for coming."

"Thank you for everything," he replied before whispering against my ear. "You have her smile. Did you know that? You have your mom's smile."

That made me hold him even tighter.

"What now?" he asked.

"I don't know." I didn't have a clue what happened next.

"We'll keep in touch, yeah? With email? Or you can call me? Or anything..."

"Of course, but also, I want you to live up college."

"And you live up your life down here, too."

"We'll check in," I swore. "On the good days and the bad."

"Always. Especially on the bad. When the hard things happen, we lean on each other. Okay?"

"Pinky promise?" I held out my hand.

He linked his pinky with mine. "Pinky promise." He slipped his hands into his pockets and swayed. "I don't know how to say goodbye to you, Ellie. I don't know how to let you go."

"No need to let go. I'm always here."

He moved in closer and enveloped his arms around me. I fell into him the same way I always did—effortlessly. Our foreheads touched, and we took our breaths together. In that moment, our timing was right. He was there, and I was there, and we were one.

"I love you, Ellie," he whispered as his lips hovered ever so close to mine. "I know it's bad timing, and I know I probably shouldn't say it, but I love you. I love everything about you, even the parts you think are too sad to be loved. I think those parts are the most beautiful. I think all the parts of you are perfect, and I just wanted you to know that you are the first person I've ever loved, and it's easy to do it. It's so easy to love you."

Tears rolled down my cheeks and I smiled because I knew. "I love you, too, Greyson. Every single part of you."

How could I not? He was him, and I was me, and we were us.

"Ellie?"

"Yes, Grey?"

"Would it make it harder to walk away if I kissed you?" he asked.

"Yes." I moved in closer, so close that his lips were millimeters from mine, so close that his breaths out became my breaths in. We were so close that my mind had already decided it was going to be the best goodbye kiss of my life. "But do it anyway."

And then he did.

19

Greyson

FROM: GreyHoops87@aol.com
TO: EGHogwarts@aol.com
DATE: September 24, 8:54 PM
SUBJECT: College

Hey Ellie,

Sorry it's been a while. College is crazy, and there's something going on every single day. Parties don't only happen on the weekends. They're on Tuesdays and Thursdays, too. Also on Mondays and Wednesdays. Every single day.
Classes are harder than high school. There are a lot of times I'm not even sure I can keep up with the work.

How are things going for you? And work? You started nannying for that new family, right?
You said you're picking up a few night classes at a campus, right?

Did you hear about this new website called TheFacebook? It's only for college students, but it's kind of cool. It's a new way to connect to people. You should get on it. I'll make sure to be your first friendship over there.

I'm mostly on that now, instead of AOL instant messenger, but I still keep signing on to see if you're around when I have free time. You never are. Night classes don't help any. Let me know if you have any free time this week for a phone chat and maybe we can schedule it in?

-Grey

———

FROM: EGHogwarts@aol.com
TO: GreyHoops87@aol.com
DATE: September 26, 7:21am
SUBJECT: Re: College

Grey,

No need for the apologies, really. I knew you'd be busy. Every time I get to hear from you is always good in my book.

Things are going well so far, but I have to admit it's a little hard working full-time and going to school part-time. I feel like whenever I do get a break, all I want to do is go to bed and sleep until the new year.

On the plus side, the kids I'm nannying are very fun! They keep me on my toes, and it keeps me busy. If I'm not busy I have to be around my dad, and he's way too sad to be around.

I wonder if he'll ever get back to normal. The more time that passes, the more unlikely it seems.

I have my night class on Tuesday and Thursday, but maybe Friday night? Call me then?

-Ellie

———

FROM: GreyHoops87@aol.com
TO: EGHogwarts@aol.com
DATE: September 26, 5:32pm
SUBJECT: Re: Re: College

Shit. I made plans with my roommate Friday night. Saturday afternoon around 2?

-Grey

———

FROM: EGHogwarts@aol.com
TO: GreyHoops87@aol.com
DATE: September 27, 7:11am
SUBJECT: Re: Re: Re: College

I have to take the kids to karate. Sunday night?

———

FROM: GreyHoops87@aol.com
TO: EGHogwarts@aol.com
DATE: September 27, 8:01pm
SUBJECT: Re: Re: Re: Re: College

I have a club meeting that night.
Damn.
We'll figure something out.

Just miss you, is all.

-Grey

———

FROM: EGHogwarts@aol.com
TO: GreyHoops87@aol.com
DATE: September 28, 7:22am
SUBJECT: Re: Re: Re: Re: Re: College

Grey,

I miss you, too.
Obviously.
Yeah.
We'll figure something out.

-Ellie

20

Eleanor

We tried our best, but it was a struggle. As the weeks and months went on, Greyson and I kept missing each other, and even though we tried our best to keep in contact, life made it harder. Our schedules clashed, our timing was off, and it always felt as if we were just one second behind.

Our emails got shorter.

Life became busier.

Greyson and I each lived our lives on different timelines.

I held on to my promise to Mom to keep finding reasons to smile, though living with my father made it a little harder. He was still drowning, and I swore each day he pushed me further away. We were evolving in different ways, and the close bond we'd once shared was slowly diminishing.

Each day that passed, I kept finding my smiles. Each day that passed, I always had conversations with Mom, filling her in on the ups and downs of my life.

Even though some days were tough, I was finding a new form of happiness.

Because that was all I'd ever wanted to be: happy.

Just like the dragonflies buzzing by, every now and then Greyson East would cross my mind, and without any more thought than that,

I'd smile. I never thought too deeply about him being on my mind. I just let the thoughts linger for however long they needed to. I learned to appreciate him somehow coming back to me, in a way. The best part of memories is how they can reappear from the most random things. I'd think of him when I saw red licorice, or whenever I flipped past a kung fu movie on television, or thought about the most defining moments of my life, he'd always show up during those moments of reflection.

I'd always be thankful for the memories and the way he'd held me up during the darkest moments of my life when all I had wanted to do was drown.

I also made a promise to myself that if life ever brought us back to each other, if the stars aligned and somehow our paths cross once more, I swore, like the waves on the shore, I'd completely crash into him.

Part Two

"Love isn't a state of perfect caring. It is an active noun like struggle.
To love someone is to strive to accept that person
exactly the way he or she is, right here and now."

-Fred Rogers

21

Eleanor

Illinois, 2019

Riley Larson was turning five years old in two months, and I hadn't stopped thinking about it. I'd been thinking about her turning five since the day I met her. Most people were excited when a child turned five. It meant they were off to school to learn and grow and become more of the person they were meant to be. To me, though...to me it felt like a kiss of death.

Because, when Riley turned five, that meant she was off to kindergarten, and what was the point of a nanny when a child was in kindergarten all day?

For after-school activities? That was when a parent brought in a babysitter, not a nanny. Soon enough I'd be replaced by a thirteen-year-old girl who would gladly accept twenty bucks to watch Riley.

I'd been dreading the day Riley's mother, Susan, asked me to meet up with her for brunch to talk while her husband had a 'daddy and me' day with Riley. Nothing good ever came from brunch conversations with your boss, except for the bottomless mimosas I was gulping down to tame my nerves.

"I really am sorry, Eleanor. You have been nothing but a saint to our family since we took on your services five years ago. I mean, heck, you've been with us since Riley was four months, and there's no way we could've survived without you. It's just that with Riley going off

111

to kindergarten next year..." Her words trailed off as she readjusted herself in her chair.

She was so nervous. I assumed it was her first time ever having to let someone go. She was struggling to actually say the words.

"I get it, Susan, really. You don't have to feel bad."

Her eyes watered over, and she clasped her hands together. "But I *do* feel bad. You've been such a big part of our family for so long, and letting you go is just so hard."

"Well, you could always get knocked up again." I was joking, but like, really. *Get knocked up again, Susan.*

She laughed a "never in the history of ever will I do that again" kind of chuckle before downing her mimosa.

"But honestly, at least we have quite a few more months before school starts," I commented. I'd take any silver lining I could find, and having that buffer would give me some time to search for new employment.

Then, Susan ripped that gem away from me. She cringed. "Actually, Eleanor, we've decided to cut ties earlier. I was able to get Riley into a 4k program this semester, and then in the summer we're taking a family trip to Italy. When we get back, we figured it might be best to just bring on a babysitter to look after Riley."

Oh.

That's a low blow, Susan.

She'd used the devastating B word.

I'd been wiping her kid's bum for how many years? And she wasn't even going to give me a few months to figure things out?

I tried my best to not allow my emotions to overtake me, but I wore my heart on my sleeve. If I was upset or hurt, people could read it on every part of my body. I had no poker face. What I felt was what you saw, and what you saw was what I felt.

I'd gotten that trait from my mother.

"Oh, that's...wonderful. That will be so great for all of you," I said.

She frowned. "Yes, I think so. But, here..." She went rummaging through her purse and pulled out an envelope. "I wanted to give you this, you know, to cover the short notice of the job ending."

She handed me the envelope, and I thanked her. "Really, that means a lot to me."

"Of course, sweetie. It's the least we can do. Also, there's a little slip in there with a reference to one of my family's closest friends, Claire. They are looking for a full-time nanny for their girls. I already called her and mentioned your name. They are interviewing for the position next week, and I gave you the strongest recommendation. It might be something worth looking into."

A bit of relief filled me up as those words left her mouth.

Silver linings are back in action.

"Thank you, Susan. Really. That's more than I deserve."

"It's not a problem at all, really." She sat back in her chair and grinned. "I'm going to need the keys to the house and BMW back now."

"Oh? I thought the BMW was a goodbye gift," I joked.

She didn't laugh this time. She just gave me a tight smile and held her hand out.

Well then.

I handed her the keys, and she stood up from the table after she laying down cash for her part of the bill. "Okay, well, good luck with everything, Eleanor! I wish you the best. Stay warm out there, and Happy New Year!"

She hurried away, leaving me a bit stunned by how fast everything had unfolded.

I picked up the envelope and opened it to see two twenty-dollar bills sitting inside.

Forty dollars.

She'd given me forty dollars after firing me without any notice.

It really was the least she could do.

I pulled out the forty bucks and placed it on the table to cover my half of the bill, feeling annoyed that, on top of everything, she hadn't even bought my lunch.

I waved the waitress over and tapped my champagne glass. "We're gonna need another round of mimosas, stat."

22

Eleanor

I wasn't good at being interviewed. I never had been. When I was a teenager and had gotten my first babysitting job for Molly, I'd cried my way through it, actually *sobbed* in front of Mrs. Lane. She'd patted me on the back, given me a tissue, told me it wasn't as serious as I was making it out to be, and then said I did a good job. I was fairly sure she'd given me the job only because she'd felt bad for me, mother's guilt or something.

My interview process for Susan hadn't been much different, but she'd been only a few months postpartum and a bit delusional, so that had worked in my favor.

Maybe I can cry my way through this one, I thought to myself as I tugged on the bottom of my black skirt.

My thighs were sweaty and rubbing against the folding chair as I sat in the living room of the employer's home. I didn't realize the skirt was too short until I'd actually sat down in the chair, and if it had been an inch shorter, I was certain parts that shouldn't be seen during an interview would've been exposed.

I wanted the job, but not *that* badly.

I kept wondering about the crying option, even though I knew that was ridiculous. A grown woman crying to get her way seemed a bit dramatic. I supposed I would have to suck it up and power through.

There were a few other women sitting around me, interviewing for the same position. They seemed much more confident in themselves than I was, which was alarming. Why weren't they puddles of sweat? And why had I worn a light blue blouse?

The sweat stains beneath my armpits were disgusting. If I had raised my hand, the whole room would be able to tell exactly how unprepared I was that afternoon.

Thank God for extra-strength deodorant.

I pulled out my cell phone and sent Shay a quick text.

Me: I'm sweating like I stole something. I'm so not prepared for this interview.

Shay: Fake it till you make it! You got this!

Me: There's not enough faking it in the world to help me make it through this.

Shay: $65k for a nannying position, Ellie. You can fake it that much. Promise.

Sigh. She wasn't wrong.

When I had applied for the position, I'd received more details on the job, and needless to say, it would be the highest-paying nannying job I'd ever had. Susan had paid me thirty thousand dollars; this was more than doubled that.

I'd already daydreamed about how I'd spend that money, how I could send some to help out my father, the trips I'd take, the credit cards I'd pay off.

Now if only I could get through the next half-an-hour without running out the door.

I shut off my phone and went back to tapping my fingers against my much-too-exposed thigh. *Gosh, is this room stuffy, or is it just me?* No, the room was stuffy. None of the windows in the living room were open, which wasn't shocking seeing how it was the beginning of January. Still, they could've turned down the heat a bit. How was anyone able to breathe in that space without any fresh air coming in? We were just inhaling and exhaling the same dirty air nonstop.

The waiting was the worst part. It felt like we were all just sitting in limbo. I couldn't wait to be moved from the waiting room to the dining room for round one of the interview.

Round one.

Seriously, who had more than one round of interviews for a nannying position? We'd already had background checks done through the nanny agency. Why did I have to meet with one family member first, and then another after that?

I'd been nannying since I was eighteen, and I was certain that wasn't the norm at all, even in Chicago.

Who exactly was the employer? Susan hadn't mentioned a name, and when I'd emailed the address she'd given me, it had gone through to the employer's assistant.

Was Beyoncé behind that door? Would I be taking Blue Ivy and the twins for afternoon walks while their parents ran the world?

It all seemed a bit odd to me, but whatever. For $65,000 a year they could be as odd as they wished.

"Eleanor Gable?" a voice called out, and I looked up toward the sound.

My arm skyrocketed into the air and I hollered, "Present!"

Heads turned my way, and eyes glanced at my armpit.

Gross, Ellie. Put that away.

I lowered my arm and got to my feet. After clearing my throat, I said, "I'm Eleanor?" My tone almost made it sound like a question.

"Are you sure?" the woman asked, cocking an eyebrow.

"Yes, I'm sure. I am Eleanor."

The woman looked at me and smiled. She was older, maybe in her late sixties, and even though I was being weird, she still looked hopeful. "Hi, I'm Claire. Please follow me back."

I started in her direction while mentally beating myself up.

Did I honestly raise my hand and yell present?

What is wrong with me?

I shouldn't have been allowed around other humans.

I fit in much better with fictional characters.

The dining room was just like the living room—massive. There were built-in cabinets that held stunning fine china, which the family probably never used outside of holidays. The table sat at least ten people, which made me think they hosted often. It had such a bohemian look to it, as if it had been carved right in their backyard and then set in their dining room. It was beautiful.

Bohemian dining room table was now on my bucket list.

"So," Claire said, taking a seat as she stared at my resumé, "it seems you have quite a bit of nannying experience. Plus, Susan spoke so highly of you."

I sat beside her and inhaled deeply. "I do. I've been at it for a very long time. I nannied while I went to night school and got my degree in early childhood education, and then when I realized working in daycares wasn't my cup of tea, I decided to stick to nannying."

She nodded and wrote something down in her notebook.

What was she writing?

I hadn't said anything interesting enough to be written down.

I shifted around in my seat, and I swore my butt cheeks were sticking to the chair.

If I made it out of this interview with a scrap of my dignity, I was going to buy myself a new skirt.

"And this is something you're passionate about?" she asked. "Nannying?"

"Very much so. I've always had a passion for working with kids, even when I was a kid myself. I started babysitting when I was sixteen, and ever since then, I've known I wanted to be a part of shaping the lives of children. Plus, my mother was a nanny, so I guess it kind of runs in the family."

That sounded good.

Write that down, Claire.

My foot kept tapping against the floor and I fiddled with my fingers.

"And before working for Susan, you nannied in Florida? Is that home base?"

"Oh, well, no. My father and I moved down there when I was a kid, just before my mother passed away, but a few years ago, I found my way back to Illinois. In my mind, this has always been home. This is where I belong." I cleared my throat and tried to ignore my sweating.

Claire gave me the kindest smile. "You're nervous."

"Shockingly nervous." I laughed, rubbing my hands together. "Sorry. I'm bad at this part, but I *am* good at my job. Actually, I'm great. It's just the landing of the job that I struggle with. My nerves get in the way sometimes."

"It's fine. I hate interviews, too, but there's no need for the nerves. I'm the easy one here. Round two is where things get rough. But, before we worry about that, I wanted to tell you more about the family. This is a bit of a different situation than what you've probably experienced in the past. There are two girls: Lorelai and Karla. Lorelai is five, and Karla is fourteen. The hours are a bit wacky, but mainly you are there early mornings to take the girls to school, you have middays off, then you pick up the girls and prepare dinner and put Lorelai to bed. We're all still trying to find our footing after losing their mother, so at times things may seem intense."

"Oh, I thought you were...?" I shook my head, a bit confused.

"The mother? Oh no. I'm their grandmother. Their mother was my daughter."

The word *was* stung my ears. "Oh, my gosh, I'm so sorry for your loss."

"Yes. She was my world. She was everyone's world..." Claire paused for a moment and looked away. It was clear her heart was still breaking over the death of her daughter. I figured a heart always kept breaking when a parent had to say goodbye first.

Claire cleared her throat. "Anyway, their father works quite difficult hours, so over the past ten months it's been my job to do the first round for hiring the nannies. I cut out the bad seeds first."

"Nannies? As in there's been more than one in the past ten months?"

"Six, to be exact," she told me, which left me a bit stunned. "Like I said, it's my job to hire the nannies, but my son-in-law finds a way to fire them pretty quickly. It's going to take someone with a lot of heart to last in this position."

"That's one thing I have—a lot of heart."

"Good, good. I'm glad to hear it. Susan told me that, too. She told me you were a bit awkward when put in situations like this but said it was worth overlooking."

"Good ol' Susan." I nervously laughed.

"She's a doll, that's for sure. Back to the girls. A lot of the time the girls will need you to help them before and after school. Get them to school, to karate practice, and therapy appointments, make their meals—you know, the usual things. The position comes with room and board in the guesthouse if you are interested. It helps, seeing how you have to be over so early and sometimes you're not heading home until nine or ten. The hours can run long due to the structure of their father's work schedule. Sometimes, he'll have business trips, and you will be paid overtime and bonuses for those times. Allison, his assistant, will notify you far in advance of said travels. If for some reason you're unable to work those periods of time, a part-time nanny will be brought in to cover you. Also, when summer comes around, the hours will be reworked so you aren't working day and night."

"Oh, okay. That all sounds good to me."

She smiled and nodded. Then, she leaned in a bit. "I just want to really make it clear, this position isn't for the faint of heart. As I said before, within the last ten months, we have had six different nannies, which is why I'm wanting to stress how important it is to understand that this family is different than most. Everyone has changed a lot since the accident. Do you understand that there may be a bit of sensitivity involved with the job?"

"I do understand that, yes. I swear I can do this, Claire, and I know me saying that doesn't matter at all because it's just words, but I believe I am the right match for this position."

"It matters," she cut in. "I think it's important, you believing you can do this."

She asked me a few more basic questions and I relaxed a little, my nerves somewhat disappearing, but they came rushing back when she told me it was time for me to advance to round two of the interview process.

"Now, this is going to be a bit hard. Lately son-in-law is a hard man, and he won't say much. You will feel as if you are being judged, but don't let him break you. You need a tough skin to work for Greyson East. Otherwise, you won't survive."

My lips parted and I sat there, stunned.

Claire raised an eyebrow. "What is it, Eleanor?"

"I'm sorry, did you just say Greyson East?"

"Yes. Greyson East, the CEO of EastHouse Whiskey. I thought I mentioned that when you walked in."

"No, you didn't." *Oh, my God.* The breeze from the window some-how stopped, the ticking clock on the wall seemed to pause, and a wave of nausea hit me.

"Are you alright?" she asked. "Do you know him or something?"

I nodded slowly as every memory I had of a boy named Greyson East came rushing back to me. "At least I used to. It was ages ago, though."

"Well, maybe that's a good thing!" Claire remarked. "Hopefully it comes in handy. Now wait here while I go update Greyson. Then I'll come back and grab you for the next step."

She headed out of the room, and the ponds of sweat beneath my arm became oceans.

Greyson East.

Greyson-freaking-East!

He had kids—two girls, to be exact. A family.

He was a CEO!

I wondered what he looked like after all this time. I wondered if those grayish-blue eyes were still as striking as they had been. Did he have the same laugh? The same smile?

My heart pounded rapidly against my ribcage at just the thought of Greyson. When I looked back on the defining moments of my life, he was near the top of the list. He'd come into my life when I had needed him the most, and he'd left sooner than I had hoped he would. Now, I was supposed to walk into an office with him to interview for a nannying position for his children.

I couldn't wrap my mind around that idea.

"He's ready for you, Eleanor," Claire said, peeking her head back into the room. She nodded me toward her, and I stood up, smoothing out my tight skirt. "And don't worry, I left out your name. I thought it would be a pleasant surprise for him to see you."

I hoped so.

She walked me down the hallway, and we turned into an actual library.

There was a library in this home, one with actual ladders. I was blown away by the concept. In my dream home, there would be a room just like this one.

"Good luck," Claire whispered once I stepped inside, and then she left, closing the door behind her.

Greyson's back was facing me as he stared out the window. He was wearing what looked like an expensive suit tailored to his body. His arms were massive, shoulders broad; he was much more built than he had been way back when. He stood straight with no curve to his body. His arms were crossed, and still he hadn't moved an inch.

Had he heard me enter the room? Did he know I was there?

I just wanted to see those eyes.

I cleared my throat, feeling my body shake. "Well, this is crazy, right?" I choked out.

"Interviewing for a job?" he asked, his voice monotone.

"Yes—I mean, no. What I mean is...it's crazy for us to cross paths again after all this time." I took a step forward, feeling the knot in my stomach tightening. "It's just crazy."

"Do we know each other?" he questioned, still staring out the window, still sounding completely uninterested in my existence.

My gosh, Greyson. Just turn around.

"Grey, it's me...Ellie."

He straightened his shoulders just a bit, reacting to my words.

With a slow turn on the heels of his loafers, he looked my way. When we locked eyes, I took two steps back, a little thrown off. His were still the same gray, but unlike before, his stare was so cold, like ice. Those eyes I'd once adored were filled with a hardness I hadn't known they could ever hold.

Those beautiful eyes.

The harshness they projected in that moment made me want to retreat from his space as soon as possible, but also, oddly enough, that same stare kind of made me want to hug him and tell him everything would be all right. This new Greyson stood there with a very Eeyore vibe to him. It was almost as if a raincloud was sitting above his head.

He didn't have the carefree personality I remembered, that was for sure.

But, the longer I looked, the more I realized what I was seeing.

It wasn't coldness from anger. It wasn't harshness from annoyance.

His stare was sadness.

Sadness didn't come with words; it ran across a person's body. It swam in the eyes. It swept across the wrinkles in one's forehead. It pushed down shoulders and sat uncomfortably at the corners of lips.

No human ever had to speak of their sadness for it to be seen. Others just had to take the time to truly notice someone to see it.

All we truly had to do was slow down and look.

Greyson's sadness was clear as day, and that was heartbreaking.

He kept staring, saying nothing at all.

I shifted around in place and gave him a tight smile. "Like, Ellie Gable, from high school. We were..."

Friends...

We were friends, Grey.

We were so much more than friends.

How could he not remember? He was the one who'd gotten me through the hardest period of my life.

My words drifted because the harder he stared at me, the more uncomfortable it all became. Did he truly not remember me? Could that even be possible? Was it even the same Greyson I'd known?

Of course it was. Eyes never lie.

"I'm sorry, this is uncomfortable." I chuckled because that was what I did when I was nervous—I laughed awkwardly. "I just thought..." I paused, giving him an opportunity to dive into the conversation.

Still nothing but silence from him.

Say something, Greyson.

"I just... It's been years, Grey. You look great! Really nice. I see you grew into your height." *What, Eleanor?* What did that even mean? The palms of my hands were a swamp and I was having a hard time thinking straight. "Claire mentioned you have two daughters, huh? That's crazy. I mean, it's not too crazy, seeing how you're a grown-up and that's what grown-ups do—they have families. I mean, except for me. Still single as a daisy," I rambled, holding my ring finger up in the air like a freaking fool.

What did that even mean? Single as a daisy?

Pull yourself together, Ellie.

I cleared my throat. "Funny how life happens, right?"

Still. No. Words.

"Well, I mean, do you want to ask me anything about the nanny-ing position? I know this is probably weird, but I really would love the job—like, really love it. Life has been pretty crazy lately, and I could really use this position. I don't want to give you my sob story or anything, but—"

"Thank you, that's all," he said. His voice was low and deep with a newfound smokiness to it. He definitely wasn't a boy anymore, that was for sure.

I raised an eyebrow. "I'm sorry, what?"

"I have everything I need."

He was so dry with his words that I truly wished he had kept with saying nothing at all. He spoke in such a monotone way that it was almost as if he weren't really even there.

I gave him my forced smile, and he responded with a grimace.

He turned away from me once more and went back to staring out the window.

Gosh, this was so awkward.

There were a million questions running through my mind, a million things I wanted to ask him. How had he become the CEO of his father's company? How long had he been married? How was he deal-ing with the loss of his wife? *Oh, my gosh, he lost his wife...*

Oh, Greyson. I'm so, so sorry.

I stood there for a while, uncertain of what to do. It seemed as if he wasn't going to say anything else to me any time soon, and the way he stared at me as if I had never meant anything to him kind of stung. So, I cleared my throat. "Well, okay. I'll get going now. It was really nice to see you again, Grey. I hope everything...works out..." I dragged out my words and waited a few seconds to receive a reply, but nothing came, so I nodded. "Okay, well, goodbye."

I turned toward the door, opened it, and felt my whole body relax. I hadn't known how tense I'd been inside that library. I was certain I had completely forgotten how to breathe for a few seconds.

How was that even possible?

How did I run into Greyson East after sixteen years only to have him look at me as if there hadn't been a time in our lives when we'd meant so much to each other? How had he not felt the things I'd felt in that intense moment?

And how could someone stand so tall while being weighed down by so much heaviness?

Claire looked at me, surprised. "That was quick. How did it go?"

"That was...an experience." I gave her a sad grin. "Thanks for the opportunity, but I don't think I'm what he's looking for."

"Oh. Well, I'm sorry to hear that. I was hopeful."

"Yeah, me too."

I thanked her one last time and walked out of the house, taking my nerves and disappointment with me. I pulled out my phone to let Shay know about the failed interview then I heard the sound of heels click-clacking against the ground.

"Eleanor! Eleanor! Wait!"

I turned to see Claire rushing my way.

"Yes?"

She was breathing heavy. "It's yours."

"What's mine?"

"The job," she said, standing up a bit straighter. "I just spoke to Greyson, and he told me to cancel the remaining interviews for the day because the position is yours. His assistant, Allison, will be in contact with you via email and will be the one to show you around Greyson's home over the weekend. And—"

"I'm...wait, what?" I was completely baffled by her words, because there had been nothing whatsoever that'd just happened during my interaction with Greyson that pointed to me landing a new job. "I'm hired?"

"Yes, sweetheart." She grinned. "You're hired."

23

Greyson

I stared through the windowpane of the library as Eleanor walked out of the house. Claire was still speaking to her, updating her on being hired for the position, and when they embraced, I turned away for a second. When I turned back, Eleanor was climbing into an old beat-up car. As she turned it on, the engine sounded like it had been a chain smoker in a past life, and she drove off in that death trap.

Eleanor Gable.

I hadn't thought of her name in years, except in passing. Now, though...now she was cruising through my mind, flashbacks of the kids we had been when we'd first found one another infiltrating my thoughts.

She had stood in the library as if she knew me.

That was crazy to me. I didn't know if she was still the girl she had been back then, but I was so far from the boy she'd once known.

Life has a way of changing us, some for the better, most for the worse.

I was the latter.

Claire came back into the library, a bit out of breath but smiling. She was always smiling, even on the hard days. I looked away from her and turned back to the windowsill. The hardest thing in the world was looking at Claire's smile, because it matched her daughter's so much.

"I have a great feeling about this, Greyson. I think Eleanor is going to be a really good match for the girls," she commented. "Did you know she lost her mother at a young age? That could be helpful for the girls."

I didn't reply. There wasn't much to say, and I wasn't one to engage in conversations that didn't matter. Eleanor was the nanny. It was a done deal. There was no need to rehash it over and over again.

"She seems wonderful," Claire commented, because she never got the hint when I wanted to be left alone. Or, perhaps she did, but she worried too much about what I went through when I was left with only my thoughts.

"She mentioned you knew each other? When you were younger?"

My body tensed up, and I fiddled with the cuffs on my suit. "Long time ago."

"Yes, but it's always nice to be reintroduced to someone from your past."

I had no comment about that either. I didn't know what it meant that Eleanor Gable had been the woman to walk into my library that afternoon. I hadn't even allowed myself to really think about the concept of her reentering my life. All I knew was that she had the best resumé out of everyone I'd seen that day, and I had more important work to get to back at my actual office.

I cleared my throat. "I have to get to work. I'll probably be late heading home, too. After you pick up the girls, can you call in the babysitter to come over and watch them?"

Claire frowned, and I hated it.

She had her daughter's frown, too.

I hadn't known it was possible to miss a person's frown until hers had been ripped away from me.

"Grey..." Her breathy voice spoke my way.

I turned to my right, and Nicole's forehead lay on the exploded airbag.

I blinked my eyes shut as Nicole came rushing back to me. It felt more and more like drowning every time it happened.

Grief was strange, how it snuck up on you, how it showed up even when you tried your hardest to avoid it. I'd kept busy because I didn't want to mourn. I didn't want to face a world where she no longer lived, but the grief appeared quietly, at random moments, even though I tried my best to drown it out. It came at me sharply with the realization of what had happened. My chest tightened as pain flooded every part of my soul.

"Greyson," Claire said, her voice soft and filled with concern as she placed a hand on my forearm, shaking me away from my darkness.

"Hmm?"

"Are you okay, son?" she asked, knowing very well that I wasn't.

But I lied.

I always lied.

"I'm fine. I'll check in later, and make sure Allison emails Eleanor with all the details about the position. Thank you, Claire, for showing up today."

"Of course, sweetheart. I'll always show up," she promised.

She didn't lie.

She never lied.

I inhaled deeply and pushed away the emotions trying to slip out from within me.

I wouldn't allow the tears.

I didn't want to mourn.

I didn't want to feel.

I didn't want to face the fact that she was gone.

So, I did the only thing I knew how to do. I went to work, and I drowned out the wildness of my mind that tried to swallow me whole every second of every day.

24
Eleanor

"You got the job?!" Shay exclaimed that afternoon as I stood in our apartment doorway fiddling with my fingers. "Oh, my gosh, we have to celebrate!"

"Um, yeah. I got the job." I hadn't really come to terms with it, actually. For the most part, I had walked around dazed and confused since I'd left Greyson's house, wondering if what had happened had actually happened or if I was having some kind of psychotic break.

"I'm sorry, are you not happy about this?" she questioned, raising an eyebrow. "Before the interview you were ecstatic at just the idea of it! What changed?"

"Oh, a lot," I muttered as I walked into our place and shut the front door behind me. We'd been living together for the past two years now, and I couldn't imagine living with anyone else. Shay was the yin to my yang.

I headed straight for the fridge and pulled out a cake. I could always count on my cousin stocking us up with the best sweets.

She did work at a bakery, after all. Even though it wasn't her dream job, she loved it there. During the day, she was at the bakery, and at night, she was on her laptop writing screenplays. Shay was beyond gifted with the written word. She could spin words in a way that made one want to laugh out loud and sob all at once. She was just looking for her big break, and she truly deserved it more than anyone. Shay was talented beyond compare. I knew for certain someday she'd make it big in the film industry. One day, her name would be at the end credits of a blockbuster film.

I plopped down on the couch with a slice of cake and two forks. Shay sat down beside me, and eagerly accepted her utensil.

"A lot as in...?" she questioned.

"Well, I found out who my employer is," I said.

"Oh, my gosh, is it Beyoncé?!" she squeaked. "I was just telling my mom how it has to be someone famous with the amount of money they offered up."

"It's not Beyoncé." I laughed, thinking it was funny how my cousin and I had the same thought process. In many ways, it was almost as if we were twins. Our minds were always on the same page. "But it is someone we know...or, well, knew."

"Shut up. What?! I'm freaking out now. Who do we know that has that kind of money?"

"Greyson."

"Greyson who?"

"*Greyson*, Greyson. Greyson East."

Her mouth dropped open, and she gasped. "No. *Way!*"

"Thank you! That was my reaction, too. I guess he's the CEO of his father's whiskey company."

"That's insane. That is *beyond* insane," Shay remarked. "Holy crap. So, how was it? What did he say when he saw you?"

"Um, nothing, really. He hardly spoke. It was weird, Shay. He was so...different, the complete opposite of the boy we used to know." The Greyson I knew was so open and willing to express himself in every way possible. He spoke with such hope in his voice, and dreamed of a bright future.

The Greyson I'd seen in the library of a mansion was different.

He was someone completely new, and I didn't have a clue how to feel about it.

"That's so crazy. You guys were so close for a while, up until you moved to Florida with your dad."

"Yeah. Honestly, he had such a big impact on me, but today he acted as if he didn't even know who I was."

"But he hired you. That has to count for something, right?"

"Maybe... I just wish you could've seen him. He was so...cold."

"Cold like mean? Or rude?"

"No, not exactly..."

Greyson hadn't exactly been rude or mean toward me. He'd just... been. It was hard to explain his whole demeanor. Calling Greyson mean felt disrespectful, yet calling him kind felt absurd. He'd just felt quietly intriguing, as if there were a million thoughts shooting through his mind, but he never let anyone else in on them.

"He's just not the person I knew, that's all. I'll just have to get used to it, I guess. Either way, it's going to be weird working for him."

"Oh, gosh, working for your first love—I couldn't even imagine that."

"I'm still trying to picture it myself."

Shay and I sat on the couch and settled in to watch some bad reality TV together. Once a week we cancelled all plans to binge terrible shows we DVRed. Our favorites were the dating competitions because they were so ridiculously over-the-top. Give us marathons of *The Bachelor* or *The Bachelorette*, and we'd be happy for days. Yet, that afternoon it was a bit hard to let go of my thoughts. A big part of my mind couldn't stop thinking about the new Greyson East. I couldn't imagine what it would be like working for a man who'd defined such a big part of my life.

It had been over fifteen years since we said goodbye, a decade and a half of growth and change, ups and downs, and moving on. Still, I couldn't stop thinking about the boy that cold man used to be. I couldn't help but think back to our first hellos and final goodbyes.

I wondered if he was thinking about them, too.

———

After Shay and I finished our TV binge, I headed to my bedroom to call my father. I sat on the edge of the bed with my cell phone in my left hand and a glass of wine in my right.

"Hello?" the deep voice said before he coughed a bit and cleared his throat.

"Hey, Dad, it's Ellie," I said, shutting my eyes. "I was just calling to check in on you."

"Oh yeah, Ellie. I was going to call you, but I figured you were busy. How's everything been?"

I grabbed a pillow and hugged it close to me as I bit my bottom lip. "Well, yeah. I mean, everything is good. How are you feeling? Did the stomach bug pass?"

"Oh, yeah. It was weird, but I'm feeling a bit better. My head was in the toilet all day and night, but I'm good now."

"I'm glad to hear that. Have you been taking your insulin each day? I know you forget sometimes." He'd been living with type two diabetes for quite some time now, and he was the worst at dealing with it properly. I used to get into screaming matches with him to try to get him to eat healthier. It got so bad that I would find soda cans hidden under the bathroom sink. I tried everything to get him to eat better, to lose weight, but it was a useless effort.

You couldn't force a man to better his life if he didn't want to change for himself, and every time I pushed him, our relationship suffered. That was why I'd left all those years ago. He had gotten fed up with my attempts to help and pushed me away.

I just had to learn to love him from a distance even if that meant me worrying day in and day out about his well-being.

"Yep, taking it every day like I'm supposed to," he said.

Lies.

I knew it was a lie, too, because I knew my father.

We both went silent, which was pretty normal.

He never said much, so neither did I. I often wondered if our silence was due to the fact that we didn't have anything to say or because we'd waited too many years to ever speak up. Perhaps our heads were filled with deep, meaningful conversations we wished to have with one another and we just didn't have a clue where to begin.

That was okay, though. At least we still had the phone calls every once in a while.

Even so, sometimes I missed the words.

He cleared his throat. "Okay, well, hey, I gotta get to cleaning up a bit around here. Thanks for calling, Ellie. I'll talk to you later."

"Oh, okay."

"And Ellie? Thanks for the money you sent me. You didn't have to do that, though. I wish you'd stop, but yeah, thank you."

"Always, Dad."

"We'll talk later, alright?"

He always did that, ending the conversations early, which was probably for the best. Otherwise, I would've just held on to the cell phone, listening to his erratic breathing and wishing we weren't the people that we were.

"All right, Dad. I love you."

"Yeah, you too. Buh-bye."

He hung up without giving me the words I needed to hear most, the ones that might've given me a bit of comfort.

I love you, too.

It was hard to believe there had been a time when my father and I were close. Time had the ability to change relationships in ways we never thought possible. Death did that to people—turned their souls into something new. Sometimes, it was for the better, and other times it was for the worst. Over time, life forced people and their relationships to shift.

Some days, I wished I could ever-so-slightly shift my father back toward the man he used to be.

I missed that man every single day of my life, and I secretly prayed to Mom that she'd help him find his way back to me.

I fully believed in my mother's love. I thought her love was so strong it could somehow beat death. I felt her love around me at all times.

I really hoped Dad felt her presence, too.

Still here, Ellie.

Those words from her were tattooed on my heart, and they kept it beating.

25
Greyson

I stayed at EastHouse headquarters as long as I could. Most of my employees cleared out by seven, and when I glanced at my watch it was half past nine.

My phone started buzzing, and Landon's name popped up on the screen. I ignored the call, but that didn't stop my best friend from instantly texting me.

Landon: Go home, Grey.

I would've said me ignoring his calls was nothing personal, but it was. Ever since the accident, Landon had checked in on me every single day, and I pretty much ignored him every single day. I was sick of lying to him by telling him I was okay when I wasn't. I was sick of hearing the concern in his voice. I was sick of him caring.

So, I buried myself in my work and continued to do so each day until I was the last man to leave the office.

When I made it home, the babysitter was sleeping on the couch. She was some seventeen-year-old kid Claire had hired for days when we didn't have a nanny. I walked over to her and woke her up.

I felt pretty shitty about it being so late, seeing how she had school in the morning.

"Hey, wake up," I said, tapping her shoulder. I didn't remember her name, because I was the asshole who forgot people's names, no matter how many times I'd met them.

She sat up a little and yawned. "Oh, hi, Mr. East."

"Hello. You can head home now," I told her.

She yawned again. "Okay. The girls did good tonight. Lorelai wouldn't take off her butterfly wings, though, and she's sleeping in them. And Karla is...well, you know...Karla."

Oddly enough, I knew exactly what she meant.

I went into my wallet and pulled out cash. She shook her head. "Oh, no. Claire already paid me."

"Here's more, for the short notice."

Her eyes widened. "But that's a hundred-dollar bill."

"Yes, I'm aware. Thank you for your time, er—"

"Madison." She smiled, giving me her name like she always had to. "Like the capital of Wisconsin."

"Right. Madison. Goodnight."

She headed out of the house, and I released a breath of air. It was always nice when there was no longer anyone around.

After I poured myself a glass of whiskey on the rocks, I made my two stops of the night. First, to Lorelai.

Her bedroom was covered in her artwork. She'd gotten the artistic skills from her mother, that was for sure. Her breaths were quiet as she slept heavily with her body balled up in a knot. I went over to her, as I did each night, and took off her butterfly wings. She grumbled and twisted a little before falling back asleep.

During the day, she was a wild girl. She never went a minute without talking and her energy level was through the roof. At night, though, she was the definition of calm. Her breaths were always so soft and quiet.

I kneeled down beside her and combed her hair behind her ear. I kissed her forehead before heading to Karla's room next.

She, too, was sleeping, but she had her iPhone lying beside her as her Beats by Dre headphones covered her ears. Whenever I checked on Karla, I first checked her heart beats. She breathed much heavier than her younger sister, and sometimes I swore her breaths took pauses that felt too long.

Or perhaps that was just my worried mind.

Karla Lynn East was born three weeks premature. She was in the NICU for five weeks, suffering from breathing issues. There was a moment we weren't sure she'd pull through, but from day one, my girl had been a fighter. The day Nicole and I brought Karla home, I sat next to her crib for weeks, counting her breaths. Each inhale and every exhale was marked down in my mind. I had slept on the floor of her nursery each day, making sure her lungs were still rising and falling at a normal pace.

After the accident ten months ago, she punctured a lung which caused her to suffer from shortness of breath. Even though her lung healed, I couldn't shake my fear away. Therefore, each night I'd check her breathing. I'd beat myself up every time she missed an inhalation, too. If it weren't for my mistake, she wouldn't have been suffering so much.

If my eyes would've been focused on the road...

Stop it, I told myself.

My brain always wandered on its own to the worst day of my life. I had no control over my own thoughts.

I removed Karla's headphones, then sat at the foot of her bed, and placed the headphones against my ears. She listened to the same thing every single night, which meant I listened to it every night, too.

I closed my eyes as the recording played.

"I love you, my beautiful Karla," the audio said in Nicole's voice repeatedly.

I love you, my beautiful Karla, I love you, my beautiful Karla, I love you, my beautiful Karla...

My wife's voice echoed on the most beautiful loop. I fiddled with my fingers and lowered my head as I listened to her words.

When it all became too much, I'd place the headphones back on Karla's ears, kiss her forehead, and head to my own bedroom.

I sat in my darkened room, with no sound except the ticking clock on the wall. Time was moving, and my mind was working against me.

The words kept playing in my mind as I shut my eyes tight and lay down to try to sleep. Though, sleep never came easy.

I hated closing my eyes, because whenever I did, I saw Nicole's face.

Nightmares had nothing on a cold reality. My current days were hard, but my memories were where I suffered the most.

"Grey…" Her breathy voice spoke my way.

I turned to my right, and Nicole's forehead lay on the exploded airbag. Her eyes were struck with fear and panic.

I shook my head, shooting my eyes open. I rubbed my hands over my face, trying to shake the real-life nightmare from my mind. There wasn't a day I didn't blame myself for not checking on my wife more closely in that car. There wasn't a day that passed where I didn't remember every single mistake that I made that night.

So, I headed to my home office that evening. I knew sleep wasn't going to find me any time soon, so I'd keep working and working to try to drown out the heaviness that was my own soul.

Around one in the morning my phone dinged.

Landon: Go to sleep, buddy.

I tried my best to listen to his request that night, but still, like all the nights that came before, I failed.

26

Eleanor

"Hi, Eleanor, welcome back to the Easts' property," Allison greeted as I walked up to join her on the front porch of Greyson's home. She had been put in charge of giving me a tour and going over all the details of the job with me. We met up on a Saturday afternoon because she thought it would be easier to show me around while the girls were at their grandparents' house. She wanted me to not be overwhelmed by meeting the girls and touring the property all at once.

I felt like she was trying to give me a calmness before the storm.

Allison was everything every woman dreamed of being—at least she was what I dreamed of becoming. She was beautiful in an effortless way and looked like a CEO as opposed to an assistant to a CEO. It was almost as if she'd been born to lead. She walked into all spaces as if she owned them and never had her chin down, moving as if she wore an invisible crown.

Her confidence was beyond impressive. Plus, on top of all that, she was nice.

I wouldn't have blamed her if she wasn't nice—she had everything else going for her. She reminded me of Shay in a lot of ways: strong.

"So, you'll have your own set of keys to come and go throughout the house. In the foyer, you'll see the keys to the car needed to help get the kids to school. Thank you for getting me all the paperwork I asked you for. We're in the process of adding you to the insurance plan," Allison told me as we walked into the house. "Lorelai is allergic to shellfish, and Karla wouldn't touch a vegetable even if her life depended on it. Mondays are always spaghetti for dinner, no matter what. That's an important one. No penne, not lasagna, just spaghetti. Trust me, it matters. Otherwise, you can get as creative as you'd like for meal plans.

"There's a no-sugar policy that is in place for weekdays, but when they go to their grandparents' on the weekend, it's a free-for-all. Come Monday morning when it's time to wake the girls, you can blame Claire if the kids are in a sugar coma. Over here is Lorelai's room, and across the way is Karla's. Down the hall to the left is the spare bedroom where you'll stay if Greyson is working late or out of town. And over here..." She clicked and clacked in her heels as she powerwalked through the home, and I tried my best to keep up with her. She showed me the kitchen, the second bathroom, the dining room, the family room, the living room—not to be confused with the family room—and a million other places while tossing other details my way.

The more she spoke, the more overwhelmed I became. Shuffling through my purse, I quickly pulled out my cell phone, opened my notes app, and started typing frantically, trying to absorb all of the information being thrown at me. Allison glanced over her shoulder and smiled.

"I'm guessing I should've told you I have a binder with all of this information included. Don't worry, I'm just going over the basics. This is the kind of job where things kind of fall into place the more you do it."

"For sure. It's just a lot, that's all."

"The Easts are a lot, especially lately. I want you to know that this is a big job. Nannying alone is hard, but nannying for this family is even tougher. It comes with its own challenges. I want to make sure you're up for the long days and sometimes longer nights."

I wasn't certain I was up for it, to be honest. It all seemed a bit much for me. "I have to admit, I was a bit surprised that I was offered the position."

"I have no doubt you'll be great. I've been with Mr. East for a very long time, and I have to believe he knew what he was doing when he hired you. Then again, you're the seventh person I've given this talk to in the past ten months, so I could be wrong again."

She continued showing me through the house, and then we stopped in front of a door. She gestured toward it, lowering her voice. "That's Mr. East's office. He's probably in there now. Most of the time while he's home, he'll be inside those four walls, working. If the door is closed, you are forbidden to enter."

"And if it's open?" I asked.

She gave me a baffled look. "Oh, no—it's never open." She continued the tour of the house and once we covered everything, she took me to the kitchen, and handed me a large three-ring binder filled with paperwork. "This should help you a bit. I put together a complete guide on how to conquer the Easts' home."

I flipped through it, impressed by the attention to detail. "Wow, this is amazing. I'm surprised you don't have this position."

"Trust me"—she smirked—"Mr. East couldn't afford me if he wanted me to nanny for his children."

She made it sound like $65,000 was chump change.

Funny given I felt as if I'd won the lottery with that level of income while she talked as if it was a piece of gum on the bottom of her shoe.

Perspective, I guess.

"Before I go, I wanted to touch base with you on a sensitive subject," Allison commented. "It's about the girls, mainly Karla."

"Oh?"

"When the car accident happened a few months ago, the whole family was in the vehicle. They all suffered injuries, but Karla was tossed from the backseat through the window because she didn't have her seat belt on."

I gasped, covering my mouth. "Oh, my gosh."

"She, um, struggles with walking sometimes. Due to the way she landed, she had to have surgery on her left hip, and there's a bit of a difference in the length of her legs. So, she limps. It's pretty noticeable, but we try our best to not call attention to it. Karla will, though. She'll try her hardest to make you uncomfortable. There are also the scars."

"The scars?"

She nodded. "Her face was cut up pretty badly. When she went flying from the car, she slammed face first against a tree before hitting the ground. There's no way to get around it. You'll notice the markings, but please try your best to not have an outward reaction. Karla feeds on that. It will make things much harder for you."

"I won't."

She smiled. "If it makes you less worried, Lorelai is an utter delight."

"Such a big part of me is hoping she was named after *Gilmore Girls*," I joked.

"One hundred percent named after Lorelai Gilmore. Nicole wouldn't have had it any other way."

That was pleasing to me. At least Greyson had married a smart woman.

Allison stood up straighter. "Okay, I think that's everything. I'm going to head out now, but go ahead and make yourself at home. Get used to the property. Mr. East knows you're here today, so don't feel like you aren't allowed to wander around a bit. If you need anything, my cell number is on the contact list in the book, or you can email me. If nothing comes up, I hope your first day goes well. Claire will be with you Monday to make sure the transition goes smoothly."

I must have had my non-poker face on, because as Allison grabbed her coat and purse to leave, she gave me a light squeeze on the shoulder.

"You're going to be fine, Eleanor. Mind over matter. You got this. Let's touch base later this week so I can check in on how things are going."

"Sounds great. Thanks, Allison."

After she left, I took a deep breath and flipped through a few pages in the binder. Then, I did a once-through of the house, familiarizing myself with whose room was where. There was something so unsettling about the quietness of Greyson's home. It was so dark with an odd gloomy feeling attached to it, haunting almost. I didn't mean dark as in the lighting situation, rather it was the energy level. There was such a heaviness in the space.

The place felt like a house, not a home.

If I hadn't known any better, I wouldn't have believed a family lived there at all.

It felt so abandoned, almost like a memory frozen in time.

That might've just been my own thoughts, due to knowing about the tragedy that had taken place in the lives of the individuals who lived there. With the number of books I'd read, it wasn't inaccurate to say my mind wandered toward the dramatics.

Perhaps it just reminded me of my father's home after Mom passed away. It had been as if he and I were both frozen in time. That was ultimately the reason I left and went off on my own—the walls had been suffocating me.

I walked back into the kitchen, flipping through the binder, completely taken aback by the girls' schedules. Between school, swim lessons, karate, piano lessons, physical therapy, and grief counseling, I wasn't sure how they found the time to live even a little.

"Eleanor."

I leaped out of my skin at the sound of my name and turned to see Greyson standing behind me with an empty glass in his hand. He was dressed in a business suit complete with a tie, which was so strange to me.

Who wore a suit and tie in their own home?

I hardly wore pants when I was home alone.

"Oh, Greyson, hi. Sorry I'm still here. Allison was just giving me a tour and she gave me permission to look around a bit more."

"She made me aware."

Wow. He had responded immediately, unlike the first time I saw him. I called that progress.

I smiled at him, he didn't smile back, and that felt like the oddest thing in the world. The old Greyson had been full of smiles.

"It's a beautiful home," I stated, unsure what else to talk about. "It's massive. I swear it's like ten times the size of mine and Shay's apartment." He blankly stared as I shifted from foot to foot. "I love the décor," I blurted out, and I hated myself the second the words left my lips. *Just walk away, Eleanor. Don't be awkward.* "Those throw pillows in your living room are to die for. Where did you get them?"

"The interior designer chose everything," he replied dryly.

"Oh, right, of course. My interior designer is normally the clearance section at T.J. Maxx," I joked. "Or on special occasions, Target."

He didn't laugh, probably because I wasn't funny.

I wondered when was the last time he'd laughed.

Did he ever find anything funny anymore?

We kept staring at one another in the most uncomfortable silence, though I didn't feel as if I could pull myself away from it. I probably stared at him too long, but how could I not? I'd gone fifteen-some years without looking at him. It was understandable that I wouldn't be able to turn away quickly.

The awkwardness of it all finally came to a halt when Greyson cleared his throat.

"Eleanor?"

"Yes?"

"I came for water."

"Oh?" I stared at him like an idiot, wide-eyed like a deer in headlights, waiting for his next words. I stood still as if he were going to expand on his interest in water. Was he offering me a drink? Were we going to sip water and catch up on things? Was I finally going to be able to ask him how he'd become the CEO of his father's company at such a young age? What had happened to his father?

His stare narrowed, and his lips turned down in a displeased fashion. He nodded once.

"Hmm?" I asked.

He nodded more aggressively this time, gesturing past me.

I glanced behind me and realized I was standing right in front of the refrigerator, blocking the water dispenser. I stepped to the side, mentally beating myself up.

Idiot.

"Oh, right, of course. Well, I think I'm done here, so I'll see myself out," I stated, scrambling to grab my binder. "Have a good afternoon."

He didn't reply, but that wasn't shocking. I was quickly learning that this new Greyson didn't have nearly as much to say as the old one.

27

Greyson

Eleanor had a way of staring and standing in front of me for too long, to the point that it was uncomfortable. It had to be uncomfortable for her, too, yet still, she kept staring as if she didn't care about the awkwardness of it all.

I also hated how she stared. She stared as if I were the saddest man alive. I wished she'd stop playing the tiniest violin whenever she looked my way. It was irritating. Whenever she awkwardly gawked, she looked at me as if I were a sad puppy from a damn Sarah McLachlan commercial.

I wasn't a sad puppy.

Just a not-so-happy man.

The weekends were hard for me, seeing how there wasn't as much work to keep my mind busy. Plus, the girls were always at Claire and Jack's house. Most of the time I tried to travel because being in different places made it harder for me to overthink too much, but sometimes travel wasn't an option and I was left home alone.

My home was eerily silent. It was always weird when it was so quiet, because there had been a point in time when all I ever heard were loud voices laughing. Sometimes I swore the echoes of the laughter still bounced off the walls, though, truthfully, I was probably just hoping the echoes lingered.

There were a million things I missed about Nicole, but her laughter had to be at the top of the list. She'd laughed in a way where tears always streamed down her face, no matter what. Nicole found everything so ridiculously funny, and she could make even the grumpiest person crack a smirk.

That was her superpower: making people happy.

It was no wonder that after she'd left this place, everything had felt a little darker. She had taken that light away with her.

My phone dinged, and there was a ninety-nine percent chance it was Landon checking in on me. Even when I told him to stop doing it, he always did.

I was somewhat thankful for that.

Even though I'd been a shitty friend for quite a few months, it was nice to know that Landon didn't take it personally.

Landon: Wanna grab a beer?

Me: Are you even in town?

Landon: I can get a private plane out to Chicago, no problem.

Me: Ha. Don't waste your money.

When the house was empty, and there were no more emails or contracts to check and double-check, I knew I was at my worst. I went for a jog on my treadmill to try to clear my head, but still, that never really did much to slow my thoughts, because the moment I stopped running, everything came rushing back to me.

She used to run, too.

She used to run, and bake, and smile.

She used to laugh, and dance, and love out loud.

She used to be everything to me.

And she was gone because of me.

On the nights when it was too much, like it was that evening, I allowed myself to crack. I fell apart when no one was looking, because it was easier to be broken when no one was around to feel bad for you.

I didn't want people's pity.

I didn't want their sincere apologies.

I didn't want their words of encouragement.

I just wanted my wife back.

So, that Saturday night, I walked to Karla's room, ignored the Do Not Enter sign on her closet door, and I opened it, which opened a world to everything that was Nicole.

Covering the walls were dozens and dozens of photographs of Nicole with the girls and me. There were a million moments frozen in time, pictures that captured their smiles, their laughs, our happiness.

Karla had set a chair in her closet and hung fairy lights throughout the space. On the floor were articles of Nicole's clothing, and I could tell my daughter had sat in the space not too long ago, because they were freshly sprayed with her mother's favorite perfume.

I shut off the main light source in the bedroom so only the fairy lights shone above me. Then, I sat down on the chair and picked up a black hoodie. Nicole had worn it to bed when she was too cold, which had seemed to always be the case. I remembered pushing her cold feet away from me almost every single night before giving in and allowing her to freeze me.

I pulled the hoodie to my face and took a deep breath as I shut my eyes.

"Grey..." Her breathy voice spoke my way.

I squeezed it in my hands as if I were somehow holding on to her.

"It's okay, it's okay." I hadn't known why those were the words to leave my lips, but they were all that had come to mind.

I held the garment as if she was somehow still there with me.

She shook her head. "No. The girls."

My hands were turning red from how hard I was gripping on to that hoodie, but I couldn't let go.

I was holding on to a ghost, a memory, a story of my past.

And then I fell apart.

When it all became too much, when my thoughts overpowered me, I left Karla's room and went to pour myself a glass of whiskey.

I stood in front of the fireplace, watching the flames as I sipped the brown liquor.

I tried to shake Nicole from my mind, but when I did my girls entered my head, and that made me sadder. It reminded me of what my mistake did to their lives. Thinking about them reminded me of how I changed their world forever.

So I thought about Eleanor Gable.

The girl who stared at me for too long, and really liked uncomfortable situations.

Those thoughts weren't as heavy as all my others.

So, I let them stay.

28
Eleanor

If you had told me five years earlier that my next employer would be Greyson East, I would've called you a liar. Heck, if you told me that a week earlier, I would've laughed so hard in your face that tears would've rolled down my cheeks. But, there I was, standing in Greyson East's dining room, meeting his children for the first time ever.

Claire was a saint to me that Monday morning. She came over bright and early, ready to teach me the ins and outs of her grand-daughters.

"I can't thank you enough for helping me out," I told Claire as she set the table for breakfast. "It means the world to me."

"Oh, darling, it's no big deal, and after all the nannies that had come before you, I feel like this is tradition. I'm just hoping you last a bit longer than the others did, that's for sure. You know what they say—seventh time's a charm!"

I laughed. "I don't think people really say that."

"Well, they should. Seven is a lucky number. So, let's meet the girls!" Claire then turned and hollered toward the back rooms. "GIRLS! BREAKFAST!"

Well, at least Claire seemed down-to-earth in an oversized house with too many rooms and not enough people.

"I swear, these girls are going to try to bully you into letting them sleep in. Don't be afraid to pull them by their pigtails," Claire said when no girls appeared. "Wait right here. I'll be back."

As she hurried off in the direction of the girls' bedrooms, I took a deep breath.

Man, I was nervous. I'd never been nervous meeting my employer's children, but this felt a bit different. I felt oddly unprepared.

"Grandma, I just don't get why I have to go to school every week," a little voice moaned and groaned as the speaker stomped her way toward the dining room. As she turned the corner, she looked up to me. "Who are you?" she asked before plopping down in front of her cereal bowl. Lorelai was dressed in mismatched pajamas. She was wearing the most vibrantly colored stripes and polka dots, and she had bright scrunchies in her hair. On her back were huge butterfly wings. She looked like an old-school Rainbow Brite ad.

"That is your new nanny," Claire explained. "Say hello, Lorelai."

"Hello, Lorelai," the little girl mocked, making me smile.

"Hi, it's nice to meet you. I'm Eleanor, but you can call me Ellie if you'd like."

"Okay." Lorelai shrugged and went straight into eating her food.

"After you finish your meal, you have to take a quick shower, okay, Lorelai? Because you can't be late to school again," Claire remarked, sitting in the chair beside her granddaughter. "Plus, unlike last week, you aren't going to put up a fight about your clothing choices."

"I just want to dress like a rainbow, Grandma. Let me live," Lorelai groaned, shoveling the spoon into her mouth.

She had truly said the words *Let me live*. I almost died laughing.

"Where did you hear that from?" Claire questioned. "Let me live?"

"Karla said it to Dad the other day."

"Sounds about right," Claire remarked. "But as far as your dress code, we're going to pick out some tamer clothes for you to wear today."

"I don't know what tamer means, Grandma, so whatever I pick out will be fine," Lorelai stated matter-of-factly.

Claire moved in closer to me. "Lorelai is the brightest personality you'll find in this place. She's sassy, funny, and so easy to love, but boy will she push your buttons some days." She turned to her grand-daughter. "Lorelai, what do you think about Eleanor being your new nanny for a while?"

She cocked an eyebrow, holding her spoon in the air. "Is she gonna let me wear whatever I want?"

"No, probably not," Claire said.

"Will she let me eat chocolate chips for breakfast?"

"No, probably not," Claire echoed.

"Will she color with me?"

"Yes," I cut in. "I can do that."

Lorelai shrugged and went back to eating. "Okay, that's fine."

Coloring—that was easy enough.

Then, from around the corner, I heard a grumbling sound.

Claire sighed. "Here comes Little Miss Sunshine." She turned to me quickly and patted the chair beside her. "Here, Ellie, come sit by me, and remember, don't take anything personally with Karla. She doesn't mean it, even if she says it." She paused. "Especially if she says it."

"Grandma, I really wish you wouldn't come stomping into my room like that. It's so annoying. Plus, I know how to wake myself up for school. I'm not a child." Karla grumbled as she turned the corner into the dining room. Her limp was very noticeable, but I tried my best to not display any kind of reaction to it. She was dressed head to toe in black and her hair was still dripping wet from her shower, stringy and hanging in front of her face. She mostly kept her head down, and when she moved to the table, she didn't look up at anyone. She didn't make one sound.

"Good morning, Karla," Claire said, walking over to her grand-daughter with Karla's meal and kissing her forehead.

"Whatever," Karla muttered. She inhaled her food quickly as we all sat there in silence for a moment.

"Karla, this is Ellie, the new nanny."

She looked up at me slowly, and I felt like a complete idiot because I quietly gasped as she moved the hair partially hiding her face.

The scars...

Allison had prepared me for them, but still, I wasn't prepared enough.

They were more intense than I could've imagined. They ran from all directions across her skin, but the one that was most noticeable seemed to start at her forehead and slice across her left eyelid, which appeared to be swollen. Her left eye had a red spot near her pupil that seeped into her potent blue stare.

I'd never seen anything like it.

God, her eyes were as cold as her father's.

"Grrr." Karla growled, clenching her jaw as she leaned toward me. My stomach knotted up and I wasn't quite sure how to react, so I just kept staring. *Oh, gosh.* Staring was probably the worst thing I could do, because Karla kept growling. *"Grrr! Grrrr!"*

"Karla Marie, knock it off this instant," Claire snapped at her granddaughter, yet Karla didn't pull back.

"Grrr! Hisssss! Grrrr!" she hollered, keeping her eyes locked on me.

"Karla, that's enough," a stern voice snapped, making my stare move from Karla to her father. Greyson stood in the doorframe wearing his suit and tie with, coffee cup in his hand and his eyes on his daughter. "Quit it."

"I'll quit when she stops staring at me like I'm a fucking freak of nature," she snapped.

"No, I wasn't...you aren't..." I started, my voice shaky as ever, but Greyson cut me off.

"Watch your language," he scolded, and she gave him the most dramatic eye roll I'd seen in quite a while. Truly I hadn't known eyes could roll so deeply.

"Sorry, Father," she mocked, standing up from the table. She grabbed her bowl of cereal. "Since I used bad language, I should be banished to my room until it is time to be driven to prison by my servant." And with that, she left.

Greyson didn't look my way once, and I didn't know why I expected him to do such a thing. He walked through the dining room toward the kitchen. From my seat, I watched him pour more coffee into his tumbler before he turned around and walked across the space. He didn't speak as he walked back through the dining room.

"Bye, Daddy! I love you!" Lorelai said, to which Greyson replied, "You too."

Then, he was off to work.

"I'm sorry about Karla. I won't lie, she's going to be the hard one," Claire remarked. "I can't blame her for her hardness, though. She's been through more than most, though, for the most part, she's physically handling her changes well. She's adapted to moving around quite quickly and is pretty self-sufficient. Now, on the emotional front, there's a bit of struggle. Don't let her exterior throw you, though. She may act tough, but our Karla has the gentlest heart. She just gets hurt easily. Don't take her moods personally. She's working through a lot."

I smiled. "Aren't we all?"

Out of nowhere, Lorelai looked up from her breakfast and turned my way. "Hey, Ellie?"

"Yes?"

"Are you sure I can't wear my pajamas to school today? I'm really comfortable, and I think I'll learn better with them on."

I laughed. "Probably not, but I can help you pick out an outfit if you want. And then while we're in your room, maybe you can show me some of your best artwork."

Her eyes lit up and the biggest smile in the world filled her face.

That smile Greyson was missing?

The one I'd once known?

It lived on the lips of his daughter.

"Okay! Come on!" Lorelai said, leaping up from her seat. She grabbed me by the arm and dragged me off to her bedroom to pick out an outfit.

Well, at least not all of Greyson's children were completely underwhelmed by my existence. One out of two was good enough odds for me.

___

When it was time to get the girls off to school, I was thankful that Lorelai was so chatty, otherwise the car ride would've been extremely silent and awkward. Faithful Lorelai talked and talked and talked about everything and nothing at all while Karla's head was down and in her phone. Her hair was no longer wet, but she'd straightened it and it hung directly in front of her eyes, blocking her face. A pair of shockingly huge Beats by Dre headphones sat over her ears, and the nosey part of me wondered what she was listening to. The logical part of me thought I should never ask, because I knew she would never tell me.

Unfortunately, my first drop-off was Lorelai, which left me in a car alone with Karla and her grimaces.

When we were about three blocks away from the high school, Karla hollered. "No! Stop here!"

I glanced back at her and raised an eyebrow. "What? Why?"

"No nanny has ever pulled up to the school and dropped me off in the past ten months."

I laughed. "What? That can't be true."

"It *is* true. The last thing I need is to be embarrassed by having an adult drop me off in an expensive-ass car like a freaking ugly diva and then have everybody watch me limp into the building. It's high school—everyone's an asshole, even to the crippled girl. So, if you could please just stop the car," she ordered, her tone filled with nothing but attitude and sass.

I pulled over to the side of the road and placed the car in park.

I felt bad for her, even though she would've hated my pity, but she was just so young and so...angry. I didn't know much about her because she seemed to mainly keep to herself, and whoever it was she'd been typing nonstop to online. Even when I cleaned her room, there wasn't much to tell me about the girl who lived in that space. She didn't have any posters, no books on her shelves, no personality. The room was as cold and distant as the girl who lay her head there.

I wasn't one to give up easily, though. I'd break through to Karla somehow, some way, even if it took forever and a day to do so.

As she began to climb out of the car, I turned to face her. "Listen, I know people in high school can be jerks, and if there's anyone who is bothering you, you can talk to me. I can be your safety net," I offered. "Or I can talk to the principal. Whatever you need, Karla, I'm here."

She rolled her eyes so hard, I wasn't sure if she'd ever see correctly again. "Can you not do that?"

"Do what?"

"Act like the 'cool' nanny. Listen, just because you work for my father, it doesn't mean you get to act like you know me. We've known each other for like, two hours. You're nothing to me, and I'm sure it won't take long for my father to find a reason to fire you, too. So, don't get comfortable. You're just another temporary thing."

Without even another breath, she got out of the car and started off in the direction of school, leaving me sitting there completely dumbfounded.

Being a nanny might turn out to be harder than I'd expected with Karla East as one of the children. Being cutthroat was in her nature, and bruising easily was in mine.

We were in for quite a ride, that was for sure.

29
Eleanor

"What do you mean she growled?" Shay laughed on the other end of our call as I prepped for dinner. I'd been quick to call my cousin, who was nice enough to take her lunch break early to listen to my crazy life.

"I mean exactly that. She growled at me, over and over again."

"No, no, no. Wait, like a literal growl?"

"Shay, she went *grrr! Grrrr!*" I attempted to recreate Karla's beautiful sounds. "*Grrrr*! Like a freaking lion."

Shay kept giggling nonstop, completely overtaken by the comedy of errors that had been my morning. At least someone was getting a kick out of it. "I'm not going to lie, I think I really like this girl," she commented.

"Yeah, well, wait until the day she growls at you."

"Well, hey, at least you're working again, you know. It's just crazy that you're nannying for Greyson's kids. I mean, holy crap, Greyson East has children—plural, as in more than one."

"I know. Isn't it nuts? They look just like him, too."

"So, is it still there?"

"Is what still there?"

"The chemistry between you and him from all those years ago."

I snickered. "You mean that teenage chemistry of hormones and grief? Uh, no. I'm pretty sure I left that in the past with most of my cardigans."

"I still think you should be rocking cardigans. It was your signature look! No one could pull off those sweaters like you could."

"Yeah, but you know after they got ruined in my last relationship, I kind of let the cardigan idea go."

I hadn't the best track record with dating. Actually, I might've had the worst track record to date. For some reason, I always found myself going toward the unhealthiest type of men. Yet the worst of them all was Alex—the therapist. When we lived together, he tried to help me through my personal issues. Even though I hated when he'd go therapist mode with me, I listened. Then, after one night of me crying about missing my mother, he thought he could help me through my issues by throwing out all the cardigans Mom made for me. He told me letting them go was a part of the healing process of grief.

I personally considered if killing him was worth the orange jumpsuit.

That day was one of the top five saddest days of my life.

"So, are you one hundred percent sure there's nothing there between you and Greyson? Does your heart skip a beat when he walks into a room? Do you two randomly run into one another and he brushes against your arm? Do you trip and he magically shows up to catch you just in time? Do you casually take note of his biceps?"

"Oh, my gosh, Shay, stop it."

"So, that's a yes."

"No, that's me saying that you've been watching too much of *Bachelor in Paradise* and you have an unrealistic view of what reality is. Greyson is a widower and I am in no way looking for a relationship. There is definitely no chemistry between us. If anything, I'm pretty sure he goes out of his way to avoid me."

"Oh, yes. Based on my knowledge, you two are right on track for a successful television series. Season one, episode one: 'The Tale of Distant Lovers'." I swore I could see her stupidly grinning from ear to ear, pleased with her cleverness.

"I'm going to hang up on you now."

"Okay, but please keep me in the loop. I need to know when episode nine happens!"

"And what's episode nine?"

"'When Lips Slip and Tongues Twist'."

I snickered. "Goodbye, Shay."

"Okay, bye! Oh, wait! I'll pay you five bucks if you growl back at the girl when you pick her up from school."

I laughed even more. "Goodbye, Shay."

"Bye!"

As I hung up the phone, I still had a smile on my face. Leave it to Shay to make an uncomfortable situation into a comedy.

———

My father had been ignoring my calls.

I only knew because he wasn't totally up on how calls worked on cell phones, and he always sent me to voicemail after the first two or three rings. I kept calling, though, because that was what I did. I kept checking on him even though he never did the same to me.

It was crazy to me how our relationship had devolved over the years, turning into something that was so one-sided. It was hard to believe there had ever been a time we were truly close. Sometimes that fact felt more like fiction, as if I had just made up the time when we meant the world to each other.

I hung up my phone after another failed attempt to get in touch with him, and then I sat down at the table for lunch on Thursday, waiting for Allison to arrive for our checkup date.

"Sorry, sorry, traffic is crazy on this side of town," Allison said, hurrying into the café looking as perfect as ever.

"No worries. I just arrived about ten minutes ago."

She took a seat and tossed her jacket off. "Well, I'm glad you weren't waiting too long, but still, I'm sorry. So, how has it been going so far?" Allison asked.

"I think she hates me," I said.

"Who hates you?"

"Karla. She hates me."

Allison laughed, shaking her head. "She doesn't hate you."

"Well, she doesn't like me very much, that's for sure."

"She's just a hard one to crack, that's all. She gets that from her father," Allison remarked.

"Greyson is nothing like I remember. It's chilling, actually, being around him. I mean, I get it, but still...when we were younger, he was a completely different person."

"If you had met him ten months ago, he'd probably have resembled the boy you once knew. At first, I thought the coldness was just from grief, from dealing with such a tragic situation, but now I wonder if this is just the new normal, if he's always going to be this way."

"How do you handle it? The coldness?"

"I don't take it personally, because it's not about me. I'm good at disconnecting my job from my real life. Whenever Greyson is in a shitty mood, I remind myself that it has nothing to do with me, because I'm really good at what I do. I'm the best assistant he could ever have. His moods are his own, so I don't take it to heart. You should do the same with Karla."

I smirked. "That sounds amazing...if only I could learn to not take things personally."

"Nothing in life is personal, not really. Some people will love you for who you are today, others will hate you for it, and none of their opinions matter either way—not the good or the bad. Only you can define who you are. No one else has that right."

"How did you ever get to that point? To the point of not caring what others thought?"

"The three Ms: maturity, meditation, and marijuana." She winked playfully, but I didn't think she was kidding at all. "Seriously, though, a word of advice: if you want to survive your job, you need to not take Karla's attitude to heart. She's been through a lot these past months, and it's made her hard. She will do her best to break you down to the point of you wanting to quit. Don't let her bully you. Stand your ground. Also, understand that some things run differently in the East household. Think of it as more of a building that holds three individuals as opposed to being a home. That homey feeling left the day Nicole passed away."

"She was their glue, their foundation," I whispered, feeling a knot in my stomach. I knew how that felt—losing the backbone of one's family. When Mom passed away, my house had come tumbling down, and Dad had been too exhausted to even think about rebuilding.

"Nicole was everyone's favorite thing..." Allison took in a deep breath, then released it slowly. It was obvious that Nicole hadn't just meant a lot to her family, but to Allison as well. "Anyway, just go into it knowing that, knowing the family isn't the normal definition of family. If you do that, you can manage your expectations. I know you probably feel the need to try to fix things, but you can't fix a home that isn't seen as broken by the people who live within those walls."

"That's heartbreaking."

"It is, but it's just their reality for the time being. Their hurts are still so fresh. The best advice I can give you is to stay in your lane and learn to bite your tongue. Stick to the to-do lists, and you'll do just fine."

"I guess you're right. It's their lives, and I'm just an employee."

"Exactly. I know it sounds harsh, but it's best that way. So, what else is on the agenda for this afternoon?"

"Well, I pick the girls up from school, then I drop Lorelai off at karate. Next I go to the physical therapy appointment with Karla. Then, I'll toss in the dinner I prepped earlier today."

"One more day of work tomorrow, and then it's the weekend!" Allison smiled. "Any fun plans?"

"Oh, you know, an exciting weekend of Netflix and reading."

"I love seeing women living their best lives," she joked, glancing at her watch. "Okay, I have to get back to work. Enjoy every second of your weekend. Call if you need anything!"

Allison paid the bill then hurried off.

As the day went on and I picked up the girls from school, Lorelai talked and talked about her day and how great her teacher was, how great her friends were. She was a nonstop chatterbox, and when I dropped her for karate, she kept chatting even when I was on my way back to the car to take Karla to physical therapy.

I much preferred when Lorelai was around, because I dreaded the silence that came when it was just Karla and me.

"So...how was school today?" I asked Karla, glancing toward her through the rearview mirror. She looked up for a split second before looking back to her cell phone.

I'd been completely ignored, though that wasn't shocking.

"Sounds wonderful," I muttered to myself.

We pulled up to the physical therapy center and headed inside. The front desk receptionist checked us in, giving big smiles to us both, and then she had us go into a back room where Karla's appointment would take place.

It seemed her physical therapy was to keep up her strength. They performed a lot of muscle exercises, and Karla was extremely good at almost every one that was tossed her way.

I waited by the door where chairs were placed for family members.

When the door to the room opened, I was a bit shocked when I looked up to see Greyson walking in. He had on the same hard expression he always did and was dressed in yet another tailored suit and tie, of course. He walked over to the empty chair beside me.

"Greyson, hi," I said breathlessly, sitting up a bit straighter. "I didn't except you to be here."

"At my daughter's physical therapy appointment? Of course I'd be here," he replied dryly.

Right. Of course.

Uncomfortable silence. I wondered if it was uncomfortable for him, too, or if I was just overthinking it all.

I had a tendency to overthink certain subjects at times.

"She's doing really great," I commented, nodding toward Karla. "Both of the girls are really. Lorelai had a fantastic week so far, and she's been talking about how she's really looking forward to going to her grandparents' house this weekend. I think it's nice that the girls get to spend that much time with their grandparents."

He didn't speak a word.

So, I kept yapping, because the less he talked, the more nervous I became. "Lorelai seems to be really into art. I looked up some art programs in the area if you'd be interested in me forwarding the information to you."

Was I speaking out loud? Were words even coming out of my mouth? Because Greyson was reacting as if I were a ghost, and he couldn't hear a word I was saying.

"She's really talented and—" I started again, and I watched his body physically cringe.

"We don't have to do this, Eleanor," he interjected, still not looking my way.

"Do what?"

"Engage with each other." He ran his hand along his jawline before dropping it and clasping his fingers together.

"Oh, right. Sorry. I just figured you'd want to be updated on my first week."

"I already received updates from Allison."

"Right, of course, but just so you know, I'm completely okay with updating you each day, since we are around one another. I can stop by your office before I head home. Going through Allison is good and all, but I feel that sometimes she just relays the information without giving you the heart of things. I think us communicating would be wise. Plus, if you think about it—"

"No," he cut in.

"What?"

"I said no. That's not going to happen. You will report to Allison, end of story."

"But, Greyson—"

"*Please*, Eleanor," he pleaded. He begged me to stop talking. As if the idea of me reporting to him was too much, as if interacting with me was a huge burden.

I took a deep breath, feeling my skin crawl. He was definitely not the boy I'd once known. "Sorry, Greyson. All I am saying is, I really feel like you should be involved with everything."

"I am involved."

Yeah, right.

Just because he showed up to an appointment once a week and waved goodbye to Lorelai in the morning before leaving for work, that didn't make him an involved parent.

But I bit my tongue.

Stay in your lane, Eleanor. Stay in your lane.

It was just so hard to do that when the boy I'd once loved would've never been so cold.

30

Eleanor

FROM: GreysonEast@gmail.com
TO: EleanorGable@gmail.com
DATE: January 18, 9:54 PM
SUBJECT: Work Standards.

Eleanor,

After our interaction this afternoon, I feel it is important to go over some guidelines on working for me. Firstly, I believe it is best that you address me as Mr. East from here on out. I believe it will make things less personal. Since you are an employee, this is appropriate behavior, and it is how all my previous employees have been told to approach me. It is nothing personal, merely a business standard that is expected. I appreciate you upholding this structure moving forward.
Please note that you are to take any and all updates directly to Allison as opposed to bringing them to me. This is of the utmost importance, as I am a very busy individual and I do not have the time or patience to be bothered at your will. I am running a huge corpo-

ration, and the last thing I need is for the nanny to occupy my valuable time speaking out of turn about piano lessons.

As to that matter, Lorelai will continue her lessons, end of story.

I believe Allison has already informed you of the three-strike process. Please respect these rules and keep them at the forefront of your mind as we move forward.

Warm regards,

Mr. East

⎯⎯⎯

FROM: EleanorGable@gmail.com
TO: GreysonEast@gmail.com
DATE: January 18, 10:16 PM
SUBJECT: Re: Work Standards.

Aye aye, Captain.
Er, sorry, I mean Mr. East.

Lukewarm regards,

-Eleanor

⎯⎯⎯

FROM: GreysonEast@gmail.com
TO: EleanorGable@gmail.com
DATE: January 18, 10:34 PM
SUBJECT: Re: Re: Work Standards.

Eleanor,

Your sarcasm is ill-received.
Please be more cognizant of acting your age.

Strike one.

Warm regards,

Mr. East

31
Greyson

ukewarm regards.

I didn't know if Eleanor was trying to be comical or sassy, but she'd missed the mark on both accounts. I simply found it childish and rude. There wasn't anything I'd said to her that was out of the norm for a professional place of employment, and for the amount she was being paid, she could've at least been respectful enough to not be catty.

I didn't have any more work to do in my home office that night, and it was only eleven. Perhaps that was why I'd found the need to send Eleanor the email at all.

I needed to stay busy. Otherwise I'd think, and nothing good came from my thoughts.

Ding.

I looked down at my cell phone.

Landon: Roses are red, violets are blue, would you stop being a dick and just call me, dude?!

Landon's best friend daily check-in message came a little later than normal that night. He must've had a long day of filming.

After high school, Landon's life had shifted in a way most people only dreamed of. He'd gone off to California during spring break to get wasted and party, and instead, he had been discovered by a Hollywood acting scout and become this insanely famous actor.

People called him the next Brad Pitt, but I still just called him Landon. The last thing he needed was to think he was a famous god. He was surrounded by enough people who praised him as if they knew him, but he and I had never had that type of relationship. I was proud of him, yeah, but I didn't treat him like a celebrity. I treated him like my best friend from childhood. He needed some people to keep him grounded.

I didn't message him back that night. He didn't expect me to.

"Daddy," a small voice said, making me look up as my office door opened. Lorelai was standing there rubbing her eyes and yawning as she walked into the office. She was once again wearing her butterfly wings on her back, even though I'd taken them off about two hours earlier when I'd done my rounds to check on the girls.

"What are you doing out of bed?" I asked, standing from my desk.

"I had a bad dream," she whined, still rubbing her eyes.

I walked over and picked her up in my arms. "Let's get you back to bed. You have school in the morning."

"Can I sleep with you and Mommy?" she asked, and her words hit me straight in the chest. I took a few deep breaths and tried to push down the hurting her words caused my soul.

"Not tonight, Lorelai."

"But Daddy," she cried.

"Not tonight," I repeated as I led her to her room.

I laid her down, and she was still crying with tiny tears falling from her closed eyes. "Will you lay with me, Daddy?" she asked, sniffling. I lay down beside her, and she wrapped her arms around me. Lorelai wasn't one to ever really show sadness except for when she had bad dreams. I wondered if they were anything like my dreams. I wouldn't have wished my nightmares on my worst enemies.

As I held her, her sadness began to fade as she fell back into a deeper sleep. I, on the other hand, lay there wide awake, staring into the darkness as her words danced across my mind.

Can I sleep with you and Mommy?

Part of me thought she'd said the words because she was half asleep and confused. Another part knew better than that, because I had walked in on her pretending to talk to Nicole. I had watched her hold full blown conversations with a mother who was not here. I had witnessed her setting a spot for her mother at the dinner table on Spaghetti Mondays.

Lorelai knew Nicole had passed away, but she had somehow managed to hold on to her, to keep going on as if her mother was still alive, just invisible.

I worried about that, wondering if it was healthy for her mind.

Then again, I also envied her ability to have that connection with Nicole in some way, her ability to believe in something bigger than what was right there in front of her.

If I could have lived in a world where I believed in angels, I'd have talked to my wife every day, too.

After Lorelai was asleep, I stayed a bit longer, holding her against me.

She needed me that night, but perhaps I needed her, too.

—————

I woke up still in Lorelai's bed, a bit confused about my whereabouts. I sat up a little as my body whined and groaned from being twisted up in such a tiny bed.

What time is it?

How long have I been asleep?

I had no clue, though, it did seem like the best rest I'd gotten in over ten months, even if my body felt bent out of shape.

I walked to the kitchen to find Eleanor making a cup of coffee from the Keurig.

As she turned around and jumped slightly when she saw me standing there. "Oh, Grey—er—Mr. East. Good morning."

I narrowed my eyes.

It's morning?

"What time is it?" I grumbled.

"Seven. I was about to get the girls up to shower," she explained. "But then I saw you sleeping with Lorelai and figured I'd let you both rest a little longer."

"Seven?! Shit!" I moaned, running my hands through my messy hair. I couldn't believe I'd slept in that long. I never slept in. I was late and didn't have time to get my morning run in. "You should've woken me," I snapped, even though it wasn't her job to make sure I was up. Still.

Shit!

"Sorry, I just figured you were already dressed for work, and went to lay with her for a little bit."

"Why would you think I was ready for work?" I barked, irritated at her, but I didn't even know why I was irritated. Sometimes my emotions ran wild before I could catch them.

"Well, you know..." She gestured toward me, and I looked down at my outfit.

My wrinkled, five-hundred-dollar suit that I wore to bed last night. I wore a five-hundred-dollar suit to bed like I had no cares in the world.

"Oh. Sorry," I grumbled, because I felt like an idiot. I turned to walk away and she called back to me.

"Mr. East, just really fast," she said, her voice low and a bit timid.

"What is it?"

"I just wanted to apologize for my email response last night. It was very unprofessional."

I narrowed my eyes, somewhat taken aback by her apology. I hadn't expected one at all. "Oh, well, yes. It was unprofessional, but it isn't a huge deal."

"It is, though. I honestly didn't know you were serious about calling you Mr. East until you replied to my next email. Therefore, my response was meant to be comical, but obviously it didn't come off that way. I crossed a line I shouldn't have crossed, and I apologize for that. I feel like you're giving me a huge opportunity with this job, and it means a lot to me. I don't want to blow it, and I'm sorry if I was rude or snappy. I take this position seriously, and I hope you know that."

I nodded once because I didn't really have anything else to say.

"And Mr. East?" she said as she combed one hand through her hair.

"Yes?"

"I am sorry, you know."

"Yes, Eleanor. You've already stated that."

"No, I mean...for your loss. I don't think I've said that to you yet, and I just wanted you to know. Everything I've heard about Nicole shows she was a wonderful woman, an amazing mother, and I am so unbelievably sorry for your loss. I know it doesn't do anything, but I am, you know. I am sorry."

I took a moment to look at her, to really see her. I hadn't done so since she arrived for the job interview. Her hair was light brown with gentle waves. It was much lighter than I remembered. Not that it mattered, I just happened to notice. And her eyes... Her eyes were still those dark brown tunnels they'd been when we were children. They were still shaped like a doe's. They were still beautiful. And now they were staring at me as if I were the saddest man alive. She made me so uncomfortable with her pitiful stare.

Deep in those eyes was a level of care and concern I didn't think I deserved. I was rude to her, cold for reasons I couldn't even untangle in my own head, but still, she looked at me as if she'd forgiven me for a harshness I hadn't found the courage to apologize for.

After all this time, Eleanor still cared, and her apology was the sincerest thing I'd ever heard.

"Thank you, Eleanor."

"Of course."

I started to walk away then paused my footsteps as stupid grief began to fill me up inside once more. I hated how it showed up whenever it wished to. I hated how it swallowed me whole, and then spat me out.

Everything in life was harder without Nicole.

Every breath I took stung a little more.

I didn't know how to explain that to Eleanor.

I didn't know if she'd even care.

I brushed my fingers against the back of my neck and cleared my throat. "We were young," I told her, making those brown eyes look my way again. "When we had Karla, we were young, and I didn't fall into the father role easily, but Nicole..." I paused, feeling her name on my lips. Even after all this time, it was hard to say it without feeling as if the sky was falling. I took a deep breath in. "She did everything so effortlessly. It was as if motherhood was something she was made for. So, what you've heard from others is true. She was a wonderful woman, and the most amazing mother in the whole world."

Eleanor's eyes watered over and she nodded, understanding how hard those words were for me to speak.

I wondered if she could see it: the crumbling pieces of my soul.

"If you ever need someone to talk to…" she started, but I shook my head quickly.

Too much.

"I don't."

I had crossed a line by sharing that small bit about Nicole, but I just hadn't been able to help it.

I just needed her to know.

The whole world deserved to know what an exceptional woman my wife had been, and the whole world needed to know that we'd lost something so damn special the day she went away.

32
Eleanor

I'd made a mistake thinking Greyson was the same playful boy he was when I used to know him. Ever since our email exchange, I did my best to keep conversations with him professional—not that we were engaging in many chats.

Over the next few weeks, I learned so much about the Easts as individuals.

Lorelai's bedroom walls were covered with artwork she'd created. There wasn't a day where she wasn't lying on her stomach, kicking her legs in the air, drawing her next masterpiece—with her butterfly wings on her back, of course. She had an imagination bigger than the whole world. With just our minds, we'd be in South Africa, running with lions, and then the next moment we were in Hawaii eating fresh pineapples.

Lorelai also wasn't afraid to hold full-blown conversations with her mother. They happened every single day. Sometimes I'd walk in on her having talks with her mom like she was right there beside her. She also put a placement at the dining room table for Nicole on Mondays, because Mondays was always spaghetti day. Spaghetti had been Nicole's favorite meal.

I loved that about her little heart, how she kept her mom close to her.

We had that in common—our daily conversations with our mothers.

Then there was Karla, my new best friend in a *Go away, Eleanor* kind of way. I couldn't even learn about her based on her room, because she didn't have anything in there other than the computer that sat on her desk. The walls were empty, and the shelves didn't hold anything on them. The only spark of personality was the Do Not Enter tape plastered all over her closet door, with signs written in sharpie warning STAY AWAY.

In a way, that summed her up completely.

Lastly, there was Greyson, though I hardly saw him.

He was never really around long enough for me to read him. I only had my past memories of who he used to be to go by, and truthfully, I hardly saw those sides of him come through. Even when they did, they were so few and far between. It was as if he tried so hard to not show any emotion, and when it slipped out, he was quick to pull it back in.

Not only did he keep his distance from me, he kept it from the girls. Even when he was around, it was as if he wasn't truly there. He seemed so checked out from reality, I was surprised he was able to even complete his daily work tasks. Yet, that seemed to be the one thing he excelled at doing. Greyson was a professional workaholic, and he took that role seriously.

If he wasn't on the phone talking business, there was a very good chance he wasn't talking at all.

He and Karla were so similar in many ways, so cold and distant, but the difference was that Karla was mean while Greyson was not. He was just insanely lost.

Whenever Lorelai and I had dinner in the dining room, I swore Greyson and Karla went out of their way to avoid coming anywhere near us. They simply grabbed their food and went to their own personal spaces.

Like father, like daughter.

I didn't think too much on it. They wanted their space, so I gave it to them. Most of my focus went toward Lorelai.

She was the blessing at the end of hard days. There wasn't anything that could keep that young girl from laughing. In a house full of darkness, she was the light that flooded each room.

Each evening after dinner, Lorelai and I would pretend we were dragons flying into a new world where our only job was to make people realize that dragons were friendly creatures. It involved a lot of jumping up and down and roaring, of course, something we both were fans of.

One night as the two of us played in Lorelai's room, our volumes reached a new height as we laughed and laughed at Lorelai's new, deep guttural roar. Tears rolled down her cheeks from laughing so hard, and every time she tried to catch her breath, she laughed harder.

Those were my favorite moments with children—the wild ones.

As the two of us lost ourselves, we were interrupted by a loud bang on the bedroom door. We all looked up to see Greyson standing in the doorway with a stern look on his face. The laughter faded away as we all noticed the seriousness in his eyes.

"Hi, Daddy," Lorelai said, her voice lower than before.

"What's with all the noise?" he scolded, his brows knitted together.

I cleared my throat and smoothed out my clothing. "Oh, sorry. We didn't know you were home. We were just having a great round of—"

"A word, Eleanor," he hissed, cutting me off. "In my office."

I stood taller, chills racing over me.

"What?"

"I would like a word with you in my office," he repeated, not waiting for me to reply before he walked away. I took a deep breath before turning toward Lorelai. Her eyes were widened and she appeared shaken by her father's aggressive arrival.

"Is he mad because we were loud?" she asked, her voice quivering. Her shoulders slouched forward, and I could see the worry in her eyes. It was as though she'd let her father down in some way.

The shame of it all was that if anyone was letting someone down, it was her father who wasn't showing up for his daughters.

"No, honey. Your father and I had a meeting scheduled, I just forgot about it." I pulled her into a hug, and she hugged me back tightly. I savored the sweet embrace. "Now go get ready for bed, alright? I'll come check on you soon."

She nodded and hurried off to pick out her pajamas. I headed to Greyson's office, where the door was wide open.

"No offense, but did you really need to barge in with such a tone? You scared Lorelai half to death," I stated as I walked in. He was pacing the length of the room, clasping his fingers together as his chest repeatedly rose and fell heavily.

"Where do you take her?" he snapped, completely ignoring my comment.

"Excuse me?"

"Where do you take her?" he barked once more, this time his voice louder, scarier.

I took a step backward, unsure of what he meant.

"I don't know what you're asking me, Grey—"

"Mr. East!" he hollered, making me take more steps backward.

He was fuming, and I had no clue why. I'd never seen him so upset. For the most part he just coasted on a nice wave of detachment. In this moment, though, he was mad—livid, even.

"What's wrong?" I asked, trying hard to not take his temper personally.

"I received an email this afternoon asking for an update on Karla. It turns out she hasn't been to school in weeks, specifically since you've been driving her. So tell me, where have you been taking her?"

"I..." My voice shook as my mind tried to catch up with the words he was speaking. How was that possible? How was that a thing? "I take her to school every day after I drop off Lorelai. I don't understand how she wouldn't be attending."

"You see her go in every day?" he questioned.

"Well, no, because I drop her off a few blocks away like the other nan..." My words trailed off and reality set in.

Oh, my gosh, I am an idiot.

Karla had lied about the other nannies dropping her off blocks away from the school building, and I was the stupid person who'd believed her sob story.

Greyson hadn't caught on to the realization I'd come to, though. He kept staring at me with a hard glance, waiting for answers. I swallowed hard and explained the situation, looking away from him.

"You're joking, right?" he said, pinching the bridge of his nose.

"I—I just thought..." I stuttered, feeling as if I'd been fooled by a fourteen-year-old. My face grew warm, and I couldn't look at Greyson. I was humiliated by my naïve mistake. She had played me. I'd been royally played by a teenager. "I'm so sorry."

"Sorry doesn't make up for the fact that she has missed weeks of schooling."

"How does that even happen, though? Don't they notify the parent if the student is missing from school for more than a day or two?"

He grunted. "That's what I'm looking into now. Until then, go retrieve Karla from her room and bring her in here so the three of us can talk this through."

"Yes, of course."

I hurried out, feeling a sharp pain in my gut from my anger with Karla. I went out of my way to treat her kindly, to make her comfortable, yet this was the result I received. The closer I got to her bedroom, the more upset I became. Greyson had blown up at me because of her lies.

Then my emotions shifted to worry.

If she hadn't been going to school, where had she been?

What was she doing?

Were there drugs involved? Alcohol?

Oh, great, now I was angry *and* worried. I wondered if this was what it was like to be a parent, feeling every single emotion all at once. It was exhausting. Each emotion came in like a wave crashing against the shore, and I wasn't sure what to do with all the emotions I was experiencing.

I felt as if there was a split personality disorder going on. I wanted to yell and speak gently at the same time. I wanted to be the good cop and the bad cop. I wanted to be her friend, and her comfort but also the drill sergeant.

There is no middle ground when it comes to parenting teenagers. You always have a feeling of being crazed.

Before Karla could even witness my worry-anger, the biggest knot formed in my gut as I walked into her bedroom only to find it empty.

"Karla?" I called out. No response.

She wouldn't have gone, would she? Snuck out to go do whatever the heck it was she did during school hours?

I walked farther into her bedroom, toward her 'Do Not Enter' closet door, and as my hand landed on the door handle, a sharp shout stung my ears.

"What are you doing?!" Karla barked, forcing me to turn around in haste.

"Karla!" A wave of relief crashed against the shore. "Oh, my gosh, where were you?" I asked, my heart racing.

"The bathroom." Her eyes narrowed. "Why are you about to go in there? Are you stupid? Can you not read?"

"Don't call me stupid," I scolded, sounding more grown up than I actually was. "Your father wants you in his office."

"Yeah? Well, I'm busy." She walked over to her desk and went to reach for her headphones to drown me out, but I grabbed them before she could.

"No, you're not. Now, get going to your father's office."

"Why?"

"Because we know."

"Know what?"

"You *know* what we *know*," I stated, narrowing my eyes as I waved a finger at her.

She cocked her eyebrow. "Or I don't."

My hands landed against my hips. "Karla, come on. You can drop the act."

"Listen, I don't know what you're talking about, and I'm getting sick of this round-about accusation stuff, so either spit it out or leave my room."

"You haven't been to school in weeks, Karla," Greyson growled, appearing behind me. His eyes were filled with anger, and his chest rose and fell harder each time he took a breath. "That's what she's talking about. That's what we need to discuss."

He was pissed off, with good reason.

The second the real parent walked into the room, I felt as if I were out of place. I was, after all, just the nanny. For the most part, Lorelai was my main duty.

"I'll take it from here, Eleanor," Greyson told me, placing his hand on the doorknob, and stepping back a few steps to make a pathway for my exit.

I took a deep breath and looked toward Karla, who looked both nervous and almost...happy? She seemed pleased with the way she was pushing her father's buttons.

Then, I turned on my heels and left the room. Greyson closed the door behind me.

Within seconds, the shouting began. The hollering match between those two made me equal parts uneasy and glad.

Even though they were fighting, I was witnessing Greyson doing something I hadn't been aware he still knew how to do—parent his children. Seeing him engaging with Karla, being so angry demonstrated that somewhere inside his cold, numb heart, he still cared so much. Somewhere within him, he was still concerned.

That had to stand for something.

I left that night before the yelling came to a halt. It wasn't my right to listen to Karla and Greyson exchange words that were filled with exhaustion and pain. It was clear that they were both hurting, but the only way they could seem to ease their hurts was by shouting at each other.

33

Eleanor

I woke up the next morning curious about what had gone down between Karla and Greyson. I couldn't help but wonder where Karla was going each day, what she was doing, and how it had slipped past both Greyson and me.

When I headed over to Greyson's house, he was already standing on his front porch with a cup of coffee sitting on the railing. He didn't seem as angry as he'd been the previous night, and I thought maybe sleep had helped him calm down. He did appear eerily calm, though.

It was freezing outside, and all he wore was a black, long-sleeved button-down shirt and a pair of slacks. How was he not an ice cube?

"Eleanor," he said, his voice tame.

I cringed a little, almost positive I knew what was coming next. "Let me guess..." I sighed, pulling my purse higher on my shoulder. "You're firing me. I get it. I made a huge mistake. I just have a few things of mine in the house. Then I'll pack up my things at the guesthouse and be out of your hair in a few minutes." I started walking past him and was taken aback as his hand landed on my forearm, stopping me.

My eyes drifted to his touch, and his gaze did the same thing before we looked up at each other. It felt as if a bolt of electricity shot throughout my entire body, leaving nothing but chills.

Oh. What was that?

I wondered if he felt them, too.

He quickly dropped his hold on me and cleared his throat. "Sorry. I just..." He took a step backward and sighed, crossing his arms. "Good morning." His words threw me for the biggest loop known to mankind.

I raised an eyebrow. "Good...morning?"

Then, he just stared at me, and I stared at him. My eyes darted back and forth for a moment, uncertain what was next for our conversation.

"Is there something I can help you with...?" My voice was low and confused.

"You're not fired."

"Oh, but I thought—"

He nodded. "I know, but you're not."

"Then what is it? Is there something else you wanted to say?"

"No. Yes. I mean..." He took a deep breath and released it slowly. Everything about Greyson seemed so complex. It was as if his heart was constantly battling his mind, making it impossible for him to really express himself wholly. "I owe you an apology."

"For what?"

"For snapping at you yesterday about Karla. It was unprofessional," he stated, brushing his hand against the back of his neck, avoiding eye contact.

"Oh, that. Well, yes, it was," I told him matter-of-factly. "But it was also understandable. I would've reacted poorly to that news, too. I just hope you know I had no clue about any of it, Greyson. I truly thought I was doing the right thing."

He nodded, he and didn't correct me for calling him by his first name. Maybe he was too dazed and confused from last night's falling out that he didn't even notice my error.

"Did you find out where she was going each day?" I asked.

He shook his head and turned his back to me, looking out toward the rising sun. "No. She wouldn't say, but I did find out she forged my signature on some paperwork, saying the family was on vacation for two months. The school even gave her all her homework ahead of time, and she's been doing it all. I just..."

His voice trailed off, and his shoulders rolled forward.

Oh, Greyson...

His sadness was so loud that morning.

"She's smart, you know?" he told me. "Thorough—like her mother. She covered all the bases. She must have had this planned before you were even hired to nanny for us, because it had been in the works for some time. I just don't know why."

"Did you ask her why?"

"No." He turned back my way with his arms crossed. "I just snapped."

He knew that was the wrong thing to do, too. I saw it, the guilt of his reaction.

"You worry about her."

When he looked up to me, his eyes told me a story his lips didn't dare speak. Those eyes looked grayer that morning. Sadder, too. The previous night must've been hard for him; his stare told that story, the tale of a broken soul.

He shifted around in his running shoes. "I just wanted to apologize for snapping. I took it out on the wrong person, and it was idiotic of me to believe you had anything to do with Karla and her evil plan."

I smiled, but I was sure he saw the sadness in the curve of my lips. "Thank you for the apology."

He nodded and lifted the cup on the railing. "I made you coffee. Two sugars, one pump of vanilla, extra cream."

My heart skipped a little as I stared his way. "You remembered my favorite coffee from when we were younger?"

"No. I just notice you making it every morning in the kitchen."

Oh. Of course. What an odd thing to even think, Eleanor. Of course he didn't remember my favorite coffee. The fact that he noticed me each day hadn't gone unnoted, though. Even more so, him handing me that mug felt a bit like a peace offering.

"Thank you," I said, taking the mug from his hands.

"No, thank you. I know I can..." He paused and released a weighted breath. "I know I'm hard to be around."

"It's fine."

"It's not. I've never been the best at this stuff—being a father. I work hard, and long, and whenever I come home, I'm checked out. It was like that before the accident, but at least then, I had Nicole there to balance me, to be the calmness to my storm. Now...without her..." He brushed his thumb against his nose. "It's just that I don't know how to do this," he confessed.

"Do what?"

He lowered his head and when he looked back up, I witnessed the saddest expression I'd ever seen in all my life. His face was pale as if all life had been sucked out of him.

He parted his lips and softly spoke, "Live in a world where she doesn't exist." His eyes looked as if his whole world was set on fire. They watered over and he shook his head once, trying to pull his emotions back together. "Sorry."

"Don't be. What you went through—what you're going through is one of the hardest things anyone ever has to deal with. And it's still so fresh, Greyson. Those hurts are still so new. It's not shocking that you feel completely lost," I said, reaching out to him. I placed my hand on his forearm, and I felt his body slightly shaking from his nerves. He was so far from okay, and I was almost certain he wouldn't be all right for a very long time.

"It's fine, I'm fine," he lied as he removed my hand from his arm. He pinched the bridge of his nose. "I just wanted to say sorry for being so rude toward you. You don't deserve it, Ellie, not at all."

He'd called me Ellie, and I didn't think he'd even noticed the slip of his tongue.

I smiled. "It's okay, really. I get it."

"Even though you get it, you don't deserve it."

I didn't know what else to say, and it seemed neither did he.

He turned to walk back into the house then paused for a moment before turning back toward me. "Every single day...I worry about Karla every single day of my life."

———

That morning, everything went back to the normal routine, except this time, I personally walked Karla into the school building. She definitely wasn't thrilled about the idea, that was for sure.

"This is humiliating," Karla whispered, hunched over, trying her best to make herself disappear.

"Yeah, well, you should've thought about this before planning a make-believe trip," I replied as we stepped through the front doors.

"Yeah, whatever. Can you go now?" she muttered, grumbling under her breath. "This is so uncool, Eleanor."

I'd never been happier to be labeled as uncool in my life. "No. First we are going to stop by the front office to clear up a few things."

"Everything has been cleared up," a voice said, making us both look up to see Greyson walking out of the main office.

"Dad," Karla groaned, slapping her hand to her forehead. "What are you doing here?"

"Doing my job as a parent," he commented back to her.

"That's a first," Karla sassed.

Harsh, yet perhaps true...

"Everything's in order. Plus, I signed you up for some extra credit in every class," he told her, standing tall.

"Extra credit?!" she hissed, her nose flaring wide. "But I did the homework!"

"Yes, you did—after lying for weeks to do God knows what on your own time. You made a choice the moment you forged that paperwork, Karla. Now I'm making a choice to keep you from thinking about ever doing something like this again. Unless..."

"Unless what?" she asked.

"Unless you tell me where you've been going every day," Greyson said.

Karla's eyes watered over and she shook her head. "This is bullshit!" she shouted.

"Language," Greyson and I said in union.

I smiled at him.

He didn't smile back.

It seemed things were back to normal.

"Don't you have a meeting or some crap to get to? Can't you just leave me alone?" she asked.

Greyson glanced at his watch and nodded. "As a matter of fact, I do." Then those eyes looked at me. "Thank you for bringing her to school today, Eleanor. If you could please take her to room 102 for her science class, that would be great."

Oh, he was really playing up the embarrassing father routine.

"Of course, Mr. East," I replied.

"It's Mr. Ea—" He stopped his, realizing I had indeed called him by his last name. "Right, of course. Well, then, goodbye."

He walked off and I continued walking Karla to her first class, even though she was completely against the idea.

"I hate when he does that," she complained.

"Does what?"

"Tries to act like my father."

"He *is* your father."

"You've been with us for almost two months now—tell me how much parenting you've actually seen."

She wasn't wrong. Just as I was about to drop her off at her classroom, another student walked up and paused in front of us. I watched Karla tense up as he looked at her.

He was adorable, a cute boy with a curly blond Afro and blue eyes that would make any girl his age melt. "Hey, Karla. Haven't seen you around lately," he said. "A few people thought you switched schools."

She shifted on her heels and wouldn't make eye contact with him. Her left hand rubbed up and down her right arm. "Yeah."

"Have you been doing okay?" he asked, narrowing his eyes.

Before she could reply, another girl called out to him. "Brian! What are you doing?" I looked up to see a sassy girl wearing more makeup than anyone her age should've ever worn, standing there with both hands on her hips.

Brian turned to the girl and shrugged. "Nothing. I just thought I'd say hi. Did you see Karla's back?"

"Saw it, don't care," she muttered. "Now get away from that thing and walk me to class," she growled.

Every hair on my body stood up as the rude little demon spoke about Karla like that. "What do you mean *that thing*?!" I started, but Karla quickly tugged on my arm.

"Don't, Eleanor."

"But—"

She looked up to me, with tears in her eyes as she shook her head. "Please. Don't."

Brian frowned and rubbed the back of his neck. "Well, I guess we'll catch up later, Karla."

"Probably not," she said dryly as he hurried away to walk Satan to class.

"Who are they?" I asked, and she grumbled as we continued toward her classroom.

"The ghosts of Karla's past," she muttered, not letting me in any more than that.

It was nice to know high school was still hell on Earth.

At least some things never changed.

34

Greyson

"How have you been sleeping?" Claire asked as we sat down for our regular Tuesday lunch date. I didn't have the desire to meet her every week, but Claire was stubborn that way. If I didn't meet with her, she'd sit in the office lobby of East-House, playing Journey songs on full blast. It amazed me how one's mind could just snap after the third round of hearing *"Don't Stop Believing"*.

So, I met her for lunch once a week. Even though it was still hard to look at her.

"I've been sleeping fine," I replied, biting into my sandwich.

"You're lying," she told me.

She was right, but it didn't matter.

My eyelids were heavy, and sometimes in meetings I'd doze off. It felt as if my entire system was running on espresso and energy drinks. It was the only thing that kept me going. Healthy? No. Good for my soul? Probably not. But I didn't really care much as long as I wasn't sleeping.

She placed her fork down and sat back in her chair, and studied me. She was so good at that, too, staring my way and being able to tell when I wasn't okay. Most people learned to leave me alone and let me be, but her and Landon always kept pushing me to open up, even though I tried my best to keep them at a distance.

"Greyson, it's not healthy, the way you're not sleeping. You should really talk to someone about it," she told me. "Jack and I have been really concerned." Jack was Claire's new husband. She'd lost Nicole's father a few years back, and for a long time she thought she'd be alone for the rest of her days. But then Jack kind of swept in and changed her mind.

Claire leaned forward and clasped her hands together. "I just worry about you not resting. Especially with the approaching days..."

"I'm fine," I told her once again, cutting off her thought process.

Still a lie, and still, it didn't matter.

Truth was I hadn't been sleeping. I fought against it tooth and nail each and every night. It appeared that the only time I had a decent night's sleep was when I was curled up in a bed with my daughter, who kicked in her sleep.

"Greyson, I know with the anniversary—"

"How's work?" I asked, cutting into her sentence once more.

She grimaced, but sat back, knowing it was time to change the subject.

She pushed me all the time, but she knew her limits. She knew when pushing wasn't going to lead to a good destination, so she pulled back. Claire had always been so good at reading people, and she knew how to read me inside and out, even without me speaking up on my feelings.

"Work is good," she told me with a small smile. She went on to talk about anything and everything else that wasn't me. I was thankful for that, because I was too tired to think about me, and I was too heartbroken to think about the days that were approaching.

———

Three-to-one.

That was how it always went. Their three votes always defeated my one.

The problem with being the only male in your family is that you are often outnumbered when it comes to votes. I wasn't even sure why my opinion was requested, as it never seemed to matter, but they always asked my thoughts on the topic at hand.

"We had Italian last weekend when we went out," I argued during our dinner debate. "Plus, we have pasta every Monday. Aren't you guys tired of pasta?"

"Nope," Lorelai said, hopping into her car seat. I buckled her in quickly before getting into the driver's seat.

"Not really." Karla shrugged.

Why did they never crave steak?

All I really wanted was a big, fat, juicy steak.

"We should go to Palmer's Italian House!" Karla exclaimed, making me groan even more, because it was over an hour's drive away, and the rain was hammering down outside. It would take even longer than normal to get there.

I looked over to Nicole and narrowed my eyes. "What do you want?" I asked her.

Please say steak. Please say steak.

She shrugged. "Palmer's breadsticks do sound amazing. Plus, it is Lorelai's birthday, so I think she should get to decide."

"Palmers! Palmers!" she hollered, pounding her hands against her legs.

Welp. There it was.

We started the trek to Palmer's, which involved a lot of twisty roads and wooded areas.

As I drove, I glanced down at my ringing cell phone to see Rob Turner's name flashing on the screen. He was an employee of mine, and I knew he was working on things back at EastHouse. Normally, I answered his calls in an instant, but it was Saturday evening, and we had a strict rule in our family: No work on Saturday nights.

Nicole noticed the name on the phone, too, and gave me a look, almost daring me to answer it, and I was quick to ignore the call. The last thing I needed was a pissed-off wife because I took a few minutes to take a phone call for work.

"Will you stop it!" Karla barked at her younger sister, who echoed her words.

"Will you stop it?!"

"Mom!"

"Mom!"

"No, really, stop it, Lorelai!"

"No, really, stop it, Lorelai," Lorelai mocked right back. That was her new favorite thing, playing copycat. It drove all of us mad, but she was obsessed.

"Girls, calm down," I scolded. "We have a long drive to the restaurant, and I don't want to hear it from you two back there."

"She keeps unbuckling my seat belt!" Karla exclaimed, her voice filled with irritation.

Nicole snapped around quickly, pointing her finger at our daughter. "Lorelai East, we do not touch the seat belts in cars. Do you understand me?"

"But, Mama—"

"No buts. Keep your hands to yourself," Nicole said, turning around as Lorelai kept pouting and Karla gloated about getting her way—which, of course, led to Lorelai's full-blown screaming tantrum.

The way that newly five-year-old could hit those high screeches made me think we might have the next Mariah Carey on our hands.

"Jesus, Lorelai! Stop it right now!" Nicole said, her voice tired, but our sweet little girl just kept throwing her fit. When a girl her age thought a situation was unjust, she made sure to make it known to the whole wide world with her shrieks.

I saw it in my wife's eyes—her reaching her breaking point. There was only so much she could take before exhaustion took over and her anger built.

Turning around, I hollered, "Lorelai! Can you just cool it?! It's your birthday and this isn't good birthday behavior and—"

"Greyson!" Nicole shouted, making me whip back around.

I blinked once, and within that second, everything changed.

It only takes an instant for one's world to be shifted upside down, mere seconds for a life filled with joy and laughter to be replaced with ultimate despair.

Those doe eyes shone bright in the headlights.

The fear filled both of our stares.

I swerved.

I swore to God, I swerved.

The deer did, too.

I swore to God, it swerved.

I missed it.

It missed me.

A shout was heard.

My skin crawled.

Whose shout was that?

Was it Lorelai's?

Karla's?

Did my wife call out in fear?

No...

It was me, my voice.

Branches snapped as the car veered off the road into the dark woods. I twisted the wheel, slamming my foot against the brakes, but it didn't work. The car kept moving until it crashed to a stop, straight into a tree.

Head-on collision.

Everything ached. Everything burned.

Smoke billowed from the engine. My head pounded, my vision blurred. I couldn't think straight as acid rose up my throat. My body was chilled as the warm, salty taste of blood slid across my lips.

"Grey..." Her breathy voice spoke my way.

I turned to my right, and Nicole's forehead lay on the exploded airbag.

"It's okay, it's okay." I didn't know why those were the words to leave my lips, but they were all that had come to mind. I tried my best to reach for her, but I was stuck. My seat belt was jammed into place, and I couldn't move. I needed to get to her, to help her. I yanked, and yanked, hoping for it to budge, but nothing was working. "I got you, just wait," I promised.

She shook her head. "No. The girls."

I turned around, and Lorelai was screaming in her car seat, seemingly in more pain than her young body could handle. As I looked to her left, my heart leaped into my throat.

The side window was shattered, marks of red streaked across the broken glass, and Karla was nowhere to be seen.

Where is she? What happened? How can I get to her? How can I save her?

Karla?

Are you okay?

I need to know you're okay.

Dammit, let me go!

I yanked the seat belt harder and harder, using all the force I could muster, and it finally released. I reached for Nicole, but she kept shaking her head. "The girls, the girls," she cried, her voice pained with fear and aches of the unknown.

I slammed my body against the door, again and again. When it finally budged, I tried to hurry out of the car, but my legs gave out on me.

I forced myself to stand and I checked on Lorelai. Even though she was crying, she seemed okay. Then, I went to find her sister. I hurried through the blinding rain in search of my daughter. "Karla!" I called once, twice, a million times. There was no reply, nothing to be heard. The thoughts that raced through my head were unwelcome, and it took everything in me to keep from falling apart.

She's here. She's okay. She's here. She has to be.

I reached into my pocket, pulled out my phone, and dialed 9-1-1.

No signal.

Dead zone.

I felt sick but couldn't just stand there and keep trying to dial the number. I had to find my daughter.

I kept shouting. I needed her to hear me. She had to be there. People didn't just disappear.

When I turned to my right, I saw her, a small figure sprawled out in front of two trees. There was blood on the tree in front of her, as if she slammed directly into it. She looked so small and still.

So very still.

The stillness was what scared me the most.

"No..." *I whispered, hurrying over and falling down beside her.* "Karla, it's me, it's Dad. Wake up, honey. Wake up," *I begged as tears streamed from my eyes, intermixing with the rain that mocked us as it fell from the sky.* "Karla, wake up. You're okay, alright? We're okay. We're okay. We're okay."

"Oh, my God," a voice called out. I turned around to see head-lights shining toward me as someone walked forward. "Are you okay, sir?" the stranger asked.

I narrowed my eyes at the figure as it grew closer. "We need help," I cried, thankful to see him. "I can't g-get a signal, c-can't call for help."

"Okay, okay." He nodded once, his fear setting in as his eyes fell on Karla. The way he stared showed me the truth I knew—she wasn't okay. I couldn't deal with that idea, though.

"She's fine. She's okay," I promised, even though my promises were much more likely lies.

"You're bleeding," the man said quietly, his tone coated in con-cern.

What? No.

I unbuttoned my jacket and touched my side, crimson staining my fingertips.

My eyes glazed over as I looked down to my white shirt, which was tainted red. Realization set in as my body began to sting with pain. Vomit began to rise from the pit of my stomach as the man moved in closer. "Let me help you."

"No, I'm okay," I told him, feeling far from fine. I felt sick, nau-seous, faint. "Just go call for help."

"But—"

"Please!"

He nodded in agreement and hurried away.

I kept holding my daughter in my arms, lowering my forehead to hers, wanting nothing more than for her to be okay, for her to open her eyes, to look my way and tell me she was going to be okay, but she couldn't. So, I kept repeating the words over and over again. "You're okay, you're okay, you're okay…"

She couldn't hear me.

She couldn't see me.

She couldn't feel that I was there.

My vision blurred even more as I waited for help to come.

"Karla…" I whispered, shaking her. "Karla, answer me… please…" I cried. "Karla!"

35

Eleanor

"Karla, do you want to join us for dinner?" I asked as she walked past the dining room to get her dinner from the kitchen. I asked her every night, and every time she gave the same monotone response: "Nope."

She picked up her plate, and when she crossed back toward the dining room, she paused. We all did.

Out of nowhere, "Karla! *No!*" was hollered from a different room as Lorelai and I sat up straighter. Karla stood taller. Our conversation stopped, and we looked up, a bit confused as the yelling continued. "*No! No!*" the voice hollered, obviously coming from Greyson's office.

I slid back in my chair and stood up. Lorelai and Karla both looked nervous, but I smiled at them. "Stay here, girls. I'm just going to go check out what's happening."

I walked off toward Greyson's office, and my stomach knotted up because it sounded as if he was in deep despair.

"Greyson...?" I called out, knocking first. No answer. I knocked again, still, nothing. Then, I twisted the doorknob and opened his office door to find a sleeping Greyson at his desk tossing and turning.

He was in deep despair, obviously having a terrible nightmare, and it didn't appear as if he'd awake from it any time soon. I walked in slowly and I tapped him once on the shoulder. "Hey, wake up."

He didn't stop thrashing. I tapped him harder a few more times. "Greyson, wake up!"

He shot up, wide-eyed and terrified.

I placed a comforting hand on his shoulder to try to shake the fear away from him. "It's okay, you're fine. It was a dream."

He looked at me, his eyes still wide as ever, and ripped his shoulder free of my touch. He looked around, alert, and then his eyes glared back at me. "What are you doing in here?" he barked, obviously shaken.

"I, um, we heard you shouting. I just wanted to check in on you to make sure you were all right."

"Are you okay, Daddy?" a small voice said.

We both looked up to the doorframe where Lorelai was standing with a worried expression on her face.

Greyson cleared his throat and tried to regain his composure as he sat up straight and adjusted his tie. "I'm fine."

"You were screaming," Lorelai commented, still concerned about her father.

Just then Karla appeared in the doorway. "What's wrong with you?" she asked him.

"Nothing. *I'm fine!*" he snapped, making all of us jump out of our skin. He slide his hands over his face and sighed. "Sorry. I'm fine. Please, go back to what you were doing."

"But, Daddy..." Lorelai started, her eyes watering over.

I offered the girls a smile I hoped would reassure them. "He's okay, Lorelai. Just a bad dream. How about you head back to the dining room and we'll finish our dinner."

"He's not okay!" Karla barked out, staring at her father. "Nothing about him is okay! Nothing about this house is okay and I'm sick of acting like everything's okay when it's just not!" she cried before walking away as quickly as she could.

Lorelai stayed still with tears in her eyes.

"Lorelai, everything's all right," I told her. "Just go back to the table. I'll be right there."

Warily, Lorelai did as she was told, and I released the breath I'd been holding. I turned back to Greyson, who was now standing and staring out his office window with his back to me. "Are you alright?"

He turned to face me. His head flinched a little as he wrung his fingers together tightly and spoke. "Yes, Eleanor. I'm all right."

"If you aren't—"

"Eleanor."

"Yes?"

"Close the door on the way out."

I did as he said, knowing he was already on edge and not wanting to push him over it. I used to have those same kinds of nightmares after Mom's death. It wasn't an uncommon thing at all. It happened to many people after tragedy struck. I remembered being terrified to close my eyes because I wasn't certain where my dreams would take me. I wasn't worried about his dreams, but what concerned me most was how Greyson didn't seem like the type to talk to anyone about his suffering.

He kept his hurts all to himself, which was the easiest way to drown.

———

I stayed a bit later with Lorelai that night after I put her to bed, because I knew she was a bit shaken up by her father's outburst. That was something that happened with aging—the older you were, the scarier life became, and Lorelai was at that age where things were becoming a bit scarier.

"You okay?" I asked her, walking over and sitting on the edge of her bed.

She nodded as she hugged her pillow. "Is Daddy okay?"

"Yeah, he's okay. He just had a bad dream."

"He has a lot of bad dreams," she whispered, her voice so low and timid.

"Really? Does he shout in his sleep a lot?"

"Yes. Sometimes it wakes me up when I'm sleeping. Is he really okay?"

I smiled, even though I wanted to frown. I combed my hands through the little girl's hair, and bent down to give her a gentle kiss on the forehead. "Yes, he's okay. He's just working through some stuff, that's all."

She nodded, being more understanding than should have been possible for such a young girl. "I miss him."

"You miss him?"

"Yeah, he used to hang out with me, but now..." Her words trailed away and she frowned. "I miss Mommy, too. She was my best friend, her and Daddy."

Oh, sweetheart...

"And Karla. She was my bestest friend, but she never wants to play anymore," Lorelai explained. "She's just kind of grumpy now."

My heart hurt for her. My heart hurt for all of them. Their lives were tangled up in tragedy, and nothing could really change that.

When Lorelai finally fell asleep, I gathered my things to head home for the night, and as I walked past Greyson's office, I noticed the door was open, which wasn't normal.

He stood in front of his fireplace with a glass of whiskey in his grip, and his stare was so hard. His brows were knitted as he inhaled and exhaled. I wished I could slide into his brain and see the workings of his mind. He seemed to think so many things yet never let those thoughts release. The amount of pressure that sat on his shoulders seemed so heavy.

"Hey," I said softly, and he snapped around to face me. When he looked my way, he looked confused as to why I was speaking to him. "I, um, I was just going to head home for the night. The girls are all in their rooms."

He nodded once. "Thank you."

"Lorelai was really worried tonight."

"There was nothing to be worried about."

"Well, I disagree..." I took a step toward him and lowered my voice. "She said it happens quite often."

"What happens?"

"Your night terrors."

He tilted his head toward me and those cold eyes locked with mine. "I don't have night terrors."

"Yes." I nodded. "You do, and it's completely normal after the tragedy your family has been through. After my mother passed away I couldn't sleep. Remember? You'd call me. You'd call and sit on the phone with me and—"

"Please don't."

"Please don't what?"

He stepped closer to me, and his voice lowered so much it cracked with his next words. "Please don't do this."

"Do what?"

"Make it so clear that I'm failing this family."

The sadness that dripped from his words was heart-wrenching. "No. That's not what I'm saying. You just have so much on your plate. I don't think I could do half of what you do, especially with everything going on. You're doing all the right things for your children. They are involved in activities, they are staying busy, they are going to grief counselors, but, you have to do something for you, too. Do you talk to anyone?"

"No. I'm fine."

He lied straight to my face, as if it were the easiest thing in the world. Maybe somewhere deep inside of him he truly believed that lie, too, but there was nothing about Greyson that was fine. He was living with an internal flame that was setting his soul on fire, yet he was doing nothing about it at all.

Maybe because he didn't know how to deal with it.

Or perhaps he thought he deserved to burn.

"It's okay to get help," I promised him. "You taught me that when I was younger. You were the person who helped me. Let me help you, Greyson."

He shook his head. "You just get tired of it, you know?"

"Tired of what?"

He inhaled deeply and exhaled slowly as he brushed his hand against his beard and he softly said, "Everything."

"Greyson—" I started, but he shook his head.

"Good evening, Eleanor." He gestured toward the door. It was clear our conversation had gone on for too long.

I nodded in understanding and took a big step away from him with chills racing down my spine. "Good night."

36
Eleanor

"So, what episode are we on with the distant lovers?" Shay asked as we sat down on her couch for our weekly reality show binge. "How are things going with our Greyson?"

"There is nothing about Greyson and I that is a reality show."

"Right, uh-huh, so we're still on episode two: 'Denying the Love.' Gah, this is so exciting! I cannot wait, because this means the 'Slow Burn Friendship' episode is coming up soon! I cannot wait for you two to accidentally become friends again."

"Are you drunk?" I laughed. "You've only had one glass of wine, so I'm guessing you're not drunk, right?"

"No, I just know these things. As a writer, you learn about story structure, and you and Greyson are the classic rom-com. It's like you're Meg Ryan, he's Billy Crystal, and I'm Nora Ephron."

"I really don't get that reference."

Her eyes widened. "What do you mean you don't get the reference? Ellie, it's *When Harry Met Sally*, only one of the best romantic comedies of all time."

"Oh, I've never seen it."

She jumped back, stunned. "What is the matter with you?"

I laughed. "Okay, so if he's the hero in the movie and I'm the heroine, who's Nora Ephron? The quirky best friend?"

Shay looked at me as if I'd just skinned a puppy alive. She held up her hand and pointed to the door. "Get the hell out of my apartment."

"What?"

"I mean it. Get the hell out of my apartment. Nora Ephron, God rest her soul, was only one of the greatest writers of romantic comedies to ever grace this planet. *You've Got Mail, When Harry Met Sally, Sleepless-In-Freaking-Seattle*, Ellie! Come on! I mean, I love you, but sometimes I worry about your intelligence when you say things like this."

I laughed. "Sorry, but not everyone's a movie buff like you, Shay."

"I'm just saying, she was a legend."

"So, did you just compare yourself to a legend?"

She smirked and shrugged her shoulders. "If the shoe fits..." She hopped off the couch and headed to the kitchen and tossed a package of popcorn into the microwave. "Back to the main topic for tonight: you and Greyson."

"No, that's definitely not the main topic, because there is nothing to talk about. The main topic of tonight is who's going to get the final rose on *The Bachelor*."

Shay groaned. "Why talk about fake reality shows when we have a real one right in front of us? Just give me a little bit more about him," she said. "What is grown-up Greyson like?"

I frowned, thinking about it. "At first, I thought he was kind of grumpy, and, I mean, I guess he is, but honestly he's just sad. Like, intensely lonely and disconnected from everything around him."

Shay grew somber. "That's heartbreaking. Kind of like Jon Snow, huh? Like a sexy kind of sad? Like the kind of sad where you want to hug someone and kind of hump their leg, too?"

I gave her a stern look.

She tossed her hands up in defeat. "Okay, okay. So, he's really that broken up, huh?" The microwave went off, and then she pulled out her popcorn. After she tossed the popcorn into a bowl, she opened a bag of barbecue potato chips and mixed the two snacks together. I swore, my cousin could eat anything in the world and remain a stick. If I even looked at a cupcake, my butt grew two sizes.

"He's like a zombie from *The Walking Dead*. Just moving along day by day with random outbursts of sadness."

"That's really sad. He was such a bright light as a kid. So, are you going to help him?"

"I mean, I want to...I really do. I just don't really know how to help, and honestly, I don't think he wants my assistance."

"Well, just keep showing up. You're like a puppy dog that people can't help but fall in love with. Give it time, and you'll probably help Greyson find his way back."

I didn't know if she was saying that because she really believed it, or because she just wanted to see episode three of our show.

But either way, I planned to keep showing up. When we were kids and I was lonely, that was exactly what Greyson had done. He had showed up for me, even when I tried to push him away.

Maybe all people needed sometimes was for someone to keep showing up for them during the hard days, even when they tried their best to push everyone away.

37
Eleanor

Each day I showed up to the Easts' home just as the sun began to rise. Every time I saw it coming up, I said a little prayer for them. I found gratitude in the little things, because that was what Mom had taught me to do. I tried to appreciate all the small moments, because at the end of the day, those were the ones that count the most.

One Friday when I walked into Greyson's house, I first made my coffee, like I did every morning, and then went to wake Lorelai. As I rounded the corner toward her room, out of nowhere came Greyson. I crashed straight into him, spilling hot coffee all over his suit.

"Shit!" he hollered, jumping back a bit.

"Oh, my gosh, I'm so sorry," I exclaimed, placing the mug down, and rubbing my hands all the way down his chest to try to sweep the spilled coffee off of him. I paused my movements as I realized I was patting down Greyson's privates.

Oh my gosh, stop rubbing coffee off his crotch.

Oh my gosh, it's moving!

I leaped back as I felt my face heating up from embarrassment. "Oh my, I'm so sorry."

Stop staring at his crotch. Ellie. Look up, look up, look...

I looked up and Greyson appeared furious.

In that moment, I much preferred the lower half of his expression.

Look down, look down, look down...

"Jesus, you need to watch where you're going!" he barked, angrier than really needed. It was clear it wasn't my intention to spill coffee all over him and grope his privates.

"I'm sorry. Obviously, it was an accident."

"That doesn't make it better. This is a seven-hundred-dollar tailored suit that you just ruined," he snapped once more, his harsh tone grating on me.

"Well, why the heck would anyone buy a seven-hundred-dollar suit to begin with?" I barked back.

Being around Greyson was so confusing. You never knew if you were going to get the heartbroken version of him, or the angry one.

"Plus, there's a thing called a dry cleaner," I said.

"I don't have time to deal with this or you."

"Why are you being so rude?" I asked.

"Why are you so clumsy?" he responded, pushing past me. He rounded the corner leaving me there, stunned.

"Way to act like an asshole, Grey," I muttered to myself, shaken by Greyson's unnecessary attitude. Sure, I spilled coffee on his ridiculously priced suit and tie, but there was no need to be nasty about it.

Mistakes happened.

"What's an asshole?" a small voice asked.

I turned around to see Lorelai yawning with her butterfly wings on, rubbing the tiredness from her eyes.

"Oh, nothing, Lorelai. I said askhole. It's like a person who asks a lot of questions," I quickly stated, trying to cover up my mistakes.

"My dad is an askhole?" she wondered, her K still sounding quite a bit like an S.

Great.

"Well, no, I mean...well what I meant was—"

Before I could remedy my actions, Lorelai went marching off, speaking loudly. "Daddy! Daddy! Did you know you're an askhole?! You're such an askhole, Dad!"

That evening I wasn't at all surprised when I opened my email and saw one letter from Greyson in my inbox.

FROM: GreysonEast@gmail.com
TO: EleanorGable@gmail.com
DATE: March 8, 7:34 PM
SUBJECT: Really?

Eleanor,

Askhole.
Really?

Strike two.

Warm regards,

Mr. East

I closed my laptop and slightly shrugged my shoulders.
Well, okay. I guess I kind of deserved that one. But still, I got a strike for saying askhole, and not one for his daughter missing weeks of school. I was starting to think this strike system was flawed.
I went about the rest of my Friday evening doing what I did best—I tried to call my father, and when he didn't answer, I went back to reading. Shay was locked away in her bedroom working on her next screenplay for the remainder of the night. Us single gals really knew how to have wild weekends, that was for sure.
I sat on the living room couch reading my novel late into the night, and around midnight, my phone dinged.

I picked it up to see a new email.

FROM: GreysonEast@gmail.com
TO: EleanorGable@gmail.com
DATE: March 9, 12:04 AM
SUBJECT: Today

Eleanor,

I apologize for snapping at you today.. I was dazed and confused after after a night of not sleping. I couldn't shut my brain off, and I took it out on you.

You confuse me.
When you're in a room I don't know where to look.
I don't know hoow to act.
I don't know how to be in the same sppace as you without feeling some kind of way.

I don't know what it means that you're here after all of this time, and that drives me insane.
.
This is a bad week.
I woke up on the wrong side of thhe bed, and I took it out on you.

Forgive me.

-Grey

I sat up, rereading the words over and over again, noting his ty-pos, taking in his words. My gut was tight and I felt nauseous as my eyes kept darting back and forth trying to process his email. It was the last thing I'd expected to receive after the day I'd had.

My phone dinged again with a new email.

FROM: GreysonEast@gmail.com
TO: EleanorGable@gmail.com
DATE: March 9, 12:09 AM
SUBJECT: Please Dismiss

Eleanor,

Please ignore my last email.
I've been drinking, and I am sorry.

-Mr. East

Please ignore my last email.
How could I do such a thing?

For a moment in time, he'd slipped. In the first email, he had signed it as Grey, the boy I'd once known so well, the one who was hurting and struggling and letting me in just a little bit to see the shadows that lived around him.

Then, minutes later he was back to being Mr. East.

Short. Closed-off. Straightforward.

It was as if his soul was swinging back and forth in a world of muddle. Parts of him were yearning to open up, screaming for help, while the other half wanted to be buried alive.

He was fighting the biggest fight against himself, and I was almost certain he was losing.

At least we were on the same page about one thing: I, too, was confused by him. When he walked into a room, I didn't know where to look. I didn't know how to act. I didn't know how to be in the same space as him without feeling some kind of way.

For a moment, I thought about responding, but then I realized I didn't know what to say to him anymore. I knew the words I would've delivered to him in the past, but he wasn't that same boy anymore, and I wasn't that same girl.

Now I didn't know what made him angry or what gave him comfort. I didn't know what made his struggles harder, I didn't know what soothed him.

So, the best thing I could do was respect his wishes.

I gave him my silence.

I ignored his emails.

———

On Monday, I showed up at work to find Greyson standing in Karla's bedroom doorframe, staring at his sleeping daughter. He looked so deep in thought as his eyes studied her.

It wasn't the first time I'd witnessed him checking in on his sleeping children. Once I swore he was even counting their heartbeats.

I wondered how long he'd been looking in there that morning. I wondered how often he studied his daughters from afar.

"Hey," I said, making him look toward me. "I know you have a flight to catch, and I wouldn't want you to be late. Plus, the roads are pretty bad with the snow." He was heading to New York for the next few days, and I was having my first stay at his house with the girls.

"Yes, of course." He broke his stare with me quicker than ever and he looked back to Karla, before turning my way. "Thank you for watching them. Allison and Claire will be around if you need anything, and if there is an emergency, please don't hesitate to call," he told me, smoothing out his outfit.

"Of course. Have a safe trip."

He nodded once and walked past me. When he did, his shoulder slightly brushed mine, and I swore for a split second, time froze.

"Oh, and Eleanor...um..." He cleared his throat and shifted around in his loafers. "About those emails..."

I gave him a small smile and shrugged. "What emails?"

A sigh of relief escaped him as his tensed-up shoulders relaxed. For the first time ever, he looked at me, and I mean really looked. His eyes locked with mine, and I swore I saw straight into his soul. "Thank you, Eleanor," he said, his words coated in gratitude. He lowered his head and sniffled before giving me a faint smile. "Thank you."

38

Eleanor

"Do you think he'll like this one?!" Lorelai exclaimed. The past week Lorelai had been spending extra time working in her craft room, creating new masterpieces to hang up in her bedroom, but the biggest project at that time was for Greyson. Ever since Greyson's night terror, Lorelai had been trying to think of a way to make her father feel better. She'd been spending hours and hours creating a collection of drawings of family memories to give to him, and it was hands down the most thoughtful thing I'd ever witnessed.

That Friday, Greyson arrived back from his trip. He didn't say anything, but came in on his cell phone and went straight to his office, and closed the door.

It was that afternoon that Lorelai finally completed her artwork. We had a bit of time before Claire would be over to pick up the girls for their weekend at her house, and Lorelai was more determined than ever, dead set on finishing the drawings before she headed out.

"Done," she said, setting down her crayon. She picked up all of her drawings and stared at them with such pride in her eyes.

"They're perfect," I said softly, proud of the hard work the young girl had put into her crafts. There were so many memories with her, Karla, and her parents, and it touched my heart deeply. I was happy she still remembered.

After Mom passed, I had struggled to hold on to a lot of my memories.

She leaped up with the biggest grin on her face and hopped up and down. "I'm going to give it to him now!" she exclaimed.

"Wait, no, he's work—" I started, but she was already dashing out of the craft room toward his office. "Lorelai, wait!"

I hurried after her and witnessed her barging straight into Greyson's office. The door swung open so quickly it slammed against the wall, making me cringe.

"Daddy! Daddy! Look what I made you!" Lorelai squealed, her voice dripping with excitement as she bounced up and down.

Greyson swiftly turned around to face his daughter, his cell phone held up to his ear, obviously on a phone call. His eyes widened with shock as he covered the receiver with his hand. "Lorelai, not now."

"But Daddy! I made—"

"Not. Now!" he hissed, sounding more annoyed than ever. He locked his stare with mine and there was such a look of anger there that I took a step back. He looked at me as if silently commanding me to do my job before I no longer had a job to do. He then turned his back to us and returned to his call. "No, my apologies. It's nothing."

No, Greyson, it is something.

It's everything.

I moved over to Lorelai and placed comforting hands on her shoulders. "We should come back after he's done working."

"But he's always working." She sighed, shaking her head. She then bounced up and down, still hopeful. "Daddy, I made you these pictures!" she exclaimed.

Her hopefulness made me sad.

I used to hold out that same kind of hope for my own father.

"Lorelai, I am not kidding! Now is not the time!" Greyson snapped, immediately dissolving his daughter's joy.

Her shoulders rounded forward, and her eyes watered over. "But, Daddy, the pictures…"

Greyson mumbled and turned his back once more. "Leave it on the desk."

Lorelai was completely defeated. She no longer danced when she moved, and her smile had faded. With slow steps, she moved toward her father's desk and lay down the art project she'd been working on with so much care. Then she turned and walked out of the room, completely heartbroken and scarred.

Wow.

There was seriously no way I could bite my tongue in that moment.

I couldn't do it. I couldn't let that slide. Lorelai was the sweetest girl alive, and the fact that her father had just treated her in such a disgusting way made my blood boil.

Therefore, it was best if Greyson quickly hung up that phone, because I wasn't going to leave until I'd given him every piece of my mind.

"*Are you kidding me?*" I hissed, still standing firmly in his office. He looked my way, his stare completely baffled.

He glanced once more before going back to his phone call. "I will have to call you back in a bit, Mr. Waken. Yes, I know, and I do truly apologize. There is a disruption I must handle immediately."

"Yes, Greyson," I stated, my arms crossed. "Handle this."

And just like that, we hit episode six of the Greyson and Eleanor show: "The Fallout."

He hung up the phone and narrowed his eyes as he turned to me. "What in the world do you think you are doing?"

"What am I doing? No, what are *you* doing?"

"Working, unlike some people around here. How dare you let Lorelai barge into my office? Do you know how important that phone call was?" he barked.

"Do you know how important that artwork was?" I barked right back, not backing down. I was done backing down. Greyson was lost and stuck and hurting and pained, but in all that he was allowing himself to hurt the ones who meant the most to him. He was hurting his girls.

He huffed. "Eleanor, please leave my office."

"*No.*"

He cocked an eyebrow. "What?"

"I said no. I'm not leaving, because you have to hear me." I swallowed hard, nervous but intent on getting my point across. "I get that it's hard for you."

"What?"

"I said I get it. I get that some days are tougher than others, but the way you just treated Lorelai is unacceptable."

"I beg your pardon?" he hissed, his voice dripping with indignance. His chest rose and fell quickly as his fingers clenched together.

"The way you just blew off your daughter is unacceptable. She worked on those drawings all week long and couldn't wait to show you."

"Her timing was wrong."

"And when was she supposed to approach you? Lately the timing seems to always be wrong with you. You're never home, and if you are you lock yourself in this office like some caveman. You don't engage with your daughters unless they are sleeping, to which I don't even understand the point. During the day you don't even look at them, Greyson. You don't even see your daughters."

He shut his eyes for a second, almost as if he knew the truths behind my words, but he fought against them, not wanting to face reality. "She knows the rules about not barging into my office."

"She's five, Greyson! Screw your rules."

He turned his back on me, again. That was his favorite move, turning his back on things. "If you can get back to your job, I'd like to get back to mine."

"She worked so hard on that artwork, and you just tossed it aside. You owe her an apology."

"You need to leave," he scolded, taking a few steps toward me.

"*No,*" I bellowed, standing tall, as I stepped toward him. Chest puffed out. Head held high. I hoped he didn't see the small tremble in my body. It was no secret that he made me nervous. He was so cold and hard that I never knew how close he was to snapping, and that was scary. Still, I wouldn't back down, because Lorelai needed me. She needed someone to stand up for her, seeing how she couldn't do it for herself. So, I planted my feet hard on the floor and stood my ground. "Your daughter is crying in the other room because you didn't even take the time to notice her artwork."

"Is that all, Eleanor? Because if you are finished I need to get back to work."

"Not everything in life is about work," I scolded.

"Maybe not for you, but it is for me."

"You didn't want to be him," I told him, shaking my head in disbelief. "All your life, you didn't want to be like your father."

"My father was a hardworking man. I was a child who didn't know the sacrifices he made to run this company in order to provide for his family."

"That's a lie."

"Eleanor, stop," he said, almost as if he were begging me to back down because I was tapping into sensitive territory, but I couldn't do it. I was going to push him. I was going to keep pushing until he woke up from this deep somber he was in. I was going to keep shoving him with my words until reality hit him.

"Your father abandoned you," I told him. "He walked away, just like your mother, and they left you alone."

"Eleanor." His voice was low, and his eyes were intense. I was doing it. I was getting under his skin, and I wasn't going to stop.

"You told me repeatedly how alone you felt after your grandfather died. You told me time and time again how you hated sitting in your house, because there was no one there for you. Greyson, this isn't you. This isn't the person you wanted to become. This isn't who you are supposed to be."

"You don't know me," he barked, his face turning redder and redder each second that past. "You don't know who I've become."

"Yes, but I do know who you were," I promised. "And I can still see that boy in those eyes sometimes, fighting like hell to come back to life."

"You don't know anything," he argued.

"I know you miss your wife."

His jaw went slack, and he narrowed his eyes. That hit him hard. Those cold, gray eyes... "You should stop speaking."

"Yes, you're right, I should, but I won't because I get it. I know you miss her, Greyson, and I know when you look at your daughters, you see so many parts of her in their eyes, and that has to be hard. I'm sure sometimes it feels as if grief is swallowing you whole, but you can't allow it to consume you. You have two beautiful daughters who are looking toward you for guidance and love, and the last thing they need is this, this *monster* version of you that randomly shows up and rocks their world sideways."

Even though my voice trembled, I stood tall before Greyson. I knew this wasn't him, this ghost of a man. Sure, we'd missed a few years, but deep down inside of his darkness was the boy I'd once loved so much, the gentle boy, the kind boy, the boy who'd saved me.

I had to believe my Grey still lived inside of this man. Otherwise, the world was lost.

"Well, aren't you a know-it-all," he sarcastically remarked.

"No, but I know enough."

He huffed at my words, obviously irritated that I had the nerve to speak to him in such a manner. "Then, please, Eleanor, do tell me. It seems you have been sent to me to tell me about all my faults. You're here to throw your truths into my face about me and my family, so tell me! Tell me what it is that my children need?!"

"Their father!" I cried, my voice cracking as I marched toward him. I still wasn't backing down, which somewhat surprised me. Maybe because this felt personal. Maybe it was because I knew what it felt like to be those girls, because all the words I'd never yelled at my father were now pouring out of my soul. So, I couldn't back down, because my heart was pounding too hard in my chest. I couldn't back down, because my soul knew how important it was to help Greyson find his way home. We were face-to-face, his breaths heavy with annoyance, my chest puffing in and out from my irritation at him being so shut off. His hot exhalations hissed against my skin, and each time he blinked, I waited for his stare to return to mine.

There was such a heavy tension in the space. Each inhale felt harder than the last, and my heartrate never took the time to slow down. I would've kept the intensity going, too, if it wasn't for one small thing.

Every so often, he'd blink, and he'd look absolutely shattered. As if every single piece of his soul was being set on fire.

Out of all of the emotions that sat within Greyson the one that shone through the most was his exhaustion. He seemed on the brink of exhaustion as he looked at me.

For the first time since I stormed into his office, I studied his face; the curves, the creases, the lines.

His lips...the way they turned upside down into sadness.

His eyes...the way they told the history of his past.

I backed down.

I was the one to break, because it was clear there was nothing left to shatter within him.

"It's you, Greyson..." I looked away and brushed my thumb against my chin. My shoulders rounded forward in defeat and I shook my head gently. "They just need you."

The room filled with silence as he kept his stare on me.

I took a step backward. "I'm sorry," I whispered. "I was out of line."

"Yes, you were."

"I just wanted to say—"

"You're fired," he blurted out.

"Wait, what?"

"It's clear that you have a problem with the way my household is run, therefore this is not the right match for us all."

My chest tightened as panic started rushing through my entire being. "But, I mean, I know I was out of line..."

"Exactly, and that's all there is to it. Strike three." He turned his back to me, and lowered his head as he gave me one last order. "Close the door on your way out."

39
Eleanor

"**H**appy birthday, sweetheart!" Claire exclaimed that afternoon as Lorelai came racing out of her bedroom toward her grandmother. She had come over to pick up the girls for their weekend get together. Lorelai leaped into Claire's arms for a tight hug as I stood there stunned.

"It's Lorelai's birthday?" I asked as Claire released her granddaughter and told her to go pick up her weekend bag. "I had no clue. We could've celebrated."

"Yes, she's six today." She glanced toward Greyson's office. "How's he doing today? I've been calling him all day but he's been ignoring my calls."

I stood in the living room, still stunned from my interaction with Greyson. "He actually fired me."

"What?" Her eyes widened with concern. "Over what?" I explained to her what had happened, and she took a deep breath. "Oh, I see. Poor Lorelai."

"She was heartbroken."

"Everyone in this house is heartbroken," she agreed. "I should've known this would be a tough time for everyone. I was just truly hoping it would bring Greyson closer to his girls, instead of pushing him away."

"What do you mean?"

"Today's the one year anniversary of the accident." She lowered her head and sniffled. "I felt it over the past few weeks, Greyson retreating a little. I know he's been cold since it happened, but I felt him getting colder."

I swallowed hard, feeling awful, knowing I'd just snapped on him while having no idea about his personal struggles. Of course he was struggling—how could he not?

"I had no clue," I confessed. "I'm so sorry. I shouldn't have pushed him."

"It's not your fault. You had no idea."

I heard her words, and yet, a tightness still remained in my chest. I felt nothing less than guilt.

When I had stormed into Greyson's office, I'd entered not only as a concerned nanny, but as a daughter who had many times been swallowed by anger at a father who'd emotionally abandoned me. I had gone in without a clear head and said things I shouldn't have said. I'd barged into his space, and snapped not only for Lorelai, but for me, for every child who felt invisible to their parents.

While I had been hollering about the unjust situation at hand, I hadn't had a clue about the storm Greyson was battling on his own.

Claire placed a hand on my shoulder and gave me a light squeeze. "You're apologizing for pushing him, but I feel like that's what needs to happen. Greyson needs a wake-up call from someone. He needs to be pushed, so thank you for that. Thank you for forcing him to break out of his slumber."

"I don't know if it helped him at all, and it doesn't matter much anyway since he fired me."

Claire gave me a smile and shook her head back and forth a bit. "Give it the weekend. He just needs to get through it, that's all. One day at a time. You've outlasted all the other nannies by months, and that has to count for something. So, don't go dusting off your resumé just yet. Let some of the smoke clear."

I should've headed home after Greyson fired me. I should've been curled up on my couch with a novel and tea, but I couldn't do it because that felt wrong. I couldn't wrap my head around leaving Greyson on what would be the loneliest, hardest night of his life.

He had stayed on the phone with me for hours the night my mother passed away, never once walking away. I owed him the same thing he'd given me—companionship.

After some time had passed, I walked to Greyson's front door and knocked, but he didn't answer, even though I could see him through the window. He stood in the living room, staring at the roaring fire, holding something in his hands.

I knocked once more, and he didn't move in the slightest.

With a deep breath, I took out my keys and unlocked his front door. I was already fired—

what was the worst he could do now? Call the cops on me for breaking and entering with the key he'd given me?

I'd take my chances with that.

"Greyson," I said softly, moving in his direction.

He didn't react to my voice, not even a flinch, as if he hadn't heard me.

"Greyson, are you okay?" I walked closer to him, my nerves building up with each step. He turned around slowly, and when I saw his eyes washed over with emotion, my chest tightened.

He'd been crying. He had to have been.

No one's eyes could've been that red and puffy if there wasn't some kind of emotion spilling from them.

In his hands were Lorelai's drawings.

"I'm fine," he replied, turning back to the fireplace.

"I... It just looks like—" I started, but he cut me off.

"I thought I made it clear that your services were no longer needed here."

"Yes, you did. I got that message loud and clear."

"Then why are you still here?"

"Because you need me."

"I don't. Please leave," he whispered the last two words, but his voice shook as they left his mouth. The pain sliced through his irritation with me.

"I can't."

I had to stay because I owed him. I owed him for staying by my side during my low days all those years ago. I owed him because when I had been floating away, he'd pulled me back to the shore.

"I can't leave you like this, Greyson, not today of all days."

He sighed. "Claire told you."

"Yes. I'm so, so sorry. I cannot imagine what you're going through, but I know you shouldn't have to go through it alone."

He lowered his head and his shoulders slumped, but he still wouldn't turn to look my way.

"If you want me to go, I'll go. I'll go and I won't come back. By morning, I'll be out of your hair, and you'll never have to hear from me again, but if there's any part of you that wants me to stay...if there's any part of you that doesn't want to be alone tonight, just tell me. Tell me, and I'll stay. We don't even have to talk. You can keep your back to me all night long, but I won't leave you. You don't have to be alone tonight."

"It's Friday night... Don't you have some place to be?" he asked.

"Yes." I nodded. "And I'm right there."

He remained still for a while longer and I was certain that was my cue to go, but as I turned to leave, he took a step toward his liquor tray. He placed the drawings down, then reached below, grabbed two glasses, and set them down.

He lifted the bottle of whiskey and turned my way.

His bottom lip twitched a little, and he locked those gray eyes with mine.

Those sad, sad eyes.

He parted his lips and said, "Do you drink whiskey?"

I hadn't expected him to ask me to stay, but when he'd reached for that bottle, a breath I hadn't even known I'd been holding had slipped through my lips.

It turned out even the loneliest souls never truly wanted to be alone.

"Sure."

He nodded once and poured the brown liquor into the glasses.

He then picked them up and handed one my way. We moved over to the couch and sat down, him on the right, me on the left, and we didn't speak a word. He sat beside me, our glasses in our hands and no words being exchanged. It was so still, silence expanding to and from each wall of the empty house. All that was heard were our small sips, and our breaths.

When he inhaled, I released a breath. When he exhaled, I took one in.

We stayed like this for a while, both getting intoxicated and not talking about it. He poured us more drinks until the whiskey was all gone. It wasn't until a bit of time passed, and drunkenness found him that Greyson cleared his throat.

My eyes quickly moved to him and I noticed how his upright posture had shifted. He wasn't as tense. His body relaxed somewhat, settling in as his lips parted.

"I owe you an apology," he confessed, his voice so low. "For the way I was treated you today."

"It's okay."

"It's not. I was an asshole, and I'm sorry." He glanced my way before looking back down to his now empty glass. "I don't know how to exist around you sometimes."

"What do you mean?"

"You stand for a period of time in my life when things were easier, when things were better, and that's hard. It's hard to look back on a time so good when things are so broken now."

"Can I ask why you hired me, then?"

He tilted his head my way and looked at me, and I mean truly stared. Before that point, it had almost been like he was always looking past me, looking through me. This time, though, I felt our connection. I felt him lock in. "Because I think the small part of me that isn't destroyed needed something good to hold on to."

"I'm a good thing?"

"You've always been a good thing, Eleanor, since the first day I met you."

My heart skipped a few beats, but I tried my best to ignore it. "I'm sorry you're hurting so much," I told him.

"How long is it going to hurt?" he asked, his voice so low.

I gave him the same answer he'd given me all those years ago. "As long as it has to."

"I'm sorry," he muttered, turning away from me, seemingly embarrassed. "I'm drunk."

"You don't have to apologize for feeling, Greyson. I would be just as lost and confused as you are, if not more so."

He nodded once and stared at the fireplace. The fire sparked repeatedly against the logs, and the flames danced around as if they were going to burn forever.

"Why did you come back?" he asked.

"Hmm?"

"After I fired you...why would you come back here to check on me?"

"Because I owed you."

"For what?"

"Saving me when I was younger and about to drown."

"Thank you, Ellie."

I smiled. "Of course. Here, let me go get us some water to sober up." I started to stand from the couch with my glass in my hand then paused when he spoke.

"It's Lorelai's birthday today," he told me. He was opening up more and more as the whiskey settled within him. *Please stay open, Grey.* His finger thumbed the rim of his glass and his eyebrows lowered as he studied it. "She's six today."

I lowered myself back down to my seat and turned toward him. "Yeah, Claire told me. I had no clue. We could've celebrated. I could've made a cake or something."

He grimaced and rubbed the back of his neck. "I didn't know how to face today."

"I don't under..." I started, but my words trailed away as the pieces clicked into place. Of course, he didn't celebrate Lorelai's birthday. "Because Lorelai's birthday is the same day Nicole died."

He nodded. "One year ago today, everything changed, and I never recovered from that. It's bullshit, right? This person I've become, the person I am. I'm a monster."

"Greyson—"

"Don't, Eleanor. Don't do that."

"Do what?"

"Feel sorry for me. I know it comes easy for you to feel sorry for me, but I'm not the hero of this story. I'm the villain."

He bit his bottom lip and wouldn't look my way.

"You're not a villain, Greyson."

"Tell that to the girl who isn't celebrating her birthday with her father—you know, the one who has more conversations with a ghost than with me, or the one whose body is battered and scarred because of my actions."

I frowned, because I saw his struggle, but I also knew it from the other side. I was both of his girls. I was Lorelai, the girl wanting nothing more than her father's attention and I was Karla—the girl who acted out just so he'd notice.

The only difference was that I'd never seen the guilt from my father that Greyson was displaying. I never saw the quiet moments where the truths of my father were revealed.

"Sorry," he muttered, pinching the bridge of his nose. "Again... I'm drunk," he told me once more.

"That's fine."

"It's not."

"I don't know how to get it back," he said, throwing me a curve-ball.

"Get what back?"

"My family."

"Do you miss your girls?"

"Every day."

"And you want to be in their lives?"

He sighed and his nose wrinkled up as he placed his glass down then put his hands on the back of his neck. "When I look at them, I don't only see their mother. I see what I took away from them. I took away the glue of this family, and I don't know how to get it back. So much time has passed now that I don't even know if I'm allowed to have them back."

"Yes, you are."

"You saying it doesn't necessarily mean it's true."

"No, you're right, but it is true. They'll take you back—without question, without hesitation." I tilted my head. "Well, Karla might have a little hesitation, but that's just because she's Karla, and I think she's stubborn."

"I don't know where she gets that."

I smirked and rolled my eyes. "Yeah, no clue whatsoever."

"I don't even know where to start, really, how to even approach bringing myself back into their lives."

"First you, then them. You need to help yourself first, Greyson. You have to get your mind right before you can be what your daughters need you to be. Plus, I can be your wingwoman."

"My wingwoman?"

"Yeah, I'll come up with excuses and events that we can all attend together. We'll do an activity once a week. Then it will give you a chance to really connect with the girls."

"You'd do that for me?" he asked, seemingly shocked by my offer.

"Greyson...you went out of your way to sit with me once every week when my mom was sick. You helped me breathe. It's only right that I return the favor. So, what do you say? Will you let me be your wingwoman?"

He kind of smirked, and I kind of loved it.

Whatever.

"Yeah, I guess so."

I held out my pinky toward him. "Pinky promise?"

He linked his pinky with mine. I tried to ignore the butterflies that began to stir in my stomach, because those butterflies had no right to even exist.

When it came time for me to leave, I stood up and walked to the front door. The night sky was deep blue and drunk with stars. Greyson walked me out to the porch with his hands in his pockets.

"Thank you for staying," he said.

"Of course. I hope you'll be okay."

He nodded once. "I'll see you on Monday."

"Does that mean I still have a job?" I asked, somewhat joking based on my new wingwoman position.

"If you're still willing to work for me, that is."

I smiled. "I'll see you on Monday, Greyson."

"Ellie..." He brushed his finger against his chin and shrugged a bit. "You can call me Grey."

40

Greyson

"Oh, my gosh, is that a pony?!" a voice that sounded shockingly like Lorelai's hollered as I sat in my office Saturday afternoon, though I was certain I was mishearing things because the girls were still at their grandparents' house until Sunday.

"OH MY GOSH IT'S A PONY!"

I sat up straight in my chair. That was definitely Lorelai's voice.

I walked out of my office and headed straight toward the noise that seemed to be coming from my back yard. The closer I got, the louder the racket was becoming. It wasn't just Lorelai's voice that was heard—it was everyone's.

And by everyone, I meant everyone.

The yard was completely decked out. Pink and gold helium balloons were tied to trees. Two barbecue grills were fired up and I saw Landon and Jack were there flipping burgers.

Friends I hadn't seen in months were in the backyard with their children, playing games, laughing, and having a great time.

"What in the world..." I opened the door, and everyone probably saw the shock on my face as they noticed me.

"Daddy! Daddy! Look! A *ponyyyyy*!" Lorelai shouted as she rode on its.

There was an actual pony in my backyard.

My mind was spinning faster than ever. When I looked to my left, I saw Eleanor, who was smiling ear to ear. She came skipping over to me with a birthday hat in her hand and she placed it on top of my head. "Great party, Grey," she told me. "It's the best kid's party I've ever been to."

My heart caught in my chest as I took a deep breath. "You did this? For Lorelai?"

She shook her head. "Not just for her. I did it for you. We did it for you," she said, gesturing to every person I'd ever cared for.

They were all there. Even though I had ignored them for months. Even though their calls always went to voicemail. Even though I'd pushed them away. They had still shown up for me.

They didn't have a clue how much that meant.

Eleanor didn't have a clue what she'd done.

"Thank you," I choked out.

"You're welcome," she replied. "Now go! Go say hi to everyone! It is a party, after all, so go party." She blew her birthday kazoo in my face and kept that big smile on her face.

I started to walk away but stopped in my tracks. I turned back toward her, and without any thought, I wrapped my arms around her. I wrapped her so tight against me that I was almost certain I'd squeeze her to death, but I couldn't let go. Luckily, she didn't ask me to. When I pulled back, I felt a bit embarrassed. Ambushing her with a hug was completely out of character for me, but it had felt right. I'd needed the embrace. It had felt like the only way I could truly show her my gratitude.

She didn't even look taken aback by my approach. She just kept smiling that gentle smile and she nodded her head toward my friends. "Go have fun, Grey," she told me.

Fun.

I wasn't sure I still knew what that was, but I'd try my best to do as she said. I walked over to Landon and patted his shoulder.

He looked at me and gave me a big cheesy grin. "Dude! Great party. You'll have to point out who the single women are," he joked.

"What are you even doing here?" I asked, a bit stunned to see my best friend back in Illinois.

He shrugged. "I was just in the neighborhood."

"You left me a voicemail yesterday from L.A. You weren't just in the neighborhood, Landon. You were across the country."

He smiled a genuine smile and patted me on my shoulder. "For you, Greyson, I'm always in the neighborhood."

That meant more than he'd ever know. I pinched the bridge of my nose. "Listen, I know I've been a bit off for a while..."

"If you apologize to me one more time, I'm going to kick you in the balls, Greyson," Landon warned.

I tossed my hands up in surrender. "Alright, alright."

"So, Eleanor really grew up, huh? Like, holy hell, she's fucking beautiful."

She'd been beautiful since day one. Most people overlooked it, though.

He scratched at the beard he was growing out for his upcoming role in an action movie. "So...is she single?"

I rolled my eyes. "Don't start, Landon. You aren't going to sleep with my nanny. Besides, you already slept with her cousin Shay all those years ago."

"Shay...Shay..." He went deep into his mind trying to connect the dots of a woman he'd slept with named Shay. When it clicked, he slapped me. "Holy shit, Shay Gable. My first love!"

I laughed. "If that's what you're calling love, we should be worried. Come on, let me get you a drink."

"I won't say no to that," Landon agreed. "Make it anything but EastHouse—that shit tastes like piss," he joked, making me chuckle as I flipped him off. It might've been the first time I laughed in months.

Everyone interacted with me as if I hadn't been a recluse over the past year. They welcomed me back in with laughter and smiles and hugs. I got so many hugs that day.

On a weekend that was supposed to be hard, they all made it that much easier.

Seeing Lorelai having the time of her life warmed me up inside. I swore she was riding the pony for the hundredth time, but Karla opted to stay in her bedroom the whole time.

After the party died down I headed to Karla's bedroom with a slice of the unicorn cake. My stomach was in knots as I knocked on her door.

She looked up from her computer and raised the headphones she wore. "What?" she muttered, staring at me as if I was the biggest nuisance in the world.

"I, uh, I brought you some cake," I told her, walking into her room.

She narrowed her eyes at me. "Why?"

"I just thought you'd want some." I set it down beside her, and her intense stare didn't ease. "It would've been nice if you were at the party today. Everyone was asking about you."

"Yeah, well," she mumbled, going back to her computer screen.

"Karla, I was thinking—"

"Look, can we not do this?" she barked, taking off her headphones. "I don't know what got into you or if the guilt of being a bad father for the past year has finally caught up with you, but I really don't have time for it. I mean, yesterday was Lorelai's birthday and you sent us away. Yesterday was the anniversary of Mom's death, and you didn't even spend it with your daughters. So, I'm sure everyone is happy-go-lucky to see you out and about and acting semi-human again, but please excuse me if I'm not interested in whatever it is that's going on with you at the moment."

My mouth gaped open, but no words left me. It was as if she'd slammed her fists into my gut and left me breathless. What was even worse about what she'd said was how true it was. I hadn't been there for her or her sister for the past year.

"Mom would've never abandoned us," she whispered, her voice shaky, and for the first time in a long time, she showed something other than anger—she showed her pain.

"Karla..." I started, reaching out to her, but she yanked her arm away.

"Just go, Dad," she hissed, putting her headphones back on. "And take the stupid cake with you."

I took a deep breath and picked up the plate. I wanted to say something else. I wanted to express myself in a way that would maybe make her understand what I'd been going through, but I didn't know how. I didn't know how to even begin fixing the damage I'd caused her, the damage I'd caused my family.

I walked away and closed her bedroom door behind me. As I walked down the hallway, I heard voices and looked into the bathroom to see Lorelai washing her hands with Eleanor's assistance. She was covered in chocolate and frosting, and the two of them were giggling like they were the best of friends.

"I think we got it all," Eleanor commented, tapping Lorelai's nose.

"Okay, good. I'm going to go get some more cake!" Lorelai hurried out of the room. She paused in front of me when she saw me standing there, and her eyes lit up. "Hey, Daddy!"

"Hey, you," I said, giving her a small smile.

She rushed over, wrapped her arms around my legs, and pulled me into a hug. "Thanks for the best birthday party ever and the ponies and the cake and the burgers and...and...you're the best dad ever." She squeezed me tighter, and then when she let me go, she grabbed the plate in my hand and shouted, "And thanks for the cake!"

Eleanor was about to stop her from running off, but I shook my head. "It's fine. We'll deal with the sugar low when it comes."

She nodded and leaned against the bathroom door frame, looking toward me. "Are you okay? You look upset." She stood up a bit. "Are you upset about the party? I just thought..."

"No, not at all. This was amazing, Eleanor. You've been nothing but amazing to my family, to me, and words cannot express how thankful I am for that."

"Then what is it? What's wrong?"

"I, um...Karla's never going to forgive me, and honestly, she shouldn't," I confessed. "I abandoned her and her sister when they needed me the most, and nothing I can do can remedy that fact. I walked away and left her drowning."

"She's just hurting, Greyson, with good reason, but she loves you."

"I don't even know if she does anymore."

"She does," she disagreed.

"How can you even be sure of that?"

"That many years of love don't disappear because of one tragic year. You just have to give her time to come around again, and for now, you have to do one thing."

"What's that?"

"Keep showing up, no matter what. She's going to push, she's going to scream, and she's going to make you want to go, but you can't walk away again, Grey. You have to keep showing up for her, even on the hard days," she said. "Especially on the hard days. Which is why I got us tickets to go to a baseball game in two weeks. I already talked to Allison and she's going to clear your schedule for the evening game. I also invited my cousin, Shay—I hope that's okay. Plus, I talked Karla into going saying it was for Lorelai's birthday. It just takes a few steps at a time to walk toward change."

"Thank you, Eleanor," I said.

"For what?"

I stuffed my hands into my pockets. "Being my reason to smile today."

41

Eleanor

After the partied ended, I stayed a bit longer to help clean up the mess. When everything was put away, and the dishwasher was running, I collected my things to head home.

As I walked to the front door, I paused as Landon spoke my way.

"Hey, Eleanor? Can I just have a word really fast?" he asked.

I turned toward him and smiled. Landon looked so grown up compared to the boy he was all those years ago. Shay would've hated how handsome he had become.

"Yeah, sure. What's going on?"

He slid his hands into his pockets. "I just wanted to say thank you for everything you've been doing for these girls, and for Greyson. I don't know how you're doing it, but thank you. Today was the first day I felt like my best friend was really here. He's been a ghost for the past year, and it has been the hardest thing to watch. So, yeah, just keep it up, okay? Whatever it is you're doing, just keep doing that."

I grinned. "I don't know if I'm much help, but I don't plan on going anywhere."

"Trust me, you're the biggest help. Also, I, uh, I owe you an apology for the asshole kid I was in the past—calling you Brace Face and stuff. That was fucked up."

I laughed. "I mean, yes, it was, but I guess since you brought a pony today, we can forgive and forget."

"For sure, and I mean, it looks like it worked out for you, ya know, those braces." He gestured toward my mouth. "It looks good. So, yeah. Good for you."

Oh, Landon. For a superstar you sure are awkward.

"Thanks."

"Okay, well I'll let you go. Make sure to tell your cousin Shay that I said hi."

I would definitely be telling Shay that as soon as possible.

"I will do. Safe travels, Landon."

The minute he left, I pulled out my cell phone and texted Shay.

Me: Landon asked about you today.

Shay: Oh yeah? Did you tell him to burn in Hell? I hope you told him to go to Hell.

I smirked, knowing it was getting under her skin a little.

Shay: How did he look? Did he look uglier in person than he does in the movies?

Me: Oddly enough, he looks even better.

Shay: Ugh. Of course, he does. Whatever, I'm done thinking about him.

Shay: But just to be clear, did you tell him I was doing great and I never thought about him again after high school? Next time make sure to tell him that.

Shay: God. I hate him. How dare he just randomly ask about me! The nerve.

She kept rambling on and on, and I felt a bit pleased about it. It was nice to have something to tease her about now, seeing how she always teased me when it came to Greyson. It felt as if my cousin and I were finally on an even playing field. Each time she mocked me, I'd be ready to mock her right back.

———

"How long are you going to walk me to class?" Karla groaned as we headed to her first period of school the Monday after Lorelai's party. It was our new normal, and needless to say, she hated every second of it.

"Until your father tells me to stop, I guess," I replied.

She groaned. "He's been extra annoying lately."

"He's just doing his job, Karla. That's all. He's been going through a lot."

"We've all been going through a lot."

"Yeah, I know."

She huffed. "You have no idea," she grumbled.

I combed my hand through my hair and gave her a small smile. "You know, I was around your age when I lost my mother, too. So, I know how hard that can be."

"Yeah? Did it leave you scarred up like a monster, too?" she asked before glancing my way and shaking her head. "Oh wait, nope. You're still beautiful."

"You're beautiful, too, Karla, and trust me, this is not what I looked like in high school. My nickname was Brace Face."

"Oh, wow, so I guess you and me are the same!" she exclaimed, her sarcasm loud and clear. "My scars are *just* like having braces. I can't wait to grow out of this stage of my life. Oh wait…" She rolled her eyes extra hard.

"Watch where you're going, freak," someone muttered as they bumped into Karla, making her stumble backward.

"Hey, watch it!" I barked, though Karla seemed pretty unfazed by it all. Those kinds of things happened to her more often than not, even with me standing right there beside her. I couldn't imagine the things they were brave enough to say to her when an adult wasn't around.

"Just let it happen, Eleanor. Muggles are gonna do what muggles are gonna do," she said matter-of-factly, keeping her head down.

I raised an eyebrow. "Did you just make a *Harry Potter* reference?"

"Yes, duh."

"You're a *Harry Potter* fan?"

"It's only the holy grail in today's world, Eleanor," she said, rolling her eyes. "I wouldn't expect you to understand."

"Um, hi, Hufflepuff here, reporting for duty. I'll have you know I loved *Harry Potter* before you were even born. I used to have to wait years for the next book to come out. Years!"

"Congratulations, you're old as dirt. And you would be a Huf-flepuff," she said with a slight tone to her voice.

Before I could reply, another person bumped into her, and when he turned to look back he said, "Sorry, Hunch," then hurried off.

"What did he just say to you?"

"Nothing," she huffed, tugging on the sleeves of her black hoodie. "It's nothing."

"It sounds like it's something."

She sighed and looked up to me, shrugging her shoulders. "Some people call me Hunch. You know, like *The Hunchback of Notre Dame*, because of my posture."

"Okay, that's where the line is being drawn. I'm going straight to the principal's office to report this."

"Don't waste your breath. What are they gonna do? Kick out half of the student body because they're making fun of the freak show?"

My heart shattered as she said those words, because she spoke them as if they were so absolutely true. "Karla, you are not a freak show." She didn't reply. "Do you hear these things from these people every day?"

She nodded slowly.

I couldn't even imagine.

"Come on," I said, grabbing her arm.

She cocked an eyebrow. "What?"

"We're leaving."

"What? I can't. I have science."

"Not today. Today we're skipping class."

"But...my dad..."

"I know, but I'll deal with your father later. For now, you and I are leaving this building and having a mental health day."

"What's that?"

"A day where you say screw high school and screw the closemind-ed muggles. Then you go home and watch a marathon of *Harry Potter* and eat food that's super bad for you until you want to vomit."

A small smile appeared on Karla's lips, and I swore it was the first time I'd ever seen her grin. She looked absolutely stunning when she smiled.

"More of that, Karla," I said without thought.

"More of what?"

I snickered. "Nothing. Never mind." I combed her hair out of her face, and nodded once. "So? What do you say?"

"Is this some kind of trap? Like some reverse psychology kind of thing?"

"Nope. Just a break from reality. What do you say? Are you in?"

She nodded slowly at first, but then it quickened as the grin stayed plastered to her face. "Yeah, I'm in."

We turned around and headed straight for the exit, not looking back once. The moment we hit the car, it was as if I could see Karla's demeanor completely shift as her body relaxed. School was stressful for the average teenaged student, but I couldn't even begin to imagine what a struggle it had to be for someone like Karla. Not only was she dealing with the bullying from her peers, she was also still grieving the loss of her mother.

I knew life wasn't fair, but it seemed extra cruel to Karla.

We stopped by the store to pick up some goodies for our movie marathon, and then we headed to the house to get started. We laid out some blankets and pillows in the living room and made it into the comfiest space known to mankind. Then we kicked up our feet and started the first *Harry Potter* movie.

For the first time in a long time, I saw Karla light up.

I knew Greyson would likely be mad at me for pulling her from school, but after everything she had to deal with, she deserved a break.

As we watched the movies, I witnessed a version of Karla emerge that I hadn't known existed. She sat wide-eyed with her focus on the television screen. I remembered that wonderment when I'd seen the movies for the first time, that excitement, the happiness.

Her lips moved with the dialogue, making it very clear that she'd seen the films dozens of time. She pretty much had it all memorized to a T.

The only times we paused the movies were for bathroom breaks.

It turned out I needed a mental health day, too. A day of magic and adventures, a day of being far-far away from muggles.

Around three, it was time for me to go get Lorelai from school, which was sad, because Karla and I were absorbed in the movies.

Karla started to stand up, and I shook my head. "You don't have to come. It will be a quick trip."

She raised an eyebrow. "Dad doesn't like me being left home alone. He doesn't trust me."

"Do you think you'll be okay?" I asked.

"Of course, I'm not an idiot."

"Well, okay then. If anything goes drastically wrong, call me. Let me put my name in your phone."

She handed her phone over. "Wow. You must really want to get fired today."

I smiled and tossed her cell phone back to her. "I'll be back in a few."

I headed off to Lorelai's school, and when I pulled up to the pick-up line, I saw the normally energetic little girl walking with her head down. I quickly put the car in park and headed over to Lorelai.

"Hey, buddy, what's going on?" I asked, my gut filling with concern.

"Nothing. Just stupid Caroline," she muttered, looking at a girl to her left who was talking to other kids their age.

"What happened with Caroline?"

Lorelai sniffled as she dragged her backpack against the sidewalk. "She just invited everyone to her super awesome birthday party except for me."

"What? That's impossible. I'm sure it was a misunderstanding, honey."

She shook her head. "No. She said I wasn't invited because I'm a weird freak who talks to myself."

Well, that pissed me off.

I stood up straight and looked over to Caroline. Then, I saw her mother call her over in the pickup line. "Wait right here, Lorelai. I'll handle this."

I jogged toward the parked car, and called after the woman. "Excuse me! Excuse me!"

The woman perked up a bit, taken aback by my approach. She held her purse close to her side and gave me a tight smile. "Can I help you?"

"Hi, yes. I'm Eleanor, Lorelai's nanny," I said, gesturing toward Lorelai, who still had her head down in disappointment.

The woman looked over and grimaced. "Oh, yes, the new nanny. I swear, that family goes through them faster than anyone. You'd think they'd figure out a way to keep someone on board for longer periods of time."

I ignored her comment. "Yes, well, I just wanted to check in with you about a misunderstanding. It seems everyone in Lorelai's class was invited to your daughter's birthday party, except for her, and I'm sure that was just a mistake."

"Oh, no, it wasn't a mistake at all," she said, pursing her lips together like a freaking prima donna. "She's not invited."

"What? That doesn't even make sense. You were just at her birthday party with Caroline. Lorelai is a great girl."

"Yes, I'm sure she's fine, but I just don't think it's a good idea to have a girl like her at my daughter's party."

"A GIRL LIKE HER?!" I hollered. Yes, I hollered at that woman, and I didn't even care. Her words stung me in a way I didn't know words could sting. "What in the world is that supposed to mean?"

"It's nothing to take offense to," she stated, a bit stunned by my reaction.

"Um, no, that is definitely something to take offense to," I argued. "What do you mean 'a girl like her'?"

"Well, sweetheart"—she said it in such a condescending way that it made my skin crawl—"you've been around the girl long enough to know she's odd. Caroline has told me stories of how she talks to herself at recess, and then I witnessed it myself at her party."

"She's not talking to herself," I argued. "She's talking to her mother."

The woman cocked an eyebrow. "Her mother?"

"Yes."

"Her dead mother?"

"Exactly."

She pinched the bridge of her nose. "Oh gosh, even their nanny is insane. Look, I'm sorry, I really am. I get that the girl has been through some trauma, but that's not my problem. I reserve the right to pick and choose the type of people who surround my Caroline."

"Yeah, well, your Caroline was very rude to Lorelai today, calling her a freak."

"Well, you know what they say—kids will be kids." She put on her sunglasses and shrugged, enraging me beyond measure. "Now, if you'll excuse me." She waved me away like I was nothing.

Then it happened.

My eyes crossed. My vision blurred.

And. I. Snapped.

"No, it's not *kids being kids*. It's a completely inappropriate action, one that should have real consequences! Your child bullied mine. She bullied her, and you are acting like it is completely okay, but I'm not shocked knowing she has a mother like you. That type of behavior doesn't just pop into a child's head, it's taught, and you should be ashamed of yourself! You're a disgusting human being who is raising a little bitch!"

I shut my mouth, but the words kept dancing in my head.

I'd just accidentally called a little girl a bitch.

I glanced around me and everyone was quiet. They were all staring my way with their mouths agape and their eyes wide open.

Then I looked at Caroline's mother, who looked as if I'd just taken a crap on her high-heeled shoes. "Your employer will be hearing about this!" she scolded me. "You can count on that!"

Then she placed her daughter into her car and drove away.

I walked over to Lorelai, who was smirking a bit. She looked at me, giggling, and smiled wide. "You're kind of crazy, Eleanor," she told me.

She wasn't wrong.

I put her into the car and buckled her in, then I combed her hair out of her face. "Hey, I just want you to know that you're special, okay? You're special, and smart, and beautiful inside and out. If anyone ever tells you anything other than that, they are a liar. Do you understand me? What Caroline told you was nothing but lies. You. Are. Amazing."

She nodded slowly.

"Can you say that? Can you say you are amazing?"

"I am amazing." She smiled, and I swore in her smile, I saw young Greyson.

"Yes." I nodded, tapping her nose. "You are."

I hopped into the driver's seat and pulled away from the curb to head back to the Easts' house.

"Hey, Eleanor?"

"Yes?"

"What's a little bitch?"

"It's a person who isn't very nice," I said matter-of-factly. I glanced toward her in the rearview mirror and shook my head. "But don't tell your father that. I'm pretty sure he'd fire me for that. Okay?"

"Okay." She went back to staring out the window, and a few seconds passed before I heard her whisper, "I know, Mom. I like Eleanor, too."

I swore my heart skipped five beats at those words.

We got back home, and in the pile of blankets on the living room floor was Karla watching the fourth *Harry Potter* movie.

She looked back toward me with an Oreo in her mouth and her eyes widened. "Sorry, I couldn't wait to start the movie."

Lorelai's mouth dropped open. "You're eating sugar and we're not at Grandma's house!" she exclaimed, pointing a finger at her sister.

"Yeah, I know. I needed a mental health day," she said, stuffing another cookie in her mouth.

"What's a mental health day?" Lorelai asked.

"It's when you eat junk food and watch movies all day," Karla replied.

Lorelai raced over to her sister and lay down, grabbing a handful of cookies for herself. "I need a mental health day, too!"

I smiled at seeing the girls cuddled up together, eating cookies and actually looking as though they were enjoying each other's company.

"Maybe a different movie for Lorelai now, Karla," I said.

She groaned. "But she just watches *Frozen* all the time."

"'Let it goooo!'" Lorelai dragged out.

"Please. Anything but that," Karla begged.

I raised an eyebrow, thinking deeply about what we could watch, and then I parted my lips. "Have you ever heard of a show called *Mister Rogers' Neighborhood*?" I asked.

"Nope, and it sounds dumb," Karla mentioned.

I didn't take it personally. Teenagers were pretty closed-off to the best parts of the world. I found the show on a streaming network, and played an episode. Karla sighed right away. "Yup, I was right. It's stupid," she remarked.

Lorelai echoed her sister. "Yup, stupid," she exclaimed.

But regardless, they sat there and watched an episode. Then another. And another.

By the fourth episode, the girls had fallen asleep on the floor with each other, snuggled up and completely knocked out from their sugar party.

I grabbed my phone quickly and snapped a few pictures of them, because it was one of those moments that shouldn't be forgotten.

It was an important one.

Around seven, the front door opened, and I was stunned to see Greyson walking in with his suitcase. He looked over to me, and then to the girls still resting in a pile on the floor.

He raised an eyebrow, then his eyes fell back to me. "Eleanor."

"Oh, hey, Greyson. What's up?"

His eyes darted back to the girls, then back to me. "Eleanor."

I swallowed hard. "Yes?"

"Can I have a word in my office?"

He headed off with his suitcase handle still in his hand, and I followed his footsteps, with every nerve in my gut twisting and turning.

He didn't speak right away, but he did gesture toward a chair, and I sat quickly. I kept fidgeting with my fingers, unsure what to do with my hands. I knew I had been out of line that day. I knew I'd made a lot of mistakes, but truthfully, I didn't regret it. For the first time in a long time, I had seen Karla smile.

That made it worth it to me.

He set his briefcase down, took off his coat, and then took a seat at his desk.

Still no words.

His hands clasped together, and he took in a deep breath. "I received a call from Mrs. Robertson today."

"Mrs. Robertson?"

"Caroline Robertson's mother."

Oh. That woman.

"Listen, I can explain. I know I snapped, and I'm sorry, but then again, I'm not actually sorry. You know why? Because she and her daughter were both extremely disrespectful toward Lorelai and I stand by everything I said." I paused. "Well, maybe calling her daughter a little bitch was out of line, but I do stand by the fact that the mother was a bitch. And I'm sorry, but—"

"Eleanor," Greyson said sternly.

"Yes?"

"You're rambling."

"Yes. Sorry. I'm just... I want you to know that even though I know I'm in a lot of trouble, that I stand by it. I stand by my words, and I know it was wrong of me and childish to snap in public, and I know it paints you in a bad light, but I just couldn't hold it in. I know you're probably also wondering why there's a big mess in your living room, and I'm just going to tell you now because whatever, I'm already in trouble, but Karla had a really shitty hard day too, and I took her out of school and we binged *Harry Potter* movies and ate sugar, and okay, I'm sorry."

He lowered his brows, staring, not really showing any type of emotion. Not anger, not disappointment—nothing really. I wished he'd stop that. I wished he'd at least give me something to go off of, just a few context clues.

"Thank you," he finally said.

"I'm sorry, what?"

"I said thank you. Thank you for being there for my girls."

I cocked an eyebrow, baffled. "You aren't...you aren't mad?"

"No. I called you in here to just say thank you for standing up for them. I know I'm not always able to be around, and I know I've been distant over the past few months. I'm not..." He took a breath and looked down at his hands. "I'm not myself. I'm trying to be myself

236

to get back to normal, but I'm not there yet. So, thank you for being there. They needed you today. I needed you today."

It was the complete opposite of what I'd thought he was going to say to me. Honestly, I wasn't even sure how to react.

I sat back in my chair, so thrown off. "Oh, well...okay. You're welcome."

"Just keep me in the loop a little next time. If you're going to take Karla out of school or cuss out a woman in front of the whole elementary school, just give me a heads-up."

"Yes, of course. It won't be a normal thing, and I am really sorry for it all, especially for snapping at Lorelai's school."

"Don't be. Mrs. Robertson is a bitch."

I smiled. He smiled back.

Greyson smiled at me.

It was the kind of smile I remembered, the kind of smile that had made me look at him time and time again in wonderment when we were younger, the kind I hadn't known I'd missed until I saw it on his lips.

My lips parted, and I spoke softly. "More of that, Grey."

More of that.

42
Greyson

After Eleanor left that evening, I continued working in my office for a while, and when Landon's call came through, I actually answered. "Hey, Landon. What's up?"

"For the love of all good things, is that what you sound like nowadays? I swear your voice got deeper," he joked.

"I just saw you at Lorelai's party."

"Still, it feels weird having you pick up my calls. For some reason, I didn't expect you to answer."

"Yeah, sorry about the missed calls—you know, all five hundred of them."

"Meh, I figured you'd answer when you were ready."

"Yeah. How's being back in California treating you?"

He updated me about how filming for his next movie was going, how crazy the paparazzi was, how he'd slept with half of Hollywood. You know, the basics.

It was crazy how different we'd become, but still, in many ways, we were the same—like how Landon couldn't keep himself from sleeping with any woman who looked his way.

"But can we talk about Eleanor for a minute? That was kind of amazing what she did for Lorelai's birthday." Landon mentioned.

"Yeah, she's been pretty amazing. Better than I deserve, actually. She's really helped the girls more than I could say."

"Yeah. So, have you seen Shay since Eleanor—" Landon started, but before he could finish, there was a knock on my door. Then it opened, and Karla was standing there.

I was somewhat stunned.

Karla never came to my office.

"Hey, Dad," she said, clearing her throat. I couldn't remember the last time she'd said Dad without anger in her voice. This was beyond strange. I was definitely going to proceed with caution. "Can I talk to you real quick?"

"Yeah, of course." I went back to the phone call. "Landon, I'll have to call you back."

"Okay! And now that I know your phone works, don't ignore my calls anymore. Otherwise, I'll start calling more. Tell the girls I said hi. Bye!"

I hung up and looked back to Karla. She seemed nervous for some reason, which in turn, made me nervous. "What's going on?"

"Listen, I know Eleanor screwed up today, and I'm pretty sure you're going to fire her or whatever because you've fired nannies for a lot less than what she did today, but...well, I just thought you should know she was just looking out for me and Lorelai. She's a bit weird and stuff, and way too nosey and interested in my life, but for the most part, I think she's pretty okay at her job. She's pretty good with Lorelai, too. So, if you could not fire her, that would be great."

I brushed the palm of my hand against the back of my neck. "You like her."

She did; I could tell. Karla didn't stand up for things or people she didn't like.

She shrugged. "She's fine, I guess."

"I'll keep her on if you tell me where you went during the school days at the beginning of the year."

Her whole energy shifted and her face dropped. I saw a flash of worry wash over her and then she composed herself and sighed. "Just forget it, alright?"

I had to try. My mind hadn't stopped thinking about the possibilities and the danger Karla could've been involved with. Each day I wondered where she had gone. Each day I wondered about the battles she faced with herself.

She turned to walk away, and I called after her.

"Yeah?" she huffed.

"I think you're right—I think Eleanor is good for our family. So, I'm going to keep her on as the nanny."

A weight lifted from her shoulders as she released a sigh. "Oh, okay, cool. Because like I said, she's okay." Karla shrugged. "You know, for a Hufflepuff."

———

I made my nightly stops to the girls' rooms, and when I passed Karla's, her bedroom light was still on, but she was in bed, reading a *Harry Potter* book. I couldn't think of the last time I'd seen her read. She used to do it all the time. It had been almost impossible to find her without a book in her hands, but after her mother passed away, Karla had kind of tossed aside all the things she loved.

That was when I knew it was happening. Eleanor was doing that thing she was so good at doing, slowly sliding into a life and making it better without the person even knowing it was happening.

43

Eleanor

Greyson did his best trying to show up for his daughters. For the most part, it was easy with Lorelai. She welcomed him back with arms wide open. He stopped working as late each night, and made time to attend her karate practices every now and again. I swore every time he walked into the class, Lorelai's eyes lit up as if her biggest dream had come true. She'd perform better, too, and always looked back toward Greyson to make sure he was watching.

Then when dinner came around, he'd sit down with us and talk. Lorelai, of course, led most of the conversations, but Greyson was there. He was engaging. He was becoming a part of his family again.

Karla wasn't having it at all, though. Whenever I invited her to dinner, she didn't even reply anymore. She simply walked off and never looked back. There came a point when it was too much for me, and I finally followed her into her bedroom one evening. She was sitting on her bed, eating her dinner with her headphones on.

"You have to stop doing this, Karla," I told her.

"Doing what?"

"*This*. Shutting everyone out. Your father is trying."

"I don't care that he's trying. He had a million days to try. I waited so long for him to try, but it doesn't matter anymore. I just don't care."

I walked over to her and inhaled deeply. "Come to dinner tonight, Karla."

"Are you deaf? I said no already. I'm pretty sure I made that really clear every single night for the past four months."

"Yes, I know, but I'm asking you right now to change your mind."

"I'm not changing my mind for him," she scolded, rolling her eyes.

"I'm not talking about for your father. I'm talking about for Lorelai."

She raised an eyebrow. "What?"

"Lorelai really misses you, Karla."

"We live in the same house—I see her enough."

"She needs you," I told her.

"She's fine," she replied.

"Okay, I get it. You're mad at your father, and I understand. You feel like he abandoned you, and you're fully allowed to take as much time as you need to work through those feelings. But you have to understand that if there is one person who understands what you are going through, it's Lorelai. She lost her mother, just like you. Please don't make her lose her sister, too. She needs her sister, Karla. She needs you."

Karla's stare shifted, and she looked down to her shoes as she fiddled with her hands. Then, she got to her feet, picked up her plate, and grumbled. "Whatever. As long as it gets you to stop bringing this up."

I smiled, pleased, and walked back to the dining room with her.

She put her plate down at the table, pulled out her chair, and plopped down. Greyson seemed beyond puzzled, and Lorelai's eyes lit up when she saw her sister.

"You're eating with us, Karla?" Lorelai inquired, clearly stunned.

"Looks like it," she mumbled with her cell phone in one hand and her fork in the other.

"That's good. I missed eating with you," Lorelai said slurping up her spaghetti. "Mom missed you, too," she said, nodding toward the untouched plate of pasta left out for Nicole.

Karla rolled her eyes. "Mom's not here, Lorelai," she said. "There's no such thing as angels."

"Karla," I snapped, but Lorelai shrugged her shoulders and leaned in toward me.

She whispered, "It's okay, Ellie. Mom knows Karla doesn't mean it."

Karla rolled her eyes again then she looked toward Greyson. "Just to be clear, I'm not here because of you," she stated sternly. "This has nothing to do with you."

"Duly noted," he said, putting his hands up in surrender.

Greyson looked my way and mouthed, *Thank you.*

I nodded once and went back to eating.

As we ate, a big part of me wanted to tell Karla to get off her phone, but at least she was sitting down at the table. At least she had showed up, even though I was sure it was hard for her to do. I was almost certain it was hard for every single person to show up to that table that night.

One step at a time, Eleanor.

One step at a time.

———

"I can't believe that after all this time, I finally get to see him," Shay remarked as we drove over to Greyson's house for the baseball game. "I mean, I know you've told me about him, and I've been tuning in the best I can to your reality show, but actually seeing Greyson after all this time is going to be surreal. It's as if I'm an extra on your show," she exclaimed.

I laughed. "You're so ridiculous."

"Does he look the same?" she asked.

"Um, yeah, but like, in a grown-up way. You'll see."

"So this is gonna be your new home when you marry Greyson, huh?" Shay said as we pulled onto the property. "Not too shabby."

"For the love of God, I just hope you avoid saying all these things in front of him."

"No promises. You know me—I'm a talker."

We parked the car, and as we began walking toward Greyson's front porch, he came out wearing a backward baseball hat and a

White Sox jersey. "Hey ladies!" He smiled and hurried down the stairs to greet us. "Shay, it's been a long time. It's great to see you." He pulled her into a hug, and Shay stood still as day.

When he let go of her, she gave him a tight smile and then turned back to me and whisper-shouted. "What the hell, Ellie?!"

"What? What's wrong?"

She pulled me in closer and turned her back even more to Greyson. "Um, how in the ever-loving-shit did you forget to inform me that Greyson, oh, I don't know, grew up to become a Greek god? Seriously, are those real biceps? Those can't be real. People don't look like that. *People don't look like that!*"

"*Shhh*, he's going to hear you. Stop being weird."

We turned back to Greyson and smiled. "Are you guys ready to head out? I figured we could all fit into your SUV," I said.

"Yeah, let me go get the girls. We'll meet you out here."

He turned around and started walking away with his hands in his pockets, and Shay moaned.

She *moaned.*

"Do you see it, Ellie?"

"See what?"

"Those cheeks of steel. *Left cheek, right cheek, cheeks cheeks cheeks, oh how cheeky Grey's cheeks can be,*" she said, mocking Greyson's butt.

"Oh my gosh, Shay, shut up, will you?"

I rolled my eyes at my cousin's comments, but heck, I did notice Greyson's behind.

A man couldn't wear perfectly fitted jeans like that and not have his bum looked at, and Greyson wasn't lacking in that department.

Not at all.

"Listen, I know there are rules against this, but if you don't sleep with him, I will," she joked.

I shoved her lightly. "You're ridiculous, but hey, I just wanted to warn you before you meet Karla. She can be a bit hard on people when they first meet her."

"Oh yeah! The growler, right?"

"Yeah. Karla is going to try to freak you out with her scars. Don't react to it, because that will just make it worse. Just try to be cool about it. Pretend you don't even notice."

Shay went to the car, grabbed her black bowler, and placed it on her head. "I'm pretty sure you're overthinking it. Don't worry, it will be fine."

Yeah, that was what I had thought, too.

Greyson and the girls came out of the house, and Lorelai was bouncing up and down with excitement about the baseball game. I didn't have a clue if she was into sports, but the moment I mentioned cotton candy, she was fully on board.

My stomach knotted as I witnessed Karla's stare move to Shay.

Karla locked eyes with her.

Shay stared back.

I swore it felt like minutes before Shay nodded. "I like your style," she said, speaking about Karla's all black attire. "Very European vibes."

"Thanks." Karla nodded back. "I like your hat."

"Do you want it?"

"Sure."

Shay took off the bowler hat, walked over to Karla, and placed it on her head.

Karla nodded once more. "Thanks." She turned and walked to the SUV and climbed inside after Lorelai.

My jaw was on the floor.

What in the world had just happened?

Shay frowned. "That was a very underwhelming growl, Ellie."

She then walked off and climbed into the SUV, too.

I turned to Greyson, who was standing there just as stunned as I was. "Is your cousin a wizard?"

"That's the only logical explanation for what just happened. Nothing else would make sense."

We all drove to the game, and the whole drive there, Shay and Karla spoke like they were the best of friends, talking about music and makeup, and oh my gosh, Karla was talking more than Lorelai.

How did we just enter the twilight zone?

The baseball game turned out to be a lot more fun than I could've even imagined. Lorelai was on a sugar high, Greyson was locked in on the game, and every now and then I swore it looked like Karla was chanting, "Let's go White Sox."

"Hey, Dad. Can I get some cash to get a hot dog?" Karla said, standing up from her seat.

Greyson sat up a bit, seeming thrown off by Karla's request. "Yeah, of course, here you go."

"Thanks. Want anything?" she muttered.

Greyson's eyes widened. He shook his head. "I'm good, thanks."

"All right."

Karla headed off to get her snack.

"Did you see that?" Greyson asked. "She asked me for money and *then* asked if I wanted anything."

I smiled. "Yeah, I saw."

"That's one of those good small steps, right?"

"Yeah," I agreed. "It was." That was the thing about small steps—they had the power to lead to big change.

When we hit the seventh inning, Lorelai was hitting her breaking point. She was coming down from that sugar high really quick.

"Just a little more," Greyson said, holding his catching glove on his hand. We'd watched four balls fly in our direction the whole game, and he was more determined than ever to catch one, too.

"But, Daddy," Lorelai yawned, climbing into Shay's lap.

"Really, honey, we're almost there. The next batter is the one who's been hitting all those balls our way. And I have a good feeling."

Lorelai groaned, but didn't put up much more of a fuss.

Then, like magic, Greyson's player delivered a ball in our direction. Greyson stood up from his seat and it all felt oddly like destiny. Greyson's eye was on the ball, and as it started to come down, Lorelai tugged on Greyson's jeans, forcing him to break his concentration for a split second. That was all it took, though. In the amount of time it took for Greyson to glance toward his daughter then back to the sky, his focus was shot. The ball was too close, and it hit him square in the face.

"Ugggh!" he groaned, tumbling backward and dropping the ball.

Everyone gasped.

"Are you okay, Dad?" Karla asked, seeming very concerned.

"Daddy, you missed the ball," Lorelai mentioned.

"Oh, look! We're on the jumbo screen! Dance girls!" Shay instructed, and the three of them began wiggling their bodies as I helped Greyson sit up straight.

"I'm sure it looks better than it feels," he whined.

"Which is scary, because it looks awful. We should get you home."

We all headed to the car, and the ride was pretty quiet. I couldn't stop from glancing over toward Greyson's reddened face. It looked like it really hurt.

During the quietest moment in the car, Karla started snickering to herself. "Hey, you guys...remember when Dad caught the baseball with his face?"

Everyone started giggling, even Greyson.

"Who needs a glove when you have a nose?" he joked.

I swore, that was the first time I'd ever heard Karla laugh.

Another small step.

When we got back to their house, Lorelai requested that Shay put her to bed—after she finished showing off all her artwork on the walls, of course.

Karla yawned as we walked into the house. "Night, everyone."

"Good night," Greyson and I told her.

When everyone was out of the living room, Greyson gave me a sheepish grin. "She said good night to me, can you believe it? And she made a joke in the car, and she asked me if I was okay when the ball slammed into my face. Small steps."

"It's a big deal. This is really good. But you know what's not good? Your face. Sit down on the couch. I'll get some ice."

When I came back with the cloth, I had instant flashbacks of younger Greyson as I sat down in front of him. "You know, maybe it's best if you stay away from baseballs," I mentioned, placing the cloth against his skin.

His arm brushed against mine, and chills raced down my spine.

"It's going to be a bit bruised, but I think you'll live to see another day."

"Thanks, Ellie."

I pulled the cloth back a little and gentle touched his skin as he took a deep breath.

"I remember it all," he said. "Everything that happened between us when we were kids. Your favorite coffee, the stuffed panda I won you, the way you nervously rubbed your arm up and down."

My eyes locked with his and I swore somehow, we were closer. Somehow, his hand was on my thigh. Somehow, my hand was on his chest.

"Do you remember anything about me, Ellie?" he whispered.

I felt his heart racing as my hand laid against him. "Only everything."

He bit his bottom lip and looked down for a split second before putting those gray eyes back on me. I'd wished he'd stop looking at me.

I couldn't think straight whenever those eyes found mine.

"You ever think about kissing me, Ellie?" he asked, brushing his finger gently against my neck.

My body was betraying my mind as it reacted to every touch he delivered my way. I shut my eyes. "Only always."

"Ellie..." he breathed out, and I knew he was closer. I felt his breaths dancing against my skin, but I couldn't open my eyes.

If he was going to lean in, though, I'd let him. If he'd moved in closer, I'd allow it. If our lips fell against one another...

"All right, I think she's down for bed," Shay said coming into the room. The minute we heard her voice, we both jumped back. I grew flustered as I leaped to my feet. Shay looked my way with a look of confusion mixed with pleasure.

"Okay, good, we should get going," I muttered. "Uh, Greyson, I'll see you, um, yeah, okay, bye."

I hurried out of the house with Shay following closely behind.

When we got into the car, Shay turned my way. "What was that about?" she asked, curious as ever.

"Nothing. Just a little bit of nostalgia," I mumbled, closing my eyes and hoping my wild heart would slow down at some point.

"He was about to kiss you, Ellie," she said, as if I hadn't known what was about to happen.

"Yes, I know."

She whistled low. "I swear...this reality show is getting better and better each night."

I ignored her comment, because currently my mind was too jumbled to tell her to shut her mouth.

Greyson almost kissed me.

And without much thought, I almost kissed him back.

44

Greyson

"What do you think about Eleanor?" Claire asked me for our weekly lunch date. I had to admit, the question threw me for a bit of a loop. Did she know what almost happened between Eleanor and me? Could she tell somehow that we almost kissed?

Was I overthinking everything ever since Eleanor's lips moved in toward mine?

Yes, I'm just overthinking. Shake it off, Grey.

"I think she's great with the girls. Lorelai is in love with her. Even Karla is getting used to her, which is insane to me. She's really good for them."

"Yes, I agree. I think she's wonderful for the girls, but that's not what I meant."

"Oh?"

She leaned in closer and gave me a smirk. "I meant what do you think of her?"

I sat back a little, confused. Then the more I looked at her, the more I realized what she was getting at. The slyness in her smile. The wonderment in her eyes.

Oh, for fuck's sake, Claire. Knock it off.

I glanced at my watch. Our hour lunch date was up. *Thank God.* "Oh, will you look at the time? It seems our lunch date is coming to a close." I scrambled to my feet, and tossed some dollar bills on the table—probably more than we needed to pay. "I have to get back to the office. Great seeing you again, Claire."

She snickered, almost pleased by my discomfort. "You, too, Greyson. I'll see you next week for lunch. And next week you're going to actually let me buy you a meal."

Never.

"And think about an answer for that question!" she hollered, but I ignored her. I definitely wouldn't be thinking about an answer for that question at all.

And Claire needed to cut back on those corny romance novels she was so obsessed with reading.

———

One Friday night after the girls went off to their grandparents' house, I noticed Eleanor sitting in her car, trying to start the engine, and it just wouldn't turn. We hadn't really spoken since the almost kiss we shared.

I almost felt like she was going out of her way to avoid me.

"No, no, no," she moaned as I walked out toward her.

"Ugh! I cannot believe this!" she hollered as she hopped out of the car and started kicking the air before pounding her hand against the hood of the vehicle.

"I don't think that's going to fix it," I commented, making her stand up straight. "Need help?" I asked, making her turn around to face me. When she did, she looked seemingly flustered, almost embarrassed by me catching her in the middle of her breakdown.

"Oh, Greyson, hey. Sorry. My car just isn't starting and I had plans to go to Laurie Lake tonight since it's my mom's birthday. Plus, I've been trying to call my father all day to check in on him, but he's avoiding my calls again. I haven't heard from him in weeks, actually, and I'm starting to worry. Especially on days like today, because I know how hard they are for him..." She released a heavy sigh. "And obviously that's too much information for you, but seeing how I'm having emotional breakdown and all..."

"Take one of my cars," I offered. "Any one you want."

Her eyes widened and filled with tears. "Really? That's okay?"

"Of course."

She rubbed her hands over her eyes and took deep inhales. "Really, really?"

"Yes, of course, as long as it gets you to Laurie Lake."

Then, she leaped forward and hugged me.

Her arms wrapped around me, and she held on as tight as she could. At first, I stood still, taken aback by the embrace that seemed to come out of nowhere. Then, seconds later, I relaxed into it and held her back. I'd forgotten how good she was at doing that, how good she was at hugging me.

As a kid, her hugs had been one of my favorite things.

When she dropped her hold on me, she stepped back and combed her hair behind her ears. "Sorry. Like I said, I'm emotional today."

"That's understandable. I'm pretty sure I've had my fair share of emotional days."

She smiled, yet I saw the sadness that sat behind her grin.

"Would you like me to join you?" I asked. "That way, you wouldn't have to go alone."

45

Eleanor

Would you like me to join you?

Greyson's words kept dancing around my head as I stared his way.

He wasn't wearing a business suit, which seemed odd. He was dressed in a simple T-shirt and jeans.

Kind of like old Grey.

"Yeah, I'm okay," I lied, giving him a tight smile.

"Fake grin," he told me. "I'll go with you," he offered once more, giving me those gray eyes that always gave me chills.

"What? Oh gosh, no. I can't ask you to do that. I'm fine, really."

"You're not asking me to do it. I'm asking if I can join you," he said, never taking his stare from me.

My heartbeats were untamed and my gosh I missed him. I missed Greyson so much. I hadn't known I missed him to this extreme until I started to see the pieces of him that made up our youth. The parts that showed up for me when I needed him the most.

"All you have to do is say okay," he told me. "Say okay, and I'll come."

I knew I should've said no because of what my heart was doing. I knew I should've walked away, because my stomach was filled with butterflies for a man that wasn't mine. Yet as my lips parted and I released a sigh, I whispered, "Okay."

He came with me, just as a friend. As a companion giving me moral support on one of the hard days.

Nothing more, nothing less.

We drove silently to Laurie Lake, because I couldn't really think of anything to say. Well, other than, *"Remember when we almost kissed? What was that about?"* Or, *"Hey, what would've happened if Shay hadn't walk into the living room exactly at that moment?"* Or, *"Well, if at first you don't succeed...try, try again..."*

So, yeah. I kept my mouth shut.

Greyson's left hand kept tapping against his thighs as he drove. If it were anyone else, I would've overlooked it, but I knew Greyson and his habits.

You're nervous, too.

We parked the car, walked through the forested area, and flashes of our teenage years came rushing back to me. Greyson and I had so many moments beside that hidden pond. Moments that saved me. Moments that defined me. Moments that would lead me through the rest of my life.

We laughed there.

We cried there.

We shared our first kiss...

"It's crazy being back here after all this time," he mentioned, shaking me from my thoughts. I was thankful for that, too, seeing how my thoughts were being disloyal to my brain.

In my head, I knew developing feelings for a widower was a terrible idea. But that heart of mine? It didn't give a damn about what my brain thought. It simply kept beating in the direction of Greyson.

We sat on the log where we always sat, and that amazed me. The log was still there, steady and grounded, as it had been all the years before.

"It's still as beautiful," he stated. "Maybe even more so than before."

"I think that every time I come," I agreed. "It's as if I notice something new every single time."

He tilted his head toward me. "Are you okay, Ellie?" he asked. "I know how hard days like today can be..."

I smiled and placed my hands on the log. "Yeah, I'm okay. I mean, for a long time this day was hard for me. But as the years go by, it stops hurting as much. You start replacing sadness with gratitude. You just kind of become grateful for the memories. It becomes easier to breathe when grief is replaced with thankfulness."

"I can't wait for that day to come," he said, placing his hands on the log, too. Our pinkies kind of brushed, and I felt the touch deep within my soul.

"No need to rush it," I promised. "Just feel what you need to feel, and over time your feelings will shift into something else. Something beautiful. The best thing about death is how it can't take away your memories. Those live on forever."

He lowered his head and took a deep inhale. "You always know what to say when I need it the most. Even when I don't want to hear it, it's as if you know the words I need."

I snickered. "That pretty much describes what you were for me when we were younger. You were my safety net that kept me from drowning."

Greyson grew somber for a moment, looking up to the darkening sky. "I still don't understand all of this..."

"Understand what?"

"Us. You and me. You showing up when you did. I don't get it."

"It does seem a bit wild, doesn't it?"

"I don't know if I believe in an afterlife," he confessed. "I watch Lorelai talking to her mother, and I pray that it's real, for her own sake. But, I don't know if there is a God, or angels, or anything of the likes. Yet when I was at my lowest... When I was so overwhelmed and broken, I went to her. I went to Nicole and I sat in front of her gravestone, and fell apart. I begged her for help, for guidance, for anything at all... I was searching for a reason to smile..." He swallowed hard, clasped his hands together, and looked at me. His eyes were so gentle, and calm. Those gray eyes... He sniffled a bit, shrugged his right shoulder, and softly spoke, "And then came you."

Oh, Greyson...

"Sorry," he breathed out, growing a little red in the face.

He was nervous. I was nervous, too. To be honest I wasn't certain if it was his nerves I was feeling, or my own.

"I'm glad I could be here for you," I told him. "Besides, I owed you."

"For what?"

"Keeping me from drowning."

He smiled and stared out at the pond. "I think now we can call it even."

We sat there for a while longer, not really saying anything at all, not needing words.

We were just there in the wilderness, calming our souls. And every now and then, a dragonfly buzzed by.

"You know how you always worry about Karla?" I asked him.

"Yeah."

"That's how I worry about my father. All the time. I just have this bad feeling that he's falling deeper into his depression, and even if he needed me, he wouldn't reach out. It terrifies me every single day."

"And you've tried to help him?"

"So much, and every year he pushes me away more. He's drowning in loneliness, and he won't take my hand."

"It's hard," Greyson confessed. "It's hard to take people's help. And the more days that pass, the easier it becomes to push people away. Most people just fall off, too. They realize that it's a hopeless cause—helping the broken souls. I know that's what I did. I pushed everyone away, and only the ones who meant the most to me stayed around. You want my advice?"

"Please."

"Keep calling. One day he'll decide to pick up, and if he doesn't, then go and kick down his door. If that doesn't work, then know that you at least tried everything. You didn't give up."

I nodded. "Thank you, Greyson."

"Always."

When it came time to leave, we both stood up from the log.

I took in a deep breath and paused. "Do you think I can take a minute alone?" I asked him. "Just to talk to my mom?"

"Of course." He stuffed his hands into his pockets. "I'll meet you at the car." He wandered away leaving me there alone with Mom.

I knew she was there, I could feel her energy surrounding me.

There were so many moments in my life when I felt lost, moments when I didn't know if I should go left or right. I doubted myself and the choices I made, felt like I was drowning, and on those days, I'd hold conversations with Mom and tell her my story.

As I stood in front of the water that gently shifted back and forth, I asked her for her help, for her guidance, for her to look over Dad in a way that I couldn't.

Then I closed my eyes, felt the light breeze against my skin, and was thankful because somehow, my mother was magic. Somehow, she had been able to cheat death. Even though her physical form was gone, I felt her spirit sweep across me every single day.

Whenever I asked for her help, she never hesitated to show me the way. Some people called it signs, others called it blessings, but I simply called it my mother's kisses.

She guided me through the darkness while promising there'd be light at the end.

So no matter what happened, I knew everything would be okay.

Because a mother's love is enough to surpass time and space.

A mother's love never vanishes.

A mother's love can always heal her daughter's heart with simple kisses in the wind.

"Happy birthday, Mom," I whispered, wiping the tears that found a way to fall from my eyes.

I didn't know if they were happy tears or sad, but it didn't matter. As long as I was still feeling emotions, I knew I'd be all right.

46
Greyson

Weeks passed, and Eleanor's and my friendship only grew more and more. Just like when we were younger. She listened to me whenever I needed to talk. She sat through the dark days with me, not asking me for anything, but just staying by my side. Eleanor was also a great wingwoman. I'd been around Karla more these past few weeks than I had the year before. Lately Karla didn't even fight against us all hanging out, and sometimes I swore she even smiled just like her mother.

When Eleanor's birthday came around, I knew I wanted to make it special for her. She'd been beyond life-changing for my family, for me, and I wanted to celebrate her for that exact reason. She was Ellie, and she was worth being celebrated.

The girls and I decorated the house for her, and Karla didn't grumble too much about it. She even baked a cake with Lorelai. I was pretty certain it was burnt and there were probably eggshells in it, but they decorated it anyway.

Claire came over, and luckily she'd brought a cake of her own for the celebration. It was probably a lot more edible.

"This is all too much," Eleanor exclaimed as she grinned from cheek to cheek once we brought her over for the celebration. "You didn't have to do all of this."

"Of course we did. You're an important part of this family, and in this family we celebrate important days," Claire said.

Hearing those words come from her lips was so meaningful. If there was anyone who was a professional at making a person feel loved, it was Claire. She loved in a way that was so loud, and she always found more love to hand out whenever it was needed.

"Girls, do you think we should give Eleanor her gift?" I asked.

"Yeah!" Lorelai cheered, hurrying over to the table and picking up the wrapped box with Eleanor's name on it. "Here, Ellie."

Eleanor's eyes widened. "You guys really didn't have to get me anything," she said.

"Of course we did—it's your birthday! Now, it's nothing big, but we all put in some work on it," I told her.

"Even Karla helped!" Lorelai remarked.

Karla huffed. "Don't make a big deal of it. It's whatever."

Oh, my angst-filled teenager. What a joy.

Eleanor began to open the box, and the moment she saw what was inside, her eyes watered over and her hand flew to her mouth. "Grey..." she whispered.

"Pull it out," I told her, nodding toward it.

She reached into the box and pulled out a crocheted dragonfly cardigan. Tears began falling down her cheeks as she hugged the fabric. She kept staring at it in awe, taking it in.

"Do you like it?" Lorelai asked.

"Oh, my gosh, I adore it, Lorelai—more than I can say." She looked over to me. "How did you...you made this?"

"Yeah. After a lot of YouTube videos and wasted yarn, it came together pretty well. The girls each put in a few of their own loops, too. The dragonflies were all Claire, though. I'm not that talented. So, it's from all of us."

"Made with love," Claire chimed in.

Eleanor covered her mouth and broke into heavy sobs as her emotions took her over. She became completely overwhelmed and Lorelai went over to hug her.

"It's okay, Ellie. You don't have to be sad."

"Oh, no, I'm not sad, sweetheart. I'm just so unbelievably happy. You see, when I was a girl, my mother used to make me cardigans, and one just like this one right here was my favorite of all. When I lost them all, I thought I'd never have one again, so this is beyond amazing."

"So, those are happy tears?" Lorelai asked.

"The happiest tears," Eleanor replied. "Thank you so much. Thank you all so much. This is the greatest gift I've ever received."

"Shay told me how you lost your other cardigans. I know we can't replace those, but I hoped this could bring a smile your way." I smiled. "Happy birthday, Ellie."

"Thank you, Grey." She smiled back, and my heart skipped a beat. I hadn't known it could still do that.

I hadn't known it could skip for another person.

And it felt kind of beautiful.

—

Later that afternoon, the girls headed to their bedrooms after a bit too much cake. Eleanor headed home to go out for a birthday dinner with Shay, and I was left to clean up from the birthday celebration.

"Eleanor's great," Claire said as she walked into the kitchen, where I was loading the dishwasher. "She's really good for you."

"Yeah, she's great with the kids," I agreed. "Even Karla is opening up to her, and we all know that's a huge deal. Eleanor has been great for them."

"Yes, I agree fully, but I was mostly talking about how she's good for you."

Her words caught me off guard, and I stood up and looked her way. "What?"

She gave me the gentlest look ever and walked toward me. "I get it, Greyson, I do. I know you're probably trying to ignore it, trying to push the feelings away, but you don't have to do that. I know you're probably scared of what it means, having these feelings coming up, but you shouldn't be afraid of them. I knew my daughter. I know what she'd want for you. She'd want you to be happy again. That's all Nicole would ever want for you. She'd want you to find happiness. If Eleanor is that for you, and I think she is, please don't pass it up."

I put down the plate in my hand, and leaned back against the countertop. "Is it that obvious?" I asked.

"Only when you look at her. When you look at her, it's as if the whole world lights up inside you." Claire moved in closer and placed a hand on my forearm. "And that's a good thing, Greyson. That's a beautiful thing."

My chest tightened and I took a deep breath as I shut my eyes. "It just feels like a betrayal...like I'm betraying Nicole."

"No," Claire said quickly, shaking her head. "No, no, no. I figured that was what has been holding you back, and I worried about those thoughts floating around in your mind. You are not betraying anyone, Greyson. You and my daughter, you had a beautiful love story. You two created a love so strong it will live on forever, and that's an amazing thing, but that doesn't mean you're never allowed to love again. Your heart is still beating, son, which means there's room for more love, and if there's anyone in this world who deserves to find that love, it's you."

I pinched the bridge of my nose and inhaled. "It's scary."

"Yes, it is, but still worth it."

"What if there's nothing there? What if Eleanor doesn't feel it back?"

"She does."

"How do you know?"

"Because when she looks at you, it's as if the whole world lights up inside her. So, trust what you're feeling, and don't let doubt creep in. Sometimes in life you just have to leap, Greyson. You have to take the leap and just trust that you can fly."

She smiled a smile just like Nicole's, and that made me happy and sad all at once.

I exhaled slowly, feeling my heart racing throughout my body.

She was right.

She was always right.

"Thank you, Claire."

"Always."

"I just..." I cleared my throat and shifted around in my shoes. "I don't think I've ever said this to you, but I just want you to know that I've always looked to you as my mother. I've never really had a motherly figure in my life until you, and from day one, you welcomed me into your life with open arms. You've given me guidance when I needed it. You talked me off the ledge when I was ready to jump. When I hit my lowest, you didn't leave my side. You fought for me when I couldn't fight for myself. You stayed by me, and I don't think you know what that means to me. I don't think you understand how much of an honor it is for me to call you Mom."

Tears filled her eyes as she walked over and wrapped me into a hug. "You are the son I always prayed for." That choked me up more than she knew. After a moment, she pulled back and placed her hands on my cheeks. "Now go," she whispered, her voice filled with nothing but love. "Fly."

47
Eleanor

Once I'd received my cardigan from Greyson and the girls, I wouldn't take it off. I wore it out to my birthday dinner with Shay. When we made it back to the apartment, I curled up on the couch with my newest novel, and even though I wanted to dive deep into the world of my characters, I couldn't. My focus was shot, and I couldn't stop thinking about Greyson.

Out of all the gifts I'd ever received, that dragonfly cardigan was at the top of my list.

After time passed and I'd only gotten through eight pages of my novel, I put the book down for the evening.

When my thoughts wouldn't remain silent, I pulled out my phone and began typing an email.

FROM: EleanorGable@gmail.com
TO: GreysonEast@gmail.com
DATE: August 24th, 10:34 PM
SUBJECT: Dragonflies

Greyson,

I just wanted to thank you for today. You have no clue how much today meant to me...how much this cardigan means to me. I would come over now to thank you again in person, but I would start crying like a crazy person, and I don't want you to have to deal with that. I love it so much, Grey. I'm going to treasure this forever.

Also, today I was talking to Karla, and I realized something that might help you with reconnecting with her. It might be a small step, but maybe it's something worth looking into.

She feels lost, and she feels like you don't really trust her in a way. I think showing a little trust might go a long way, even if it's just letting her take care of Lorelai for a few hours a week. She's really great with her sister, and I think it might make her feel a bit more independent and useful in a way.

Again, just an idea. Feel free to ignore it. I just wanted to pass it on.

-Ellie

⎯⎯

FROM: GreysonEast@gmail.com
TO: EleanorGable@gmail.com
DATE: August 24th, 11:02 PM
SUBJECT: Re: Dragonflies

Eleanor,

I'll take any tips and tricks you can think of.
Thank you.

Also, there's this big launch party happening for EastHouse's new line of whiskeys. My friend Landon is coming to host it, and it's going to be a big event.

Would you and Shay like to attend? I remember parties not really being your scene, but you are more than welcome to bring your own book.

I'll make sure you have an antisocial corner to hide in.

-Grey

———

FROM: EleanorGable@gmail.com
TO: GreysonEast@gmail.com
DATE: August 24th, 11:09 PM
SUBJECT: Re: Re: Dragonflies

Grey,

You had me at antisocial corner to hide in.
We'll be there.

-Ellie

———

FROM: GreysonEast@gmail.com
TO: EleanorGable@gmail.com
DATE: August 24th, 11:17 PM
SUBJECT: Re: Re: Re: Dragonflies

Happy birthday, Ellie.

I hope all of your dreams and wishes came true.

-Grey

48
Eleanor

The night of the whiskey launch, Shay and I got ready at Greyson's guesthouse. Greyson had arranged for the three of us to ride there together in a limousine, so it made sense for us to get ready at his place.

The event was supposed to be one of the biggest of the year, and with Landon being the celebrity guest and inviting his other celebrity friends, I knew it was going to be a wild night.

Even so, I brought a big enough purse to hold the novel I was currently reading, because the introvert within me was still alive and well.

"Does this look okay?" Shay asked, smoothing out the black gown that fit her perfectly. She looked freaking incredible, but that wasn't hard for her to do. She could've worn a potato sack and looked like a million bucks.

"It's amazing," I said, stunned by her beauty. I turned back to my mirror and put on red lipstick, the finishing touch to my whole look. "And me?"

I was wearing the fanciest golden dress I'd ever seen, thanks to Shay. She took me shopping for it, and once I tried it on and noticed it sparkled alluringly when I turned, I thought it was overwhelmingly over the top, but Shay had convinced me that Hollywood was too much, which meant the dress was perfect.

We finished getting ready, slid on our high heels, and then headed over to Greyson's. The limo was already sitting outside waiting for us, and when I saw that, a knot formed in my stomach. This was going to be the weirdest night of my life, I was certain of it.

"Do you think Chris Evans is going to be there?" Shay asked as we approached the front porch. "I need Captain America to be there. Or Chris Hemsworth, or hell, Chris Pratt. Honestly, I'm not picky. I just need a Chris."

"Are you sure you don't need a Landon?" I joked, mocking her first high school crush.

Her face tensed and she made a gagging sound. "You know what's worse than dating a boy who becomes a famous celebrity and therefore being forced to see his face everywhere? You know what's worse than that?"

"What?"

"Nothing, nothing at all. I bet you he's still the same ol' Landon he was all those years ago, except with more expensive cars."

She said the words as if she didn't care, but I knew she was nervous. Shay picked at her fingernails when her nerves were high, and she hadn't stopped doing so since I'd told her about the party.

We knocked on the front door, and Greyson opened it, giving us a small smile. "Hey, you two, you look amazing. I'm just finishing up my hair," he said as he brushed gel into it to slick it back.

He wore an all-black tuxedo, and it fit him like a glove, showing off every muscle on his body and his best...well, *assets*.

He turned to walk away and Shay lowered her voice. "Left cheek, right cheek, cheek cheek cheek..." she whispered.

I nudged her, feeling my face blush, because yes, I had noticed his butt.

Oh, how cheeky Grey's cheeks can be.

When he came back out, he was sliding his wallet into his back pocket with a bright smile on his face. "Okay, I'm ready."

"Wait, you're all going?" Karla asked, coming into the living room. "Don't tell me Madison is coming over to babysit us."

"No," Greyson told her, fixing the cuffs of his sleeves. "I figured you could look after your sister."

Karla's eyes widened, and I swore I saw her jaw hit the floor. "What? You want me to watch Lorelai?"

"Well, yes. I just don't think it makes sense to have someone come and babysit, when you're old enough to do it. I mean, if you're up for it," Greyson said, cocking an eyebrow. "If not, I can call—"

"No!" Karla shot back quickly, tossing her hands into the air. She then realized her exaggerated response, lowered her arms, and cleared her throat. "I mean, it's whatever. I'll watch her."

"Thanks, Karla. That means a lot to me. Have a good night. Call if you need anything," Greyson told her.

"Yeah, okay, bye."

As Greyson turned away from his stunned daughter, he looked at me and smiled as he mouthed, *Thank you.*

I nodded once, feeling as if that win was exactly what both he and his daughter needed.

Greyson led me and Shay to the limo, and he opened the door for us to climb in.

Gosh, I felt like I was going to prom—a really expensive, star-studded, high-class prom.

Greyson climbed in, and the driver shut the door for us. "Okay, so, I didn't want to freak you out, Ellie, because I know you're an introvert by nature, but there is a red carpet we're going to have to walk—you know, for promotional purposes. There will be a lot of people from the press there, especially with the list of celebrities Landon had invited, so I just don't want you to be overwhelmed."

I cringed at the thought.

Seriously my biggest nightmare.

Greyson must've noticed, and he placed his hand on my knee, squeezing it lightly. "Don't worry. I'll be there the whole time to get you through it."

And just like that, I was taken back to when he was a teenager escorting me to my first dance, telling me everything would be okay. It was funny how memories came so quick to leave impressions on one's heart.

I smiled and nodded, trying to ignore my wild thoughts.

"What about you, Shay? Are you comfortable with walking the red carpet with us?"

Shay laughed, shaking her head. "Greyson, I've been pretending to walk the red carpet since I was two years old. This is history in the making. I was born for this."

She wasn't lying. When we were kids, she'd dress up in my aunt's heels and walk back and forth, posing as if the paparazzi were following her everywhere. This was Shay's dream come true.

As we pulled up to the venue, everything looked make-believe. There were dozens upon dozens of people walking the long red carpet. Flashes of light popped up everywhere, and the amount of security was beyond insane. There was a fence to keep the public from getting too close to the celebrities, and *oh my gosh I am going to vomit*. Right there, in front of all those cameras, I was going to freaking vomit.

Greyson squeezed my knee again, and I pretended it didn't make every inch of me melt into his touch.

"Okay, ladies, ready? It's showtime," he said as the door of the limo was opened. He stepped out first then reached for Shay's hand. He helped her out of the vehicle, and then he reached for me next.

My body was trembling.

My forehead was sweating, and I was really angry at myself for not wearing extra-strength deodorant. Just when I was about to fall apart, just when I was about to dash away and break into an awkward run, Greyson's hand landed on my lower back. He leaned to whisper against my ear. "Don't worry, Ellie. I got you. And also..." He pulled back a little and locked eyes with me "—you look beyond beautiful tonight."

Chills.

Chills all across my body.

"Ready?" he asked.

"Ready," I replied.

As ready as I would ever be.

Greyson linked one of his arms with Shay's and the other with mine as we walked to the red carpet. We posed in place every so often as cameras flashed. I was certain my smile was awful. I was positive that my knees were buckling. I knew when I saw the images online the next day, I'd be mortified, but Greyson kept holding me up, so I didn't try to run away.

"Mr. East! Mr. East! Over here!" a reporter shouted.

"No, over here, Mr. East!" someone screamed.

"Who are the ladies with you tonight?" another asked.

"Two old high school friends," Greyson commented with a smile.

Yup, that was me, just an old buddy of a really successful man. Honestly, I hadn't realized how successful Greyson was until that moment right there.

"Does it feel weird being here without your wife? How are you dealing with her death?" another reporter asked.

"How are you coping with the loss? Is that why these two women are your arm candy?"

I felt Greyson tense up, but he kept that smile of his in place. He thanked them for their time, and we walked off the carpet toward the party.

"That was freaking rude," I hissed, annoyed with the carelessness of the reporters.

Once we made it inside, Greyson released our arms and gave me a small smile with a slight shrug. "Just a part of the job."

"Well, that's ridiculous. You know, if you want, I can go kick their asses for you. I've been doing Pilates, and I'm really building up my strength," I remarked.

Greyson smiled as we walked into the room. "Or, we can just forget them, and take shots of the new whiskey," he said as a tray of them was presented in front of us. Greyson pointed out the different types. "This one is cinnamon flavored, this one is apple, and this one is kind of like a citrusy-thing. You have to try all three. It's the rule," he said.

Well, bottoms up.

The three of us picked up shot after shot, and even though it burned a bit, it was smooth on the way down. Apple was my favorite.

"Oh, my gosh, Greyson! Those are amazing!" Shay exclaimed.

"Which is your favorite?" a voice asked from behind us. We turned to see Landon standing there in a tailored navy suit, looking as dapper as ever. His blond hair was combed back, he wore a burgundy tie that matched his shoes, and I couldn't lie—he looked amazing.

I was guessing Shay thought the same, because her mouth was currently agape.

I leaned into her. "Shay?"

"Yes?"

"Close your mouth or you're going to catch flies."

Her lips formed a tight line and she pulled herself together, standing tall.

"Eleanor, it's good to see you again." Landon slid his hands into his pockets, and gave Shay that sly Hollywood smile. "And Shay, long time no see. You look as beautiful as I remember."

"Whatever, Landon. You look fine."

He chuckled. "I see you still have that fiery personality."

"And I see you still haven't grown into your ears," she shot back.

They shared a glare for a while, almost as if they were in a staring contest and whoever looked away first would be the loser.

It was becoming very odd, to say the least.

"Uh, okay. Well, I'm gonna go show Ellie around," Greyson said, placing his hand on my lower back.

I wished he'd stop doing that.

He didn't realize what kind of nervousness it provoked within me.

"Why do I get the feeling Landon and Shay are going to end up sleeping together by the end of the night?" Greyson whispered against my ear. I swore his lips gently brushed against my lobe. Or maybe I just dreamed of such a thing happening. Either way, my body reacted to his close proximity.

"Oh, because Landon and Shay are totally going to end up sleeping together," I explained.

We started walking off, and every time a tray of whiskey passed me, I took a shot to help my nerves. The drunker I was for this, the better off I'd be.

Someone bumped into my shoulder and apologized, touching my forearm lightly. I swore it was Captain America and *oh, my gosh, I am never washing my arm again.*

"I want to show you something," Greyson said, walking me through the crowd of people. We headed toward the VIP area, and when we walked through a door, there was a long hallway with more closed doors. We walked down the halls, and when we reached one of the rooms, I raised an eyebrow. The door was tagged with my name.

271

"What is this?" I asked.

Greyson pulled out a key card to open it, and when he did, my eyes watered over.

There were strings of white lights hanging across the room, and the floor was covered in blankets and pillows. There was a table with snacks and another with stacks of novels.

"What is this, Grey?"

"I know how overwhelming parties can be for you. So, I made you a reading nook. You know, so you could escape if you needed to."

He made me a reading nook...

He made me a reading nook!

Goodbye heart. You now belong to Greyson East.

"Thank you, Grey. This is..." I breathed in deep as I saw the stack of *Harry Potter* books. "This is beyond perfect."

"I have to go do some press work, but here's the key card. You can come and go whenever you want. Just show security that and your VIP landyard. There will be a big confetti drop at midnight to celebrate the official launch of the whiskeys, just FYI in case you want to see it. There are also going to be fireworks outside. I know it probably sounds stupid, but it's actually pretty neat."

"I'll be there," I said, smiling. I could tell how much it meant to him, and I didn't want to miss it. "I'll find you."

He smiled, and I loved it.

"Yeah, come find me."

With that, he left, taking my heart with him.

———

I stayed in my reading nook until the clock hit 11:50 p.m. I read the words of a fictional land that was far, far away for hours, but still, Greyson kept crossing my mind. I didn't even try to fight the thoughts. I let him stay there.

I stood up to go meet him, and I gasped slightly when I opened the door to see him standing there.

"Greyson," I said breathlessly.

"Hi, Ellie."

"What are you doing here? I was just coming to find you for the confetti—"

"I can't stop thinking about you," he confessed, placing his hands against the frame of the door and leaning toward me. "I haven't been able to stop thinking about you for some time, and I don't know what that means. When I close my eyes, I see your face. When I daydream, it's you who's there."

My heart was racing at a pace I hadn't known hearts could achieve. I felt hot and cold all at once as my hands fell to my chest and I stared into those beautiful eyes.

"Sometimes when I'm around you, I feel it," he said.

"Feel what?"

He looked up at me with the sincerest stare, parted his lips, and whispered, "Everything."

Why wasn't my mind catching up fast enough? Why weren't my thoughts forming?

"Tell me I'm crazy, Ellie. Tell me you don't feel it when you look at me. Tell me you don't see it when we lock eyes. Tell me I'm insane and there's nothing between us."

"I can't tell you that, Grey."

He tilted his head up a little. "And why's that?"

"Because I can't stop thinking about you, either."

He dropped his hands from the doorframe and moved a little closer to me. "You feel it?" he whispered, moving so close that his breath danced against my skin.

I nodded. "I feel it."

There were so many reasons why we should've walked away. He was still mourning, and I hadn't known how to make my heart beat correctly for a man.

We were still broken, and cracked, and growing and learning. We were mistakes and perfection, flowing streams and hurricanes.

But for how long could I deny what I felt? How could I pretend that the feelings weren't there? Truth was, I thought the feelings for the man in front of me had never really disappeared.

How could they?

He was him, I was me, and we were us.

This was us.

This was our story.

He took my hands in his, linking our fingers together, and I was certain I was seconds from passing out, seconds away from my legs giving out. I was shaking, or maybe it was his chills I was feeling. Honestly, it was hard to tell what were my feelings and what were his.

He moved closer still and rested his forehead against mine. I closed my eyes as his hands glided against my lower back and my body effortlessly arched toward him.

"I want to kiss you," he whispered as his eyes dilated.

"I want to kiss you back," I replied, my words falling faintly from my tongue.

"I need you to understand that if I kiss you, I won't stop. Everything will shift, and nothing will be the same. If I kiss you, we're going to be something new."

"Yes, I know," I said, sighing against him as I opened my eyes and stared into those gray eyes. "But do it anyway."

And then he did.

His lips slammed against mine, engulfing me fully as I kissed him back. He kissed me hard, as if he was making up for all the missed time. I kissed him back for all the moments our lips had not been locked. He closed the door behind us and led me into the reading nook.

I stepped back a little and looked at him with a smile.

I tossed off my high heels.

He removed his suit jacket.

I began to unzip my dress.

He loosened his tie.

My dress fell to the floor, and his eyes danced across my body. "Jesus, Ellie," he muttered, moving in closer, placing his hands on my skin, pushing his body against mine. His mouth moved to the curve of my neck and he kissed me gently, whispering, "I want you so bad, I want this so much…"

I unbuttoned his shirt and slid it off his body. My fingers trailed up and down his chest. Half of me thought I was dreaming and half of me thought I was back in my world of make-believe fantasy, but I didn't care.

This felt too good to stop.

He unhooked my bra and slid it off. His hands cupped my breasts, and he lowered himself to gently suck on them, worshipping me with every touch.

Next, his pants came off, and we tossed them to the side of the room.

My nerves were live wires, and I thought he could tell because every now and then he'd tell me I was so beautiful.

Once the clothes were off, we moved like the wild.

Everything became faster as we grew more determined with our actions.

He laid me down slowly upon the blankets. The strings of lights shone above us as my hands rested against his chest. I watched his heavy inhalations and exhalations move through his body, and silently I begged him to take all of me. I wanted him to give me his all, every piece of him—the good, the bad, and the broken.

He rubbed his hardness against my thighs, and I arched in his direction. He bent down low and swept his tongue against my earlobe before gently sucking it, sending chills down my spine.

"Please, Grey..." I begged, breathless as he teased me, rolling himself against my core as anticipation built. "Please..." I cried, wanting it all. Wanting him. Wanting us. Wanting love.

And then he gave it all to me.

He slid into me slowly, rocking his hips against mine. My fingers dug into his back as I moaned out in pleasure. He pushed himself in deeper and pulled out slowly, keeping that tame rhythm going for a while, making me feel every inch of him as he pushed himself into every part of me.

"More..." I whispered, and he picked up his speed. He rocked into me, as I held on to him. "More..." I cried as I stared into his dilated eyes and saw his wants, his needs, his passion.

Harder, deeper, faster...

Greyson made love to me as if he'd been waiting to claim my body as his, and I was his to claim. Every inch of me was his. Every part of me belonged to him.

"Ellie, I'm going to..." he whispered, pounding into me again and again. He kept hammering as my hips arched up. "I'm going... *Fuck*."

He shut his eyes and I fell into the deepest bliss as we hit the greatest high together.

Eventually, he slowly climbed off me and rolled over to my side. I was completely out of breath, trying to control my breathing the best I could. "That was…" I whispered, wiping my hands against my forehead.

Greyson laughed. "Yeah, exactly." I turned to face him and he gave me the smile I'd always loved. He leaned forward and kissed my forehead, and then he pulled me into his arms and held me.

We were quiet for a minute, just taking in the silence of the night.

"We missed the fireworks," I joked.

He rolled me on top of him and looked straight into my eyes with a small smirk. "Don't worry," he said confidently. "We can make some of our own."

And then we did.

— · —

When we finally got dressed, I found three missed calls from Shay. I hurried out of the room to go track her down as Greyson went to get the limo for us all to go home.

The moment I saw Shay, I cocked an eyebrow. Her lipstick was smeared and her hair was wild. When she looked at me, she mirrored my expression.

"Did you…?" she asked in a knowing way. My hair must've looked as crazy as hers.

I pointed toward. "Did you…?!"

She smiled.

I smiled.

"We're screwed," she muttered, walking over to me and linking her arm with mine. "But I'm glad episode nine finally happened."

I snickered. "Shay?"

"Yeah?"

"I think I have feelings for Greyson."

She rolled her eyes so hard, I wasn't certain she'd ever be able to see properly again. "No shit, Sherlock."

"What about you and Landon?" I asked.

She made a grossed-out face. "Me and Landon? Fuck Landon," she said with such distain.

"Uh, pretty sure you already did that," I joked.

"It was a one-time thing and whiskey was involved. It doesn't count. I still hate him to my core. The cocky asshole."

I smirked.

She was smitten.

———

We all drove in the limo back to Greyson's place. Shay and I were going to stay the night in the guesthouse before driving home in the morning.

The ride was quiet. It was as if Greyson and I were both still processing what had just happened. When we pulled up to his property, he climbed out of the car first, then offered a hand to help Shay out.

She thanked him and hurried off, allowing both Greyson and I to have a moment to ourselves.

As he helped me out of the limo, I thanked him.

"You're welcome. I hope tonight was..." He brushed his thumb against his bottom lip and somewhat blushed. "I hope tonight was as good for you as it was for me."

"It was perfect."

Beyond perfect.

"Good, good. That's good." He smiled his shyest grin I'd ever seen. "Good night, Ellie."

"Good night, Grey."

As I started walking toward the guesthouse, he called after me one more time.

I turned his way, and he was swaying back and forth a little with his hands stuffed in his pockets. "No regrets?" he asked me.

"No." I shook my head as my heart began to explode into a new form of happiness. "No regrets."

49

Eleanor

We fell together quickly, and we fell together fast. Once we started the descend, there was never a moment of regret. There was simply respect and understanding. We worked through the hard parts together, and we found our way around the tough days.

And boy, did we learn to embrace the good days wholly. We welcomed them with open arms.

When the girls fell asleep, Greyson would crash into my world. We'd laughed, we'd kissed, we'd made love.

Love...

I was falling in love with him, and it came effortlessly, too. Almost as if all I was ever supposed to do was love a man like him.

"Good morning," Greyson greeted his daughters as he walked into the dining room for breakfast. He looked refreshed that morning, and I couldn't help but think it had something to do with *our* early morning greetings.

He moved over to Lorelai and kissed her forehead as he grabbed a banana from the table.

"Good morning, Daddy!" Lorelai exclaimed, shoving cereal into her mouth.

Greyson walked into the kitchen to get his coffee, and he hummed to himself as he did so.

Karla cocked an eyebrow. "What's wrong with you?" she asked him as he walked back into the dining room, still humming.

"What do you mean?" he asked.

"I don't know, you're acting...weird."

Greyson tossed the banana in his left hand into the air, and caught it in his right. "Don't know what you mean, Karla."

She narrowed her eyes, still suspicious, but she went back to eating. "Whatever, Dad."

Greyson headed off to work, leaving me and the two girls there to finish our meal.

"He was super weird," Karla mentioned again, pouring herself another bowl of cereal.

"How so?"

She shrugged her shoulders. "I don't know. He just seemed like... old Dad. The dad he was before everything happened. Like he was himself again. After Mom died he never hummed anymore."

I tried my best to not react too much to her comment, but Greyson was humming again.

And I thought that was beautiful.

———

Greyson and I together felt like a dream. It felt like the best dream in the world. Each day we connected, my breath was swept away from me. Each day we touched, I prayed he'd be mine.

One night after a lot of conversation and a bit too much wine, we began losing ourselves against each other in the guesthouse. I moaned as he kissed me all over. His hands roamed my curves as if I was the only body he'd ever wished to touch again. Each time his lips found my inner thigh, I arched toward him. Each time he swept his tongue against my core, I cried out for more.

Then, I always returned the favor, turning him onto his back, and lowering my mouth to his hardness. I loved how whenever I touched him, he'd moan. I loved how whenever I sucked, he'd show his delight.

"Yes," he whimpered, pushing his hips toward my face as I worked to show him how much I craved every piece of him. "Mmm," he moaned, twisting his fingers within the sheets. I felt his need. I felt his want. I felt his desire every time he spoke. "Yes, yes, please…"

I love how he moaned, how he craved me.

Once I finished, we put on our underwear, held one another, and I was sure I'd found heaven.

We talked, laughed, and I fell ever more for the first love of my life.

"Are you ticklish?" he whispered, running his fingers against my sides as I squirmed in the bed.

"Oh my gosh, stop!" I giggled as I tried to get away from his grip. When I failed to escape, I fought back and began tickling him—and boy, was Greyson ticklish.

"Okay, okay!" he laughed nonstop as I kept my fingers moving at full speed against his sides. I loved that sound—I lived for his laughter.

"Alright! You win! You win! Stop it, Nicole!" he chuckled.

I froze in place at his words and then I felt the pain of them.

It stabbed me right in my chest, forcing me to pull away from his body.

The moment I stopped, he sat up, and I saw realization hit him as the reality of the situation slid into place.

"Oh, my God…Ellie, I'm sorry," he breathed out.

I was on the brink of tears. They were sitting there, begging for me to let them fall, but I pushed out a tight smile.

"It's fine," I said, shaking my head.

He parted his mouth more, though nothing come out. That made sense. What more could he say?

He'd called me by her name.

My mind was spinning as embarrassment settled in deep in my gut. I felt foolish, idiotic, even. Was that what he was always thinking of whenever we touched? When his lips found mine, was he thinking of hers?

Oh my gosh…

I needed a shower.

"I—" he started, standing up, but I shook my head.

"It's fine, really. I think we should just call it a night, though," I said, snatching the sheet from the bed and wrapping it tightly around my body. "I'm just going to shower here first before heading home."

I felt hurt.

Used.

Embarrassed.

He looked as if he had so much to say, but he knew nothing could fix that moment. There were no words that could heal my humiliation, so he simply gathered his clothes, and got dressed.

As he walked away, he muttered another apology, but I couldn't even reply to it.

I shut the front door, headed straight for my shower, and dived inside, allowing the water to wash all over me. I turned up the heat, too, letting it slightly burn my skin.

I wanted it removed from me. I wanted his touches that weren't crafted for me to be gone. I wanted his taste to leave my mouth, I wanted his name to escape my mind.

The water hammered against my skin as the water crystals intermixed with my tears.

I guessed that was the thing about dreams.

The biggest problem with dreams was the fact that one day, you were forced to wake up, and once you awakened from the slumber, you could no longer return to the make-believe world you were creating.

Reality set in, and you were left to face its truths all on your own.

―――

"He called you by her name?" Shay blurted out, stunned as I sat on our couch with my knees pulled to my chest.

"Yup."

She lowered her brows. "After you two had ...?"

"Yup."

"Crap," she breathed out, stunned. "I'm so sorry, Ellie. I can't even imagine how hard that was for you."

"Well, I just sobbed in the shower. No big deal," I joked, but Shay didn't laugh. She just kept frowning. "I'm okay. I mean, we're okay, Greyson and I. I'm sure it's just something we have to get over together. Just a speed bump."

"Wait, what? Ellie, that's not a speed bump. That's a red light. That's a stop sign. That's a 'Do not pass go, do not collect two hundred' moment. You can't seriously think that you and Greyson are still...something."

"How could I not? It feels like we were brought together for this, for us to be an us."

"But you aren't an us," she argued. "Eleanor...he called you by his dead wife's name. That just has toxicity written all over it."

I shifted around in my seat and shook my head. "You don't understand, there's something there with Greyson and me. There's always been this thing between us."

"Yeah, I know, and trust me, I was there for it through and through, but this changes everything."

My stomach flipped as I listened to her words, and anger began building more and more. "You were the one who'd been pushing me toward this idea! You and your reality show talk."

"Yeah, I know, but this...this is more than just a mishap in the beginning stages of a new relationship, Ellie. This is unhealthy. I know how you feel about Greyson. I've known ever since we were kids, I get it, but he's not in a place where he can give you what you deserve."

"I deserve him," I told her. "He's the right one for me."

I knew it, too.

I knew it deep down in my soul.

"Yeah, you do. You deserve the completely healed Greyson, not who he is right now. Plus, he deserves to completely heal before he can learn to give himself away again. Don't take his broken pieces and call them love."

I stood up, irritated at her.

How could she say this?!

She was the one who'd pushed this. She was the one who'd been so loud about me allowing myself to fall for Greyson, and now she was backtracking. Now she was being realistic.

I didn't need her to be realistic.

I just needed Greyson and me to be okay.

"I think it was a mistake with me telling you," I told her, grabbing my purse and walking toward her door. "I think I need to get some air."

"It's never a mistake telling me anything, Ellie, and you know that. I'm sorry if I upset you, but I'd rather upset you out of love, then tell you what you want to hear. I love you, Ellie. You are the most important person in my life, and you are worthy of having more than someone's mediocre love. The best kind of love is the kind that fills one up completely, leaving reassurance, not doubts. You deserve that. You deserve to be someone's whole."

"I really believe we're meant to be, Shay."

"I know, honey. I believe that, too, but just because two people are meant to be together, doesn't mean it has to happen right this second. Sometimes the best love stories are about those who waited."

She said the words, and they broke my heart, because I knew she was right.

50

Eleanor

"Are we just avoiding one another now?" Greyson asked as I walked past his bedroom door after putting Lorelai to bed for the night. He was unhooking the cuffs on his sleeves as he stared at me.

I took a few steps toward his room and stood in his doorway. "I'm sorry, I just…" I took a deep breath. "I didn't want to make you uncomfortable."

"Make me uncomfortable? Ellie, I called you another woman's name. If anyone should be uncomfortable, it should be you. I'm so sorry." He rolled up his sleeves on his button-down, and sat on the edge of his bed. His hands gripped the edge of his bed and every muscle in his arm became visible.

I wished he'd stop looking so much like himself. I was still unable to get the taste of his lips off my mind, and the more I saw those gray eyes, the more I wanted them to stare into mine.

I shook my head, trying to keep myself together. "It's not your fault. It's no one's fault. We had so much wine that night, anyway. Things got carried away…"

He lowered his head. "I wasn't that drunk," he truthfully whispered.

Sigh.

Me either.

When those eyes looked back to me, every butterfly came rushing back. I slightly parted my lips and reminded myself to breath every now and then.

"I'm so sorry, Ellie," he said quickly. "I didn't mean for that to happen. I'm horrified and such an asshole, and I don't know what is happening between us..."

I wanted to push him to give us a chance.

I wanted to tell him we could try again.

I wanted to hold him.

To kiss him.

To have him as mine.

But I also knew that those thoughts were selfish, and wrong. Also, I didn't want to hurt him like that, because I knew he wasn't fully healed from losing her. He wasn't able to fully love, and I knew Shay was right, even though it made me sad. The best kind of love was the kind that filled one up completely, and Greyson couldn't do that for me at this time.

If I couldn't have all of his love yet, I didn't want to keep falling for someone who wouldn't be able to catch me.

"We go back," I told him, walking over toward him and sitting beside him on the bed. My hands gripped the side of the mattress, just like him, and I gave him a slight nod. "We go back to how it was before that night."

"But..." He stared at me so apologetically and I wanted to shake the guilt in his eyes. I needed him to know that I fully grasped how much his soul was struggling. Greyson was at war with himself, fighting to move on while still trying to hold on to the past.

He wasn't ready to let her go, and I had to respect that.

My love was patient. For him, I'd wait forever.

"It's okay, Grey. I swear, I'm okay. We're okay."

He gave me a half grin, and I gave him the other half. "I meant everything I said, Ellie, about how I feel about you. I just want you to know that I meant all of those words."

I believed him, too. How could I not? He was my Grey. The first boy to ever leave his mark on me. "I know you did, but you don't need a lover right now, Greyson. You need a friend. Let me be that. Let me be your friend."

He cleared his throat and rubbed the back of his neck. "You have no clue how much I need that, how much I need a friend."

I knew, because I needed one, too. We each needed the other, maybe not lips against lips, but hearts against hearts. Maybe we'd both needed someone to talk us through the hard days, to get us closer to the light.

"You don't talk about her, do you?"

"No."

"Because you don't want to?"

He shook his head. "No, because people get tired of a person's sadness. They all start moving on, and expect you to do the same."

I tilted my head and looked up into those gray eyes that I've loved so long ago. "Tell me."

"Tell you what?"

"Everything single thing about her."

51

Eleanor

"Hey, Eleanor? Can you come get me?" Karla asked as I answered the phone. It was around ten p.m. on Saturday, and I was beyond confused by her call. Claire and Jake were on a trip, so Lorelai and Karla stayed home for the weekend, which made the fact that she was calling me pretty odd.

"Please," she cried.

Her voice was low and shaky. I sat up straighter in my bed.

"What do you mean, come get you?" I asked. "Aren't you in your room?"

"I was, but I, um, I snuck out to go to a party. I..." She started to sniffle. "Please just come get me, okay?"

"Where are you?" I questioned, hopping out of my bed and tossing on a pair of jeans and a T-shirt. I scrambled around to get my shoes on, and I grabbed my purse and keys as she gave me the address.

"Are you hurt? Are you okay?"

"I'm fine, it's fine. I just...I just want to go home," she started sobbing into the receiver and it broke my heart.

"I'm on my way. I'm coming."

"Just don't tell Dad, alright? He'll never trust me again," she warned through her tears.

"Just stay there, Karla, okay? I'm on my way," I said once more, trying to give her all the reassurance that I could over the phone.

I hung up the receiver and dashed out of the house, and drove straight to Greyson's. I rang the doorbell repeatedly until he answered.

He raised an eyebrow. "Eleanor? What is it?"

"It's Karla. She's at a party, and we have to go get her."

"What? No. She went to her room a while back," he explained, rubbing the back of his neck.

"No, she just called me. She snuck out a while ago."

"What?!" he snapped, his eyes widening from shock. "I'm going to kill her," he hissed, hurrying over to get his shoes on.

"First let's just make sure she's okay. She sounded really upset on the phone. I'll grab Lorelai."

"Okay, I'll meet you out front."

When I grabbed Lorelai, she was yawning, asking what was going on, but I just told her we were going for a quick ride. We headed outside, and Greyson already had the car running. I placed Lorelai into her car seat and buckled her in, then I hopped into the passenger seat and closed my door.

"Where are we going?" Greyson asked with his hands gripped tightly around the steering wheel. "Where are we going?" he repeated, his voice stern.

I gave him the address and he took off, not speaking a word. I glimpsed the anger in his tense jaw and the way he gripped the steering wheel. The stress that was flying through his mind.

"That is the last time I give her a bit of responsibility," he hissed beneath his breath. "She just proved—"

"Greyson," I said lowly, placing my hand on his forearm. "There's plenty of time for you to be upset. But right now, I think she's just going to need you to be there for her. She sounded so distressed."

He let out a quick huff and went silent, not speaking another word.

When we arrived at the location Karla had given me, we found her sitting on the curb. She was balled up, with her arms wrapped around her legs and her head down, rocking back and forth.

Lorelai was fully awake now, glaring out of the window at her sister. "What's wrong with Karla?" she asked, confused.

"Stay here, Lorelai," Greyson ordered as he and I got out of the car.

We walked over to Karla, and looked at her, and a strong stench hit our noses as we grew closer and closer. There were some liquids all over her and what looked to be pieces of trash, stuck to her clothes.

"Karla?" I whispered, and she jumped, alarmed, as if someone was going to attack her.

"Leave me alone!" she hollered, wide-eyed as she looked around. When she realized it was me, she took a deep breath. "Eleanor." She stood to her feet and then saw Greyson and her eyes filled with fear. "You told him? I told you not to tell him!"

"I had to, Karla, he's your father."

She looked at Greyson and began shaking, as if she knew exactly how much trouble she was in. "Dad, look, I'm sorry, okay?" Tears started streaming down her face as her small frame shook. "I know you're upset and you won't trust me ever again, but look, you don't get it. Nobody gets it."

"Gets what, Karla?' I asked, because Greyson was standing there speechless, and I wasn't even sure what emotions were running through him. I couldn't tell from his stance. I couldn't tell from his facial expressions. He just seemed frozen in place.

"I'm lonely!" she cried out, tossing her hands in the air. "I have no friends, and everyone hates me and makes fun of me every day. Every day is hard, and you guys don't understand. Nobody understands! I just thought when my old friends called me to hang out that maybe I was being let back into our friendship group, I just thought, I thought, I th..." Her words were so jumbled and shaky that they grew harder to understand as she sobbed nonstop. "I'm sorry, Dad, okay? I'm sorry. I'm sorry, I'm—"

Before she could continue, before she could push one more apology out of her mouth, Greyson stepped in and wrapped his arms around her. He pulled her in so tightly that she wouldn't have been able to let him go if she wanted to. She kept saying the words *I'm sorry* to Greyson, and he held her so close to him.

"It's all right, Karla. You're all right, I got you." He held her as she sobbed into his arms.

"You're never going to forgive me," she cried. "I keep messing up."

"Hey, hey, look at me." Greyson pulled away from her and bent down to look her in her eyes. "You are my daughter. I am always going to be here for you."

That just made her cry harder and wrap her arms around him, burrowing herself against him.

My heart was breaking for Karla. I couldn't even begin to imagine what she'd been going through.

"Karla. What happened tonight?" Greyson asked once he and his daughter finally let go of each other.

She rubbed her left hand up and down her right arm, that was covered in some kind of junk. "Missy called me and asked if I wanted to hang out. I thought it was some kind of joke because she spent the past year ignoring me since she started dating Colton Stevens, a senior jerk, and well, Colton said he wouldn't date her if she hung out with a freak like me."

"Who's Missy?" I asked.

"Karla's old best friend," Greyson answered. "Go on. She called you and what?"

"Well, she and Colton came and picked me up, saying they wanted to make up for not talking to me. They wanted to take me to a party at his parents' house, since they were out of town, so after some convincing, I agreed to go. Then, I got here, and everyone just started calling me a freak, and they...they..." Her eyes watered over and she shivered, clearly reliving what had happened. "They said that my face looked like trash, so I should smell like it, too. And they all started dumping stuff on me, and rubbing raw meat and crap against me."

Greyson was visibly livid. He glanced to the house. "Stay here, Karla."

"What? No, Dad! You can't—"

"I said stay here," he ordered, marching straight for the house where the party was currently taking place. He pounded his fist on the front door. When a boy answered it, he had a smug look on his face.

"Uh, yeah?" he said, looking at Greyson.

"Are you Colton?" Greyson asked. "This your house?"

"Yeah?"

Greyson pointed to Karla. "Did you do this to my daughter?"

Colton looked down at Karla and then chuckled a little. "No, I think the tree did that to her when she got fucked up last year."

Greyson tensed up and his hand formed a fist. The moment I saw this, I hurried up to the porch and stepped between the two.

"Greyson. Breathe."

"Yeah, old man. You might have a heart attack," Colton remarked, looking smug as ever. I wanted to hit him, too. "Hey, look everyone. Hunch called her daddy to come save the day. He smells just as bad as she does," he joked, looking back into his house and making his friends laugh.

"Listen, you little shit," Greyson hissed, his hands gripped tighter than ever before. "If you ever come near my daughter again, or say some bullshit about her, I'm going to—"

"Going to what? Kick my ass? Newsflash, old-timer, I'm seventeen. If you lay a hand on me, I will call the cops. You can't hit a minor. I'm not stupid."

"Let's find out," Greyson said, pulling his fist back, but I caught it midair.

"Greyson, you don't want to do this," I whispered.

"Trust me, I do," he argued, his eyes piercing into Colton as if he was seconds away from murder.

"Greyson, look at me," I ordered.

"No."

"Greyson, look at me," I demanded once more.

"No." He tightened his arm even more, and I could feel the intensity coursing through his veins.

"Grey!" I placed my hand on his cheek and forced him to look my way. We locked eyes and I lowered my voice, feeling chills race over me as I stared into his fiery eyes. "This isn't you. This isn't you," I softly spoke. The force of his arm began to relax and he began to lower it right as Colton decided to speak again.

"Yeah, and how about you get off my porch and go take a shower? You smell like your disgusting daughter," Colton huffed.

For goodness' sake, it was as if this little prick wanted to get his butt kicked.

Greyson's strength resurfaced as Colton's words hit his ears, instant anger rising once more throughout every inch of his body. He was so tense that I wasn't certain I could hold his arm down much longer, but luckily I didn't have to.

Lorelai came marching pass me, with butterfly wings on her back, and she kicked her leg up in the air, right between Colton's legs. "You leave my sister alone, you little bitch!" Lorelai shouted, kicking Colton straight in his privates.

Greyson's arm dropped as both of our jaws practically hit the ground in shock.

Oh my gosh, Lorelai just kicked a seventeen-year-old's ass.

I'd never been so proud in my life.

Colton tumbled over, howling as he placed his hands over his junk. "Oh, my God!" he cried, whimpering in pain. "What the hell?!"

"Dude! Colton just got his ass kicked by a kid!" a guy hollered, and everyone started laughing their heads off.

Greyson bent down to the crying boy and nudged him with a shoe. "Like I said. Leave my daughter alone. Or my other daughter will do that again. Only harder." He turned to Lorelai and me. "Come on, girls. Let's go."

We headed back to the car and all climbed inside. Before putting the car in drive, Greyson pulled out his cell phone.

"What are you doing?" Karla asked him, wearingly.

"I'm calling the police station to report a noise complaint," he said matter-of-factly. When the call was picked up, Greyson cleared his throat. "Hello? Hi. I'm calling to report a noise complaint at 1143 W Shore Street. There seems to be a party taking place, and I'm pretty sure there is underage drinking going on. Thank you."

He hung up the phone, and when I glanced back at the girls, I noticed there was a small smile on Karla's face.

"Thanks, Dad," she whispered.

"Always, Karla," he replied. He turned around to face her, put a hand on her knee, and gently squeezed. "Always."

"Why does it smell like farts in here?" Lorelai shouted, making us all laugh a little.

"Let's get home to shower," Greyson said. "But first, Lorelai, I'm very proud of you for standing up for your sister, but in the future, let's not kick people. And we can't call people those names, okay?"

"But Daddy, he was a little bitch," she insisted.

"Where did you even learn that word?" he asked, baffled.

Don't say me, don't say me.

"Eleanor said it to Caroline's mom, but she said don't tell you because you might fire her," she said.

What a traitor.

I had to turn my head to keep her from seeing me laughing. Greyson glanced my way with a smirk before putting his grown-up voice back on.

"Yes, but it's not kind or appropriate. Especially for a girl your age."

"Which part isn't kind? Little or bitch?" she asked, seeming truly confused.

"The second part," he told her.

"So bitch?" she asked.

Karla started snickering. "Yeah, Lorelai. Don't say that. But thank you for having my back."

"I'll always have your back, Karla. You're my best friend."

I noticed Karla smiling from Lorelai's comment and she whispered, "You're my best friend, too, kiddo."

We drove home in silence, other than Lorelai mentioning the smell, and when we pulled up to the house we all climbed out of the car. I was planning on putting Lorelai back to bed while Greyson and Karla took their showers. As we were walking, all of our footsteps stopped as Greyson spoke from behind us.

"I owe you an apology," he said, making us all turn to look his way.

His shoulders were rounded forward as he rubbed his hand over his mouth, and his eyes were locked on Karla.

"What?" Karla asked.

"I let you down, and for that, I owe you an apology."

"Dad...I'm the one who snuck out without telling you." Karla rubbed her shoulder, nervously swaying. "If anyone's sorry, it should be me."

Greyson shook his head. "No, I haven't been here for you this past year. I checked out, and fell into work, just to keep from facing the fact of what I took away from you. What I took away from us all. And I am sorry, Karla. If I would've been around, maybe tonight wouldn't have happened. Maybe you wouldn't have felt abandoned or lonely... I, um, I know you won't forgive me right away. Truth is, I don't deserve your forgiveness. But, I want you to know that I'm here now. Okay? I screwed up, and I abandoned you, I abandoned this family, and I am sorry, but I'm here. So, even when you feel lonely, I just want you to know that you aren't alone. I'm here, Karla. I'm back, and I won't leave you again."

Karla appeared as if she didn't know how to react. She bit her bottom lip and wrapped her arms around her body. "I hated you, you know. For leaving." She sniffled and wiped the back of her hand against her eyes. "I needed you and you weren't here."

He walked toward her, nodding. "I know. I can't change the mistakes I made, but I promise you from this point on I will spend each day trying to make it up to you."

She still seemed unsure as she looked down at the ground, her figure slightly shaking. "You promise, promise?" she asked, glancing back toward her father. "You won't keep working all the time?"

He held his pinky finger out toward her. "Pinky promise," he whispered.

My heart about exploded when Karla walked over to her father and linked her pinky with his.

Greyson nodded over to Lorelai and held his other pinky out toward her. "You, too, Lorelai."

She hurried over to him and locked pinkies with her father and with her sister, making a small circle. "What about Eleanor, Daddy?" she asked, glancing my way.

Everyone turned to me, and I stepped back, feeling fully out of place. That was their family moment, and in a way, I was intruding just by being there. "Oh, no, Lorelai. I think it's just a family pinky promise."

Karla gave me a halfway grin and slightly shrugged as she dropped her hand from Lorelai's and held her pinky out toward me. My emotions began building up from the small gesture, and Karla sighed. "I swear to God, Eleanor, if you start crying, I'm taking my pinky back," she warned.

"Sorry," I laughed, wiping at my eyes and hurrying over to the circle. I linked my pinkies with Lorelai and Karla, and we all held on as Greyson spoke.

"From this point on, we work as a unit, okay? We're a team, and we are there for each other all the time. Through thick and thin. If we fall, we fall together. If we break, we shatter as one. That's who we are. That's our promise. Promise?" he asked.

"Promise," Lorelai replied.

"Promise," Karla echoed.

Greyson looked toward me with those eyes that healed me, and I released a quiet sigh. "Promise."

———

That night after I put Lorelai back to bed, I stopped by Karla's room, just to check in on her. She was sitting on the edge of her bed, scrubbing her hair dry with such a somber look on her face.

"Hey, you okay?" I asked, knocking lightly on her door and making her look up.

"You'd be surprised at how hard it is to get the smell of fish out of your hair," she grumbled.

"Karla, what those kids did to you was beyond disturbing. I know your father is going to speak to the principal come morning, but is there anything I can do right now? Anything I can do for you?"

She hesitated a minute before shaking her head. "No. I'm fine."

"Okay, well, if you need anything just let me know. You have my number, and you can wake me up at any time. I'm here for you."

Her bottom lip twitched a little. "Thanks, Eleanor."

"Always."

"You're not just faking it because it's your job, are you? You actually really care about us, huh?"

I laughed. "More than you know. Try to get some sleep."

"Will do. And Eleanor?"

"Yes?"

"Thank you," she said, running her hand through her hair. "You know, for bringing my dad with you to pick me up. I really needed him there. I needed you both."

My eyes welled up. "Can I give you a hug?"

"No, probably not," she flatly replied.

Oh, well, then.

That seemed about right.

———

"Hey, how are you doing?" I asked, checking in on the final member of the family.

Greyson was sitting on his bed with his hands wrapped tightly around the edge of his mattress. His foot was tapping repeatedly as he stared at the carpeted floor.

He looked up to me with so much emotion in his eyes. "She's lonely," he whispered before looking back down at the floor. "She's lonely, Ellie."

I sighed walking into his room, closing the bedroom door behind me. His thoughts were probably spinning with everything that happened that night. How could they not be? His daughter was attacked, abused, belittled. All because she was lonely.

I sat beside him and noticed his shoulders were rounded forward.

I knew his looks so well. I knew when he was beating himself up. I knew when the world was too heavy on his shoulders. I knew when he was thinking the worst thoughts. "It's not your fault, Grey," I promised, but he tensed up as if he didn't believe me.

"If I was here, she wouldn't have been alone. If I hadn't abandon her, this wouldn't have happened. If my eyes would've stayed on the road..."

He couldn't slow down his mind. He couldn't hear anything except his rapid flawed beliefs, so I wasn't certain any words would help him.

"What do you need from me?" I asked placing a hand of comfort on his leg. "What do you need me to do?"

He turned his head toward me as tears streamed down his face. His lips parted slowly. His voice was so low and broken, I wasn't certain that I even heard him. "Stay," he breathed out. "I just need you to stay."

So, I did exactly that.

We lay down in the bed, facing each other. We weren't touching, but I swore I felt him. I felt his heartbeats. When he hurt, my heart cried. When he was in pain, my eyes were the ones to weep. That's how close the two of us were. Our love story was so much more than a romantic tale. Our story was about friendship. About family. About looking out for those who always looked out for you.

His soul was born to be loved by mine.

We fell asleep that night, and whenever he awakened from night terrors, I would be there to soothe him. I held him tightly as he hurt with empathy for his daughter.

I needed him to know it was okay to break. To fall apart. To crash and burn. Then when it came time for him to stand again, if he ever needed a hand, I'd always give him mine.

"Still here, Grey," I whispered as his head lay against the curve of my neck.

Still here.

52

Greyson

"Daddy, wake up! It's morning and Grandma always makes us chocolate pancakes on Sunday mornings." Lorelai walked into my bedroom, yawning. I was exhausted, and could've easily slept for a few more hours. But, Lorelai kept talking, and her next words forced me to open my eyes. "Why is Eleanor in your bed, Daddy?"

My eyes shot open and I looked to my left where Eleanor was still sound asleep. My arm was wrapped beneath her body, and when I sat up a bit, she stirred.

"Lorelai, what did I tell you? Just let Dad sl— What the hell?" was muttered, and I knew it wasn't from Lorelai's mouth. Karla stood in the doorway behind her little sister, but they both held such different expressions.

Lorelai stood there with wonderment while Karla wore the strongest look of betrayal.

"You and Eleanor?" she breathed out quietly, stunned.

"No, it's not what it looks like," I bellowed, yanking my arm from beneath Eleanor's body. "Eleanor, get up," I said, nudging her arm.

She stirred a bit more before waking up, and the moment she collected her whereabouts, the moment she saw the girls, panic filled her eyes.

Tears welled in Karla's eyes and she repeated herself. "Oh, my God! *You* and *Eleanor*?!" she hissed, this time pissed. "How could you?" she pressed me. "How could you do that to Mom?" she cried before hurrying off toward her bedroom.

"Shit," I muttered, standing up from the bed.

Lorelai looked at me with such bewilderment. "What did you do to Mommy, Daddy?" she asked me, scratching her head.

"Nothing, I'll explain later. Stay here."

I darted toward Karla's door, which was already closed, and being blocked by her body. Every time I tried to shove it open, she'd shove it shut. *"Go away!"* she shouted, and I could hear the heartbreak in her voice.

I laid my fists against the doorframe. "Karla...it's not what you think," I tried to promise.

"Oh, so you weren't just cuddled up in bed with the freaking nanny?!" she hollered.

Well, okay.

It was what she thought.

Eleanor walked up, combing her hair behind her ears. She looked at me with a frown, and then lightly knocked on Karla's door.

"Karla? It's me, Eleanor."

"Go away, whore!" she barked.

I parted my lips to discipline Karla's words, but Eleanor held up her hand, stopping me in my tracks.

She went back to speaking. "Karla, I know what you're thinking, but—"

"You're a liar! All you do is lie! You said you really cared about me, but you were just trying to get to my dad. You don't care about me or Lorelai at all."

"That's not true." Eleanor sighed.

The door swung open and Karla's face was covered in rolling tears. She crossed her arms and huffed heavily. "Look me in the eyes, then. If you're not a liar, look me in the eye and tell me that you two haven't hooked up at all since you started working here."

Both of our mouths opened, and Karla began shaking more as she pushed her door closed. "Just go away! I hate you both. I hate you. I hate you..."

We both stopped trying to push her door open, because we were guilty. Me more so than Eleanor.

I'd fucked up.

"Maybe you should go for a little bit," I told Eleanor, unable to look at her, but I could already imagine the hurt that was in her eyes. "We should just give her time to cool off."

"If it's okay, I'll like to wait in the guesthouse for a few hours—just to see if I can talk to her later and explain."

"Yes, of course."

Eleanor nodded slowly, and placed a comforting hand on my shoulder, but I still couldn't turn to see her. "Come get me if you need anything, Grey," she whispered before walking away.

I lay my hands against the door as my forehead fell against it and I closed my eyes. "I'm sorry, Karla," I softly spoke. "I'm sorry, I'm sorry..."

Deep breaths.

Erratic heartbeats.

I'm sorry.

53

Greyson

"She's gone," I breathed out after pounding my fist against the guesthouse front door. Eleanor stood there with a look of concern. My mind was spinning and I hadn't any tools to slow down the speed at which my thoughts were shooting through my mind. "I just went to check on her, to see if she was ready to talk, and she was gone."

Eleanor's eyes widened with worry, which only made me more scared. Her hand landed on my forearm and she released a breath. "Okay, okay. Don't worry, we'll find her. So, where would she go? We can go looking for her. What are some of her favorite places?" I asked.

"I don't know, I don't know where she would go. She was so upset, she could be anywhere," I said, pacing back and forth, racing my hands through my hair. "This is all my fault. I did this. I made her run away," I muttered, falling apart second by second.

I needed Eleanor, because I couldn't stop myself from being wild. My thoughts were running away from me, and each one that came felt worse than the one before it. I needed her to give me some reassurance that everything would be okay.

She stepped back and narrowed her eyes. "Okay, so where would I go if I felt betrayed...where would I go if I felt lost? Where would I go? What would I do? Who would I run..." She paused and realization hit her brow. "My mom. I'd go to my mom. That's probably what she'd do. She'd go to her mother."

"What do you mean?" I asked, pausing to raise an eyebrow.

"When I'm lost and confused and at my lowest, I always go to Laurie Lake, because that's where my mom is in my heart. That's where I'd go. I'd go to my mom."

The pieces clicked in my mind. "The cemetery," I spat out. "Can you watch Lorelai?"

"Of course. Go. Call me if you need anything."

"Okay, thank you," I said hurrying down the steps.

"And Grey?" she called after me.

"Yeah?"

"Breathe."

———

I know she said breathe, but I hadn't taken a breath since I took off toward the cemetery. My thoughts were surrounded by fears. My throat was tight, and it took everything inside of me to keep from falling apart right then and there.

The past kept flashing in my mind, memories pushing to the forefront of my mind.

I forced myself to stand and I checked on Lorelai. Even though she cried, she seemed okay. Then, I went to find her sister. I hurried through the blinding rain in search of my daughter. "Karla!" I called once, twice, a million times. There was no reply, nothing to be heard. The thoughts that raced through my head were unwelcome, and I had to do everything to keep from falling apart.

"No," I muttered to myself. "She's fine. She's okay. She's okay," I kept repeating over and over again. She was okay.

She had to be okay, because if she wasn't, I wouldn't know what I'd do.

My eyes blurred over, but I blinked away my emotions. I wouldn't shed a tear until she was with me. I wouldn't fall apart before I knew she was all right.

I parked the car and rushed through the cemetery.

The closer I grew, the more worried I became.

There was a small figure laying still in front of Nicole's tombstone. My heart ached as I moved faster, dashing through the space, praying to God for her to be okay. But she looked so still, so small...

When I turned to my right, I saw her. A small figure laid out in front of two trees. She looked so small, and still.

So very still.

The stillness is what scared me the most.

"Karla," I called out, "Karla!" I cried.

The moment her body moved, a breath of relief hit me. I kept dashing, faster and faster, running to get her.

"Dad?" she asked, turning to face me.

I collapsed to the ground the moment I reached her, pulling her closer to me, holding her so close that I could hear her heartbeats. So close that I was certain there was no way we could get closer.

"What are you doing here?" she cried, pulling away from me. Her eyes were bloodshot from crying, and I touched my hands against her face. I felt every inch of her head. I touched every inch of her, making she sure was okay.

"Kar..." I couldn't speak the moment I felt her pocket. I went to reach into it, and my heart split in half as I pulled out a bottle of her prescription pills and stared at them in my hand. Then I looked to Karla.

Her body began to shake.

Her lips trembled.

My heart shattered.

"What are you doing with these, Karla?" I asked, my voice low, so low so she couldn't hear the fear feeding on my soul.

"Dad..."

"Karla. What were you going to do with these pills?" I asked again.

Her eyes welled up and a flood of emotions spilled out of her as she began sobbing uncontrollably into the palms of her hands. "I hate this!" she hollered. "I hate all of this. I hate being me. I hate being alone. I hate how much I miss Mom. I hate how hard everything is. I hate myself so much, Dad. I hate this world. I wasn't going to do it, though, Dad. I promise, I wasn't. I just..." Her words became so jumbled up, and every piece of me shattered as I watched my daughter fall apart. "I'm tired, Dad. I'm tired."

I wrapped her tightly in my arms and held on for dear life. "I got you, Karla. I got you. Just you, Lorelai and me, okay? From this point on."

"Just the three of us?" she asked with wonderment in her eyes.

"Yeah. Just the three of us. There is no one, and I mean no one, more important to me than you and your sister. You are my world, Karla. You are my complete, and only world."

I meant that down to the deepest parts of my soul.

I'd give up my world for my daughters.

I'd surrender it all if it meant their hearts would be okay.

53

Eleanor

later that night, Greyson came knocking at the front door of the guesthouse. I waited there until I knew Karla was all right—there was no way I'd be able to drive home without knowing. As I opened the door, I wrapped my arms tightly around my body. "Hey, is she okay?"

"Yes and no," he commented, looking down to the ground. "Claire is over there with her right now, and we're looking up some treatment centers for her mental health. She, um—" he swallowed hard "—she had a bottle of pills with her, Ellie. She didn't take any of them, but I think she thought about it. It turns out some bullies at school told her to kill herself."

"Oh, my gosh, Grey..." I couldn't wrap my head around how people could be so cruel. Where did humans learn to be so dark? How could those words ever leave anyone's lips?

"Everything she's been through on top of seeing you and me together, I think that was her breaking point. I can't have her struggle anymore, Ellie, which is why I'm asking if you could..."

"It's fine," I told him, cutting him off. "I know it's not good for her health for me to be here, so I'll find a new place to work, Grey."

"I just want you to know all this was more than a job, Ellie...you were more than the nanny."

"I know, but it's okay. Karla matters most. When I lost my mom, there was one big thing that kept me going each day, and I'm sure it will save Karla from drowning, too."

"And what's that?"

"You. It was you, Greyson. And who knows? Maybe this is our thing. Maybe we come together when we need each other most, and then we move on again."

"Yeah, maybe. There were moments when I thought we could be us again, though. But like, more than us. A new kind of us where falling together would be our norm."

I smiled. "Yeah, me, too." *Dream a little dream with me.*

"But truth is, I'm not okay, because I can't be okay if my daughters aren't. Honestly, I don't know when we'll be okay, but I'm working on it, Ellie. I'm working on bringing my family back together. And then, I want to find you again."

My body began to shake as he said those words. "Grey..."

He shook his head and looked up toward me. "My world is better with you in it. I just need you to know that. I just can't be what you deserve right now, but I promise to my core that I will work on becoming the man worthy enough to love you. Because at the end of the day, you're the one I want to fall asleep beside. You're the one I want to wake up to come morning. Now I know that it's not fair of me to ask you to wait, but—"

"I'm here, Greyson," I cut in. "I'm here, waiting. It's been over fifteen years since I've been dreaming of you," I joked. "What's a little more time?"

"So is this the point where we say goodbye again?" he asked. "It feels like we're always saying goodbye after we say hello."

"Not goodbye, just until we meet again. Until then, can we keep in touch? With email?"

"Yes, of course. Or you can call me, or anything. I'm always here for you, Ellie, even when I can't physically be there."

He moved in closer and enveloped his arms around me. I fell into him the same way I always did, effortlessly. Our foreheads touched, and we took our inhales together. In that moment, our timing was right. He was there, and I was there, and we were one.

I shut my eyes and tried to tame my heartbeats. We were so close that I swore I felt his lips graze across mine.

He softly said, "I want to kiss you, but I can't. Not now. Not yet. But I just need you to know, when I kiss you next..." his breaths danced against my skin as his words spilled into my soul, "It will be forever."

—

After watching everything that unraveled with Greyson and his family, I knew I had to make a trip of my own. As Greyson worked hard to fix his unit, I felt as if it was finally time for me to fix mine.

I packed my suitcase to make a trip down to Florida to see my father. I hadn't even told him I was coming, because if I did I was certain he'd make up excuses to not see me.

But before going to the airport, I made an important stop first.

It took me a while to find the tombstone, but when I did I took a few deep breaths before speaking. I held the bouquet of roses in my hands as I stood still.

"Hi, Nicole. I know you don't know me, but my name is Eleanor, and I am in love with your family. Every part of them is loved by me, but I won't be able to watch over them for a while. So, I wanted to stop by here to just ask for a little help. Can you keep looking over them? I'm worried about Karla, but I know if her mother is watching over her, then she will be okay, because that's what mothers do—they make everything okay. So, please keep an eye on her heart, because I know it's such an important heart to have in this world. This world needs Karla, so if you could wrap your light around her, I'd be so thankful.

"Also, thank you for keeping your conversations with Lorelai going strong. She loves you more than you'll ever know. Lastly, if you could look after Greyson for me, that would be great. I know there are parts of him that probably thinks he needs to let go of you in order for him and I to fall together, but I don't believe that's true at all. You showed him a love that made him the man he is today, which is a beautiful thing to see. It's because of you, that Greyson is strong, so please stay with him. Protect them all for me, Nicole, and I know they'll feel your love in the wind."

I lay the flowers down on her grave, and thanked her once more.

"Oh, and if you see my mother, can you tell her I love her?" I asked. "And no matter what, I'm still here for her always."

As I spoke to one angel about another, a dragonfly danced right past me, and I swore the broken pieces of my soul slowly began to heal.

54
Eleanor

After I landed in Florida, I felt a giant knot form in my stomach as I picked up my rental car. It had been over a year since I'd seen my father, and I wasn't certain what to expect. Yet when I pulled up to the house and walked up the front porch, my heart instantly broke.

"Eleanor," Dad muttered, stunned to see me standing there. He looked wrecked, as if he hadn't showered in days. His hair was wild, his beard not trimmed, and he'd put on a bit of weight since the last time. "Hey. What are you doing here? Are you okay?"

I glanced past him, and saw his house was trashed. The coffee table was covered in junk food wrappers, and there were clothes tossed all over.

I raised an eyebrow. "Are you okay?"

He shifted over a bit, trying to block my view, but I already saw everything I needed. He began coughing into the palm of his hand, and I swore it sounded like he was going to lose a lung any second now.

"I'm good, I'm good. Just getting along day by day," he said, scratching the back of his neck.

His eyes looked hollow. He looked a bit pale. And sad.

He looked so sad.

But that was nothing new. My father had been sad for the past sixteen years. It was his new normal.

"Can I come in?" I asked, stepping forward.

He grimaced and blocked my entrance. "It's a mess in here, Eleanor. Maybe we can go out and grab a bite to eat." He was embarrassed by himself, but I didn't care. I was his daughter, and I loved him.

Whatever he was going through, I could help.

"Let me in, Dad. I'll help you straighten up the place. Plus, I was hoping to stay here a few days before heading back home. Just so we can catch up."

"Oh? Well, I don't know. I just wish you would've told me, Eleanor."

"Dad. Let me in."

He shook his head. "It's bad..."

"Dad," I argued. "Let me in." I pushed my way past him, and walked into the house to see that it was a million times worse than when I simply peeked inside.

There was trash everywhere. Crumbs of food through the carpet. Emptied soda cans, bottles of liquor, cookie containers. Wrappers of all sorts. His clothes were tossed into a junk pile in the corner of the living room, and the kitchen sink was stacked high with dishes.

I'd seen my father during some of the lowest points of his life, but never like this. He was living in filth, and it was almost as if he didn't care.

He started scrabbling around, picking things up, obviously completely thrown off by my arrival. "It's not always like this," he lied. "Things have just been a bit crazy lately," he muttered.

"You can't live like this, Dad," I said, stunned. "You deserve more than this."

He cringed. "Don't start on me, Eleanor. You showed up with no warning. I didn't have a chance to straighten up."

"It should've never been this bad! And look at you...Dad...have you been taking your medicine?"

He grimaced. "I'm fine, Eleanor. I don't need you coming down here and belittling me because of my choices."

"I'm not trying to belittle you, Dad. I'm honestly just worried. This isn't healthy, and you look weaker than the last time I saw you. I just want to help you."

Now his embarrassment was shifting to anger. "I didn't ask for your help! I don't need your help. I'm fine."

"No, you're not. You're broken, and you have been for years now."

"See? This is why I don't like to visit. This is why us living together didn't work out. You always end up pointing out my flaws."

"Dad, that's not what I'm doing! I'm just saying, I'm worried."

"Yeah well, stop worrying. I don't need your pity."

"It's not pity, it's love. I love you, Dad, and I want you to be the best you can be."

He didn't say I love you, too.

That always stung.

He lowered his head and scratched the back of his neck. He didn't look at me very often, and I was almost certain it was because I looked like Mom. Maybe it was too hard for him to face me. Maybe it made his hurts hurt a little too deeply.

"Maybe it's best that you don't stay here. I'm not in a good place right now, and I just don't want you to have to feel bad for who I am, alright? Maybe it's best if you head out, Eleanor."

He dismissed me.

Without even looking my way.

He pushed me away, and told me to go, and that was all there was to it.

The whole flight back to Illinois, I cried. I sobbed for him out of fear. Out of worry. Out of heartbreak. And then I prayed to Mom to look over him, because I was certain there was nothing I could do to make him come back to me.

⸺

When I returned to Illinois, I began my search for a new job. I was picking up the pieces of my broken heart, and learning to teach them to beat on their own again.

Every now and then I thought of both my father and Greyson. I thought about their hearts, and I hoped they were still beating on their own, too. I did the only thing I could truly do for the both of them due to the muddy waters we were all floating through: I loved them from a distance.

55

Greyson

I missed her.

I missed Eleanor every single day since she'd left, but I did my best to keep moving along for my girls. They were my main focus, and until everything was right with them, I couldn't think of anything or anyone else. Though, sometimes Eleanor freely raced through my mind, and I allowed it to happen. Truthfully, thinking about her made some days easier.

When December came around, it was our second Christmas without Nicole. Holidays were still so hard for us all to face, but the girls and I were facing it together. That Christmas morning, the grass was frosted, and the temperature was beyond chilled. I tossed on my winter jacket and gathered some blankets from the back closet, and headed to the living room where Lorelai and Karla both were sitting.

They both looked up at me with confusion in their stares.

"Where are you going?" Karla asked.

"I thought we could go visit your mom to wish her a Merry Christmas," I told them. "Want to go grab your coats?"

They went off to do as I said, and we drove in silence to the cemetery. As we pulled in, I noticed others visiting their loved ones on the special day, sharing stories and memories.

The girls and I walked to their mother's gravestone, and we lay the blankets down on the ground before sitting next to one another, squeezing close to keep warm.

We were quiet at first, just staring and reflecting.

"This is where I came," Karla whispered, staring at the tombstone. "When I was skipping school, I'd come here to be with her," she finally confessed. "It's where I felt the most okay—when I was around Mom. It felt like she always had something to tell me, but I couldn't hear her. I couldn't figure it out."

I looked at my daughter and gave her a smile. "I used to do the same, after she passed. And I felt the same way. Like there was something she was trying to say to us, but I couldn't even figure it out."

"Why didn't you guys just ask her?" Lorelai questioned, confused. "I ask Mommy stuff all the time and she answers."

I smiled at Lorelai and I truly hoped that gift she had to hold on to her mother would never disappear. I pulled her closer to my side. "For some people it's easier, I guess, Lorelai. Some people are able to hold a very tight relationship with their loved ones after they passed away."

"Yeah, Mom and I are best friends," she frankly stated. "You should try just talking to her."

"How do you do it, Lorelai?" Karla asked. "How do you talk to her and know that she hears you?"

She shrugged her shoulders. "You just gotta believe."

Karla took a deep breath and closed her eyes. "Hey, Mom, it's me, Karla. I just wanted to say that I miss you a lot. Every day, and it never really gets easier. I miss your bad jokes, and your laugh, and your terrible taste in music. I miss how you could make my bad days better. And how you could stop me from hurting whenever someone was mean to me." Tears started rolling down her cheeks and I wiped them away as she kept talking. "And I miss hugging you. I miss hugging you so much, but Dad's been doing a pretty good job of being there lately for the hugs. So, yeah. We're not okay with you gone, but we're okay. We're looking out for each other, and I just wanted you to know that. We're okay, and I love you."

She opened her eyes and wiped the tears away.

"See, Karla?" Lorelai whispered. "Did you hear it?"

"Hear what?"

"Mommy said she loves you, too."

And for the first time in over a year, I think Karla finally felt her mother's words.

———

"You knew her before?" Karla asked as she walked into my office the evening after Christmas. She held an envelope in her hands and fidgeted with her fingers. Nicole always said Karla got that nervous habit from me.

"Knew who?"

"Eleanor. You knew her before she was the nanny?"

Just hearing her name made my chest tighten a bit. "Yeah, when we were in high school."

"She was your girlfriend?"

"Well, no, not exactly."

"So she was just a friend?"

I brushed my hand against the back of my neck. "No. Not exactly."

"You're confusing me," she said, arching her eyebrow.

"I know. It's just hard to explain what exactly we were. She was her, I was me, and we were us. There was no label for it. We were just two people helping each other breathe."

She nodded slowing, walking to the room. She sat in the chair across from me. "That's what she said, too."

"What do you mean, that's what she said?"

"Um, I wanted you to read this." She laid the envelope down on my desk. "It's from Eleanor. She wrote it to me the night she left, and slipped it under my door. I didn't read it until last night, and I think you should read it, too."

She sat back in her chair, patiently waiting as I opened the envelope. Inside it was a letter and photograph that I couldn't take my eyes away from.

It was Eleanor and me, the night of the homecoming dance. We both looked so young and completely unaware of where our lives would take us. We were so happy, so free.

"That was an ugly suit," Karla mentioned, making me snicker.

"Yeah, well, back in my day it was pretty dope."

She groaned. "Dad, people don't say dope anymore."

"What are we saying nowadays? Fly? Hip? Happenin'? Groovy?" I mocked.

She rolled her eyes. "Just read the letter already."

I placed the picture down and unfolded the sheet of paper. As my eyes darted across the page, I was reminded of every single thing I loved about Eleanor Gable.

Karla,

I feel like there are not enough words in the universe for me to express how sorry I am for how everything unfolded, but I am going to try my best to do exactly that. I guess the best way to approach this is to go back to the beginning.

I was in high school when I lost my mother to cancer. I was young, lost, and broken. That was exactly when your father came into my life. He showed up during my darkest days, and brought me his light.

He knew of my hurting, and he called my scars beautiful.

He was my first love, but it wasn't simply a romantic thing. He wasn't even my boyfriend, and I could count on two fingers the amount of times we kissed in our youth.

He was just him, I was me, and we were us.

Your father saved me. Without him, I'm certain I would've drowned.

Losing a mother is a unique kind of loss.

A mother understands your heartbeats when you cannot even interpret their sounds. They see you as magnificent, even when you feel like you're so unworthy of love. They calm the doubts that wreak havoc on your soul. They show you what unconditional love is from the day you take your first breath.

Sometimes it feels like they know you better than you'll ever know yourself, and then, one day, they are gone.

You feel cheated. Cheated on the things that they haven't yet taught. Cheated on the lessons you still needed to learn. Cheated out of laughter, and smiles, and comfort, and love.

But what I've learned with time is that my mother is still around me. I see her in everything. Whenever there is beauty, that is where my mother exists.

I know she's never gone, no matter what reality tries to tell me, because my heart is crafted from her love, and as long as it beats, she lives on.

So, that heart of yours? The one you think is damaged and bruised and unworthy of existing? That heart is perfect, and it cannot wait to show you how much love is waiting for you in this world. And whenever you need that reminder, place your hands over your chest, and feel your mother's love in every single beat.

You're going to be okay, Karla.

You're going to be more than okay.

But I need to ask you to do one thing for me: watch after your father. Truth is, he's going to need you more than you need him. Because he doesn't have her heartbeats in his chest. No, his reminder of Nicole lives in your eyes. In your smile. In your love.

You are saving your father. Without you, I'm certain he would drown.

So, even if you never forgive me. Even if you continue to hate me. Even if I never cross your mind again...I want you to know that I am here for you. Day or night. Night or day. Whenever you need me, I'll be there, Karla, because you mean that much to me. Not just as Greyson's daughter, yet as another human being who just needs to know they aren't alone.

I'm one phone call away, and I will always answer.

I'm still here.

-Eleanor

P.S. I know you're hurting, but your scars are so beautiful.

I placed the letter down on the table, and sat back a bit, stunned. "Wow."

Karla nodded. "Yeah." She raced her hands through her hair and then leaned toward me. "So...when are we going to go get her?"

"What?"

"Eleanor. When is she coming back?" I raised an eyebrow, and she gave me a dramatic sigh. "Dad, are you kidding me?! Didn't you just read that letter?"

"Yes, and it was perfect, but that doesn't mean Eleanor is coming back."

"What? Of course, it does."

I wanted to agree with her. I wanted to rush out of the house and run to Eleanor to tell her we were ready. Yet, I couldn't do that. Not yet. "Karla, we've been through a lot these past few months, and we still have a long way to go to heal. My concern is you and your sister. If Eleanor and I are meant to be, it will work its way out down the line. But for now, it's just the three of us against the world."

"Look, I know things haven't been easy for us, and I know I've made them even tougher sometimes, but you deserve to be happy, Dad. I know it's been hard for us all, but that's the truth. I'm sure you think I deserve to be happy, and if I deserve it, you do, too."

I gave her a smile. "I am happy. I have you."

She groaned, slapping her hand to her face. "Why do you have to be so corny sometimes?"

"I'm a father. Being corny is part of a father's job."

She stood up from the chair and started walking away, but I called after her.

"Yeah?" she asked.

"What made you open the letter today?"

"I don't know." She shrugged. "Maybe it was just Mom whispering in my ear."

She walked off, and I picked up the letter and read it over and over again.

"Thank you, Nicole," I whispered into the wind, and I did as Lorelai instructed me to do.

I believed to my core that Nicole could hear me that night.

"So, I received a call from Karla saying you were being stubborn," Claire mentioned during our Tuesday lunch date.

"Is that so?"

"Yeah. She said you had a good thing in Eleanor and were tossing it to the side because you were a chicken shit—her words, not mine."

I smirked. "Sounds like my daughter."

"So, why aren't you going to get in touch with Eleanor? Wasn't the main reason you were keeping your distance because of Karla, and now with her blessing..." Claire's words trailed off.

"It's more complicated than that," I argued. "It's a long story."

"Well, luckily I get an hour of your time every Tuesday. Unless you want me to start singing Journey songs again."

I sighed and pinched the bridge of my nose. 'I made a huge mistake when I was drunk... Eleanor and I were involved, and I accidentally called her by Nicole's name. It was stupid. It was a huge mistake, and I don't think I can really come back from that slip."

She nodded slowly, in understanding. "When I first started dating Jack, I was terrified. I'd been married to my husband for forty years before Jack had come into my life, and I was certain I'd never love again. There was no way I could love someone the way I loved my husband, and in a way, I was right. My love for that man was its own creation. It was our special thing.

"Then when Jack showed up..." Claire's eyes watered over with so much hope, I almost began to tear up. "Jack taught me how to trust again. He taught me that I didn't have to be perfect, I just had to be me, scars and all. He taught me that being myself was all that I ever had to do. Truthfully, I didn't think my heart could beat for another man, but I was wrong. What I learned was that hearts are resilient. They always remember how to beat again. We just have to be willing to give them something to beat for. And the only way to do that is to let go of fear."

"But my mistake..." I whispered.

She smiled. "I called Jack by Randy's name a handful of times. It wasn't on purpose. I remember being horrified, and certain that I was going to run him off forever. But do you know what happened?"

"What's that?"

"He stayed. And oh, boy, please believe that I gave him a million reasons to run, but he wouldn't. He stayed." She crossed her arms and kept grinning my way, as if she knew something that I hadn't known. "What happened after you said it? Did she run away after you two talked it through?"

"No, she didn't. She talked me through it. She listened to my pain. She stayed."

"Then sweetheart..." Claire placed a comforting hand on my shoulder and shook her head. "Why are you running?"

I wanted to stop running. I wanted to call Eleanor and ask her to come back to me. But then I thought of my girls and all of the healing we still had to find.

"It's too soon," I said, shaking my head. "I just need more time."

"I get that, son, I do. Just be careful to not let the time in the sand glass run out. Our lives are short, and tomorrow isn't promised. If there is one thing we all deserve, it's the right to be happy. Perhaps you deserve that even more than most, Greyson."

Happy.

That's all I ever wanted, and I was sure I'd get it someday.

Just not now.

56
Greyson

Two days later, the doorbell rang, and I stood up from the living room couch to go answer it. The moment the door opened, confusion hit me. Eleanor stood there with eyes full of worry.

"Ellie, what are you—"

"Is she okay?" she asked, her voice shaky.

I raised an eyebrow. "Is who okay?"

"Karla. She sent me a text message saying she was in trouble and needed my help. I came over as soon as I could."

"Oh, I'm fine," a voice said behind me. I turned to see Karla standing there with a smirk on her face.

"Then why did you text Eleanor?" I asked.

"Because I do need her help. We all do."

Eleanor looked bewildered, not having a clue what was going on, but I was slowly catching on. My hand brushed against my neck. "Sorry, Ellie. It seems my teenage daughter is acting up."

"Only because you were being stubborn, Dad. Just face it...you like Eleanor. And Eleanor, you can't even deny that you like him, too, because you can't hide your emotions for anything. So, you two should just...be together."

"Karla..." My voice dropped and I grimaced. "You know why we can't—"

"Yeah, Dad, I get it. You're fucked up, I'm fucked up, Eleanor's fucked up—we're all fucked up! But we might as well be fucked up together."

"Language," Eleanor and I said in unison.

I smiled, she smiled, and damn, I loved it.

More of that, Ellie...

I missed those smiles.

"See? You both are even corny together. So, you have to be together." Karla shrugged. "Look, I get it. I sometimes fall apart, and make things hard, but I just want you to know that I want Eleanor here. So does Lorelai. We don't need to wait until we are perfectly healed, Dad. We can be a team with a few cracks still left to fix. Through the good and the bad. Besides..." She gave Eleanor a hesitant grin. "We made a pinky promise."

She turned and headed back to her bedroom.

I parted my mouth to speak, but no words came to mind. Because this was what I wanted, Eleanor was who I craved.

I locked eyes with Eleanor and brushed my thumb against my chin. Nerves filled me up as she kept smiling my way.

"Grey, if you're not ready for this, I—"

"Ellie?"

"Yes?"

I stuffed my hands into my pants pockets. "You've been my true north since the day I met you. You've healed my family in more ways than I could count. You brought me back to life after my soul had died. You save my life each and every time you cross my mind. Just the thought of you heals me. I know there are things we have to figure out. I know there are hurdles that we have to jump, but if you're willing, I am willing to take the leap. I want to leap and fly with you and only you for the rest of my life. So, what do you say?"

She moved in closer, and wrapped her arms around me. I placed my hands against her lower back and pulled her in even closer. Our lips brushed against one another, and I swore my whole life lit up with our possibilities.

"Okay," she whispered against my skin. "Let's fly."

My mouth crashed against hers as I pulled her to me. We kissed for our past, we kissed for our present, and we kissed for our future.

Her lips took mine as if they were promising me forever.

Forever.

This kiss meant forever.

And I was okay with that fact.

We made it. After all these years, we began to descend on to our beautiful chapters. The chapters where pain became beauty. Where heartaches began to heal. Where always met forevers.

She was she, I was me, and we were us.

This was our story.

This was our always and forever.

And it was going to be beautiful.

57
Greyson

Eleanor didn't talk about her father as much as she used to, but I could tell that it still ate at her soul. Whenever I brought it up to her, she'd smile and tell me, "He is what he is, and there's not really a place for me in his life."

That broke my heart, because I knew it broke hers. And if her heart was breaking, mine cracked, too.

"I have to travel today for business," I told Eleanor as we lay in bed a few weeks after she came back into my life. "Do you think you can watch the girls until I get back? I fly out early, but will be back home late tonight. It's a really quick trip. I feel a bit odd about leaving with everything going on with Karla, but it's a very important issue."

"Yeah, of course. I'll take care of them."

I leaned in and kissed her. "I love you," I whispered, and the words came so effortlessly. Almost as if we'd been saying it all our lives.

She kissed me back. "I love you, too."

Of course we loved each other.

I was certain when our love began all those years ago, it never really stopped.

I found myself in Florida, standing on Eleanor's father's front porch. Shay had given me the address. I stood there for a minute with a book in my hand before I built up the courage to knock.

"Can I help you?" Kevin asked, raising an eyebrow as he opened his front door.

Eleanor might've had her mother's smile, but she truly had her father's eyes.

"Hi, yeah, I'm Greyson. I don't know if you remember me, but we met many years ago through Eleanor. I was her friend from high school. I took her to homecoming."

He narrowed his eyes. "Oh, yes, Greyson. Long time."

"It has been indeed."

"How can I help you?" he asked, somewhat closing his door so I couldn't see the mess that existed behind him.

"I'm actually here on behalf of Ellie. You see...I love her, sir. I am in love with your daughter for a million reasons. She is truly the greatest gift this world has given to me, and she is currently heartbroken because she misses her father."

Kevin grimaced and huffed. "Now, look, if you came here to make me feel bad—"

"That's not why I'm here," I cut in. "Not at all. Trust me, if anyone knows what you're going through, it's me. Over a year ago, my wife passed away, leaving me with my two daughters. I shut down completely. I pushed everything and everyone away, because I couldn't face a world where Nicole no longer existed. But then, against my stubbornness, Eleanor Gable came back into my life, and she saved me. She's the most patient person in the world, Kevin, and I bet she gets that trait from her mother. I bet she gets a lot of her best traits from Paige."

The moment I said her name, I saw Kevin react. The heartache that lived inside of him was still alive and strong. But I wouldn't stop speaking, because I knew he needed to hear my words.

"Eleanor is nurturing, and kind, and her smile can light up a whole room. When she laughs, she does it with her whole body, and when she cries, it breaks every part of your heart. She's forgiving, even when she shouldn't be. She's understanding, even when people are hard to understand. She's gentle. She's sensitive. She's beautiful inside and out, and I know that came from her mother. So, that makes it hard for you."

He closed his eyes and took in deep breaths. "You don't understand..."

"She has her eyes," I softly said, because I did understand. I understood more than he knew. "Which makes it hard to look at her. She has her smile, which makes you want to frown. She has so many parts of the woman you lost, so you push her away, because it hurts so much. But Kevin, you'll have to come to realize that what you think is a curse, is actually a miracle. I get to see Nicole each time I look into my children's eyes. I get to see her smile. I get to hear her laugh, and that is the greatest gift this world could ever offer."

He opened his eyes, and I saw the same despair that I'd lived with before. The sadness that had been swallowing him whole for the past sixteen-some years. "How did you get there?" he asked. "How did you begin to heal?"

"That's easy. I let Eleanor in, and you should do the same."

He shook his head and grumbled as he wiped away his tears. "No. I can't. It's been too long. Too much time has passed. I can't fix our relationship."

"You can't, or you won't try? All I'm saying is, if you ever want to fix things with Eleanor, she'll be there to listen."

"How do you know that? How can you be so sure?"

"Because that's the woman you've raised. You brought a woman into this world who breathes unconditional love."

Kevin lowered his head, and I could almost witness the wheels turning in his head. I reached into my pocket, and pulled out one of my business cards. "Listen, I don't want to take up any more of your time. I just wanted to stop by and let you know that your daughter's love is worth fighting for. And when you are at your lowest, you can give me a call. Give me a call, and I'll walk you through it. From one widower to another, I promise you, Kevin, the sun can shine again. All you have to do is wake up."

He took the card from my hand and nodded slowly. "Thanks, Greyson."

"Of course, and here, take this." I headed him the novel. "Just in case you two need to find something that you have in common to talk about."

I turned to walk off and he called my name once more.

"Greyson?"

"Yes?" I rotated around to look at him.

He brushed his hand under his nose and cleared his throat. "You'll take care of her?"

"Yes, sir," I promised. "For as long as we both shall live."

58

Eleanor

On the anniversary of my mother's death, I found a moment to give thanks to her because I knew she probably had a lot to do with bringing Greyson and me back together. I knew she always had a way of showing me her love.

"We should go to Laurie Lake," Greyson suggested as he walked up and wrapped his arms around me. "You know, to celebrate her memory."

"I'd really love that."

The girls were at Claire's house, so we made the drive to the lake, and as we approached, I felt calmness. It was as if I could sense her being there. As we began walking through the trees to our hidden oasis, my heart came to a halt as I looked up to see my father standing there with his back to me.

"Dad?" I asked, stunned and confused.

He turned and gave me the saddest smile. "Hey, Snickers," he whispered. Surrounding him were wrapped boxes and a stack of card envelopes. In his hands was a novel and he waved it. "I finally got around to reading this *Harry Potter* thing you were always talking about. It's pretty good."

I tried to speak, but my voice cracked. When I tried again, it came out as a whisper. "What are you doing here?" I looked over at

Greyson, who gave me a knowing grin. It was clear he'd had something to do with it.

"I think I left something in the car. I'll be back," Greyson said. I reached out to him, nervous, unsure of what to do, and he gently squeezed my hand. "You don't have to forgive him, Ellie, but it's okay to listen. You'll be okay, and I'll be around the corner at the car, ready and waiting for you, okay?"

I nodded. "Okay."

He left us alone, and Dad kept alternating between looking at the water and looking at me. I moved in closer but still didn't say a word. I had so many things I'd wanted to say to him, but nothing was coming out.

He coughed a little and brushed his hand against the back of his neck. "I think I'm a Ravenclaw, based on all the details. I'm guessing you're a Hufflepuff, based on what I've read and what I know about you."

"What is all this stuff?" I asked, looking around, as confused as ever.

"Oh, it's...um, well, it's..." His thoughts were jumbled, and I didn't blame him. My thoughts were in the same state. "It's sixteen birthday cards and sixteen Christmas gifts, for all the years I missed. I, um..." He scratched his head and then pounded his fist against his mouth. "I missed out on so much, and I know you aren't going to forgive me for that, but I just wanted you to know that, I...I'm so sorry, Ellie."

"You abandoned me," I whispered. "You abandoned me for years, and you think some cards and gifts are going to make up for that? I didn't want your gifts, Dad. I wanted you."

"I know, I know, and I don't deserve your forgiveness. I don't know if I will ever get it, but I want to work at it. I want to do my best to earn you back into my life. Ellie, after your mother passed away, something inside me snapped. It completely broke, and I didn't want to figure out how to put it back together. Seeing you...your smile, your eyes... Every part of your mother lives in you, and I wasn't strong enough to deal with that. I wasn't strong enough, and I screwed up, and I'm sorry. I know it doesn't change all these years, but I am sorry for being a shit father. You deserve more than me."

"Yes," I agreed, "I do."

He lowered his head, stung by my words.

"But, regardless of that fact, you're still the only thing I've ever wanted." When he looked up, tears were streaming down his cheeks, which in turn made me cry.

"I'm a mess, Ellie."

"I know you are. I've been a mess, too, and I'm not going to lie; I'm still really mad at you. I'm still hurting, and it's going to take a long time for me to get to a place where I feel as if I can forgive you completely."

"Yes. I understand."

"But if you're willing to try..." I offered.

His eyes lit up. "Yes, I am. I am more than willing. Anything it takes."

"If we do this, we do it together," I told him. "If we fall, we fall together. If we break, we shatter as one, but we don't leave each other anymore, okay Dad? We fight for this. We fight for our family. We fight for us."

"All for one," he whispered.

"And one for all," I finished as I wrapped my arms around him.

The healing process with my father was going to take time. It was going to be more than one conversation, more than ten conversations. I knew it might take years, knew we might never return to being the father and daughter we'd once been, but having something was better than nothing.

At the end of the day, family was worth fighting for, scars and all.

———

When I went back to meet up with Greyson at the car, Dad came with me. He was going to stay with us a few days before heading back to Florida, just so he and I could get a conversation started toward the healing of our relationship.

That night as I climbed into bed with Greyson, I held him closer than I'd ever held him before. "You did this for me?" I asked, speaking about bringing my father back into my life.

"Of course, I did, Ellie. There's nothing I wouldn't do to make sure you were happy."

"Grey?"

"Yes?"

"Would it be all right if I kept you forever? I know I said that before, but like, really this time? Can I keep you?"

"Yes, Ellie." He chuckled lightly, and kissed my forehead as both of our eyes began to shut. "I'm yours."

59

Eleanor

It had been almost a year since Greyson and I decided to let our love story grow, and it was a beautiful story to partake in.

Life became easier. Even though my father went back to Florida, he checked in more often. We talked more, and when he said he would visit, he actually came. He was putting in the effort that was needed, and I was more than thankful for that.

When months passed, and he showed up for Christmas, I was amazed.

"Can we open gifts?!" Lorelai shouted darting into the living room on Christmas day.

Claire, Shay, and I had just finished preparing brunch together while the guys all sat in front of the television, watching sports. Landon even stopped by for Christmas brunch, stating that he was simply in the neighborhood again. I knew how much it meant to Greyson for his best friend to be there, and if there was anything Landon was excellent at, it was showing up. He always showed up whenever Greyson needed him.

Even though he wasn't great for my cousin, he was the best kind of best friend.

"After we eat and make our wish ornaments," Claire told Lorelai, who groaned about not being able to rip open her presents yet.

Shay walked past me in the kitchen after peeking her head into the living room to look at the guys for the fifteenth hundred time. Or, mainly to look at Landon.

"You know what I hate most in this world?" she asked me.

"What's that?"

"Landon Harrison. I mean, can you believe that? When I showed up today he had the nerve to say, 'Merry Christmas,' to me. Can you believe that asshole?"

I snickered. "How rude."

"Exactly! It's like he's trying to play some crazy mind games." She huffed as her cheeks reddened. She was so flustered around him. It was actually pretty cute.

"Or maybe he simply meant Merry Christmas," I offered.

She lowered her eyebrows, going deep into thought. "Yeah, maybe. Maybe that's it. Okay, yeah. It was just a Merry Christmas. Nothing more, nothing less."

Just then Landon popped his head into the kitchen and gave a big smirk. "Need any help in here, ladies?" he asked.

"You cook?" Shay asked, sassily with her hands against her hips.

"Yeah, sometimes."

"Why do I find that so hard to believe?" she mocked.

"I don't know, but if you give me a few minutes, I'm sure I can bring some nice sausage into your life." He winked her way, making me chuckle.

Shay groaned. "You're disgusting."

"I'm just saying, it will probably be the best meat you've had in a while. And if memory serves me right, which it does, you kind of already told me how much you loved my sausage."

"Shut up, Landon," Shay hissed, turning redder than ever. "You're so cocky."

He smirked, pleased with how he was getting under her skin. "I know, right?"

"Oh, piss off, Landon," she breathed out, hitting him with a dish rag, making him hurry away.

She stayed flustered as she combed her hair behind her ears. "What a dick," she muttered. "I can't wait until he goes back to California."

"I can't wait for season one, episode one of the Landon and Shay show," I joked. "I love a solid enemies-to-lovers storyline."

She pointed a stern finger at me. "That will never in the history of ever happen. *Never.*"

A part of me knew she was lying, though. Shay and Landon had this intense game of cat and mouse they played together, and for some reason I felt as if the story between the two of them was just beginning.

Once the food was prepared, we all gathered around the dining room table, and feasted on the meal. There was so much chatter, laughter, smiles, and peace going around the table setting, and it warmed up every part of me. After the meal, Claire handed out pieces of paper, and clear, glass ornaments.

She had the idea of making wishes for the upcoming year. In the clear, glass spheres, you were supposed to place a wish for the year to come. Then when the year was over, you opened the ornament and you'd be able to see how your wish had come true. Then, you'd use paint to decorate the ornament however you wished.

As everyone sat there decorating with looks of joy on their faces, I sat back in my chair, in complete awe.

This was it.

This was all I'd ever wanted. All I wanted was this moment. All I wanted was this family. All I wanted was us.

As I put my wish for the coming year in place, I thought about the words I'd written down about what I hoped for. I looked around at the happiness surrounding me, and I felt beyond blessed.

This was all I wanted for the upcoming months.

More.

More happiness, more laughter, more smiles.

More of him, more of me, more of us.

Greyson pushed his chair away from the table, and cleared his throat as he stood up. "Hey, everyone, I just wanted to take a moment to thank you all for coming out today. You have no clue what it means to me and the girls to have each chair at this table filled. There was a time where I thought we'd never get this back. There was a time I thought happiness was gone forever, but then a light came back into my life, and everything changed. So, I just wanted you all to be here when I show my gratitude to the woman who saved my family, to the woman who saved me."

My heart skipped a beat as he turned toward me and reached into his back pocket, pulling out a small box. He then lowered himself down to one knee.

"Greyson, what are you doing?" My voice shook and tears floated my eyes.

"Ellie, you are everything good in this world. You've treated my daughters with nothing but love. You've respected the time we needed to heal. You showed up whenever we needed you. You've always been there, even when you had every reason in the world to walk away. You stand for peace in the chaos. You are the sunbeams breaking through the clouds. You are the definition of happiness, and that's all I've ever wanted. I wanted to be happy. Which is why I want to spend the rest of my life in the arms of you." He opened the box, showing me a beautiful engagement ring. I gasped as I studied it. Tears began falling down my cheeks as my emotions became unsteady.

The ring was a series of small diamonds shaped like a dragonfly.

As I looked over at Greyson, he smiled.

I loved it.

Whatever.

"Eleanor Gable, you are my heartbeats, my laughter, and my love. Will you marry me?" he asked, but before I could reply, my heart began to cry even more as Lorelai hurried over, holding a small box in her hands, too.

"And me?" she asked, getting down on one knee. She opened the box and showed me another dragonfly ring.

Karla walked over next, and got down on one knee beside her sister. She opened her ring box next. "And me?"

My heart was exploding into a million pieces. The three of them and their love was what made this life of mine whole.

With ease and so much love, I replied to each and every one of them. "Yes, yes, a million times yes," I cried as the room burst into celebration.

Greyson placed the ring on my finger, and then he pulled me into a tight embrace, holding me closer than ever. He kissed me deeply, and I felt forever against his lips.

Forever.

This kiss means forever.

As he pulled back, he smiled, and I smiled back.

"More of that, Ellie," he said as he leaned in and kissed my lips once more.

Yes, exactly.

More of that.

The end.

Acknowledgements

This book would've never happened if it wasn't for my mother. I almost gave up on this story after having an emotional breakdown over it. I almost threw it all away, but my mother looked at me and told me to keep going, to trust myself, to trust the process. So, this book exists because of her love and endless support. Thank you, Mama. You're my best friend.

This book is for my family, who always has my back no matter what. They love my fully—always and forever.

This book is for the man I love: More of you, more of me, more of us. *More of that.*

Thank you to Hang Le for the most amazing cover design I've ever had! I'm still blown away whenever I look at it.

To Talon, Christy, Allison, and Maria: the best betas in the world.

This book is for the editors and proofreaders who always show up when I need them Caitlin, Ellie, Jenny, and Lisa: you have no clue how often you save my life. Thank you.

To Elaine: Thank you for your beautiful interior formatting of the paperback.

This book is for my agent, Flavia: You are heaven sent. I'm the luckiest author in the world to have you in my corner.

To every reader and blogger who continues to show up for me, thank you. This story isn't for everyone, I'm sure, but it *is* for the broken-hearted and the healing souls. This is for those who have lost the ones who mean the world to them. This is for those who are dealing with a heavy grief that some days feels unbearable. This is a sign that one day you'll find your smiles again. You'll remember your loved ones and feel completely filled with love. Because even when it doesn't feel like it, they are still here. They live within your heart and soul.

Thank you for reading my words. Thank you for supporting my dream. That you for understanding my messy mind.

And thank you for seeing my heartbeats.

Until next time.

-BCherry

Made in United States
North Haven, CT
26 February 2022

16536931R00209